A HAUNTING OF WORDS

Published by Scout Media
Copyright 2017
ISBN: 978-0-9979485-0-9

Cover: **Sydney Blackburn**
Interior graphics: **Amy Hunter**

Visit: **www.ScoutMediaBooksMusic.com**
for more information on each author and future anthologies.

Table of Contents

Anesthetize
(or A Dream Played in Reverse on Piano Keys)

Brian Paone

Mark Crowley fumbled with the medication bottle's childproof cap as another gust of wind ripped open the front of his unzipped jacket. Using the large tree branches' shadows as cover, he tossed back his head and swallowed an uncounted number of white pills. He punched his chest once to help the tranquilizers slide down his esophagus.

Mark found a nice-size rock—one not big enough to break her window but large enough to get her attention—and juggled it haphazardly in his hand. He aimed at Samantha's second-story window and let the rock fly. Its trajectory was right on the money, clinking loudly against the pane. He waited a few moments to see if the sound would summon her to open the window. Seconds passed; nothing.

He surveyed the ground for something larger. Maybe she was in her bathroom and couldn't hear the *plink*. He needed something that made a *thud!* Hell, at this point, maybe she deserved to have her window fucking broken.

Mark noticed a baseball half hidden underneath a bush beside the front steps. He nonchalantly strolled toward the bush, sifted the ball from the dirt, and placed it under his armpit. Illuminated by the motion-detector spotlights secured to the corner of the first-story roof, he reached into his pocket and removed a different pill bottle. He unscrewed the cap and tapped a handful of pills into his palm. He shrugged, chomped on the medication loudly until it was just dust clinging to the roof of his dry mouth, and then whipped the baseball through her window.

Bitch, he thought.

The front door opened, and Mark sprinted toward the tree line, using the shadows to hide from the moonlight.

— • • —

Mark could have found his special spot deep in the woods even if the moon hadn't flooded the trees with light. Hell, he could find his way with his eyes closed. He stutter-stepped over the decrepit and rotting railroad ties and maneuvered around the overgrowth consuming the rusted double rails. He placed his hand on the caboose of a passenger train, half off the tracks and leaning like the famous Tower of Pisa. Standing on his tiptoes, he placed his other hand on the yellow-tinted window to the train car and raised the glass just enough to slip his hand through.

His fingertips found the corner of the Ziploc bag, and he slid the stash through the slit of the windowpane. Planting his feet level on the ground, he separated the pills, through the plastic, with his thumb and index finger. Content they were all accounted for, he turned his back on the long-forgotten derailed train and stared at the back fender of his mother's car, camouflaged under a thicket of small trees and shrubbery.

"How many have you taken already?"

"Fuck, man. Don't do that," Mark said.

"Sorry, thought you knew I was here," Dawson replied.

"I never know when you're here."

Dawson laughed. "I'm always here. You should know that better than anyone."

Mark sat down next to his best friend. "These are the only things that help me through the day."

"How many prescriptions do you actually have?"

"Legally?" Mark asked, reaching into his coat pocket for the two bottles.

"Whichever."

"These two"—he handed Dawson the bottles—"and these are the ones I bought from Neil at the mall."

Mark handed over the Ziploc bag, a smorgasbord of different-colored pills of various sizes.

Dawson looked at the labels on the two bottles. "Mogadon?"

"Yeah, it's a tranquilizer. And this one is my antidepressants."

Dawson returned the two bottles and the baggie to Mark. "Are they helping?"

"Well, they curb the desires and urges. I also pretty much stopped caring about anything. So, yeah, I'd say they're doing their job just fine."

Mark opened the bag, pinched three different pills—none of them similar—and sent them down the hatch.

"Did you go to school today?"

Mark shook his head. "Nah, I don't concentrate when I'm there. I can't seem to focus. Plus next week is prom and then graduation. What's the point?" He unscrewed the bottle of Mogadon tranquilizers and flicked one into his mouth.

"Dude, fucking slow down. You're gonna kill yourself the way you're eating those like candy. I'm the one who wanted to die, remember?"

"You're a little neater and more concise with stuff like that than I am. Plus I can just blame the genes. As the son of two pill-heads, there was never any real hope for me anyway. I inherited their problems," Mark replied. "Oh, I went to Samantha's tonight. Broke her fucking bedroom window with a baseball."

"Jesus, you have zero regard for that restraining order, don't you?"

"It's just a stupid piece of paper."

Dawson stood up. "A piece of paper that will get you arrested if you go within one hundred yards of her house or work."

"I don't think it says anything about staying away from Baldock & Ashford."

"Go get it. I'm sure the order includes her work. Doesn't matter if she only works there on weekends. I can't imagine her parents not including it, after what you did."

Mark rose to his feet and headed toward his mother's car tucked in the woods. "Doesn't matter anyway. I won't lie. The sex was kind of fun, but really it was just one more way to kill the boredom. And, if she made me fucking listen to Radiohead one more time, I was gonna hurt someone."

"Sometimes I don't get you, man. I mean, you're my best friend, but you certainly go out of your way to be disliked."

Mark reached the passenger side door and yanked on the handle to get it open. The doorjamb was crusted with dried mud and sticks. He opened the glovebox and removed the folded yellow paper. When he slammed the door, startled birds took flight across the large lake in front of the abandoned car.

Mark scanned the glasslike water and tried to focus on the shoreline across the lake. A tightening in his stomach took him by surprise. He wasn't ready to become sentimental or nostalgic of times past. Not now. Not ever again. He forced himself to look away from the clearing across the water, grabbed a large stone, and tossed it into the lake, shattering the calmness of its serenity.

Need to lay off the tranquilizers and load up on those antidepressants instead, he thought as he shook the memories and emotional response from his brain.

"Let me see," Dawson said.

Mark handed him the paper, and Dawson unfolded it. Scanning with the tip of his finger, Dawson's lips fluttered slightly as he silently speed-read the provisions of the restraining order.

"See, right here. It states you are prohibited from going within one hundred feet of her house or her place of employment."

"No worries. I'll just stay away from Baldock & Ashford whenever I hang at the mall. I hate that store anyway."

"Now there's the right attitude. Don't be accountable or sorry for what you did. Just find a way to cut it out of your life altogether. You're a piece of work sometimes. Do your parents even know about this?"

"Give me that," Mark said and snatched the restraining order from Dawson's hand. "And I didn't tell my parents. They don't care about anything anyway."

He crumpled it and hurled the balled-up paper, like an outfielder, through the trees.

"And, for the record, your band sucks," Mark added.

"You only heard that one song."

"Well, you guys sound like a crappy version of Pearl Jam."

"Hey, don't knock Pearl Jam," Dawson defended.

"I'm not knocking Pearl Jam. I fucking love Pearl Jam. I'm knocking your shitty band's attempt at being Pearl Jam. And what's with all the black clothes? Jesus, could you guys be more cliché? Fucking goth-looking band sounding like early nineties grunge. And you tell me that I'm the one who's confused?"

"Are you done?"

After a moment of silence, Mark answered. "Yes."

"Thank you."

"But your music's still crap."

"For fuck's sake, man. Why do I even still hang out with you?"

Mark snickered. "Because you have to."

"I made a decision. It wasn't an easy one, but I made one."

"You mean the curse. The curse of 'there must be more,'" Mark said and peered over Dawson's shoulder, making sure Dawson knew where he was looking.

Dawson turned and looked at the silhouette of his own hanging body, swinging in the breeze from a thick branch, still undiscovered by any of the search parties.

"Yes, the *thought*—not curse—of there being more than this shitty life," Dawson answered.

"Have you tried to leave Jupiter Island?"

"Not yet. Something about going too far away from my body until they find it bothers me. Jupiter Island was always the happiest place of my childhood. My family would camp in these woods, and we'd fish in the lake. I'd have laser tag tournaments with the other kids who were also camping. I learned to swim in that lake as a kid." Dawson looked across the water just beyond the top of Mrs. Crowley's car. "I'll stay here until someone cuts me down."

"I'll cut you down."

"I already told you, Mark. I want them to find me. I want them to be so sorry for the way they treated me. I want them to find their dead son, decomposing on the rope. I want to drive the message home. That will be their penance."

Mark snickered. "And you think I'm fucked in the head?"

"I never said that. Are the pills helping at all?"

"I'm not really sure. I keep having these thoughts. I own all this stuff, material shit, but so what?"

"Hey man, in the end you can't take it with you. I'm a case in point." Dawson waved his hand down the front of his body like he was Vanna White on *Wheel of Fortune*. "But you need to get your shit together. I made one decision that changed everything, and I can't take it back. Not that I want to right now, but, if I ever did, it's a no-go. I think I damned my soul, if you believe in that kind of thing."

"Are you trying to save my soul? Okay, so tell me. What happens now? I want to hear it with conviction."

"I don't follow."

"I could be on a plane, and someone could have a bomb in their suitcase. And *BOOM!* The plane rips apart, and my body disintegrates across the sky and through the clouds, and my ashes fall over some park in Wales."

"Why are you going to Wales?"

"I hate you sometimes, you know. I mean, what happens now? What is the difference between what you did to yourself and some horrific natural disaster? Does it affect what happens to us afterward?"

"Are you talking about whether it's the difference between being a ghost trapped here, like me, or being whisked away into the heavens? Dude, I don't fucking know. I haven't left Jupiter Island since I cannonballed off that branch last month."

Mark shook a few more unmarked pills from the Ziploc into

his mouth, like they were a handful of sunflower seeds. "What good are you then?"

"You know what? You just keep popping those pills. Let me know how that works out for ya."

Dawson slowly faded until Mark stood next to the train tracks alone; the rope holding Dawson's body creaked as it swung in the distance.

Mark walked toward his mother's car and leaned backward on the hood. He inserted his earbuds and closed his eyes as he pressed Play on the iPod in his pocket, inhaling the welcoming smells of Jupiter Island's lake. A rush of happy memories swarmed his head, then were stifled by the medications—doing their job by regulating both happy and sad into a flat emotionless line.

Keeping his eyes shut, he dreamed of an escape. Arriving somewhere but not here. Maybe fleeing on the derailed train behind him. Maybe the train tracks could be his proverbial yellow brick road. There must be something better than this.

Mark hadn't realized how long he had been draped over the hood of his mother's car until the last track on Jimi Hendrix's *Are You Experienced?* gave way to The Beatles' *Sgt. Pepper's Lonely Hearts Club Band.* Mark opened his eyes, disregarded the fantasy of ever escaping the industrial cityscape of Golders Green or the throes of the pills, and headed home.

— • • —

Mark awoke to the sound of a chromatic scale played on the piano outside his bedroom door. His shutters were closed, and his curtains were drawn; just a peek of sunlight pierced through the haze of his room. He rubbed the sleepies from the corners of his eyes and heard it again. The banging of the notes sounded like untrained fingers randomly running down the keys.

He crawled from bed and found his way, using the small bit of morning sunlight and the flicker of his television to guide his path.

He opened his bedroom door and grunted when he saw the family cat, prancing back and forth over the piano keys.

"Bonnie, you shithead, you woke me up. Get in here."

He stepped aside while the cat jumped off the piano and scurried into his darkened room. He stopped in front of his television as some actress screamed. *Stupid horror movies.* He grabbed his earbuds from the floor and looked at his iPod's display screen. Radiohead's *The Bends* had been set on Repeat at some point during the night, replaying in a vicious cycle on his floor.

Mark clicked the input button on the television remote and switched the movie to his Xbox. He coughed, shook a few tranquilizers into his mouth, and searched for the controller somewhere within his unmade bed. He caught a glimpse of himself in the mirror and didn't recognize the guy there. He glanced at the bottle of Mogadon and then back to his reflection. He stood and approached the mirror slowly. He opened his mouth wide and scraped his fingernails along his stretched cheeks. He half expected to claw his skin from his bones, like the idiot had done after seeing a maggot-filled steak on a kitchen counter in the movie Mark had just switched off.

Mark flicked his cheek hard, just to make sure he could feel pain. He looked at the pill bottles on his nightstand and shook the cobwebs from his brain. Bonnie curled herself into a fuzzy ball on his pillow and purred. Mark nodded, content this was reality and that the pills hadn't tie-dyed the fabric of life just yet.

He sat on the floor, his back pressed against the foot of his bedframe, and loaded Halo. As his finger flicked the switch, slaying the Covenant, Bonnie relocated from his pillow to his lap. He patted her absentmindedly as he continued to battle with the alien enemy on-screen.

Just as he gritted his teeth and pivoted his torso downward and to the right—as if body language ever helped anyone move their game character faster—his mother burst into the room without knocking. Bonnie whimpered and scooted underneath the bed. Mark didn't even look up from the game.

"Where's my car?"

Mark's trigger finger worked overtime as he proceeded though the level. His left eye twitched, concentrating on the impending enemy assault.

"Mark. Did you hear me? Turn that shit off. Where's my car?"

Mark raised his left hand in a *not now* signal.

"Don't you ignore me, young man," she said and stepped farther into the room. "Where . . . is . . . my . . . car?"

Mark shrugged and glanced at the Ziploc bag of treats. Those were what he wanted right now. Not the shitty prescription tranquilizers and antidepressants. The *Matrix*-looking shit that rendered his body void of a person.

Mrs. Crowley noticed her son's distraction and stormed across the room. She snatched the plastic bag and sighed. "Turn the game off."

Mark stoically continued to blast the threat on the screen.

"Mark, please," she pleaded and stared at him and stared at him and stared at him and stared at him and stared at him . . . while he shot and killed, shot and killed, shot and killed, shot and killed, shot and killed; . . . and she stared at him and stared at him and stared—

"All right. Christ! I can't take the staring or your silent sympathy," he blurted out.

"How do you feel?"

"I hate that question," he answered, returning to shooting and killing.

"How's it going in school?"

"Mom, school is a fucking joke. You know I can't concentrate."

Mrs. Crowley sighed. "Do you wanna talk about it?"

Mark dropped the controller and glared at her. "You are such a bitch! Your mouth should be boarded up. You talk all day long, and you don't say anything relevant to anything. Even when you try to act smart with your drinking floozies, your points are all based on misinformation. And Dad should get a fucking medal for trying to talk to me. That man just won't let up!"

Mrs. Crowley threw down the bag of pills and balled her hands into fists. "You should just shut up and be happy. Stop fucking whining. Please. And where the hell is my goddamn car?"

"I don't know. Maybe it's been stolen, repo'd, sold to a chop shop. How the hell should I know?"

"Because you were the last one to have it!"

Bonnie peeked from underneath the bed and scampered through Mark's open door into the living room.

"Samantha issued a restraining order on me."

"What? Why? What did you do to her?"

"She's a bitch, Mom. She wouldn't leave me alone about having sex with her. I think it was just spiteful revenge because I wouldn't sleep with her again. And I'm paying for it."

"Are you crazy, Mark? You and Samantha have been like two peas in a pod since elementary school. A restraining order? A judge must have believed something was happening to issue that. And why didn't you tell us? Do we need to adjust your meds?"

"Oh, for Christ's sake, Mom. Me and Samantha are . . . complicated."

"Well, you get points for being a cliché."

"You know what? Go fuck yourself, Mom."

Mrs. Crowley headed for the door. "Nice. Great language. I want my car back in the garage before you go to bed tonight."

As she closed the door, Bonnie squeaked back into the room and jumped into his lap. He used the input function on the remote to switch his Xbox to cable. He flipped through the channels until he came to MTV2. He tilted his head as he watched a video from a band he had never heard of before. They reminded him of a more melodic Tool, and the vocalist sang about stripping someone's soul.

He pressed Input again, switching to the DVD signal. Without further manipulation, he heard the DVD player whirl to life, and images appeared on-screen.

He flexed his hip to knock Bonnie from his lap and then unzipped his pants. As the woman moaned in pleasure, he grabbed himself in an attempt to feel any sort of arousal. Nothing. Lifeless. When the actors were done with their melodramatic scenario, they returned to a fake dinner party, where it appeared other characters in this fabricated orgy were about to get their turn at some fun. Mark stopped touching his limp self and chuckled embarrassingly at the losers forced to recite this god-awful dialogue.

Bored with the calculated sex on his television, he stood and walked toward his desk. Mark's foot kicked a shoebox sticking out from underneath his bed. The box skidded across his floor and stopped just shy of his stereo. Bonnie lifted her head, whimpered, and nuzzled down for a nap on his pillow.

Mark bent and picked up the shoebox. A layer of soot decorated the cover. He brushed away the ashes and rubbed the residue on his jeans before opening the box. He was forced to sit on his bed as he studied the first few layers of photographs.

Not yet. Just not ready yet. He reached for the Mogadon, the antidepressants, and the Ziploc bag of candy pills. He siphoned through each bottle and the bag, collecting a conglomerate of varieties before swallowing them in multiple gulps. *Now I'm ready.*

Mark pinched a photo of himself as a boy and brought it to eye level. He rode his first bicycle, his maiden voyage without training wheels. And he looked miserable. No smile. No excitement. No joy of accomplishment. Void of emotion, even then.

His hand covered his closed mouth in lightning speed as he picked the next photo to inspect. The image displayed him and Samantha as toddlers on the shoreline of the Jupiter Island lake, frozen in a sloppy kiss forever. Mark could see the Novaks in the foreground, laughing as their two-year-old daughter planted a big juicy one on the Crowleys' son. How adorable. But that's how they had met. That kiss, fifteen years ago, was the start of their friendship . . . and the trouble.

Mark sifted deeper into the offset pile of photographs until he found one that injected a little bit of life into his heart. The picture portrayed Samantha, the summer between eighth grade and high school, holding her hat as the wind tried to pry it from her hands. Mark had taken that photo, and it was the pinnacle moment of his love for her. He studied the bottom of the photo where the water lapped the shore and counted the waves. One. Two. Three. Three ripples broke on the shoreline at Samantha's ankles as she tightly held her hat, and her hair was like a flag in the wind. Her mouth was captured in midspeech. She was saying something to Mark when he had snapped the photo, but he couldn't hear her. Even in the picture it was obvious she was trying to convey something. Was it a mouthed *I love you*?

In the next photo he commandeered from the box, Samantha had turned away from him. He studied the top corner of the picture as Bonnie slithered into his lap, hoping for a petting. He ran his finger across the photographed sun. The picture seemed to depict noontime, but the sun was black in the photo.

He subconsciously petted Bonnie, and, when he leaned his face closer to study the black sun, the cat arched her back and hissed at the shoebox. The sound snapped him from his trance, and he placed the box in his lap.

Rummaging urgently through the rest of the photos, he noticed they all contained images of happier times, of more innocent times. The pictures of him and Samantha growing up together through the years showed a happy, smiling Mark. The other, strictly family photos showed otherwise.

He flipped the shoebox onto the floor, spilling the contents. He frantically separated the pictures into two piles: one having anything to do with Samantha and one being just family photographs of him and his parents.

Mark leaned over and opened his nightstand drawer. He located a pair of scissors and a lighter. Focusing on the Samantha pile, he cut out her face from every photo she was in. Picture by picture, he discarded photos with almost perfect circular holes where her face had been. Next to him was a rounded pile, like poker chips, of Samantha donning every emotion possible throughout the years.

Mark only stopped to chomp on a handful of mystery pills from the Ziploc before continuing to desecrate his childhood memories of the only girl he had ever loved.

"I will forget you eventually," he said, maneuvering the scissors around her head in yet another happy photo. "I know that I will. It might take a thousand years. It might take one week. I'll even forget the sound of your name . . ."

Mark wiped the first glimmer of a tear in a long, long while from the corner of his eye as he mutilated the last of the photos containing Samantha's image.

". . . or the way you look when you're sleeping and dreaming of something more."

Mark collected all the discarded yet intact photos, the desecrated photos, and the circular cutouts of Samantha's face, and returned them to the shoebox. He reached for his lighter and lit the corner of the cardboard. Dropping the box onto the hardwood floor, he watched the shoebox and the memories inside burn; the heat from the flames stabbed his cheeks, as if begging and pleading to be saved.

He stomped out the last of the flickering flames, ash ballooning upward into his face and clinging to the curtains. After he was satisfied the fire was extinguished, he tossed the remnants of the shoebox into the trashcan next to his Xbox and crawled under his bedcovers to drown in his torpor.

Bonnie snuggled under the sheets as Mark wrapped an arm around the fuzzy cat. His last thought before he drifted to sleep was, *I wish I was a little bit more sentimental.*

—··—

Mark awoke to the sound of diminishing piano notes again. He glanced at the digital clock atop his television and pressed his palm against his temple to ease the throbbing inside his brain. He hadn't been asleep long, but the sun had begun its descent on Golders Green. The piano notes reversed and climbed up the scale.

"Bonnie," Mark whispered with aggravation.

He opened the door and grabbed the cat off the keys.

"Why must you insist on waking me up with your terrible Stevie Wonder impression, huh?"

Bonnie meowed and licked his cheek.

"Mom? Dad?" Mark listened for a reply. Nothing. The house was still. "Mom?" Still nothing.

He placed Bonnie on the floor and looked through the parlor windows. His dad's car was not in the driveway.

"Looks like it's just you and me," he said to the cat.

Mark lifted his mattress and removed the bags of LSD and pre-rolled marijuana. He threw the bags on the bed and released the mattress; it *whomp*ed onto the box spring. He picked a joint and an LSD tab, and then retrieved the Ziploc of treats from his pocket. After studying the remaining pills in the baggie, he chose an orange and purple one he hadn't tried yet. He swallowed the pill dry and sublingually ingested the LSD blotter. Lighting the joint, he sat on his bed and inhaled three quick puffs as Bonnie jumped into his lap. He exhaled in pleasure, as if he had just drunk a large glass of water during a heat wave.

"You wanna go to Alton Towers with me, girl? I can't deal with all this boredom."

The cat didn't look at him.

"Nah, I guess not. I think the mall is pretty fucking lame too." He took another hit of the joint. "But I wanna see if Samantha is working today."

Bonnie slid off his lap as he stood. He entered his parents' bedroom and opened their walk-in closet. Using a stepstool, he opened his dad's shoe cabinet and pulled down the gun safe.

"Stupid fucker left the key in the lock."

Mark turned the latch, and the cover popped open. He holstered his dad's pistol under his belt at the small of his back and returned the safe to its spot in the cabinet.

"I'll be back, Bonnie. Don't wait up for me," he yelled across the living room as he closed the front door behind him.

The LSD trip started the moment Mark grabbed the glass doors of Alton Towers' main entrance. The people bustling around inside the mall swirled together, and the colors of the storefronts collided and merged with violence. He steadied himself and fought to control his equilibrium. Once the initial phase passed, he stepped inside Alton Towers Mall.

He patted the bulge of his shirt's backside to make sure the weapon was still there. His shoulder bumped into another shopper.

"Uh, sorry," he slurred.

The shopper continued walking, seemingly unfazed by the collision or returning any sort of apology.

"Fucker," Mark whispered and lost his balance.

He entered Metanoia Books and absentmindedly shuffled through the aisles. He stopped and touched the front cover of Bret Easton Ellis's *Lunar Park*. Scanning the aisle for any spying employee, he quickly stuffed the paperback into the front of his pants and headed out the door. *What's the point of money anyway?* he thought as he adjusted his belt to maintain the weight of both the weapon and the stolen novel.

Mark shambled toward Samantha's workplace and sat down on a bench directly in front of Baldock & Ashford. He removed *Lunar Park* from his waistband and surveyed the clothing shop's interior through the large storefront windows. After flipping through the novel, he hiccupped and tossed the paperback into the trashcan next to the bench. Returning his attention to inventorying which employees were currently working, he unholstered the gun from the back of his pants.

The passersby didn't seem to notice the black firearm in Mark's lap. Or, if they did, they didn't seem alarmed. He counted six female employees but no sign of Samantha. He fondled the trigger guard and noticed his palms had become sweaty. He thought about saving the paperback from the trashcan to have something to read while he killed time waiting.

Mark bent over and reached into the wastebasket just as black spots invaded his peripheral vision and the world shifted on its axis. He closed his eyes and prepared for the inevitable fainting spell.

When he regained consciousness, he realized he had slumped forward in a manner where the gun had been hidden, tucked between his stomach and thighs. He stiffened his body to help exterminate any residual dizziness from passing out.

Still no Samantha.

He sighed in defeat, secured the pistol into his pants again, and exited Alton Towers, leaving the shoplifted novel in the trash.

━ • • ━

"Dawson!" Mark almost stumbled over the railroad ties again as he crossed the tracks toward his mother's car. "Dawson!"

"Calm down. I'm right here," Dawson answered, materializing.

Mark removed the firearm and tossed it to the ground.

"What the hell is that?"

"My dad's gun. I just came from Alton Towers."

"You went to see if Samantha was working, didn't you?"

"Maybe."

"You're such a shithead. You were rejected by her, then she issued a restraining order—a lawful order to stay away from her—and you keep going back for more. Are you trying to ruin your future?"

"I never wanna be old, and I surely don't want any kids."

"Why? Because you think all your troubles are the result of bad parenting? You can't blame your parents anymore, dude."

"Well, that's no fun. Who can I blame then? The pills?"

Another dizzy spell overcame Mark as the LSD took full effect; the sky seemed to move sideways, and he tried frantically to stop the moon from touching his shoulder.

"You can blame the fucking drugs you seem to be on right now."

"Oh, don't go all Goody-Two-Shoes on me, Dawson, now that you're all dead and clean. When you were alive, you were a junkie, and you knew it."

Mark pulled his cell phone from his back pocket and tapped the screen.

"What are you doing?"

"Deleting Samantha from my life—text messages, emails, unfriending her on all my social media accounts. Sucks that a friendship with the history we had ended this way."

"You did it to yourself, bro."

"Don't I always?"

Dawson smirked and shrugged.

A twig snapped behind them.

"Was that meant for me?" Samantha asked, pointing at the discarded gun.

"Sam! What—what are you doing out here?" Mark asked, taking a step forward.

"I was waiting for you to come back so we could talk."

"Come back? How did you know I was coming back? How long have you been waiting?"

"Dawson told me that you always visit him out here. It was just a matter of time. Again, was that meant for me?"

"Nah, babe. I was just gonna fire some rounds into the trees. Bored. Ya know."

"Dawson explained everything to me."

Mark glared at his friend. "Oh, yeah? What did Dawson explain exactly?"

"Follow me. I think you are suffering from short-term memory loss."

"I'm not going anywhere."

"Yes, you are."

"Fuck you, Sam."

Mark didn't move. When a few moments passed, and Samantha realized he wasn't going to do what she had asked, she lunged for the gun.

"Okay, okay! I'll follow you."

She turned and headed toward the derailed train. When they reached the locomotive, she slid aside one of the entry doors.

"I know this is where you keep your stash."

Mark remained silent.

She entered the train's cabin. "And other things."

"Sam, don't. Don't go in there," he pleaded.

"I already have, Mark. I want to see your face when you see what they look like now."

He swallowed hard and stepped into the train. The putrid smell was overpowering. He gasped and placed a hand over his mouth to prevent bile from rising in his throat.

"How can the smell not bother you?"

Samantha slid open the divider door between the two cabins and pointed into the darkness. "There. Look."

"Sam, I know what's in there. I put them in there myself."

She shoved him into the darkened cabin, and he stumbled over his mother's darkened and decomposing foot.

"Fucking look at them! Those are your parents! You did this— to your parents!"

Mark shook his head. "I didn't know what I was doing. I didn't mean it."

He rummaged through his sweatshirt pocket for the bag of pills. His fingers found the tranquilizers, and he removed the bottle. Samantha slapped the bottle from his hand; it rolled across the train's floorboards and came to a stop against his dad's burnt earlobe.

"How long have they been out here?" she asked.

"I don't remember. Dawson could tell you. Time seems to move differently for me when I'm on the meds."

"And Bonnie? You had to fucking kill your cat too? Mark, you are some monster."

He allowed his gaze to move to the pile of lifeless fur by his mother's torched right arm.

"When did you burn them? Before or after you killed them?"

"After. I killed them at the house and burnt them here. I did a good job covering my tracks. But they don't seem to know they're dead. I had a fight with my mother about her car this morning. And Bonnie and I have been snuggling all morning too."

"Are you sure it's not just the meds? Or all the drugs? Or your twisted little brain?"

"No. I don't know. Maybe. How do I know you're really here? How do I know that any of this"—he fanned his arm across the space above his parents—"isn't a hallucination?"

"Because I'm here, and I know I'm real."

"Is that what you think? Are you completely sure about that?"

"Excuse me?" she asked with an attitude, cocking her head.

Mark grabbed Samantha by the forearm and dragged her from the train, closing the door of his parents' train-tomb. Not releasing his grip, he stopped and grabbed the balled-up restraining order from a pile of leaves and opened it, smoothing the crinkles.

"In the end, this yellow piece of paper did you no good," he spat.

Samantha tried to take a step backward and free herself from his vise grip. Mark clenched her arm tighter.

"I don't understand." She sounded terrified.

He dragged her to the rear of his mother's car and punched right next to the license plate. The trunk slowly opened.

Samantha gasped. "Oh . . . my . . . God."

She snatched her arm from his grip and placed all ten fingers against the sides of her lips and took a step forward. She reached into the trunk and brushed her hair away from her dead body's forehead.

Mark laughed. "And you thought some signature on a piece of paper would keep me away."

She leaned closer to her corpse and touched the ligature marks around her neck.

"You . . . strangled me?"

"You wouldn't stop flopping around like a fish."

Samantha fell to her knees in a heap of sobs and undecipherable screams.

"Now it's time to say goodbye," he said.

She collected herself for a moment and looked quizzically at his face.

He closed the trunk, sealing her cadaver inside, and pushed the car toward the waterline. The vehicle gained speed as the downward slope of the ground became steeper. Mark took his hands off the back of the car and watched it careen into the water. Massive ripples crossed Jupiter Island's lake as the sedan floated and then slowly sank.

He turned to Samantha. She rocked back and forth while trapping her knees with her arms.

Dawson offered her his hand. She accepted, and he helped her to her feet.

Mark started to cough. A deep, guttural cough. He lunged forward, grabbing his chest and heaving. He doubled over and fought with every ounce of energy to inhale. Water projectiled from Samantha's mouth as she panicked, trying to catch her breath. They both fell on the ground, gasping for any bit of air they could drag into their lungs. Mark convulsed and clawed at his chest. Samantha's lips were pressed against the dirt; with every breath she easily exhaled, she struggled to draw any new air into her lungs.

Dawson looked at the lake. The car was almost completely submerged. He returned his gaze to the two people flopping on the ground at his feet, drowning in air. He looked back at the car and then again at Mark and Samantha. The farther the car sank, the more frantically they flailed, unable to squeak even the slightest breath into their mouths.

The top of the car completely disappeared, and Mark and Samantha spewed water from their noses and mouths. Samantha started to seize; her body twitched and spasmed, like she was being electrocuted.

Mark reached for Dawson and gurgled with one last dying effort. "What . . . have . . . you . . . done . . . to . . . me?"

Dawson looked at Samantha. She had stopped moving. Her eyes remained open. He kicked her to make sure her phantom body was just as dead and drowned as her physical body in the trunk of the car.

He looked across the lake and noticed even the bubbles had stopped floating to the surface where the car had sunk. Then he kicked Mark's lifeless body, again to make sure his revenant body was also just as dead and drowned as his corporeal one in the backseat of the car.

"It's a shame murder victims don't ever know they're dead," Dawson said and kicked the gun into a leaf pile, the muzzle still warm from the shot he had fired moments earlier.

Bonnie jumped into his arms and purred when Dawson lovingly patted her.

Mark released the last batch of air he had kept trapped in his lungs. Water poured from the bullet hole in his forehead, like a faucet. He thought he could hear the creaking of the rope attached to Dawson's hanging body as it swung in the breeze, but the sound of rushing water as the car landed on the lake floor was too loud for him to be sure.

Then nothingness and silence.

Silence.

Silenc .
Silen .
Sile .
Sil   .
Si   .
S   .

    .

———

Brian Paone was born and raised in the Salem, Massachusetts area. Brian has, thus far, published three novels: a memoir about being friends with a drug-addicted rock star, *Dreams are Unfinished Thoughts*; a macabre cerebral-horror novel, *Welcome to Parkview*; and a time-travel romance novel, *Yours Truly, 2095,* (which was nominated for a Hugo Award, though it did not make the finalists)—all three novels are available in paperback, eBook, and audiobook. Along with his three novels, Brian has published three short stories: "Outside of Heaven," which is featured in the anthology, *A Matter of Words*; "The Whaler's Dues," which is featured in the anthology, *A Journey of Words*; and "Anesthetize (or A Dream Played in Reverse on Piano Keys)," which is featured here. Brian is also a vocalist and has released seven albums with his four bands: Yellow #1, Drop Kick Jesus, The Grave Machine, and Transpose. He is married to a US Naval Officer, and they have four children. Brian is also a police officer and has been working in law enforcement since 2002. He is a self-proclaimed roller coaster junkie, a New England Patriots fanatic, and his favorite color is burnt orange. For more information on all his books and music, visit www.BrianPaone.com.

Rowdy

D.W. Vogel

I was only five when Mom brought home a puppy, and for me it was better than winning the lottery. Snow blew in the front door when she entered, and the pup was such a tiny thing that Mom carried him inside her coat, snuggled warm against her body.

Dad wasn't as excited. "A puppy? A Labrador? Really, Bev, don't we have enough going on right now?" He looked at me when he said it, but I was too excited about the puppy to feel the slight.

Mom set him on the floor and he yawned, all squinty eyes and puppy breath. He looked around for a moment, sniffed the carpet, and made a beeline for one of my stuffed animals. When I took it away from him, he blinked at me and peed right there, in the middle of the living room.

I wanted to call him Tinkles because, for the first week or so, that's almost all he did. But Mom said his name was Rowdy, and he became my very best friend.

That was eleven years ago.

His breath doesn't smell like puppy anymore. It's gotten foul over the past few months because his kidneys are failing. He takes a long time to get up now, and it's painful to watch him stumble after a ball, even if it's just rolled across the kitchen floor.

I've known since he was a puppy that this day would come.

We start with a car ride to the dog park early in the morning so no one else will be there. Rowdy can't run with the younger dogs, and it breaks Mom's heart to see him wobble after a happy pack that leaves the old gray-faced Lab behind. We sit under Rowdy's favorite tree with a view of the pond, the fields just starting to green up for spring.

After the dog park, we go for ice cream, but Rowdy only takes a couple of licks, and anyone can see he only does it because he can tell how much Dad wants him to. He hasn't really eaten much of anything for a week, and the vet said that's how we'd know it was time.

Mom cries the whole way from the Dairy Hut to the vet's office. It breaks my heart to see her cry, but there is nothing I can do to make it better.

The doctor is a kind woman who gets right down on the floor with us.

"Oh, old man," she says to Rowdy, who is lying on a fuzzy fleece blanket. "What a good boy you've been." She pats his bony head, explains the procedure, and leaves us alone in the exam room while she gets everything ready.

I lean over and whisper into Rowdy's ear. "It's just a shot, buddy. You'll just go to sleep. It won't hurt or anything."

His hearing went a long time ago, and I know he can't hear me, but his tail thumps a little at the nearness of my face to his.

"It never gets easier," Mom says, and Dad kneels behind her, sniffling into her hair. "I thought I'd do better this time, but . . ."

Dad squeezes her shoulders. "I know, honey. Just can't imagine the house with no dogs in it, you know?"

The vet comes back in, and Rowdy doesn't even move when she pokes his skin with the first shot. In a few minutes his eyelids go slack and his breathing slows.

"Are you ready?" The vet holds a syringe full of bright blue liquid.

Mom and Dad nod.

The liquid flows into Rowdy's vein, and before it's all in, his breaths go silent.

Mom collapses over his still form, and Dad wipes his eyes.

"Thanks," he says to the vet. "We appreciate everything you did."

The vet nods, her hand resting on Rowdy's still chest. "Two dogs in two years is too many. Wish we'd had fifteen years, like Ranger. I'm so sorry we didn't get longer with Rowdy."

She leaves and Dad bends over Mom, whose tears wet the fur on Rowdy's soft ears.

They don't see when Rowdy jumps up out of his body. He yawns and blinks at me, just like that very first day they brought him home.

"Go see Ranger," Mom whispers. "He's waiting for you on the other side."

But I'm not on the other side. I'm right here where I've always been. With Mom and Dad and my best friend Rowdy.

We sniff a greeting, and Rowdy leaps across the room, free of painful hips and sick stomach. Dad helps Mom out of the hospital, and Rowdy and I bound after them into the warm spring sunshine.

D.W. Vogel is a veterinarian, marathon runner, SCUBA diver, and cancer survivor. She was raised on Cincinnati chili and is a terrible bowler. She lives in Cincinnati with her husband, Andrew, and a houseful of special needs pets. Novels include the #1 bestselling *Horizon Alpha: Predators of Eden* (Book One of the *Horizon* series, available from Future House Publishing), and *Flamewalker*. Her short story, "High Wire," set in the world of *Horizon Alpha*, is available in the *Future Worlds* anthology. Join the party at: wendyvogelbooks.com.

Widower's Choice

Virginia Carraway Stark

I watch you from the walls, and I see your pretty life playing out like a shadow show. I watch you whenever I can because I have nothing else that I can do. I'm sorry if I scare you, I don't mean to. If I could, I would be part of your life, and I would learn to love you. I speak this to each of you who have lived in my house, to all those I have tried to love, and lost.

Time doesn't move the same for me as it does for you, although each moment for me is honey-sweet or bitter with my own mistakes.

I've had a long time to think. When I was living in this old house, I knew every creak of each board of the floors that I scrubbed gray, cleaning on my hands and knees. They walk across the floors, and I try to stave off the deep anger that I feel when I see how little they care for the planks that came from living trees, that were carefully milled and installed by my father, still so rough they gave me splinters.

In those days, there were no mops on sticks. Now I see lazy cleaners putting rags on sticks and smearing the filth around, then they say they have cleaned the floor.

Not only have they not cleaned the floor, but by being haphazard in their ways, they show a disrespect for what had once been towering trees that danced in the wind. They had lived and died as summer turned to autumn turned to winter and then, like a miracle, they were reborn each spring with infant buds. The same could not be said for me. I aged and my life turned into the grays of a winter sky, and spring never came to renew me.

My sister and I were only a few years apart: pretty Alice who could do no wrong and me, the elder, the spinster. My name is Elizabeth. The difference between us was that she was sugar that melted away and vanished in death, leaving nothing of herself behind. Meanwhile, I was, and am, a salmon bone that stuck in the throat of death and refused to leave anything behind and move on to wherever those fragrant blossoms who move on go.

Beautiful Alice, who had married Lawrence, the boy two years younger than me, who had thought I was an old lady when I was eighteen and he was sixteen. How I had loved him, his ochre eyes and his curly dark blond hair that fell into those same earth-toned eyes. I thought about the color of ochre his eyes might be; it's a family of tones and in some lights, they shone like sienna and others—like ferrous ochre. I thought about his colors while scrubbing the floors even after their wedding. Pretty Alice with her smiling children. She never grew old, she only dimmed her light, and I tended her until her light dimmed and then went out. There was no horror of death in her. It wasn't violent or disgusting anymore than a flower dying for want of water is anything but a sorrow rather than a visceral showing.

I thought Lawrence would marry me after her death. He cried on my shoulder like a little boy, and Alice's son held my hand while I held her infant daughter in my arms, and they lowered her into the rain-soaked earth. Earth the colors of ochre. Sienna, ochre, umber—the ground was colored like layers of cake as they laid my beloved sister to rest. I envied her ability to rest when I must go ever on, but still I thought of Lawrence and how he needed me and how I needed him.

Alice and Lawrence had moved back to the family home when I was twenty-three. Alice had married Lawrence at the respectable age of seventeen, only a few days after Lawrence had turned eighteen. I was twenty, and after Alice married, everyone whispered behind their hands that I would never marry. They were right, but the ones who said I would never know the embrace of a man were wrong.

My parents' deaths, sudden and brutal, were the catalyst that had brought Lawrence and Alice back home. It was a big old house that cried out for a family. The gray boards chattered merrily to the sound of the children's feet. The boards had ceased to be trees a long time ago, they had ceased to feel the wind blowing on their hardened skin or the rain caressing their cheeks. Their leaves caught the raindrops, and the old roots, gray under the earth like worms or the dead boards or my dress, were the only reminder to them that they were alive.

Then, like a girl who realizes all at once that her dreams will never be realized, the trees were cut down and crashed to the earth, their branches broken under their fall and sap leaking from their wounds. They were fed into the board planer and laid out by my father while I watched the wonder of something built where once there had been nothing.

When my mother taught me how to scour the boards with damp sand and then wash the boards, oil and repeat—something I would do for the rest of my life—I had taken to the task with joy. I didn't notice how the sand roughened my hands, even as it smoothed the boards, or how my dresses slowly merged to a uniform gray that blended with the aging planks.

"I don't know why you do that every day," Alice said. She was leaning on the doorjamb, flowers entwined in her blonde hair and pulled back in a crown of braids. Golds and pinks were the colors that surrounded her the way I was shrouded in gray and Lawrence always the colors of the earth.

"To keep it clean. Doesn't it look lovely?" I answered, my mind thinking cross, petty thoughts I would never speak. *Brassy-colored hair,* I said internally, instead of *Golden tresses,* as was only fair, proper, and true.

"It looks clean," she offered.

I sniffed. "You don't get splinters in your delicate, pink feet anymore. I should think you'd be happy."

"Beth—" She knelt beside me, careful to lift the hem of the white lace that trimmed the rose pink of her dress from the floor. "—there's more to life than the floors and the gardens and the dishes."

"I know that. There is needlework, quilting, embroidery—"

She had been fifteen then, and I still dreamed that Lawrence would ask me to marry him. I was seventeen, but my birthday was only a few weeks away.

"Have you thought about a husband?"

"Of course I have. You've seen my hope chest," I said proudly. I wished she would stop talking to me. I wanted to get the floors done so I could check on the garden and then get in to work on some squares for my new quilt before the bugs started to come out for the evening.

"There's a dance tomorrow. I'm going to ask Father if I can go. You could ask to come too. Put away your gray dress and put on something pretty." She brushed a loose dark hair out of my eyes. "You're so beautiful, Beth, but you insist on being so plain."

She had asked Father to go, and he had let her. She had asked for us both to go but I refused. I was tired, and my back was sore. I had only a few more squares to finish before I could begin the edging of my Bachelor's Despair quilt. I had anguished over the design and saved for the fabric to make it perfect. What man could resist a woman clever enough to make a flawless, complex quilt such as the Bachelor's Despair?

That night Alice and Lawrence danced together while I sat at home and sewed. The charcoal-colored seams at the edge were thick where the layers of fabric gathered together to make the border with the crimson edging, and I pushed the needle hard into the fleshy pad of my index finger. A large drop of blood dripped like a ruby onto the virgin-white central square of the fine quilt I had made for my hope chest. I knew then that I had made a mistake. It was not for Lawrence to despair for me, it was I to despair for all. The only color I had put into my quilt was blood red and blue, all the rest was grays, whites, charcoals, and black.

It was the last quilt that I made for my overflowing hope chest, although not by far the last quilt I would make. When the nights are right and the realm between your world and mine is particularly thin, I can leave the attic door at the top of the stairs open and hope that someone from the pretty world of life will follow me and look at my hope chest with the specter of me. Few of them follow me. Most curse the wind or the foundation of the old house that makes doors open and slam with my humors. The ones who come, and the very few who open the chest, find a box of rags. The Bachelor's Despair is now faded all to grays, like the wood, like my dress. They are eaten by moths, despite the cedar the chest is made of, and fall to pieces like forgotten dreams in the hands of the living.

Why do I keep showing them to the living? What insanity besets we, who are dead, to repeat the same actions while failing again and again?

After Alice died, Lawrence came to me for comfort. He was no bachelor; he was, in fact, a widower, and there is a different quilt that one makes for a widower. He came to me, first in the garden, and then in the kitchen, and finally in the sterile sanctity of my maiden's bed. I spilled blood again, this time on my white sheets. The quilt that covered my twin bed was a simple Roman Cross. I had made it from one of my old dresses and two of Alice's, so her gold and pink brightened my room like a gust of wind in a stale attic.

I didn't mind the spilled blood or how quickly Lawrence fell asleep. I traced out the Roman Cross with my fingers, the dusty rose satin soft under my coarse finger tips. When I woke in the morning, somewhat later than usual I confess, Lawrence was gone. He had returned to his own bed, and he thanked me coldly and distantly when I served him his coffee and eggs. The children stared at us as I froze midway toward kissing his cheek and turned awkwardly away beneath his hostile stare. There was no love for me in his eyes; they were the color of winter dirt.

I wasted no time for weeping. Instead I walked into town and picked out fabric: blue, gray, black, and red; the same colors I had chosen so many years ago for Bachelor's Despair. I would make a new quilt; a quilt for a widower: Widower's Choice.

I stayed up most of the night cutting out squares and organizing the pieces into neat piles. He did not come to my room that night.

I told him in a chill tone to tend his own children when he came to ask me what was for lunch. He watched me. I felt his eyes on the back of my head. I sat on the floor, my dress the same gray as the boards. I was part of the house. I was an angry part of the house.

Blue for Lawrence, gray for me,
Black for death, and red
For love for me and thee.

I repeated the little verse to myself, making a tune of it as I did.

I sewed day and night until the squares were made, and I breathed a sigh of relief. It was time to begin assembling them. Lawrence was relieved when I returned to my fulltime duties as nurse, nanny, housekeeper, cook, and concubine. His visits to my bed became nightly, only to have him flee each morning.

I sewed my squares together. *You must make a choice, Lawrence. Widower's choice: love or death, but choose before my heart breaks.*

Alice was dead, his children needed a mother, he needed someone in his bed, why did he hesitate? Was I so repugnant to him that he would rather choose death than love with me?

Now, as a spirit, I walk to the windows, and the fog that is my breath congeals on the windowpanes. I watch the family that lives here now spill out of a new vehicle. Talking and laughing, they look at glowing screens more than each other. None of the children clean the floors or sew or even have a hope chest to leave them desolate and alone. They are nearly a different species from me.

Back then, when I had finished my quilt at long last and spread it on my bed, Lawrence had come into my room with a lamp turned low. "That's a new bedspread."

"No, it's a new quilt," I corrected.

"It's very nice," he offered and kissed my neck.

"What color do you like best?"

"It's too dark in here to see the colors properly," he protested.

"Then turn up the light," I urged.

echo through the chimney. A woman rocks her own golden-haired, pink-hued daughter and tells her, *Hush, it's only the wind, little one.*

I like to remember when everything was beautiful and I was young. Even the gray ones deserve to have memories like that. Even the murderers deserve to remember what it was to be loved. I tell myself this, but all I can see are rags in an old hope chest and quilts buried deep in the trees. A Widower's Choice quilt stained black with blood in the moonlight and the struggles of the children to resist me.

I bite my ghostly knuckles and weep for a dance never gone to . . . and all the other choices I never made . . . and all the ones I did.

Virginia Carraway Stark started writing professionally with her first screenplay, *Blind Eye*. Her award-winning series, *Carnival Fun*, has received international attention. She is a prolific writer and has dozens of short stories in various presses, including a story in *Chicken Soup for the Soul: Think Possible*. She has been nominated for many awards and won several. She is the Editor in Chief for StarkLight Press, where she also coordinates collaborations and publishes novels and anthologies as well. You can find her work on Amazon and brick-and-mortar stores, as well as in libraries and schools. Find out what is new and recent by going to www.virginiastark.wordpress.com.

The Blue
Amberol
Turns Again

K.N. Johnson

The Turners called their home a farm, but to most folks in Buchanan County, they lived on an estate with one hundred acres of premium land close enough to town that electricity lit up their big farmhouse with its second story and inside toilet. No one held their good fortune against them. The Turners earned every bit of it, got their own hands dirty breeding quality horses in their round red barn. No one wished them a bad turn. No one figured one was coming.

"This way, Benji. You've gotta see why we're skipping the piano tonight." Pearl Turner tugged at the watch chain draped across Benjamin's vest. "It's bonafide."

The Edison Amberola had arrived that morning, carried in a crate by the postal delivery wagon. Just in time for their Friday night shindig, Pa Turner gave the new phonograph a place of honor in the addition he was keen on calling the "ballroom." He'd rubbed the dark cabinet down with wood soap, like liniment on a prized racehorse, tenderly wiping packing dust from its mahogany girth. He'd opened the storage door and organized the bright blue cylinders of music, each label printed with the face of Thomas Edison. He turned them all so Edison's eyes faced forward, peeking over the shelf edge again and again.

The Turners and friends huddled around the Amberola at the far end of the large room. Heels tapped on the hardwood floor, gazes drifted to the crystal chandelier.

Albert, the Turner's oldest, used all six-foot-four of his lanky frame to command attention and held up one of the wax cylinders. "You know, my buddy up in Wisconsin says these blue Amberols are getting rinky dink. He's buying diamond discs. They're flat and take up less space."

In the lull of new music, the younger Turners rolled their eyes, clasped their friends' hands, and giggled their way into a rowdy spin of ring-around-the-rosy.

"These are Edison." Pa took the cylinder from Albert's hand. "I don't care about those other talking machine jobbers."

"Edison's making discs too, Pa."

"Applesauce." Pearl raised her voice over the children's singing *"ashes, ashes"* and squeezed her way between her father and brother. "Don't listen to him, Pa." She knelt to read the cylinder labels. "He doesn't know music like you and I do."

She handed her father a cylinder, and he lifted the top lid to slide it into place. Band music trickled from the cabinet and filled the room with the earnest pleas of a beau to his sweetheart, begging her to *go a-walking*. Pearl yanked Benji into the middle of the room and led him into a slow foxtrot. She had learned all the newest dances.

Ma Turner raised her eyebrows and leaned into Pa. "It's a good thing they're engaged."

Pa chuckled, then elbowed Albert and pointed out the window to a cloud of dust. An automobile horn honked, and four goggled figures emerged from the billowing dirt.

"See that machine?"

Albert nodded.

"Son, do we get rid of all our horses just because we bought a horseless buggy?"

Albert shrugged.

"Course we don't. Course we don't, son."

Pa Turner's second son, Grover, entered the front door with another fellow and two young ladies. A chorus of laughter and the ruckus of goggle, glove, and motor coat removal broadcast their arrival. The young ladies used a small brush to tidy their dresses. Grover bounded through the parlor into the ballroom to his father.

"You lost one of your music doohickeys." In his outstretched hand lay a bright blue cylinder.

"The Amberola only comes with a dozen." Pa Turner took it and frowned at the label. "It's not an Edison."

"Well, it was on our porch. This must be number thirteen."

— • • —

The Fieldings moved into the old farmhouse with a gusto indicative of city dwellers getting to stretch their legs on a patch of green in suburbia. The house came with a round red barn on its three acres, situated close enough for a stroll to the quaint downtown coffee and gift shops. While Fiona appreciated the bargain and proximity to her job at the hospital, Max envisioned converting the round barn into a sound studio. That is, once he got the house renovations squared away.

Max sat on the second to last step of the staircase and sighed. The more boxes he unpacked, the more worn the old house looked. With a little elbow grease, he knew vintage hardwood floors hid beneath the orange vinyl flooring. And he couldn't decide whether he preferred the idea of a real wood-burning fireplace or if he should convert it to gas; set blazes with the flick of a switch. The screen door in the kitchen slammed and in skipped his son, Jack.

"Dad? What's this?" He tilted backward so his father could reach into the hood hanging down the back of his sweatshirt. The boy had been rummaging in the barn since that morning, insisting he got dibs on treasures.

Max gripped the brown paper parcel and loosened the twine.

Meg hopped down the stairs, pink headphones resting at her neck, and peered over her father's shoulder. "Oh, how are we going to play it?"

He stared at the blue cylinder, its wax surface speckled with white clouds, its label browned and torn. "This will only play on a very old record player."

As they marched into the backyard, Jack kicked at a length of concrete jutting from the ground. "Why's there an old parking lot in the yard?"

Max gave the concrete a kick too and explained it wasn't a parking lot. "This house used to have an extra room."

Meg tiptoed along the crumbled foundation, balanced on one foot while holding the other aloft, and tilted forward into the shape of a capital letter *T*.

Max pointed to the large picture window on the back of the house, and both of his children stared. "That used to be a doorway into a huge ballroom."

On the back of the house, a faint line revealed the mystery room, a dingy charcoal halo around the siding less dingy than the rest.

Meg shoved her hands on her hips. "A ballroom? I could have had a ballroom to practice in?"

In the dim light of the barn, the three Fieldings sorted through wooden crates and dusty cardboard boxes but found no Amberola.

Jack grumbled and refused to open another box. "I'm telling ya, there isn't one in here. I would've seen it, Dad. I know what those record players look like."

Max Fielding rattled the ladder to the loft. "Take a break, Jack." He pointed his thumb at the loft. "If I don't find anything up here, we'll try the shops downtown and hit that ice cream place before Mom comes home."

Jack grinned and raced from the barn as his father climbed the ladder.

Meg skulked to the door as well and yelled as she left. "I'm taking a break too."

Max rolled his eyes. Kids. Didn't they want to witness the reveal, the great moment of discovery? He crawled beneath the cobwebs sagging from the ceiling and reached a small stack of boxes.

Meg and Jack reappeared, their eyes wide as they crammed against the doorframe.

"There's music. Old music coming from the house."

Meg gripped her brother's shoulders.

He hummed and tried to sing. "*Long way to* . . . where's Tippa Larrey?"

Despite his efforts, cobwebs clung to Max's black T-shirt. He cupped his hand around his ear. In the distance, the distinct strain of an old song wobbled, the male tenor belting out about it being a long way to go.

He shifted his body, closed his eyes to focus on the faint music, and felt his knee sink into a soft plank of wood with such speed, he failed to grab anything to stop his long, long fall.

— • • —

Grover and Benji marched around the room, the younger Turners keeping step, and Albert sang out with an exaggerated Irish accent, "*Tipper-ra-ry!*"

Ma Turner forced a smile. "Our Grover. Joining the army." She clutched Pa's arm. "Going to war."

"It's not our war." Pa retrieved the cylinder after the song ended. "It's a Mexican revolution." His words echoed in the large room. His eyes drifted to the window, the nightfall. "The army's just protecting the border. Making sure they stay on their side of the Rio Grande." He tucked the cylinder into the cabinet, spun Edison's eyes forward. "We've got four men running for president this year and not a one are talking war."

Grover clambered into his mother. "No war for me, Ma. I'm gonna catch bandits." With his fingers bent in the shape of a handgun, he aimed at the chandelier.

One of his guests giggled.

Pearl yanked at her fiancé Benji's hand. "Don't you forget you're just tagging along. Don't you sign a thing." She rested her head on his shoulder. "Pa, was that the last one?"

Albert sidled to the phonograph with the thirteenth cylinder. "We haven't tried this one."

Pa grumbled at the label, running his fingers over the stark lines and two dots until Pearl leaned over his shoulder.

She pointed at the symbol. "It's a repeat." She smiled and placed the cylinder in position. "On sheet music. When you see it, you repeat the whole thing all over again."

The new cylinder spun. Even the young Turners held their breath. A ship's horn blared and Ma's startled jump made the children laugh. A golden trombone played and a man sang:

They built her big, and they made a guarantee,
Big cheers for her un-sinka-bility . . .

Pa crossed his arms over his chest as the chorus rang out:

Oh Titanic, sunk is she,
Poor Titanic at the bottom of the sea.

And he wrenched the cylinder from the machine before it could finish.

The children held hands and circled, the catchy tune easy to sing. "*Oh Titanic, sunk is she . . .*"

But the older Turners and friends brooded, speaking over each other: "The Titanic? The unsinkable ship?" "She only set sail days ago." "Who writes such a thing?"

"Bunk. Pure bunk." Albert took the cylinder from his father. "We've heard it wrong." He positioned the cylinder to play again. "It can't possibly be about the Titanic."

The cylinder turned and a jaunty tune jingled, music entirely different from the trombones of the Titanic ditty. This song called one of them by name, bade him a foreboding farewell.

"It's singing about Benji." Pearl's voice rose in pitch, her words rushed, crammed together in disbelief. One hand hovered over her mouth, the other pointed at the phonograph. "Benji?" She gaped at her fiancé, then each of her family nearby. "You hear it, don't you? This is, it's—"

"Bunk." Pa Turner flung the cylinder across the room where it remained as guests departed and the family tucked in for the night.

In her bed, Pearl tossed and turned, her ears insisting music played downstairs. A voice taunted, *Bye-bye, Benji, boy.* She trembled. The trombones moaned. From beneath her door, the song stuttered. *Buh-buh-buh, bye-bye, Benji.*

Edison's eyes peeked over and over the footboard of her bed.

—・・—

Max, his arm in a cast and sling, sat on the floor surrounded by tools and tiny parts. Jack squatted nearby, reaching as his father requested them.

"Still no stove?" Fiona hung her tote bag on the stair post, slid her shoes off, and stepped over a blue cylinder near her husband's knee.

"I've almost got it." Hunched over the contraption, Max tightened a screw.

Fiona settled onto the floor beside them.

He straightened his back, patting her socked foot. "Tomorrow. The stove is tomorrow's project."

Jack held up a black wax cylinder. "Dad bought a punk rock song, and they sent us the instructions."

Fiona pursed her lips, and Max tapped the black cylinder. "This cost less than an Edison phonograph at the antique mall. Way less."

She leaned closer. The pine box only had two sides and, across the open top, a rod between two pine blocks and a rubber tube. It looked nothing close to an Edison Amberola.

Max placed the new black cylinder, not on the rod, but on two rails in the box. He took a deep breath. "It's been bouncing everywhere, but I think this is it."

Jack wobbled closer and showed his mother the hole he'd cut in the bottom of a cone-shaped measuring cup. He fitted it to the end of the tube while Max pushed a button on a motor small enough to fit in the palm of his hand. The cylinder began to spin. Jack beamed, nodded at his father, and from the cone came the sounds of a crowd mumbling, then humming, and the clatter of mugs on a pub sideboard.

No instruments, just a man's Cockney English accent singing

a tale about his father's grave getting moved for a new town sewer. The song ended with the voices joining in harmony to draw out the word *grave*.

Max laughed as his wife and son exchanged looks.

Jack dropped the cone. "That's it? That's punk rock?"

"Well, they're steampunk." Max adjusted his sling and switched the black cylinder for the moldy blue one. "Here's the real mystery. The lone blue Amberol." He nodded at Jack to refit the cone and tube.

The cylinder spun and assailed them with a swooshing sound, the swirling of a brush or broom that refused to keep time with the static click of each rotation. Fiona grimaced. Jack gritted his teeth, stretching his arm with the cone as far from his ears as he could reach. Horns and clarinets played a merry, if crackling, opening. A man's voice warbled, rolling his *R*s, proclaiming his love for an Irish gal named Meg.

Fiona smiled. "Of all the songs." She hurried to the stairs and called for Meg. "Come down and hear this."

Jack caught his dad's attention and pulled a face, but his father half shrugged. "We sang it to her when she was a baby."

His son rolled his eyes as Meg hopped down the last stair to the finale of happy horns and clarinets.

"I'll play it again."

Max reset the cylinder and frowned when, through the sweeping static, piano notes pounded. He stared at Fiona with wide eyes as a woman's voice sang a nursery rhyme with flair. "*Little Jack Horner . . .*"

Fiona kneeled at the contraption. "It's not the same cylinder."

Max Fielding held up the black cylinder. "We've only got two." He pointed at the spinning blue Amberol. "And that's the only blue one."

"What's wrong?" Meg crossed her arms.

"That's my name." Jack turned the horn toward his face, as if he could watch the lyrics exit. "How'd you do that, Dad?"

Fiona's eyes grew wider as she scanned the room. "You didn't order any extras? Was there a freebie in the box?"

She scavenged through the packing peanuts in the cardboard box as the woman repeated the rhyme. "*Little Jack Horner. . .*"

Fiona took the handmade machine, pulled the tube and horn from Jack's hands, and dropped it into the box with a *thud*. Before Max and the kids could protest, she carried it out the back door and tossed it into the yard.

No one dared to retrieve it.

— • • —

Pearl charged at Benji in the Turner's foyer, her face almost bumping his. "Look." She pressed a newspaper into his chest. "The Titanic. It sank." Pearl swooned and he gripped her arms. "The unsinkable ship sank. And that, that thing knew."

Benji guided her to the parlor, to a velvet chaise, and shook the wrinkles from the paper where the headline confirmed her ramblings: *New Titanic Sinks. 1800 Persons, Watery Graves.*

Pearl clutched his pant leg. "It's a jinx. A jinx." She bit her lip. "You can't, you can't leave with Grover."

Ma Turner hustled into the parlor but pulled back into the doorway as Benji took Pearl's chin in his hand. "We're not going in a boat, honey bunch."

She twisted her hands into her skirt, pulling and wringing at the delicate chiffon.

He cupped her hands with his. "I'm tagging along. Grover will enlist and I'll come right back home to you."

"The second song said you'd wreck, Benji." She squeezed his hands. "It's a jinx."

"No such thing." Ma entered and stroked her daughter's shoulder. "It's just a silly song, dear. No one's going to wreck."

— • • —

Meg rustled her bedsheets, kicking her comforter to the floor. The muffled voices of her parents tapered off before midnight, the television in her brother's room silent for more than an hour. She pressed her eyes closed and tried to count sheep. One, two, three, four.

"*It's a long, long way. . .*" Someone wailing for home. The voice too manly to be Jack, too warbled to be her father.

Meg's eyes shot open. Downstairs, something rolled across the floor. Not heavy like a bowling ball, but lighter, like a rolling pin. The song stopped and her heart pounded so loud in her ears she wasn't certain if the rolling, rolling sound continued.

She crept to the top of the stairs and listened. Something rolled. Crouching behind the rail and spindles, she tiptoed to the last step and cowered behind the large newel post. Moonlight cast a large bright rectangle from the window to the side of the staircase.

With the rhythm of a wheel, a faded blue cylinder trundled, trundled into the light, and with each rotation across the floor, a man's voice crooned a different tune. No more words of a long trip to Tipperary.

Meg froze; the air chilled. The man called out, called out for Meg. Two, three, four times.

— • • —

In the Turner's ballroom, the children pulled at Pearl's arms, tugged at her skirt, and dragged her into ring-around-the-rosy to distract her while she waited for Benji and Grover's return.

"Sit here." Young Nellie Turner forced her big sister into a chair, the narrow back topped with pointed finials—a starburst carving.

Little Tommy, arms behind his back, pressed into her kneecaps. "Promise you won't tell Pa?"

Pearl held her palm in the air, pointed her index finger, and crisscrossed over her heart. "Cross my heart." She tilted her head. "Now, what have you got there?"

Young Mabel snuck behind Tommy and snatched his hidden treasure. "You promise?"

Pearl sighed as Tommy stomped on Mabel's toe. "Hope to die," she reassured them.

Mabel and Nellie skipped to a corner of the room and placed something on the floor. They waited. And then, with no one having touched it, it rolled. They pointed as it meandered from the dark corner, and the rolling pushed forth a melody of faint trumpets.

Tommy climbed into Pearl's lap as the bright blue cylinder rolled closer. A man sang as if his nose were pinched in a clothespin. He wailed about Benji and his demise. Pearl glared and kicked it.

With Tommy on her lap, her foot didn't land as hard as she'd intended, but enough that the cylinder rolled back to her sisters. But this time, a woman screamed with every roll, and her shriek pierced the air until the cylinder rocked to a rickety, restful stop.

— • • —

The old blue cylinder sat in the middle of the living room floor. In their rock concert T-shirts, softened from years of washing machine cycles, the Fieldings circled the Amberol.

Max cradled the sling on his arm. "Could you have been"—he tapped the cylinder with his toe—"sleepwalking?"

Meg shook her head.

Fiona strode to the window, a window which years ago would have been entry to the Turner's ballroom. She peered into the night, into the dead space of foundation scraps behind the house. She shot a long stare at Jack, who frowned and waved his arms to fend off her silent accusation.

Max tapped the cylinder again. It rocked like a warped paper towel tube. "Maybe an animal sniffed around the backyard and jiggled the phonograph?"

In the kitchen, he rifled through drawers and retrieved a flashlight. Fiona opened the back door and they stepped outside.

From inside, Jack and Meg watched their parents amble over concrete and uneven ground, the beam of the flashlight bobbing. Something in the room rustled. The cylinder rolled, a crackling static announcing its journey. They turned, wide-eyed, as the cylinder wheeled over the floor.

Accompanied by the swoosh of a brushing broom, it moved closer, closer, and stopped at their feet. Jack reached for it. The cylinder rolled from his grasp and stopped. Meg gulped and lifted her hand. The cylinder darted backward. There was no mistaking it for a breeze or uneven floor.

As it whirled across the room, a scream escalated. They pressed their hands to their ears as the cylinder rotated, each spin driving the scream into the pitch of a siren.

— • • —

Albert hitched a carriage to two of their best horses and raced Ma to the hospital to sit at Grover's bedside. Pa's heart squeezed tight in his chest as they left. He couldn't shake the tune rattling around his head. *Buh-buh-buh, bye-bye, Benji.*

He lit the fireplace in the parlor, fixed his attention on the wood crackling in the flames, and tried to stave off the chill of spring and grief. Pearl rested her head on Pa's shoulder, her face pink and pinched. She wadded one of his cotton handkerchiefs.

"Everything turned sour after we got that Edison Amberola." She sniffled. "Benji loved the piano."

"Now, Pearl." Pa took a deep breath. "The Amberola didn't make things go bad." Soft music drifted from the ballroom. "It didn't write the songs. It just plays the music."

"It's that one blue Amberol." She wiped her eye. The music grew louder. "The one that's not an Edison." She scowled, looking over her shoulder. "It doesn't just play the music. It twists the songs."

Pearl dropped the handkerchief and strode to the ballroom. Pa followed. A tenor sang about his home in Tipperary, sang with a tempo teetering between a march and a pub drinking song. Pearl bumped the Amberola, skipping the singer into a repeat of his long way home. She wrenched the cylinder free and, before she could toss it, Pa saved it.

"That one's an Edison."

He sucked air through his teeth and tucked it beside the other watchful eyes in the phonograph cabinet.

A voice boomed, "I have just been shot."

Pearl gasped and Pa slammed the cabinet. Teddy Roosevelt. They knew his voice from town hall—the speeches heard from the phonograph that convinced Pa to buy his own.

Roosevelt continued, "But it takes more than that to kill a Bull Moose."

With hands on her hips, Pearl scanned the room. From the corner, the thirteenth Amberol rolled, reciting a speech they had yet to hear. Pearl seized it, pinched the rim between two fingertips, and carried it to the parlor.

Pa followed, and when Pearl stood before the fireplace with the cylinder raised, he nodded and she hurled it into the flames

———• • •———

Jack and Meg fled to the back door just as their parents reached the step, just as the shriek died. But they had heard it too. The door trembled on its hinges as Max and Fiona burst in, their mouths gaping as they gasped for air. Fiona huddled their children into a hug, and Max inched closer to the cylinder sitting in the other room. He stared at it for a moment, then picked it up. He turned it around, inspected the worn surface, and dropped it in the box with the pine board phonograph bits.

"Throw it out." Fiona wouldn't let go of the kids. "I don't even want it in the house."

Max took a deep breath. "I know it's disturbing, but there's got to be a scientific explanation. There's got to be. . ."

Jack touched his dad's arm, the arm bound in a cast and sling. Max tried to smile, and the two of them walked out with the box of bits and the blue cylinder. Jack lit their path with the flashlight and pushed open the barn door.

As his father searched for a spot to place the banished items, Jack piped up. "Wish I'd never found the thing."

Max turned to his son, trying to avoid looking into the beam of light. "Where, exactly, did you find it?"

Jack swept the light across the space, lighting up graffiti painted on the wall.

"It was in that hole." He pointed and scuffed at the dirt floor. "The hole with the chicken bones."

Max frowned. As he moved closer, he recognized the graffiti. A music symbol. The repeat sign. And in the hole lay a small wooden carving. A woman in a blue dress with a golden halo, resting on a bed of brown bones and a skull with a tiny pointed beak.

▬ ▪ ▪ ▬

A spark ricocheted from the fire, and Pearl shook it free from her skirt. Balanced on the oak logs, the cylinder crackled, but the blue wax did not melt. Pa leaned closer, watching it glisten in the heat. The logs shifted and the cylinder rolled, rolled from the fire to the ashes under the grate, then to the ashes on the hearth.

Pearl cried out, "Pa!" as it hopped from the hearth to the floor, and the familiar marching song began to play.

Pa shuddered, grabbing the mantle to stop his fall.

"*It's a long way to Tipperary . . .*"

The cylinder rolled, aflame as a log on the fire, trailing a line of hot embers for Pearl to chase and stomp.

"*It's a long way to go. . .*"

It rolled from the parlor and through the grand doorway. It rolled into the ballroom and nestled under the velvet drapes.

The tenor swelled into the chorus. "*But my heart's right there.*"

Flames climbed the fabric, licking at the ceiling.

Pearl's screams brought the young Turners running. Pa gathered his wits and a bucket of water from the kitchen and waved the older girls into an assembly line so they could drown the fire. Little Tommy scampered to fetch help from the neighbors while Pearl dragged a rug from the parlor and smothered the flames daring to spread from the ballroom.

Soon, folks arrived pulling wagons of water, and even sand. Swifter than a team of horses, the new town firetruck veered up their dusty drive, the iron bell clanging and the siren stuck in an ear-piercing howl.

—••—

Meg and Jack Fielding hadn't slept in their parents' room for years. But tonight, their mother didn't want them out of her sight. Meg stretched between an overstuffed arm chair and a makeshift ottoman of two boxes and a throw pillow. Jack snuggled on the floor in a sleeping bag of robots and spaceships.

When everyone seemed settled in, Max turned off the lamp and uttered in the most convincing voice he could muster, "Everything will make more sense after a good night's sleep."

Crickets chirped outside and the occasional late night driver sent headlight beams across the wall.

Meg tried to sleep, but a knock, knock, knocking kept stirring her awake. "Jack, could you stop it?"

"Jack, please stop kicking the floor." Fiona wondered if the family sleepover had been a bad idea.

"It's not me," Jack whimpered.

The knocking stopped, replaced by a rapid rattle and a thump, as if something had fallen down a tube or tumbled down the chimney flue.

Fiona sat against the headboard and prodded Max. Jack cozied between them, and Meg crawled onto the end of their bed. They sat in the darkness and listened for silence, listened with breathless hope that the past had surrendered its relentless pursuit. But downstairs, something rolled across the floor.

With the rhythm of a wheel, it trundled. And with each

rotation, a woman's scream pierced the air, until the cylinder rocked to a rickety stop.

K.N. Johnson won first place in *Mythraeum's* Pygmalion contest, and her story, "Frigid," is now in the running for development as a short film. Her short stories have appeared in *Proximity Magazine*, plus the anthologies: *A Journey of Words*, *Polterguests,* and *Incandescent Mind,* the literary journal of Sadie Girl Press. She has served as an acquisitions editor for Mighty Quill Books and worked as a local reporter. Johnson is a member of the HWA and slated to serve as a juror in the anthology category for the Bram Stoker Awards. Follow her progress at: www.facebook.com/knjohnsonauthor.

IF IT'S NOT OKAY, IT'S NOT THE END

TRAVIS WEST

Radio stations across the country all said the same thing, and the one coming through from Wichita was no exception.

"Still plenty of time left in the day if you wanna see Daddy's Girl live in Kansas City," the DJ raved. "They'll be shaking up the Hurricane tonight. I'm telling you now, folks, this may be your last chance to see 'em in such an intimate venue. Starting in May, they'll be playing the big houses, as they open for The Cars all summer long. They're the next big thing, I promise you! Everybody's talking about 'em. *Rolling Stone* is talking about 'em. Check out the latest issue. Check 'em out, up close and personal, at KC's Hurricane tonight. It's not *that* far a drive, boys and girls. Here they are now with their new single, 'Radio Kisses.' It's Daddy's Girl."

Billy Cherry kept a hand on the steering wheel as he lowered the volume. "Two more weeks, guys, and we're out of this shitty van. We'll get a nice big tour bus. With a driver. We'll play to thousands every night, all summer, with The Cars. I can't wait. These radio jocks, the magazines . . . they're preaching the word, doing all the work for us. All we gotta do is show up and play."

Keeping his eye on the road, the guitarist passed his joint to his childhood friend and Daddy's Girl's bassist, Solomon Scott. Solomon drew a lungful of smoke.

"Yeah," he said, exhaling. "You know what I can't wait for? Skimming on those Cars groupies. Seriously, man. It's gonna be a nightly smorgasbord. All you can eat."

Billy and Solomon laughed at the quip, but not everyone in the van shared their humor.

"Hey, Sol," Billy said, meeting his friend's eyes in the rearview mirror. "I don't think Howie finds you funny."

Solomon leaned forward, offering Howie the smoke. "How, c'mon, man. You're the drummer for the hottest new band of 1982;

Rolling Stone says so. Enjoy the ride, man. Fortune has opened her legs to you. Get fucking."

Howie eyed the joint with annoyance. "No, thank you. Is that all you think about, Sol? Getting laid?"

"When I'm not thinking about music? Absolutely! What else is there?"

"I don't know. How about financial stability,"—he pointed to the joint, now back in Billy's hand—"good physical health? True love?"

Billy feared where Howie might be steering the conversation. "God. Who let the geezer into the van?"

Sol leaned forward again. "You mean, who let the geezer into the band? Your question offends me, Howie Benton. I do believe in true love. I *truly* love rock 'n' roll and pussy. Do not doubt me, sir. Billy, pass that over."

"How long of a break do we have before this arena tour starts?" Howie asked. "A week and a half?"

"Roundabouts," Billy said. "Two more weeks of club dates, then yeah, about a week and a half off. Why?"

Howie sighed and Billy knew exactly what he was about to say.

"Guys, I think I'm gonna try to get Ashley back."

Billy and Solomon groaned.

"Howie, come on," Billy said. "Didn't she make things clear enough for you? Ashley gave you an ultimatum: her or the band. Mind you, the band she spent a decade supporting in every way possible. But once a contract was signed and she realized this was more than some weekend fantasy, boom, gone; out the fucking door she went. A decade, Howie, and she didn't know how serious we were about this band? How much it meant to us? C'mon, man! You know what that tells me? That deep down, she either, *A*: never believed we, including you, ever had what it took to succeed; or *B*: never wanted us to succeed. Fuck that, man. Fuck her. How long's it been? Seven or eight months? Eight? It's time to move on, bro, and enjoy our success. Your success."

Solomon patted Howie on the shoulder.

"Billy's right. Look at Chad, here." He pointed to the band's new keyboardist, passed out in the seat next to him. "He's been with us as long as you've been single, and you know what? I don't even miss Rich, man. Rich who? Sure, Rich was with us from the beginning, but he ran as soon as shit got real, didn't he? Personally, I prefer the new guy. He puts out more."

Howie shook his head. "Rich's wife was pregnant. What would you have done?"

"Did you see this beast last night in Tulsa?" Solomon asked, pretending not to have heard Howie. "Those two little Okie chicks he ran off with? Rodeo shirts knotted in front, cowgirl jeans with the pocketless asses."

"Pink and yellow roses embroidered across those asses. *Mm-mm*," Billy added, making a show of biting his fist.

"Hell, yeah. Take a lesson from our new brother, Chad," Solomon said and smacked Chad on the rump.

Chad uttered an incoherent groan and turned in his seat.

"Those two cowgirls? Could have been you, Howie. I'm sure Chad would have been more than happy to share."

Billy nodded. "Here's another way to look at your situation, bro. We're poised for the big time. The whole world is screaming our name: *Daddy's Girl! Daddy's Girl!* No one can fuck it up now but us. You know how many rock stars wind up marrying models or actresses? That chick you liked from *Nancy Drew* and *BJ and the Bear*, Janet Louise Johnson? You could meet her. After this summer, that's a real possibility."

The Wichita station faded into squalls of broken static. Billy spun the dial, but surrounded by the rolling Flint Hills of Kansas, the radio picked up nothing.

"Hey, Sol. Grab me a tape. We need some tunes."

"Sure thing. Whatchya feeling?"

"The Police. No, some Joe Jackson."

"Joe Jackson, the man says. Which one? We've got three."

"Is that a real question? *Look Sharp!*"

Solomon handed the cassette to Billy, who popped the tape into the player. The scattershot guitar of "One More Time" filled the van; Solomon and Billy howled and bobbed their heads to the beat.

Howie lowered the volume. "So, I think I've got a surefire way to win Ashley back. Wanna hear my plan?"

Billy gave him a disdainful smile. "No. I do not want to hear your plan, How, because your plan is worthless."

He cranked the volume to the fine line between loud and incomprehensible and turned his attention toward the endless tidal waves of grass-covered hills. He couldn't look at Howie. He was disgusted with How's day-in/day-out whining about Ashley. He was also disgusted with himself for treating his friend so horribly.

Screw it, Billy told himself. Howie needed to hear how he felt. The band was bigger than any chick, and he was damned if he would let one pull away Howie like one had done to Rich.

Watching the green hills pass by calmed him, and the effects of the marijuana took hold. He cracked the window to get some fresh air, nodding his head to the music and becoming one with every beat, note, and vibration. He was Billy Cherry, he was music, he was rock 'n' roll.

A loud bang sounded from beneath the van, and a thousand springs recoiled through his right arm as the steering wheel ripped from his hands. Even as he flailed for the steering wheel, he knew his wrist had broken. He managed to find purchase with his left hand as the van veered off the road.

The vehicle careened into the ditch, shot up and out the other side, and the world ended.

— • • —

Birds singing. The sun's warmth. Blood-orange cream soda glow flooding his vision.

Billy opened his eyes and looked around. He sat on the

highway's shoulder, legs splayed out, leaning backward on his hands. He tried to comprehend the scene—the van wrapped around a big cottonwood so tight the tree reached the third row of seating.

Gravel crunched from behind. He turned to see Howie approaching along the shoulder in full-on panic mode, his searching arms outstretched, chin quivering.

Ah shit, Billy thought. He rose to his feet and moved to intercept his friend.

"Breathe, Howie. You're okay."

"Wh—what? What happened?"

"We wrecked the van, How. But,"—he noticed Solomon walking toward them—"but we're all right, man. See? Here comes Sol now."

Solomon kept looking around as he came nearer. He wore a white blazer over a turtleneck, and his hair was perfect. Solomon Scott: *The New Shining Star of New Wave*. That's what *Rolling Stone* had called him.

Even after a tour van accident, he looks every inch the part, Billy thought. *He'll either leave us behind or lead us to the goldmine.*

"Jesus, what the hell?" Sol asked. "I can't remember anything except I was searching for a tape to play and then I'm standing in the road. You okay there, Howie?"

"I don't know. How the hell did we escape?"

The three men looked at each other and then at the van, with its now compacted front end and brand new tree-antenna sprouting from the roof.

"We were obviously thrown clear," Billy said. "What's important is we're fine."

"Were we thrown back here? Before the van smacked the tree?" Sol asked. "Because I was sitting next to the new guy, and—"

"Chad! Where's Chad?"

They searched the roadside for Chad, taking turns calling his name and avoiding the area around the wreckage. Unable to locate him, they accepted the inevitable conclusion.

"One of us has to look, just to be sure," Billy said.

Howie started to lose his shit again. "Not me! I can't. I don't want to see that."

"Then don't." Billy turned to Sol. "I'll look. Can you stay and keep him together?"

Apprehension amplified as he approached the rear of the van. He looked back to Howie and Sol, then made his way to the driver side door. What he saw was not what he had expected. Billy knew the scene wouldn't be pretty. He knew he would find a body. But four? Well, that shit was too farfetched.

At least I still look good, he thought. Like Solomon, his hair was perfect; auburn and exquisitely feathered. His light freckles were more apparent than ever on his bloodless skin. If it wasn't for his pallor and bluing lips, he could almost believe he was watching himself sleep. The other three bodies weren't in such good condition. Especially Howie. Howie had been sitting directly behind the point of impact.

Sitting beside me and yakking about that damn girl for the millionth time, Billy remembered. *That's what he was doing.*

The big tree had destroyed him, coming to rest between Solomon and Chad, who weren't looking too pretty themselves.

"Billy?" Howie called.

Billy raised a hand. "Stay there. You guys don't need to see this."

"Is he in there?"

"Yeah, Howie, he's here."

"Oh fuck."

"Damn, how are we gonna tell his family?" Sol asked.

"We're not. I mean, somebody will. It just won't be us."

The van slipped from the tree, listing fast and heavy to the right. Billy jumped backward at the unexpected movement.

"Shit, Billy, you okay?" Howie asked.

"Fine as I can be."

The shifting vehicle must have released some pinched hoses;

trickling sounds emitted from beneath the van. Billy got on his hands and knees, searching for the source.

"Hey man, if that thing's leaking fuel, you'd better get away before it goes up."

No, Howie, Billy thought. *Not leaking fuel, just leaking you.*

He rose and returned to his bandmates. Howie eyed him with anticipation, but Solomon was preoccupied with the ground behind him.

"Is it bad?" Howie asked.

"Really bad. Guys, we need to talk. Sol, what's up?"

Sol pointed to the asphalt. "See that?" The highway was littered with black rubber. "Blowout's what got us, I'd say."

"It got us, alright. All of us. Listen—I—well, we—"

"What? Spit it out, bro."

"Chad's not alone. We're in there too."

Sol gave him a look that said, *Oh you poor, crazy fool.* "No, buddy. We're all standing right here. Did you hit your head, maybe?"

"Most likely. Sol, we're here, but we're also in the van. We're dead, guys. Like, ghosts or . . . some shit."

"Like hell we are. Billy, you just saw some rough stuff, but you've gotta listen to me, man. We are not dead. Chad is, but not us."

A car traveled around the curve from the direction they had come. The driver had evidently seen the accident because the car barreled onto the shoulder.

"Sol, watch out!" Howie warned.

The car passed through and beyond Solomon, leaving him shaking where he stood, mouth hanging open. He looked at his guitarist with unmitigated understanding.

"Oh. We're dead. Billy—we . . . Fuck! We're dead!"

A muscular *WHOOSH* arose from behind Billy. He turned in time to see a fireball rolling through the branches of the cottonwood, igniting twigs and leaf buds along its path, sending the would-be rescuer scrambling. The van and the four dead men inside were fully engulfed.

"Goddamn it," Billy groaned, his arms spread in exasperation. "There goes my open casket."

— • • —

The coroner arrived to collect the bodies. Billy Cherry wasn't sure about his bandmates, but he was pissed.

"Either of you interested in seeing what you look like Kentucky-fried? I'm not. Ambulances will be leaving soon. There's no need for them. They say Emporia. I'm gonna catch a ride; you guys coming with me?"

"What would we do there?" Howie asked.

"What would we do here?" Sol countered.

The three men approached the rear doors of the ambulance.

"Here goes nothing, or everything," Solomon said. He grabbed the handles and pulled. Nothing happened. "Fuck."

He leaned his head against the doors and laughed slowly, barely audible. His laughter grew in volume, his entire body convulsing with each guffaw.

"*Rolling Stone* called me 'the New Shining Star of New Wave,'" Sol said. "We never talked about that part of the article, but you guys read it, right?"

"We saw," Billy said.

"Total bullshit, of course. We were a band, not a solo act. But they liked us, they thought we were the future. We were going to tour with The Cars and sell millions of albums. We'd make another killer record, maybe do our own tour. Now it's all gone; there is no future. In a couple years, we'll be forgotten, and our record will collect dust in thrift store bargain bins."

"Or," Howie said, "all the kids will wear black armbands and turn us into legends. The magazines eulogize us, and we sell millions more copies."

This time they all laughed.

"At least our families will be set," Sol said.

"Don't forget about Rich," Billy added. "We shared songwriting credits. Rich will own those now."

"Lucky bastard," Howie said, "with his hot wife and new family. We die and he'll reap the we're-into-them-now-that-they're-dead benefits."

They all agreed. Rich was the lucky one.

"Excuse me, Sol," Billy said. "You mind if I try something?"

Solomon stepped aside. "Be my guest."

Billy grabbed the door handles with both hands, placed a sneaker on the foot rail, and lifted himself off the ground.

"Well, that works. Here goes nothing."

"Or everything," Sol added.

"Or everything."

Feet together on the foot rail, he readjusted his hands on the door handles, closed his eyes, and leaned forward. He encountered no resistance, and opening his eyes, found himself inside the ambulance. He stepped inside the rest of the way and turned. This time he only passed his head through to the outside.

"Come on in, guys. The air is cool and sterile."

— • • —

The ride to Emporia was quiet, each man lost in his own thoughts. Billy recalled the moments leading to the crash. Staring at the grass-covered hills, he had tried to ignore Howie's constant talk about Ashley and had asked Sol to find a Joe Jackson tape to drown out How's blathering. His last memory was Solomon asking which one, and then . . . nothing. Maybe there was some kind of divine safeguard, a spiritual aegis protecting souls from traumatic memories of violent death.

Souls. Billy was an atheist who laughed at the idea of such a thing. Yet here they were, three lingering revenants hanging out inside an ambulance in the middle of fucking nowhere. If they were ghosts, then perhaps they did have souls, per se, or there was an unknown scientific explanation. Residual energies able to communicate with one another, wax nostalgic, and pass through walls. Maybe their brains fired final synapses, creating made-up information to provide a cushioned landing into death. Billy figured those would have sputtered out during the fire. Besides, the tree had exploded Howie like a June bug on a windshield, so that theory didn't hold much water. Yet again, if all this was a mind-created memory cushion, then the fire never really happened.

Or did it happen? Billy had to accept he knew nothing or he would think himself through circles.

They exited the ambulance when it arrived at the hospital. A map of the city, with landmarks, hung on a wall in the main lobby. The Greyhound station was only a couple miles away; the walk there wouldn't be too long. They could board a bus and ride to their hometown.

Leaving the lobby, they came across a bit of luck. As they passed an older couple in the waiting area, the husband rose, glancing at his watch.

"Lorraine, I'm heading to the bus station. Craig's bus oughta be coming in anytime. Are you waiting here?"

"Yes. I'm staying," Lorraine said. "I should get back to her room, soon."

The man kissed his wife and left the hospital, unaware of the three specters following behind. He had barely moved the car from the parking lot when he activated the heater.

"Goddamn its cold," he told himself.

———

The bus depot was empty. The three friends sat on a bench, away from the man who had unknowingly given them a ride. A bus arrived twenty minutes later. A few passengers and the driver exited and went into the depot. The marquee in front read, *Kansas City*.

A young college-aged kid approached the man from the hospital and embraced him, sobbing. Although invisible to the men, the bandmates were loath to encroach upon such a private moment. Leaving the building, they boarded the bus.

Kansas City sounded as good a destination as any other.

—· ·—

Kansas City's Greyhound station was larger and busier than in Emporia. The place was teeming with people. Some sleeping in their seats or in private conversation, while others chastised station employees over late arrivals, as if making another person's day worse could bring their bus sooner.

The members of Daddy's Girl would have to wait an hour to board a Chicago-bound bus. In Chicago, they would have to board another to their hometown of Rockford.

"Why are we going back home?" Solomon asked. "Really, what's waiting for us there? What are we gonna do, go to our own funerals? I really don't want to see my parents grieve. Sounds like a real blast."

"Where else do we go?" Billy retorted. "We don't have any other home."

Solomon paced, hands aflutter. "We were about to travel the world, man, and we can still do so. We've proven to ourselves we can ride anywhere we want, am I right? Let's just go."

"Your idea is tempting for sure, Sol. But I'd been planning on doing all that with . . . you know, beautiful women and champagne. Maybe a *few* drugs. Dead isn't quite how I'd imagined."

"But you're still saying yes, right?"

"I want to see Ashley," Howie said, cutting off the conversation.

Billy wanted to throw something. If only he was able. "Jesus Christ, Howie. It's fucking over. It's been over. She couldn't handle being with a traveling musician, man. Ashley's a great girl, I've always thought so. But seriously, she waited for the record to come out before she left? She figured it out then?"

"I could've stayed behind, you know. I would've been happy living a regular life with her, instead of being stuck in a van with you guys, only able to shower every few days, stinking to shit."

"Then why didn't you stay?"

"Because you wouldn't let me."

"Wouldn't let you?"

"Yeah. I tried to leave, but you guys laid such a heavy guilt trip on me."

"Nobody tied your hands, Howie. We laid an even thicker one on Rich, and it didn't stop him from bailing. We could've found a new drummer, just like we found Chad."

The mention of Chad shushed them all. Why wasn't he with them? He was every bit as dead.

Someone in the lobby chuckled, followed by, "*Tsk, tsk, tsk.*"

Along the back wall, in the corner, sat a man dressed in black. A black hat was pulled over his face. One dark boot rested on the floor, the other on the edge of his seat, with his arms wrapped around his knee. He made no further sound, and the dead men continued their talk.

"Come on," Billy said. "What would you do? Creep around her house and follow her everywhere? You're dead, Howie. There's nothing you can do anymore. Ashley will mourn you for a while, because she loves you. That, I've never doubted. But she'll move on, bro. She'll get married, have another man's children. Because you're dead."

"I know, Billy. I just need to leave her a message."

"How? We couldn't even open the ambulance doors."

"No, but we were able to grab the handles and stand on the foot rail. Walk through walls. Sol had a car drive right through him, yes? But tell me this; how were we able to walk up the steps of the bus? How are we able to sit without falling through the chair to the floor? I think there's rules to this whole being-a-ghost thing; certain allowances are being made. Whether it's science or divinity, I can't say."

Billy and Sol stared at him, dumbfounded.

"So I'm thinking," Howie continued, "there's gotta be a way. I'm sure it's possible. My old man bought this book a few years ago. It's called *Strange Stories, Amazing Facts*. From *Reader's Digest*, maybe. There's all these stories on ghosts, how they can move objects. This stuff is supposedly true, with quotes from researchers and shit. I'm sure I can manage something."

"I think it's a stretch," Billy said.

Solomon rubbed his cheek. "I don't know; suppose it's possible? Maybe there's a learning curve?"

"Okay, let's say it can be done. Have you thought about how leaving Ashley a message might affect her? Are we sure it's worth doing?"

"Of course it's worth doing," a voice with an English accent said. "For love, anything is worth doing."

The guys turned to see who had spoken.

"No way," Howie said.

A spasm of machine-gun laughter escaped Billy, and he quickly covered his mouth to stifle any more outbursts.

Standing before them was the man in the black hat.

"If I wasn't dead," Solomon said, "I swear I'd piss myself right now."

John Lennon gave him a look of amused disgust. "Then be glad you're dead, mate. Soaking your trousers is no way to show admiration."

— • •—

Billy could not stop staring. The ghost of John Lennon looked exactly as he had in the photos taken outside of the Dakota on the night he had been murdered.

"Please lift your chins, gentlemen, before you drool over my boots. I couldn't help overhearing your conversation. Tell me, how long ago did it happen . . . dying?"

"Just this afternoon," Solomon said. "We're a band. Were, anyway. Our van blew a tire, and we hit a tree."

"Ah, fresh wrapped fish," Lennon said. "Well, let's get to the business, shall we? Your friend deserves his chance to reach his girl.

It's absolutely possible. You lot weren't able to open doors because you don't know how, not because it cannot be done. You're new to death; practice makes perfect."

"So we can open doors and move things around? How?"

"I told you. Practice, like playing music. Now, where are you lads going?"

"Rockford, Illinois," Billy said.

"Does your bus go there, straightaway?" Lennon asked.

"Chicago first, then another bus to Rockford."

"Fantastic. I'll go with you. Need to return to Chicago anyway. Gotta see a friend."

"And you happened to be in Kansas City?" Howie asked.

"Right! How lucky are you lot?"

"I'm only asking because, well, you're John Lennon. Why Kansas City?"

"Friends here, as well."

"You have friends here?"

"I do now. A jazz pianist named Benny Moten—one of the original greats—was from here and still checks out the local jazz scene. Even after death, he couldn't bear to leave what he helped create. Last night, I met The Bird,"—he nearly danced with excitement—"Charlie Parker, Jr. The one benefit, really, of being a spirit: meeting those who've come before and inspired you. The ones who have held on, anyway."

"Guys," Howie said. "Keith Moon is one of my drum heroes. I'd love to meet him."

"Can't happen," Lennon said. "As far as I know, overdoses don't hang around. I'm unsure why. Maybe it's because the dope pulls 'em under before they go. Most who die sleeping don't hang around either. They just slip through to whatever, if anything, is on the other side. Too bad, Keith was a good mate o' mine. I'd like to see the nutty tosser, tell him how I feel about the end of his story."

"That's the reason Chad isn't with us," Solomon said. "No wonder, he was asleep. I remember now."

Lennon nodded. "I've gone into libraries at night, researching. I've talked to others along the way, those who've remained. Some stay, some go, none of it makes any sense. There's no patterns or rules I can tell, except I've never met an overdose. The majority of lingerers are those who've died violent deaths. Again, I don't know why. The suddenness, perhaps; although for some it's"—he snapped his fingers—"lights out. Like the three of you. Some of us struggle to cling to the rope while it slowly slides through our hands, burning our fingers along the way. I can't tell you how long we'll remain, I just have a kind of faith everything will be okay in the end. And if it's not, well, then it's not the end."

Everyone pondered the late Beatle's words.

"Hopefully," Lennon continued, "your friend is in a better place, wherever he may be. On a sunnier note, I've spent the last year and a half traveling your country. I've met a lot of great musicians: Buddy Holly, Patsy Cline, Sam Cooke, Otis Redding. I caught the feeling Patsy is ready to move on soon and probably will. Buddy told me only he and the pilot stood in the field after their plane crashed. Everyone else had gone to the wherever."

"Elvis, what about Elvis?" Billy asked. "Have you gone to Graceland?"

"I have," Lennon said. "He wasn't around. Chicago, you say? I think our bus is about to leave the station, lads."

— . . —

The bus ride from Kansas City to Chicago was a grueling twenty-four-hour trip as, unbeknownst to the four former musicians, the bus traveled first to St. Paul. They used the opportunity to learn more post-life lessons from Lennon. One could sit in any seat he wanted, and no living person would try to sit in the same space. People naturally avoided the dead.

"They know you're there," Lennon said. "They just don't know they know you're there. You know?"

He also taught the guys a game where they would sit next to

a live passenger. Not knowing why, the poor living soul would feel cold and move to a new seat, whereby the offender would sit next to them in *that* location, forcing the passenger to relocate to yet another seat.

Eventually tiring of Freeze Out, they took to asking their guide about his former band. For instance, was the original Paul, as rumors had supposed, dead as well?

"Of course not. What rubbish. Paul McCartney is alive and well, making music. We did run with that one, however. Why not play into the mystique? No, Sergeant Pepper is just fine."

Solomon laughed. "If Paul is Sergeant Pepper, does that make you Billy Shears?"

"The Billy Shears character sang 'With a Little Help from My Friends.' Ringo would be Billy Shears, no?"

"What does that make you then?"

"Lance corporal?"

— • • —

Most of the passengers were asleep. With St. Paul two hours behind them, Billy and John Lennon sat at the rear of the bus. Solomon and Howie were in the front, watching the road and the passing headlights under a moonless sky.

"You lads are a band?"

"We were."

"Successful?"

"We were getting there. *Rolling Stone* loved our album; hailed us—well, mainly Sol—as the next big thing. The band to watch in '82. We were wrapping up a club tour, then we were supposed to open for The Cars all summer."

"The Cars? I like The Cars. What did you call yourselves?"

"Daddy's Girl."

Lennon's eyes grew huge, and he smacked Billy on his arm. "'Radio Kisses!' I love that song. You wrote 'Radio Kisses?'"

Billy laughed. "Sol and I wrote all the songs. Wow. You like our song?"

"I do. I hear things here and there. Love the band name too. Androgynous, like New York Dolls or Alice Cooper."

"Yeah, except we were new wave."

"What a bullshit label—like punk or heavy metal. I did all of those, and it was called rock and roll."

Billy didn't argue, he knew the man was right.

"For what it's worth, I'm sorry you lads died before you made the big time."

Billy sighed. "Yeah. Me too. Now I've just—"

"Got regrets," Lennon said.

"I've had a few."

John Lennon chuckled and Billy was glad he had gotten the joke.

"About how you and Solomon have treated your friend Howie over this young lady."

"Mister Lennon, how do you know all this? How I'm feeling? Death make you a mind reader?"

"What? No. I've just seen it before. All of it. You live the life of a Beatle, you see and learn more than you ever cared to. I know how people tick. I may not always know *what* makes them tick, but I know the hows. You weren't fighting over this girl, were you? Love triangle?"

"No love triangle. Our keyboard player quit after we recorded the album. His wife was pregnant. We laid into him hard but he left anyway. An admirable decision, I suppose. We got a new guy, Chad. Then Howie's girl, Ashley, broke up with him. She can't be with someone who's never gonna be around and always on the road. He was ready to quit, himself. He couldn't bear the thought of life without her. This time the guilt trips worked. Shitty of us, I know, but I didn't care. How dare he? We hadn't come this far to merely shrug our shoulders and say, *Nah, I don't think so.*"

"You feel guilty?"

"Fuck yeah, I feel guilty."

They rode several miles in silence.

"You know," Lennon said, "fame gets old really quickly."

Billy laughed. "Easy for you to say, you were only in the most popular band of all time."

"It was awful. No, seriously. You laugh, Billy, but I'm telling the truth. I loved making music with the guys, but the lack of freedom to do as we pleased, whenever and wherever?" He shook his head. "And to think, I was finally able to reclaim my freedom, my music, my family, everything cohesive and peaceful. Then . . . *BAM*."

"Mister Lennon . . ." Billy felt the fragile support of eggshells beneath the weight of the moment. He had to tread carefully or risk crushing it all.

"Cut the Mister Lennon shit. Just John, please."

"John . . . did you ever think of paying him a visit?"

Lennon cocked his head to the side. "Him, who? Who would I be visiting?"

"You know, Chapman. Have you thought of haunting him?"

John Lennon gave a sneer that tried to be a smile. He looked away, directing his gaze to the darkness beyond the window.

"John, I'm sorry if I—"

Lennon whipped his head back around, locking eyes with Billy. "Why would I ever do such a thing?" he asked, a restrained quake in his voice.

"Payback? To make his life hell after what he did to you."

"Payback for what? For being a weak, doughy, feeble-minded man who hears voices in the walls? For thinking it was his duty to kill because he considers it hypocrisy to sing about peace and love and have money at the same time? I was a musician and a songwriter. People paid me for my product. Is that so fucking wrong? Why shouldn't I cash the royalty checks? I earned them. I never cared about the critics; the only way to stay honest in that business was to make your art as you saw fit. I made my art. I battled my demons to fuck-all and won. You understand?"

Billy nodded.

"'He went away,' they said. I went nowhere. I took the time to stay home with my wife and child, was a father for the first time in my life because I fucked off my first go-around being a goddamn Beatle. I was living my life right for the first time, and along came some twit playing Jehovah with a book and a gun, claiming to be the second coming of Holden Caulfield. Did you ever read it? *The Catcher in the Rye*? Well I have and what a pot of piss! Some spoiled little rich brat mad at Mum and Dad, for what? Phoniness: 'phony this, phony that.' And who was the real phony? Some little broken man trying to be someone else, claiming to do God's work. Piss on Mark Chapman, and piss on his version of God!"

Even in death, Billy's face was hot with shame. "Mister Lennon—John, listen. I'm so sorry."

Billy glanced toward the front of the bus. Solomon and Howie were still watching the road. He couldn't tell if they had overheard any of the conversation.

"Billy, I'm not angry with you. I've been holding in this garbage for almost a year and a half, and you were unfortunate enough to be in the way when it spilled over. Look, I haven't even been able to check on my own family. It hurts too damn much. Like I said before, I have no idea how long you or I will be stuck in limbo. For all I know we could be lingering a hundred years from now or we could pass to the other side in an hour. I know I don't want to see that man again, and I won't be wasting my time in some prison, haunting a mental case who already has a hard time with reality. What I will do is help that young man sitting there reach through to his beloved. Maybe all his pining sounded silly a couple days ago, but now it's all he has left. There is nothing else."

In Rockford, Illinois, the setting sun played a final waltz upon its crown of clouds, then settled into repose; a touch of blush the only clue of its passing. The last group of family and friends exited the Rigby home, unaware of being watched by the dead ex-boyfriend of the bereaved, his equally dead friends, and a Beatle.

"This is where your Ashley lives?" Lennon asked.

"Her parent's house. I'm sure she's here now," Howie said.

Solomon laid a hand on his shoulder. "We sure spent a lot of time here, bro."

Howie laughed. "Hell, I lost my virginity in this house."

Billy joined them. "Happened on a Friday. I know, because Sol and I raided the cereal cabinet and watched *Donnie & Marie*."

Lennon scowled. "You watched *Donnie & Marie?*"

"Only because we thought Marie was cute," Billy said, defending himself. "Besides, didn't the Beatles have a Saturday morning cartoon?"

"We had nothing to do with that drivel, and it was still better than *Donnie & Marie*."

"Yeah, but you're nowhere near as cute as Marie."

"You're right. Paul's cuter."

The two men traded laughs and nudged elbows.

"Guys," Howie said, "I'm going inside. Are you all coming with me?"

"We're with you, lad. Whenever you're ready."

"I'm ready. Keep up."

Howie ran up the porch steps and passed through the front door. The others followed, almost running into the back of Howie, who stood in the middle of the foyer. Looking over Howie's shoulder into the living room, Billy saw Ashley seated on the center cushion of the sofa. Her head hung in despair, fingers woven into her black hair.

Her mother entered the room, prim and straight-backed.

"Ashley, honey." Her voice was soft, yet firm. "Sweetie, your father and I are going to see the Bentons. Would you like to come with us?"

Ashley turned her head slightly in her mother's direction. "Not tonight. Please tell them I'll visit tomorrow. I need to be by myself a little while."

"Understood. We'll return in a couple hours."

Mrs. Rigby kissed the crown of her daughter's head and left the room.

Howie kneeled between the sofa and the coffee table, less than a foot from the woman he loved. Ashley lifted her head and wrapped her arms around her torso in an attempt to warm herself. Billy and Solomon kept their distance, out of respect. John Lennon watched over their shoulders.

Howie smiled at his friends. "Here goes nothing."

"Or everything," Sol answered.

"Ashley," Howie began, "our movie was never supposed to end this way. I'm sorry it did. The happy ending would have gone something like: boy drummer and his buds become huge rock stars, conquering the world. And something corny, like: the girl goes to one of their concerts—a homecoming show—and our drummer boy-hero stands up, confessing his love in front of thousands of people. And—and then she takes him back. The end." Howie stopped. Long seconds ticked away. "Instead, some asshole screenwriter decided the band would drive their van into a tree at seventy per, turning our drummer boy into hamburger." He turned to face Billy. "Don't think I didn't notice where the tree plowed through the van. I was toast. Well, we all got toasted, but I was French toast. I'm sorry you had to see us all like that."

"I'm okay, How," Billy said.

"I know. You're always okay in the end. But I'm not. I'm not okay."

"Then it's not the end," Lennon said.

"No," Howie said. "But I wish it was." He returned his attention to Ashley. "I'm here and so are the guys. They came all the way across the country with me, and, get this, Ash . . . John-fucking-Lennon is with us! Sorry, John."

"It's quite all right. I met Chuck Berry once, blabbered my way through the entire conversation."

"Baby, I'm so sorry. I never blamed you for wanting a different life for us. I know you'd have preferred raising a family here in Rockford. I wish I would've stayed with you. Sol and Billy wrote all the songs; they could've replaced me like they replaced Rich. They could've still been stars. The world would never have known. And maybe if I hadn't been there to distract Billy with my bitching and moaning, he could've kept from hitting the tree."

"This isn't your fault, Howie," Billy said. "I was stoned. You can't blame yourself."

"Either way, here we are. I'm so sorry, Ash. I love you. I'm so sorry."

Ashley lifted her head from her hands, unaware she was staring into Billy Cherry's eyes. Nevertheless, Billy felt them piercing through to his soul. *I'm sorry too*, he thought. *You're alone because of me. You let him go because I wouldn't, and I'm sorry too. Please forgive me.*

She rose from the sofa, shuffling away from Howie in that way the living have of naturally avoiding the dead. She walked down the hallway and entered a bedroom. Reemerging with a stack of clean, folded clothes, she went into the bathroom. A moment later, the shower started.

"Stay beautiful," Howie said to the door. Then to his friends, "There's nothing more I can do. Let's go, guys."

Solomon put his arm around him, and they passed through the door to the front porch.

"Well," Solomon said, "you did what you could, man. I have no doubt she'll be just fine. She's always had a level head on her."

"Yeah," Howie said, dejected.

"At least you know she felt you. Did you see her trying to cover herself?"

Howie stopped on the porch steps. "Freeze Out!"

"What are you talking about?" Sol asked.

Howie turned to Lennon. "John, on the bus you taught us that game. Freeze Out. You sit next to someone long enough, you freeze them out. Ashley couldn't hear me but she felt me. She can feel me again."

"What would be the point?" Billy asked. "You'll make her cold, so what?"

Not hearing, Howie was already back on the porch. This time he missed the door, traveling through the wall where the mailbox was mounted. The mailbox rattled and the lid . . . raised, then . . . dropped down into place.

"Holy Jesus," Billy said. "Did you guys see that?"

"Indeed," Lennon said. "The boy's got it now."

He ran after Howie; Billy and Solomon directly behind.

Howie waited outside the bathroom door while the others gave him space. Ashley turned off the water. They heard the shower curtain being pushed aside, followed by sounds of rustling clothes and items moving around on the bathroom countertop.

Billy licked his lips. If they weren't already dead, the anticipation surely would have killed them.

The door opened. Ashley trekked the hallway to the bedroom. She returned a moment later with a makeup bag. Howie preceded her into the bathroom and stood against the wall as she entered the room. She tossed the makeup bag onto the countertop.

Ashley grabbed a hand towel from a wall rack. As she reached to wipe the condensation from the bathroom mirror, Howie made his move. The three men in the hallway watched in awestruck horror as Howie stepped into his ex-girlfriend. Their two forms— hers physical, his spectral—occupied the same space. Ashley's body stiffened with shock, chest hitching as she fought for air.

"I love you. I love you, I love you." Howie's voice.

Ashley gasped and hugged herself. Howie stepped forward, releasing her; the separation causing them to stumble in opposite directions. Ashley plopped butt-down on the bathtub's edge. Flung forward, Howie caught himself, his hands hitting the vanity mirror above the sink with an audible *smack*, rattling the glass against the wall. Careful to avoid Ashley, he backed away, taking a seat on the opposite end of the bathtub.

"Oh." Lennon stepped between Billy and Solomon, his mouth guppy-ing. "Oh," he said again.

Two clear handprints had been left in the middle of the steamed mirror. Howie's handprints. A single rivulet of water ran from the bottom of each.

"Howie?" Ashley cried, scanning the bathroom. "I heard you in my head. You were inside of my soul!" She laughed, heavy tears flowing. "Baby? Howie, are you still here?"

Howie stood and returned to the mirror. Using a finger, he traced through the condensation. A large Valentine's heart appeared on the mirror.

Ashley nodded. She wiped at her face, trying to keep up with her tears, and failing. "I love you too, Howie. I miss you."

Miss you, he wrote above the handprints.

"Shit, no one is ever going to believe me," she said, more to herself than to Howie.

No, he wrote. He followed with a little smiley face.

Ashley began to cry again. "Howie, what am I going to do without you?"

Howie set his finger in the middle of the heart. He waited a long while, and Billy wondered if he was okay. Finally, he wrote, *Live Well.*

"I will, Howie. For you, I promise."

Howie started making smaller fist-sized hearts all over the mirror. He only finished seven. A quarter of the way through the eighth heart, the line narrowed. Three-quarters through, his finger ceased affecting the layer of condensation, and his hand passed through the mirror and wall.

"Damn, it's gone," Howie said.

He gave another try, and again his hand went through the wall.

"You ran out the battery," Lennon said.

"What?" Howie asked.

"She charged you, like a pair of jump leads. You've run out the charge."

"Howie? Are you still here?"

They all turned to Ashley, who was slowly raising herself from the tub's edge.

Howie looked past his friends to the legend standing between them. "What should I do?"

"You'll have to take more from her if you want to continue. I think so, anyway."

"I can't do that, can I? Won't she be hurt if I keep taking from her?"

Lennon shook his head. "I can't tell you. I don't know."

"I don't want to hurt her."

"Then you'd better step aside, lad."

Ashley raised her hands, searching. If her hands found Howie, she'd feel the decrease in temperature and know he was there. Howie slipped behind her and out the bathroom door as her hands reached the countertop.

"Howie? Howie, are you here?" She searched from side to side and turned around, looking for further messages or clues. "Howie?"

"I'm here," Howie whispered.

Billy could barely hear him.

"I always will be."

Ashley studied the messages on the mirror, then switched off the exhaust fan in an attempt to keep Howie's words a little longer.

"Goodbye, Howie," she said.

She expelled a short laugh. Covering her mouth, she laughed again. This time she allowed her emotions to carry her away, and she jumped up and down, laughing and squealing.

Smiling, Howie walked to the front door and his friends followed. They passed, one by one, single file, to the porch where Howie sat on the top step.

He looked at Billy, his face beaming and his eyes sparkling with victory. "I did it. I'm ready to go now."

"You sure did. That was amazing, Howie. We'll leave in a second. Let me talk to the guys first and figure out where we want to go next."

Walking to the end of the huge wraparound porch, Billy rejoined Sol and Lennon.

"Do either of you have folks you need to see here?" Lennon asked.

"No," Sol said. "Like I said before, the last thing I want to see is my mother grieving for me. I don't know what to do next, but I'm ready to coast the hell out of Rockford. The sooner, the better."

"You?" Lennon asked Billy.

Billy had no reason of his own to stay. His mother was the only one, other than his bandmates, who thought him worth a shit. Like Solomon, Billy had no desire to witness his mother's bereavement.

"No. Wherever you guys want to go, I'm game."

Sol looked to Lennon. "What about you? Chicago?"

John Lennon sighed. A whimsical smile spread across his face. "After everything we've seen tonight, I think the best place would be New York. I need to see my family, perhaps leave my own message. Who knows, maybe I'll even catch a plane for a hop across the pond. I'd love to see my old mate, Stuart. My oldest boy plays music, I hear. I should check on him as well. You lads ever been to England? We'll have some fun, see the sights. What do you say?"

Billy looked at Sol, who nodded.

"I'd say we're in, John," Billy said. "Hey Howie, John's invited us to . . . Howie?"

Howie was no longer on the step.

Billy ran around the porch, looking over the railing for his friend. "Howie? How? Where are you, man?"

Solomon went into the house. He returned shaking his head. "She's alone in there."

"Where is he?" Billy asked. "Howie! Come on, man. Where you—"

"Stop," Lennon shouted. "Howie's not here. And he won't be coming back. Gentlemen, your friend has moved on."

"What do you mean?" Billy asked.

"Moved on. To heaven, reincarnation, whatever is waiting for us."

Billy shook his head.

"I think John's right, Billy," Solomon said.

"But he wanted to meet Keith Moon," Billy pleaded. "Or somebody. This can't be his end."

"And yet it is," Lennon said.

"But why?" a distraught Billy asked, the finality of Howie's absence sinking in. *I'm ready to go now.*

John Lennon smiled. "Because he's okay."

Travis West lives in Lawrence, Kansas, with his wife, Angie, and their three children. Only one of two *Of Words* threepeat authors, Travis has two previous short stories available through Scout Media. "The Most Beautiful Boy" appeared in *A Matter of Words* (2015), followed by "The Errandsman's Folly" in *A Journey of Words* (2016). A huge fan of literature and music, Travis continues to write and is very slowly working on the "next Great American Rock 'n' Roll novel," which he hopes will become the first novel to stuff a kielbasa down its pants, terrify parents, and impregnate young actresses the world over. Follow Travis at www.facebook.com/TravisWestWrites.

ONLY THE DEAD GO FREE

J.M. AMES

The shower's hiss behind me competes with the roaring inferno raging down the hallway. Breathless and without thought, I gaze with lifeless eyes into the bathroom mirror. This gore-drenched nightmare of a witch is no longer recognizable. What have I done? What was the lesson here? I never wanted this.

Questions bubble up like water-borne carcasses until I hear his final words thunder in my head. "Only the dead go free," he had said, right before he—

No, there's nothing left for me now.

I raise the imbrued hunter's knife to the side of my neck, fingers tightening, hand shaking. My palm sticks to a bloody strip of leather matted on the handle. Sinewy bits of his flesh dangle from the blade's tip that now presses into mine. A tiny droplet of blood wells where the point pierces the outer layer of skin. Will I die if I never look away or will time freeze me here forever?

Fiona's whispered prayer echoes in my mind—*in reparation for all of my sins, for the souls in Purgatory*—and I question again if she was correct in her faith. Is there a Heaven, Hell, or Purgatory? Fuck it, it doesn't matter. Nothing real can be changed, anyway; the die has been cast. Sweat trickles down my temple from the growing heat. An acrid stench of burning flesh and gasoline assaults my nostrils.

With my eyes still locked onto their dead reflection, I plunge the knife into my neck. Its warm blade slides through my skin, slicing tendon and esophagus until it strikes bone. In a single swift motion, I bring it around the front of my windpipe. The blade squeaks as it scrapes across my vertebrae. A new mouth opens where one should never be. Crimson sprays onto my ghoulish doppelganger.

What must be gallons of blood splashes into the rusted sink, maroon on brown. Wells of saline liquid spring from the back of my throat and pour from both the slit in my neck and my mouth. Copper stink masks the smoke.

Fiona, oh my Fiona, I miss you more than anything.

The mirror clouds. Is it steam from the shower or is my vision failing? Is it like this every time? I sense there is truth in the answers flashing across my heart, but just as I am about to reach them, they elude me once more.

Weakness overtakes my legs; I stagger, then fall into my own gore. My head cracks open on the white tiles like a ripe coconut. Life drains from me in a widening lake of sanguinity.

The world evaporates and the answers disappear.

— · · —

"Are you sure he can't find us here?" Fiona's voice cracks on her last word.

She tucks a wave of brown hair behind her ear with a trembling hand and grimaces. Bruises the color of moldy plums cover her wrist. Wide, bloodshot eyes scan the driveway and what little of the road is visible through the dense pepper trees. Her other hand clutches the gold cross necklace I had bought her for her Confirmation, what, three months ago? Her thumb caresses it with care.

"Yeah," I said. "I never told him about this place. Grampa died and left it to me before I ever met Earl. Police should've cleaned up all the nastiness by now. Hard to believe the renters killed each other like that, after being here so many years. Who knows why? Anyway, we ain't had any new takers yet. Should be good here for a bit."

In the distance, a coyote yips and howls at the setting sun, eager for the darker side of day to end so its nocturnal hunt can begin. Fiona shudders at the sound. "We haven't been here since I was, what? Five? This place still creeps me out. I hated those weekends we would come up here."

A sense of familiarity mingles with stark dread within my soul.

Walking to the front door with keys in hand, I hear a faint

buzzing behind the aged wood. A hive crawling with bees doing insect things in insect ways must be on the other side. Keys tumble from my hands onto a dirty pile of leaves before the door. Every heartbeat feels like a hammer to my skull.

"God-fucking-dammit, which key is it?"

I stomp my foot and bend to retrieve the metal ring, which seems to hold passage to every door but the one before me. I crouch low and retch in a wave of nausea as a thick stench of rot and death slams into my nostrils.

Must be a dead raccoon or somethin' under the porch.

Straightening, I fumble with the tangled key mess again. Smoke puffs around the cigarette dangling from the corner of my mouth.

"I gotta fuckin' piss like a goddamned racehorse, and this motherfuckin' key must not exist!"

I kick the door before collapsing on the peeling wooden porch in a sobbing heap. My arms cover my head as my body rocks back and forth.

Why can't anything ever go my way?

"Here, Mom, give me the keys." Fiona sighs, prying them from my hand with care. Her eyes avoid the reddening track marks dotting my arms. "I'll get the door open, and you can go in and lie down for a while."

"Screw that, I need a drink." *Or a fix.*

"Let's just figure out our next move first, okay? Afterward, maybe it's time you—there we go."

With a loud creak, the door opens and stale, smoke-scented air wafts out. The fly-buzzing ceases. Fiona helps me up, kisses me on the cheek, and we step inside.

Fiona flicks on the light switch. From the corner of my eye, I see a shadow dash behind the faded brown sofa in the middle of the room. Maternal instinct kicks in, and I step in front of Fiona, my arm barring her at the door.

"Stay here."

I step toward the couch with fists so tight my fingers ache, and my acrylics dig into my palms. Stepping around the sofa, I see there is nothing behind it, aside from a large brown stain matting the carpet.

"Huh. Guess I'm seeing things." Though I am pretty sure I saw *something.*

"I think this might be a good time for you to get completely off all that stuff, Mom."

Fiona steps behind me and wraps her arms around my waist. Love, pain, and disappointment resonate in her words. A parent should never disappoint their child.

"It would be good to have my mother back, full time again."

Anger flashes across my heart before it melts into agonizing regret. I've not been there for her, not for a long while. No Mother of the Year awards are on display on *my* shelf. She deserves so much more than she's gotten. How did Fiona manage not to become a fuck up? Thank God she didn't end up like me. Only fifteen and already a stronger person than I. My vision blurs as tears well up and threaten to fall.

"I'll get clean, honey. I am so, so sorry for what I've put you through. I'll make it up to you."

And I mean it, with all my heart.

— • • —

Early next morning, Fiona limps down the hallway from the bathroom and plops into an armchair in the corner, her bell-bottoms swaying with the motion.

Fiona furrows her brow. "Something's up with that bathroom. It smells like smoke and old farts and pennies. And the mirror, it must have a crack behind the glass or something. Like, I keep seeing a brief doubling of my reflection in it."

"It's an old cabin, prob'ly has *a lot* wrong with it. Anyway, I'm going to go into town now to get groceries and carpet cleaner to try to clean up that nasty-ass stain."

I scratch my arms and moan at the relief it barely brings.

The burning, maddening itch keeps getting stronger, as does the headache.

Goddamn I need to find some heroin.

"No booze. No self-medication. Okay, Mom? You know what? I'm just going to go with you," Fiona says, easing herself off the couch, hissing and wincing.

"Honey, no. I'll be fine. I'll be good. Besides, we don't need to draw attention to ourselves. You're all bruised up, limping, and with one helluva shiner. Ya think no one's gonna notice? Let me run around for now, at least until you're better."

I can't let her see me shaking, or this house of cards will fall.

Fiona stares at me for a long while before speaking. I'm suspicious about that look in her eyes; it doesn't look like the unconditional love a child should have for their parent.

"I guess we need to start trusting each other. You know we can't afford for you to get wasted right now. Make sure you get a lot of aspirin, please."

I beam a forced smile in her direction. "Ya ain't gotta tell *me* that."

"One hour. If you're not back by then, I'm going to go looking for you. On hobbled foot." Fiona's eyes plead with me. "Maybe after you get back we can go to the theater to see *Escape to Witch Mountain?*"

"An hour or less. I promise. And it's a date."

I shut the door behind me and take a deep breath of fresh air.

I don't need the dope. I don't need the booze. I just need Fiona.

— • • —

I veer off the dirt road and swing wide into the driveway more than two hours later, no longer burdened by the shackles of sobriety. The car cruises in at an odd angle and hits the parked Harley Davidson with a delicate impact, just hard enough to tip it over onto the brown lawn.

Breathing seems impossible, and my belly aches as if jabbed

by Muhammad Ali. The bitter taste of stomach acid replaces the heavenly juniper flavor of the gin I had been guzzling a few minutes earlier.

Earl's Harley.

Fuck! How could he have found us . . . ? Fiona!

My ancient Datsun's rusted door flings open with a loud screech, and I try to rush to the house. I don't even make it out of the car when a tight pain in my chest blooms, my breath gets pushed out of me, and I am pulled backward into the seat.

Stupid fucking seatbelt!

I fumble with the belt and somehow escape its clutches. In my rush to reach the front door, I miss seeing the pepper tree root protruding from the earth. My foot catches it, and I hit the ground, hard, releasing an *oomph* as my lungs compress and empty. The car door sways open, and I can see groceries spilling onto the floorboards. I stand and try to hurry to the front door, but everything is now rubbery and painful, and my ankle screams in agony with every step. I'm vaguely aware of dirt and leaves sticking to my face, and I'm bleeding from somewhere but I don't care. I need to reach Fiona, to stop him from hurting her again.

I throw open the front door.

He's got her pinned to the couch. Blood trickles from her mouth, and her right temple is swollen. Her blouse is open and ripped, her bra missing and breasts exposed. Apparently he hasn't heard me enter—his backside still faces me. One hand holds his precious hunter's knife to her belly while the other is undoing his belt. Earl always keeps that knife as sharp as a razor.

Fiona's eyes widen when she sees me. She shakes her head ever so slightly as if to stop me, but it's too late, I can't stop myself. Nobody hurts my baby. *Nobody.*

With an inhuman cry of blind fury, I charge at him.

Earl stands straight and pulls Fiona in front of him. The flat steel of the blade presses hard against her stomach. His other hand pulls her necklace tight enough for her to start turning red and gagging. The end of his now-undone belt flaps against the bulge of his erection under his jeans.

I stop and extend my hands, palms displayed.

"*Ah-ah-ah*. Not another step or I gut your bitch of a daughter." Earl is breathing heavy, his voice deep and gruff. Spit flies from his sneering mouth with every word. His nostrils are powdery and white, sweat drips down his mutton-chop sideburns—he's clearly flying high. "Nice cabin you got here, Wendy. Betch'ya thought I didn't know about it. You're not exactly careful about your secrets when you're living it up with your lovers, Black Tar or Beefeater, are you? No, you have no fuckin' clue what goes on in your own house when you're drunk 'n' stoned."

Rage like I've never felt builds. My face flushes with its heat as sobriety comes rushing back. "You let her go right now you motherfucker, or I'll—"

"You'll what, Wendy? Take another drink? Look at you. You're fuckin' wasted right now, as always. I bet you didn't even know what was happening all this time, did you? Right under your nose, ever since she hit puberty. You paid more attention to bottles and needles than me or her. But hey, that's okay. You tend to your needs, and I'll tend to mine."

He pulls Fiona's necklace tighter and leans forward, taking her earlobe into his mouth. Fiona grits her teeth, eyes closed, and turns away from him.

My resolve breaks. "Please, just set her free!" I beg, hoping beyond reason he actually will.

"Free? Darlin', don't ya know by now? Only the dead go free."

Fiona squeezes her eyes shut and starts croak-whispering one of her prayers. "Most Sacred Heart of Jesus, I accept from Your hands whatever kind of death it may please You to send me this day with all its pains, penalties, and sorrows, in reparation for all of my sins, for the souls in Purgatory, for all those who will die—"

Earl's message registers as Fiona sputters that last word, and it echoes in my head like a church bell summoning the choir.

DIE! DIE! DIE!

Before I realize what I'm doing, I charge at him, screeching those same words.

Everything takes a familiar slow-motion aura. Earl's eyes widen. Fiona's mouth opens in a hoarse shriek as she elbows him in the gut. The blade of his knife slides fully into her belly button and then slashes upward, splitting her open until it crunches well into her sternum. Blood and multi-colored organs spill out of her like a gutted deer. The stench of shit and bile as her torn intestines empty onto the carpet should be nauseating, but I hardly notice. All three of our screams are almost mute to my ears.

I tackle Earl and my knee squashes his testicles against the floor; one of them bursts under the pressure. He roars in agony. His fist slams square on my jaw, throwing off my balance. My thumbnail jabs into his eyeball with an audible *POP*. Pinkish-clear jelly oozes out as my thumb slides in. He screams and reaches for Fiona's twitching, wrecked body and tries to remove the knife embedded in the center of her ribcage. I grasp at his hand to stop him, but the knife wriggles free and he slashes at my face.

That's okay, he missed.

Only he didn't. Wet warmth pours from my cheek, and every breath burns as it passes through the new gash. He slices at me again, and I instinctively try to block it with my hand. It takes a moment to realize the crayon-like objects flying through the air and rolling into the corner are three of my fingers.

I grab his knife-wielding arm with my good hand, pull it backward, and place my leg underneath the elbow. I rise as high as I can and drop all my weight on his arm. With a snap, like fresh celery stalks breaking in half, his elbow bends the wrong way, and his hand goes limp. The knife rolls to the floor, and I lunge for it.

Earl sits up, headbutts me, then bites my hanging flap of cheek and tears it from my face with an agonizing wet rip. I wail while my good hand grasps the knife and plunges it deep into his precious leather Motorcycle Club vest, over and over and over again. The blade penetrates with a *CRUNCH* . . . withdraws with a *SLURP*. Droplets of blood soar higher into the air with every strike.

At some point, I realize I'm still screaming and that his chest is nothing but a sticky, spongy ruin. The wheezing that had been bubbling from new holes in his chest has stopped. Blood covers every surface of Earl and me, most of Fiona, the carpet, and the couch. Only Fiona's pale face is prominent in this scarlet sea.

I roll off Earl to check Fiona and find no pulse or breathing. Her face is so beautiful, even still. I sit and hold her hand for what seems like a long time. My heart rips apart with the knowledge I will never see her face smile again. Memories of the lifetime it took for us to get here—for the moment of freedom we got to enjoy—play on a loop in my brain. All the hope I had when we arrived here of fixing myself and repairing our relationship dies with her.

Her skin begins to cool and becomes an ashen gray color. The only thing left in this world I haven't fucked up beyond repair, the only thing I still care for, is now gone.

Lightheadedness drains my brain of thought as my wounds drain my body of blood. Without knowing or caring why, I stand and trudge to the garage. I drag the red plastic gas can from beneath the shelving that lines the walls with my five-fingered hand.

Seems full enough, should do the trick.

I return to the living room and splash gasoline across their bodies until the can is empty. I reach for my Zippo, but that hand only has one finger and a thumb, so I reach across with my other hand and awkwardly remove it from my pocket. I flick the fire to life and toss it onto Earl. Blue flames crawl across his body, tasting him before devouring him completely.

Thoughts aren't coming so easy now.

So filthy. I need to get clean.

I head to the bathroom and turn on the shower. I face the sink, and sudden clarity hits me. Multiple reflections of myself are transposed onto each other in the mirror. In some of these broken silhouettes, my face is destroyed; in others, it's untouched; in yet others, it's somewhere in between. One is nothing but a maggoty death's head.

For a brief moment, I can remember all this happening many times before. Panic steals my breath. How many times has he killed her? How many times have I killed him, before I took . . .

And as quickly as they came, the answers disappear. Once again, my mind goes blank.

The shower's hiss behind me still competes with the roaring inferno raging down the hallway. Breathless and without thought, I gaze with lifeless eyes into the bathroom mirror—again. This gore-drenched nightmare of a witch is still not recognizable. What have I done? What was the lesson here? I never wanted this.

Questions bubble up like water-borne carcasses of my past until I hear his final words thunder in my head. "Only the dead go free," he had said, right before he—

— · · —

A shiny blue Oldsmobile pulls off the road and parks askew in the driveway. A striking woman with black hair and copper skin exits the driver's seat and raises her hand to shield her eyes from the setting sun. A couple and their young son follow suit. The boy hums Judas Priest's "The Ripper" as he plays with a toy motorcycle.

"I think you'll love this floorplan and location. Not too far from town, but secluded enough to guarantee your privacy. The bank is quite motivated to sell—you won't find a better deal, I promise you!" Rebecca flashes a bright smile. "Watch the grass please, sweetie. We just had that put in."

Quinn glares at her. Adults are no fun at all. He throws his motorcycle on the lawn, where it lands on its side, and he sticks out his tongue at her.

Still smiling, Rebecca walks across the fresh-painted porch to unlock the lockbox on the door, but her keys tumble from her hand. She bends to pick them up and is overwhelmed by a strong odor of rotting meat.

Great, how am I supposed to sell the house with that *stink?*

There is a humming behind the door, like a swarm of bees. Foreboding replaces her disgust. Hairs on the back of her neck prickle and her shoulders tense. The coyote yipping and howling in the distance is not helping her mood. This place *always* gives her the willies.

She shakes it off and reapplies her fake smile. This time her key penetrates the box without a hitch and the humming stops.

"Ms. Church," the mother says, "I was told this place is haun—"

"Dawn, let's not even *say* that word. You don't really believe in all that tomfoolery, do you?" Michael clucks his tongue at her.

"Well, there is *a* truth in that." Rebecca leads them into the house, still smiling, and flicks on the lights. "By California law, I do need to disclose to you that there was a death on the property last year. That's why the bank has reduced the price by thirty percent. There was also some heavy fire damage to the structure, but that just means most of it has been rebuilt. I can assure you there are no gho—"

Michael shakes his head while waving his hands in front of him. "Please, I don't even want to hear that word."

"Did you see that? I think someone's here. I saw something dart behind that sofa." Dawn points at the brown floral-printed couch in the center of the room. Her eyes bulge from her skull, her mouth draws into a horrified *O* shape.

"Jesus, Dawn!" Michael says and strides into the room and peeks behind the sofa. "Nothing back here except some big, old stain on the carpet. You really need to stop reading those stupid horror stories."

Rebecca frowns. *How could there be stains on the new carpet? The agency will not be happy about this.*

Dawn scowls. "Well, I saw *something.* I'm not the fool you think I am. Ms. Church, how did you say the previous resident passed?"

"Uh, well, you see, there . . ." Rebecca stammered.

"Wasn't just one death. There were three. No, there were

more—going back a *loooong* time," Quinn says in a voice much deeper and gruffer than should come from a small child.

All heads turn to him. His eyes roll backward to whites, and his eyelids begin fluttering.

He points to the stain. "It always starts right there, but ends up in— "

The shower hisses to life down the hallway, startling all three adults. Dawn puts a shaking hand to her mouth.

"—there." Quinn points down the hallway to the steam bilowing out of the bathroom, and his lips retract into an uncharacteristic sneer. He bends to grab a large, mottled hunting knife from the carpet stain, then smiles sweetly. "And it usually ends with this."

The front door slams shut. Everyone jumps and gasps. Smoke wafts into the room from nowhere.

Michael runs to the door and struggles to open it, but it won't budge.

The lights go out.

Dawn screams.

"Open the door!" Rebecca yells. "Open the door and set us free!"

"Free?" the gravelly voice behind her asks. "Darlin', don't ya know by now? Only the dead go free."

J. M. Ames is an author native to southern California. He published his first short story, "The Last Ride," in 2016 in the anthology, *A Journey of Words*. When not working his day job or enjoying his fatherly adventures, he writes short stories and novels, including an upcoming series. J. M. resides in southern California with his lovely wife, two daughters, and an ever-growing zoo of dogs and cats.

The Unimportance of Being Oscar

Mariana Llanos

Oscar walked the crowded streets of New York, the city he'd called home for the past two years. His legs dragged and his bloodshot eyes burned. His joints creaked like the hinges of an old door. He'd had too much to drink the night before, and his forty-year-old body couldn't handle it like it could when he was younger. His arms hurt from waving a rainbow flag from his friend Jeff's balcony in the East Village. But it had been well worth it. Gay marriage was legal now, and several of his friends would marry soon.

Not that being married was a good thing. No, no. He had been married to a woman before. They were doomed to fail though. Turned out she knew he was gay even before he did. Would it be different if he married a man? Sure, it was legal now, but strangely he still had that feeling he was being judged. But marriage was something he needed to push out of his mind—at least for now.

He hobbled down the grimy concrete stairs to the subway station, stopping to spare a couple of dollars for the old trumpeter who played bluesy licks every day in the same spot. He was missing both legs and sat on a worn-out bluish rug in front of a coffee can. Everything about him was gray. His eyes, his hair, his skin. He'd blend with the wall if it weren't for the vibrations of his trumpet, which seemed attached to his mouth. Oscar's money clanked at the bottom of the can. He saluted the man with a brief smile and went on.

The station stank like sweat and booze—atypical for a Monday morning. It seemed as if everyone had partied the night before.

I belong here. New York. Hell, I'm not going back. New York, rats and all . . . , he thought, spotting a naked tail behind a trash can. His stomach swirled. "Not going back," he said aloud through clenched teeth.

Oscar pushed through a group of students and locked his arm around the metal pole inside the train car. The train closed its doors and started a slow, rhythmic motion toward his destination at 59th and Columbus Circle.

"Damn work permit," he growled, and his gut dropped as it did every time he remembered his was about to expire. The nightmare couldn't be real—him being sent back to London. He fisted his hand on top of his mouth as tension crushed his stomach. "Gawh!" he let out, resting his weary head against the pole.

A plump old woman—the only one in the train whose eyes weren't glued to a smartphone—eyed him and clutched her purse a little tighter.

The train stopped and Oscar quickly exited the sliding doors. Uptown roared like a rusted machine made of rushing people, honking cabs, and gawking tourists. A few feet away from the station on Columbus Circle stood a massive glass and steel building. Oscar had visited it before to sign a one-year work contract with Judy Swift. *Basher, Dancer & Co. Publishing* was engraved on a shiny metal plaque.

Oscar smoothed down his clean yellow shirt and wiped some dust off his leather shoes. He ran a hand over his unruly hair. He wanted to look tidy, but casual—like most authors on the back covers of children's books. His reflection on the glass wall seemed to wink at him. Oscar knew deep inside, no matter how much he tried, he'd always look old-fashioned. Too late to think about that. It was now or never.

Troy Harris, *the* Troy Harris, had requested his manuscripts. This was a good sign. More than that, it was his chance to keep working in America. Maybe he'd get a book deal on top of a renewed ghostwriting contract. His heart pounded; he was ready.

He pushed the Up button on the wall repeatedly, as if that would make it hurry. Going back to London to write more nonsense gossip and rumors for the celebrity magazine wasn't an option. Not at forty.

"Twenty-second," he told the elevator attendant. His voice

resounded like a drum. The hangover was dwindling, and now his chest burst with hope.

Troy Harris, Editor-in-Chief—as it read on the plastic sign—opened the door a few seconds after Oscar knocked. He was white, round, middle-aged, with a scruffy face and a head that shined like a crystal ball. Troy smiled briefly and pointed Oscar toward his cluttered desk.

"I've been waiting for you," Troy said, sitting on an oversized office chair.

"Sorry if I'm late." Oscar took one of the guest chairs on the other side of the desk. The immenseness of Central Park rolled down like a royal green carpet at his feet, on the other side of the glass wall. It was a powerful feeling to be so high over the city.

"Judy Swift said you are one of the most talented ghostwriters in the fantasy-erotica department."

"Thanks, that's kind of her," Oscar said, crossing his legs, then uncrossing them immediately. He didn't want to look too confident. He realized the palms of his hands were sweating.

Troy cleared his throat and opened a folder. Oscar recognized it at once: the manuscripts he had sent to Judy.

"What makes you want to write children's books, Oscar?"

"There's magic in writing for children—"

"Yeah, yeah . . . But what makes you *think* you can write for children? I mean, have you actually studied the market?"

Oscar's blood rushed to his cheeks. "I suppose I haven't." *Maybe I should've.* "But I've read and written all my life."

Troy smiled and nodded. "Sure. All writers have. They think that gives them the ability to write for children."

Oscar opened his mouth, but Troy broke in before he could speak. "Look, Octavius, I'm trying to do you a favor here, since you're such a good friend of Judy's. She's my best editor, and I want to keep her happy, know what I mean?"

Troy took a look at one of the pages in front of him and tapped a finger on the desk while reading it. *Click, click, click,* like a dripping faucet. Like a freaking dripping faucet in the middle of the night. For a few minutes, Oscar held his breath, trying not to shout in the bald man's face.

Finally Troy said, "I don't think these are children's stories."

"They're fairytales," affirmed Oscar instinctively.

"Fairytales? Beautiful princesses and enchanted carriages . . . all that crap that little girls dream of? Not your stories!" Troy flipped some pages of the file in front of him. "*The Happy Prince*? Seriously? I've never read anything more depressing."

"The prince is happy to bare his soul to help the poor—"

"Eight-year-olds don't want to know about poverty! They want to read about people like them—like, I don't know, what to do with your teeth if the tooth fairy doesn't show up."

"So what are you saying?"

"Rewrite this, man! Make the Happy Prince happy. Have him meet the joyful princess. Too much violence in your stories, Oliver, way too much violence—"

"Oscar."

"Look, it's not that you aren't a good writer. You have your moments, but no one wants to hear about people dying in children's stories."

"There are deaths in fairytales, Troy . . ." Oscar cleared his throat. "Can I call you Troy? Cinderella's father dies almost at the beginning—"

"But she marries a prince! And not just any prince—a charming, handsome, rich prince! That's what we want to see. Happy. Or at least funny."

"Okay, you have a point." Oscar inhaled deeply, willing to listen.

"Here, *The Nightingale and the Rose*. What's that? The bird stabbing herself with a thorn? I think the student should be the main character. Make him a little wimpy kid. Kind of a nerd. Kids love the underdog. Parents would give us crap if we put a dying bird in one of our books. And what kind of bird is this—" Troy said, fluttering his hand in the air as if looking to grasp an answer.

"It's a nightingale. They have this powerful song—" Oscar explained, leaning toward the desk.

"Look, just change it for a parrot or something more exciting— that's an idea! What if they're pirates? Well, I'm just brainstorming here. You're the writer, after all."

"Okay," Oscar said. He pulled a small notepad and pen from his back pocket and scribbled: *Parrot—pirates—no deaths.*

"Let's see . . . *The Selfish Giant* . . . Oh, yeah, he dies too. I kind of liked it in the beginning. It reminded me of *Jack and the Beanstalk*, but then all that about the Christ-like child. We're not a religious imprint."

"It's not a religious story," Oscar assured him, looking up from his note taking. "It has a moral, like most fairytales—" He stopped when he noticed the sardonic look on Troy's face.

"It's just not happening. Look, your writing is sharp, but it's not commercial. Put that in your notes. It feels . . . old-fashioned, almost." He tapped the table again, harder this time.

Old-fashioned. Not from this era. I've heard that before. Oscar's stomach knotted painfully, and he wished once more that he hadn't drunk so much the night before.

He caught a glimpse of his reflection on the glass and saw his rebellious hair sticking out. His reflection looked older, so much older. And tired. He breathed in and said, "That's one of my best stories, I've been told. It's about forgiveness."

"Five-year-olds can't even spell forgiveness. It just wouldn't sell. Believe me, I've been in the business for more than twenty years. Children's books sell as good as candy but not if they have a moral, too many words, or dead people in them."

Oscar stopped writing to look at Troy. "Then you're not going to publish any of my stories?"

"No, no. I didn't say that." Troy went back to the opened manuscripts. He moistened his thumb with his tongue and turned over the pages. "Here it is! *The Remarkable Rocket.* I think it has a lot of potential. I kind of like the idea of a huge party thrown for the prince's wedding, told from the firecracker's point of view." His green eyes softened. "Look, I didn't mean to be rude before, but I have children and I know what they want to read."

Oscar glanced at the picture frames on the top of Troy's desk nestled behind a pile of books. Three chubby children were rolling on the sand of a deserted green-water beach.

"They're beautiful," Oscar lied.

"Thanks." Troy nodded. "I'm not insensitive, you know? I understand you think your stories will sell and all that romantic crap writers think." He chuckled and then lowered his voice as if to confide some deep, dark secret. "I was a writer too, once. I wrote day and night when I was in college. I even thought I'd have a career as a writer, but . . . someone has to pay the bills. This job allows me to do that and more. I know a lot about children's literature, that's why I tell you that *The Remarkable Rocket* should be more about the beautiful Russian bride. And magic! Make the rocket cast spells. Make it vibrant. Make children want to grab dollies out of the remarkable rocket! You know what I mean?"

"Sure," Oscar said, sounding unconvinced.

"Oh, and the word count. A short story should be short. Give me the story in less than five thousand words. Cut it to seven hundred. We won't publish anything for children with more than seven hundred words—children's attention spans are short, you know? If you want more words, then give me a chapter book for middle graders. But short stories? Please. No one reads them. No one buys them!"

Oscar scribbled once more on his notepad. *700. Short.*

"But before you go, I have some bad news for you," Troy said, closing the file with the stories inside. "Judy didn't want to tell you, but . . . your ghostwriting contract—the one that is expiring—won't be renewed. Sorry. We just have other expenses."

Oscar jumped out of his seat. "But you said I was one of the best ghostwriters!"

"I didn't say that, Olaf. Judy did."

There was an awkward silence in the room.

Oscar put his notepad on the chair beside him. "It is Oscar."

"What is?" asked Troy distractedly.

"My name. Oscar. Oscar Wilde."

Troy pulled another file in front of him. "Come back when you've rewritten *The Remarkable Rocket*. Make it ready for the big screen."

Oscar saw the trees and lampposts of Central Park below him through the glass wall. The cars looked like beetles and the people like ants. He wanted to smash them. Dizzy, he turned toward the door.

"Oh, Oscar?" Troy called from his desk.

He stopped and turned slowly, his leather shoes squeaking on the tiled floor.

"I read the manuscript of your *Dorian Gray* novel. Speculative fiction is not your thing, buddy. I'm telling you this from one writer to another. Think *50 Shades of Grey* instead. Now, that sells."

Oscar quietly walked to the elevators. He felt as if he were being carried by an invisible current. Everything around him became a blur, and every sound turned into a screech. He didn't feel his legs moving, yet he moved, and soon he found himself sitting on one of the plastic seats of the train that took him home.

His name wouldn't be famous after all, like his mother had once predicted. His gut gurgled and churned. He'd have to return to London being the same loser he was when he left. *Shit*. Even worse, he'd have to go back to a place he didn't belong. But where did he belong?

His distorted reflection seemed to laugh hysterically on the shiny metal pole. His grotesque mouth rippled around it, his tongue contorted like a red snake. Oscar turned his head and ignored it.

He wouldn't stop writing. He'd write until his fingers cracked and bled, even if his stories didn't please anybody but himself. Maybe he'd marry Jeff to stay in America. He had said something about marriage the night before, but Oscar hadn't been paying attention at the time.

Marriage can't be that bad. Not this time.

The train stopped to let more passengers on. Oscar quietly chuckled in his seat. Now he could picture Troy picking up the little notepad on the empty chair. He imagined Troy reading the words he had scribbled there. *F-U-C-K-I-N-G A-S-S-H-O-L-E.* He could see Troy's face turn red with anger. He laughed out loud, pounding his fist on his knee. His mouth rippled on the metal pole.

A woman in front of him eyed him and clutched her purse a little tighter.

Mariana Llanos was born in Lima, Peru. The daughter of two journalists, Mariana developed an early passion for writing and reading. Mariana wrote poetry, short stories, and plays all the way through school and high school. She studied theatre in the prestigious school, CuatroTablas, based in Lima. Mariana moved to Oklahoma in 2002. After her second child was born, Mariana began working in a preschool center, where she stood out for her creativity and passion for arts education. In 2013 Mariana published her first book, *Tristan Wolf,* which won a finalist spot on the 2013 Readers' Favorite Book Award and a spot in the 2013 Gittle List Independent Book Awards. In 2014 Mariana decided to pursue her dream of becoming a fulltime writer. Since then, she has published seven books independently in English and Spanish and has visited more than 150 schools around the world through virtual technology, to promote literacy. Just recently, Mariana signed a contract with the publishing company, Penny Candy Books, for the publication of her new children's story, *Luca's Bridge*. Her work geared toward an adult audience has appeared on Writer's Resist and Blackbirds Thirds Flight, among others. Visit www.marianallans.com to learn more about her.

Knock, Knock

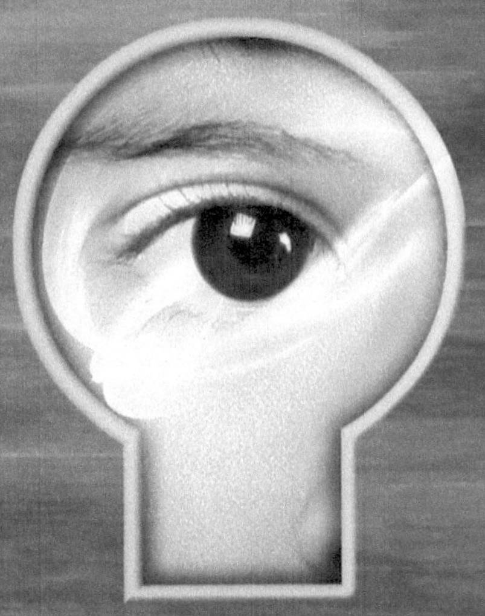

D.L. Smith-Lee

The high-pitched squeal and crashing of a frying pan against the kitchen floor was indicative of yet another fight between Charlie's parents. He lay in his bed in his upstairs bedroom with a pillow covering his head. The pool of tears beneath his head was nothing new, nothing unlike the night before or the night before that.

Charlie's parents argued every night, and it always seemed to happen just a few hours after his mother would put him to bed. He'd grown accustomed to awakening at an hour a normal seven-year-old child shouldn't, when his father chose to arrive home with slurred speech hardly recognizable to Charlie's ears. The noises he would hear would consist of similar things: his mother yelling with colorful words he knew only grownups used, his father yelling back the same, and pounding noises that surely meant physical contact. Where that physical contact was, he didn't want to know. He just wanted them to love each other like they had before. He wanted his father to pay attention to him again; Charlie could hardly remember his face.

Over the loud yelling and continual arguing, Charlie heard the first two knocks at the door. He lifted his head from under the pillow and wiped the tears from his wet face. Charlie climbed out of his bed and took a peek out of his bedroom door. The rowdy screams of his angry mother became clearer, and he could make out words, but there was no one in the hallway. He closed the door and listened more closely.

The knocking came again, this time he was sure of it. Two knocks. Charlie walked to his closet and stood before the great white door with the shiny brass doorknob. He waited for the knocks to come again but nothing happened. He felt his heart throb in his small chest as he raised his hand to the switch outside of the door, watching as the light illuminated the threshold.

If it was the Boogeyman, then light would get him, Charlie thought.

But Charlie knew the Boogeyman wasn't real, his mother had told him so. He just wanted to take simple precautions before opening the closet. His hand rested on the brass knob for only a moment as he twisted the knob and snatched it away, allowing the door to swing open.

His school clothes remained on their hangers untouched, and his board games lay in a pile on the top shelf. His shoes were still lined neatly on the floor. Charlie closed the closet door and turned out the light. He was still not satisfied and wanted to know where the knocking had come from.

Charlie tried knocking on the closet door and waited for a moment. He didn't know what to expect. Maybe the closet door would fly open by itself and the monsters would come out. Maybe he would enter an enchanted land he'd read about in storybooks. He didn't know, but he waited.

It seemed like forever until he heard three knocks at the door. Charlie's heart jumped at the sound, but he didn't rush back to his bed.

"Who's there?" Charlie asked.

"A friend," a shrill child's voice told him.

"Why are you in my closet?"

"Because I wanted to meet you, Charlie."

"You know me?" Charlie asked eagerly.

Charlie's bedroom door opened as the lights came on, flaring his sensitive vision. At the door stood his mother.

"Baby, why are you up?" she asked, her voice trembling.

Surely her throat had swollen from sobbing so hard. Charlie hadn't realized the argument had stopped.

"The boy in my closet," Charlie said explanatorily, pointing at the closed closet door.

"Honey, we've talked about this," his mother said, walking to the closet and opening the door. "See, there's nothing there, okay? Now it's really late, let's get you back to sleep."

She picked Charlie up and laid him in his bed, not taking note of the wet spot beneath his pillow. His mother retrieved some cough syrup from the bathroom medicine cabinet and gave him the proper dosage so that he would sleep soundly.

It was playtime again, and Charlie was sitting on the floor by the classroom cupboard stacking dominoes. The other kids played games with one another. Some built starships, ray guns, and swords with Legos as they traveled on their various adventures across the galaxy. But Charlie only wanted the dominoes. He would stack them, building intricate lines and patterns, and topple them just at the end of playtime. He wanted to play with the other kids, but they didn't seem to like him very much.

Charlie set down his final domino in the intricately built swirl pattern he'd worked hard to create over the last thirty minutes. As he stared down, carefully studying the dominos, two knocks came from his side. He looked up at the closet door, perplexed for a moment before remembering the night before. He stood, careful not to destroy his hard work. He returned the knock with three of his own before receiving three more from the other side.

"Is it you again?" asked Charlie.

"Yes, it's me again," the childish voice answered.

"You still never told me your name."

"I don't know my name."

"Your mommy never gave you a name?" The thought of it was absurd to Charlie. Every child had a name, even if some were names he found funny.

"No," the voice replied ashamedly.

"Do you go to my school?"

"No, I just wanted to come play with you, Charlie."

"Then why don't you come out of there?"

"Because I'm scared. Why don't you come in here?"

"I don't know. Why are you scared?" Charlie asked, not realizing that the room around him had gotten quieter.

Footsteps behind him drew closer as the teacher stood over him; her flowery dress and matching glasses seemed a bit out of date. Miss Greckski was a woman in her mid-forties with salt-and-pepper hair that flowed just past her shoulder blades.

"Charlie, who are you talking to?" she whispered. She didn't want the other children to stare.

"The boy in the closet," Charlie replied.

Miss Greckski waited for further explanation, but when the innocent brown-eyed child just stared back at her smiling sweetly, she opened the closet door, knocking over Charlie's dominoes in the process.

Charlie looked at the piled papers and old crayon drawings and then looked down at his swirled creation, ruined.

— • • —

Jessica worked at the help desk at South Suburban Hospital. This had been her job since Charlie had been eight months old. She knew eventually Ronnie's drinking problem would be too much to deal with. Jessica had thought she could change him once he got back on his feet. Being in the Navy for six years, then getting discharged for too many DUIs, should have been warning enough for her, but she wasn't ready to give up on her husband. She loved him before the Navy and she would love him after.

Only now Jessica had her son to worry about. She knew why her baby boy couldn't sleep at night, the reasons why he would lie awake. Her marriage was crumbling before her eyes, and she knew there was nothing she could do about it.

"Jess, would you mind—" Jessica's co-worker, Stacey, stopped her words in their tracks.

She tried to look past the bluish shine on Jessica's eye that was poorly covered by foundation that didn't match her crème-colored skin. Stacey sighed, knowing that there was little else she could do since her hundreds of words of advice had already been ignored.

"Jess," Stacey repeated, placing the folder on the desk before Jessica, her head cocked to the side, her eyes sorrowful.

"I know, Stacey," Jessica replied, already knowing what she would say.

Stacey sighed to herself, feeling helpless. "Could you run these through? I've got a patient to see," Stacey said dryly.

"Of course," Jessica replied.

Stacey walked away a moment later.

Jessica's phone vibrated as a reminder came across:

PARENT TEACHER CONFERENCES TODAY.

She cursed, forgetting that this was the day. Ronnie wouldn't be there, so she knew she had to do this herself. She would be off shortly.

—   •   •   —

"Mrs. Easton, I'm aware of the situation with you and your husband," Miss Greckski said to Jessica. "Has Charlie shown any negative behaviors at home at all?"

"No," she said. She felt guilty thinking of the nights her son would lie awake while she fought with her husband over his lack of employment and increasing drinking habits. It was only the night before that she'd ever seen him at his closet. What was it that he said he was doing? Something about a boy? "Has he been acting out in class?"

"No, quite the opposite actually. He's become very withdrawn from the other students. He's very quiet and well mannered, even when the other kids are mean to him. Don't worry, I assure you, bullying does not occur in my classroom," Miss Greckski explained confidently. "But with that withdrawal, do you think he's found some other way of coping with his loneliness?"

Jessica's mind instantly flashed to the night before.

"No," Jessica lied. "He's just trying to come to terms with the loss of his father at home. Charlie rarely sees his father, and as of last night, my husband and I are separated. I've been seeking lawyers for quite some time now."

"I see," Miss Greckski said. "Well, Mrs. Easton, I would just recommend trying to find him playdates. Any relatives his age?"

"Well, yes, but they're out of state. I can definitely try my best to pay more attention to him."

Miss Greckski pursed her lips together, biting back her words. Maybe being with his mother was what he needed most, but she knew there was more that he needed. She nodded in response, and the two shook hands and said their goodbyes.

—— · · ——

The boy in the closet didn't come the night after. Charlie wondered if he'd been scared away by the adults. He lay wide awake late each night since the habit of waking to his parents' arguments had been formed, awaiting the two knocks at his closet door. Some nights, Charlie would climb out of his bed and knock on the door himself just to see if he would get a reply. Nothing.

He would try it in school during playtime as he built his perfect domino structures. Still nothing.

A week had passed as Charlie sat before his closet again as his mother ran his bath water. He still wore his school clothes, ready to don his bathrobe. Before he changed, he closed his bedroom door. Charlie stood before the closet again and gave the door two knocks.

Charlie jumped when he heard the sound of three knocks in response. He immediately responded with three of his own.

"Who's there?" the familiar voice asked him.

"It's you!" Charlie said, overcome with joy. His knocking friend had returned. "I want to come play with you now. I don't like it here anymore."

"Really?" the voice said excitedly.

"Yeah, let's go over to your house, and we can play there, if you're too scared to come here."

"Okay, but you have to open the door first, Charlie."

"Okay," Charlie said, grinning from ear to ear as his mother snatched open the bedroom door, viewing the back of Charlie's dark curly head of hair.

She crossed her arms and frowned a bit as her son opened his closet door earnestly, then stepped slowly inside while closing the door behind him. Hiding from bath time. Although he hadn't done it in a while, he had done it many times before.

Jessica pushed the door open. "Now where is that boy?" she said with exaggerated earnestness. "Is he under the bed? Is he behind the dresser?" She feigned looking under the bed and behind the dresser respectively. She inched to the closet door carefully. "I know where he is," Jessica said with a grin.

She knocked on the door three times before turning on the light. She swung the door open with a playful, *GOTCHA!* But her smile faded at what she saw. It was more of what she didn't see that presented the problem. The clothes remained in their respective places with the shoes stacked neatly, but Charlie was not there.

Jessica shook her head and began tearing the closet from bottom to top. Maybe there was a trapdoor or a secret passage of some sort. She knew the thought was ridiculous, but something had to explain this.

She immediately called the police. The police doubted that the boy went missing in his closet but sent out the AMBER Alert anyhow.

— ﹒ ﹒ —

As the months dragged on, Jessica's divorce was made final. Ronnie blamed her for their missing son but didn't stay around long enough for him to be found. He moved to Wisconsin with his brother. Jessica wanted to keep the house and was allowed to do so. Stacey moved in with her to help pay for the house.

Jessica would sit in Charlie's room after she came home from work. She would sniff the empty sheets and blankets that remained tousled on his bed exactly the way he'd left them, just to absorb his scent.

Images of him standing at the closet door would come to her mind as she stood before it. She would knock on the door, waiting for an answer, but she was only met with silence. Jessica opened his closet occasionally, remembering the days she would pick out and iron his clothes for the week.

Even as the months turned to two long years, she would still go to his room every night, praying that he would come back to her. His room still remained in the exact condition he had left it. Jessica made sure that dust would not collect on his toys and dresser so that when he came home, they would be ready for him to use.

Stacey was sure—everyone was—that Charlie was dead, but she didn't have the heart to tell Jessica to accept it. She knew that had to come on her own terms.

Jessica lay on the floor of his bedroom one evening, awaiting sleep to take her off into dreams of her baby boy, when she heard two knocks.

"You don't have to knock, Stacey," she said.

The door didn't open, and Jessica ignored it until two more knocks came. Jessica shot upward, suddenly aware that the knocks hadn't come from the bedroom door.

She walked to the closet, listening for another sound. She raised her hand and knocked on the door three times and waited. A long moment passed before the three knocks came back. She slapped her hand over her mouth as tears came bursting from her eyes.

The closet door swung open as she hopped out of the way, stumbling across the room onto Charlie's bed, ruining the tousled blankets the way he had left them.

"Mommy!" the screechy voice came as the boy rushed to wrap his arms around her.

His sleeved shirt came to his elbows and part of his lower back was showing, it was clearly too small for him. His curly dark hair was unmistakably familiar. Jessica stood and wrapped her arms around her son. She had no words, only tears of joy. Charlie had returned home.

He pulled away, standing before her as not the little boy she remembered, but now nearly a preteen who was clearly outgrowing his clothing.

"How? Where have you been?" Jessica asked frantically.

"I'm happy now, Mommy," Charlie said. Not an ounce of his childish innocence had been scathed. "He found me."

"Who?"

"Him," Charlie replied, rubbing his mother's belly at the words. "Somebody hurt him and he says he's lonely. But we're both happy now, Mommy. He found me. And he wanted me to give you this."

Jessica barely processed the words her son spoke as he set the blackened rope-like object in her hand. She could feel something familiar about this item. Something so close it should've been comforting, but it only gave her chills.

A noise came from the closet door; two knocks, like before.

"I have to go back now," Charlie said, his voice severe, his bright smile fading.

"Go where?" she said, and Charlie pulled away.

"Bye, Mommy."

The knocks came again, this time like a battering ram attempting to smash down the door. Jessica nearly leapt across the room, but her socks slipped on the hardwood floor. Charlie returned the furious bangs with three knocks of his own and opened the closet door.

Rushing to her feet, Jessica chased her son to the closet door like a fading dream, begging for it to last longer. She reached the door only a second after Charlie had closed it behind him. Jessica opened the door to find nothing again. She turned on the light, taking in the mess she'd made of the closet on that night two years before.

—・・—

Jessica still sits there in Charlie's room, watching and waiting. Occasionally she raises her old bones from the rocking chair she's placed in the room and goes to the closet. She knocks twice and waits for the knock to be returned. Nothing. She tries three times and waits. Still nothing.

But she won't give up hope. She still feels the warmth of her son's arms around her. She still hears his juvenile voice developing into that of an adolescent. His toothless smile is replaced with adult teeth. Surely her son is grown now. And she knows that one day he will come back to her.

She sits rubbing her stomach, holding the black rope-like item close to her belly.

Never again, she thinks.

No matter how long it takes, she will be waiting.

D.L. Smith-Lee grew up in the wilds of urban and suburban Chicago in the chaos of the new millennium. A US Navy Sailor, a lifelong lover of fiction and creative freedom, and a passionate video gamer, D.L. seeks nothing more than to create fiction and media for folks of all backgrounds to immerse themselves within. He has had several works of short speculative fiction published online and in print, including: "The Were-Traveler," "In Creeps the Night," and "Rococoa." The first installment of his dark fantasy *Blood Sorcery* novelette series, *Blood Curse,* is available on Amazon through Kindle. D.L. Smith-Lee resides in the great city of Chicago.

Gunpowder & Wool

Kari Holloway

Cool winds blew across the field of dying grass. The breeze withered and danced through the trees. An orange leaf drifted from the sycamore before crunching under worn soles. The men sweated beneath their wool uniforms. Bandanas trapped what moisture they could from the company of men.

The campfires had burned to red embers, yet silhouettes of smoke rose to greet the dawn. The hot, bitter coffee was the only comfort on these endless days. Some of the men ate fried pieces of salted pork and grits.

Corporal Hulett examined the first men standing ready near their tents. All seemed in order. Neat. Tidy. Accessible. He prepared for his squad's inspection. He straightened his sack coat's collar and checked the five brass buttons down the front. His slouch's wide brim hid his short cropped hair and the scar above his ear.

Some of the men fought with the instep tab—the fabric that hugged the arch of the foot. The small buttons were easy on the instep but hard to button on the outside of the foot. The choice was between ease and preventing some hard thing clinging to their socks and into their boot.

Sergeant Kelly bustled through camp. He muttered under his breath and pulled on his gloves. As he walked near Hulett's squad, the men snapped to attention. The sergeant paused, and with a glance, moved down the line of men, inspecting their uniforms. With a curt nod, his men returned to their duties, and he resumed his agitated walk.

The short musical notes sounded, and the men, ready or not, began to muster. Squad by squad, the platoons formed. Corporal Hulett and the other squad leaders sounded off. *"Present and accounted for."* Sergeant Kelly about-faced and saluted First Sergeant Traux.

With a nod, Traux's weary eyes peered over his men. He

returned the salute, and Kelly marched to his place. Traux looked at the young boy, ten years old, proudly holding the flag. The bright colors now faded but that didn't diminish the pride in these men. His men.

"Reports have come in from Sergeant Major. The Yanks have breached the river north of here. We are to deploy at once." First Sergeant Traux's words stirred passion in some men and fear of the coming clash in others.

A horn sounded across the way, and the men nodded a solemn glance at their brothers-in-arms. As quickly as calloused and water-blistered feet could handle, the men assembled into neat, tight ranks. Their weapons were heavy, and the bayonets were dented and discolored in spite of maintenance. As they moved out, the rifle barrels swayed to their march through the forest where nature once reigned. Their cadence kept time with the steady tap of the drum.

The drummer, a small boy of eight who walked beside the color bearer, had a job more important than even he realized. They brought morale to the tired men. The steady *thump, thump, thump* reflected the hearts of men who were willing to die for their freedom from government dictation. The wind rippled through the flag, snatching the fabric taut before moving to other haunts.

Halos of sunlight speckled the ground. The gray wool soaked the sun's heat, like a rock in the desert. Men licked their chapped lips and wished for rain. Wet wool wasn't any more enjoyable, but at least it would bring some relief.

The men broke through the forest's embrace. For a mile or more, the grassy knoll stretched under the sun's light. The bugle echoed as the man in the commander's hat raised his sword with the decorative hilt to the sky and hollered, "For the South, by the Grace of God."

The first line of men knelt. The rifle butts pressed against their shoulders. Some hands shook with nerves. Manly men sighted down the barrels, no different than if varmints were their target.

Corporal Hulett leaned over Private Sherman, first man in the squad, before shouting into his ear. "Brace more, you son of a bitch. Control your hand, boy, before you shoot out your eye."

The first volley of ballistics shot across the field. Overhead, the whizzing lead balls made men flinch. On either side, dirt exploded as the mortars buried themselves into the dirt. The tiny flecks of sand and clay stung as they showered upon the men. The squad behind the kneelers took aim and fired with the commander's orders.

The men Hulett had been commanding hurried to grab their powder horns. The tiny black grains looked like sand as they poured into the barrel. Metal slid on metal as the ramrods encouraged the musket balls into place.

The scent of gunpowder grew in the field as the men fired again and again. Colleagues fell, and nothing could be done until the final warble of the horn sounded tonight. The men closed the gaps and began to march forward. The drum's pulse increased to match the beat of the battle.

The thrill of battle rang through Hulett as he raised his short sword in rally fashion. "Give no quarter to these yellow-bellied fledglings."

Doty laughed at the corporal. "What are you doing?"

"Giving encouragement. What are you doing to help turn these boys into men? Besides how to lay in a tree?" Hulett smirked. He found it hard to remember exactly how long they had been friends.

Doty's laughter rumbled from his belly and shook his whole body. "Not wasting my breath. You do remember you're a ghost— they can't hear you."

"But what's the fun in that?" Hulett countered, with a face-splitting grin.

Doty raised a bushy brow. "Shouldn't you be haunting World War II? After all, you served in that one."

"The same could be said about you, swabbie," he jested with the petty officer. "There's a lot to be said about reenactments."

Doty faded from the tree and rematerialized beside Hulett. "Well then, don't let me stop you."

Hulett smirked at Doty. "You wanna join in?"

Doty laughed. "And risk becoming a bullet sponge, like you?"

"What's it matter? We're ghosts." Hulett found joy in echoing what Doty had pointed out minutes prior.

By the time the ghosts exchanged their jolly greeting and decided to join the fray, the show was finished. The crowds clapped. Little girls marveled at the bonnet-covered women dressed in Victorian-era garb whose skirts graced the ground like a waltz. Little boys dressed in replica cotton coats and kepis used imaginary pistols and foam swords in recreation.

As the weary reenactors departed for grilled food and healthy beverages, Hulett spoke. "There's another show at two." He nudged Petty Officer Doty's shoulder and wagged his brows.

Doty laughed and shook his head. "Count me in."

A typical cusp Cancer, **Kari Holloway** is quiet until she gets to know you. As a fourth-generation farm girl, she specializes in southern fiction romance and fantasy, using her experiences, as well as her studies in psychology from her time at Georgia Southwestern State University, to really get into the minds of her characters, helping her to create people in her stories who are true to life. Especially cowboys, for which she has an affinity. A native of Leesburg, Georgia, Kari spends her days writing, cuddling with her daughters, and baking delicious treats. She's also a bit of a shutterbug, taking kids and camera to some of her favorite places: aquariums, theme parks, museums, and zoos.

Thief

Laurie
Gardiner

The rain fell so hard the day Luna died it bounced off the hot pavement before slowing to a gentle mist, perfect for running through on a muggy summer day. The sun peeked from behind a cloud, and steam wafted into the air.

Luna sat in a shallow muddy puddle in her underwear, naming worms according to size. The long one with the fat middle was Papa. Mama was long and thin, pale, stretched out, and tired looking.

Luna searched through a wriggling, slimy pile for another. The worm slipped away and slithered through the mud toward freedom. Gently, she picked it up and wound it through her fingers to hold it in place. It was small, but robust and fierce. Definitely a Luna worm. Smiling in triumph, she placed it carefully into the box full of dirt with the others.

Now to find a Cira worm. Luna's breath hitched at the thought of her twin sister. She stared up at the second floor of their white Colonial home—intimidating in size and austerity—and rubbed at the sudden knot of anxiety in her chest. The curtains on her sister's bedroom window were closed tight to the daylight. "So Cira can rest," Mama had answered when Luna once asked why the room was so dark.

The anxiety turned to resentment. Cira should be outside with Luna, imagining away the day, not alone in bed with tubes running through her body. But Papa had told her to let him do the worrying, so she shook off the anger, and the knot slowly untwisted.

There! A tiny worm caught her eye. She scooped it into her palm and cupped it, afraid to pinch the delicate creature between her fingers. The worm was perfect for Cira: tiny and flawlessly formed, yet nearly translucent in its paleness.

She held it to her face, speaking softly as she ran a gentle fingertip along its body.

Mama grabbed Luna's arm and pulled her to her feet. "Luna Fiore! What are you doing out here in your underwear?"

The worm flew from Luna's hand. She watched in horror as it landed on the gravel below.

"Mama, no . . . Cira . . ."

She wrenched her arm free and kept her eyes on the tiny worm as she moved to retrieve it.

Mama stepped toward her. "I've told you before, you are too old to be playing outside nearly naked."

Luna's eyes widened in horror as the Cira worm disappeared beneath Mama's foot. Choking back a sob, she swung to face her mother. "You killed her. You killed Cira. I hate you!"

The blood drained from Mama's face for a moment before hot anger crept up her neck and flushed her skin crimson. Her open hand sliced through the air and connected with Luna's cheek, turning her head with the force of the blow. The sharp *CRACK* of the slap hung heavy in the air between them.

Luna put her hand to her cheek and glared at her mother, silently daring her to do it again. Why did it matter what Luna did, out here in the country with no neighbors for miles and not yet old enough to need a bra?

Papa traveled for work, and Mama spent her days tending to Cira. Why should they care if Luna sat in a puddle and played with worms? The only time it mattered—the only time she existed—was when Mama needed to vent her anger. She was beyond angry now. Luna knew by the twitch of the scar beneath her eye.

The silence stretched as they glared at one another. Luna refused to look away first. Finally, her mother turned and strode to the house.

When the sun sank below the trees and her stomach growled in hunger, Luna crept into the house and peeked into the sitting room. Mama sat at the piano, staring at a well-worn photo of Cira on the music rack. One hand rested unmoving on the keys, the other held a tumbler of scotch. The half-empty bottle rested on top of the piano.

Luna knew enough to avoid her mother when the bottle was nearby. Ignoring her hunger pangs, she snuck up the stairs and into the bathroom to fill the tub. She could only hope her mother forgot her earlier rage as she drank herself into oblivion.

The bathroom door banged open as Luna stepped into the tub. She jerked at the sound, put a hand on the wall to steady herself, and turned to see her mother slouched against the doorframe, drink still in hand. Her robe hung open, revealing a booze-stained silk negligee. Stray strands of brunette hair fell from a bun, curling around her face.

She waved her drink toward Luna. "Why did you say I killed Cira?"

"That's not what I—"

"Don't lie to me." Mama straightened and took an unsteady step toward Luna. "You think I don't know the stories your father fills your head with?"

"Papa doesn't—"

"Of course he does. I see you two when he's home, sitting with your heads together, whispering about me. He lies, Luna. He lies, and he cheats, and he blames me for being cold." She waved her drink in the air, spilling amber liquid onto the white marble floor. "Tell me, what kind of father stays away when his daughter is dying?"

Luna shook her head. A ball of resentment coiled in her stomach. "That's not true! Papa loves Cira. He wants to be here with her, but he has to work to pay the medical bills."

Mama smirked. Ice clinked as she took a long swig. "You're just a child, what do you know of it? Only what he tells you."

Luna stood tall and locked eyes with her mother. "I know more than you think. I know you're happy when Cira's sick."

Mama's eyes widened briefly before narrowing to angry slits. "You think giving up two years of my life made me happy? I sacrificed my nursing career, my friends, my marriage—everything—to take care of Cira. My child is dying, and you think that makes me happy?" Her voice cracked on the last syllable. Tears brimmed in her eyes.

Luna had already pushed too far, and yet her mother's emotion made her bold enough to push even further. Mama never cried. She rarely laughed either. In fact, the only emotions she seemed to possess were normally reserved for Cira. Luna had long ago learned to take anything she could get, even anger.

"I know you don't want her to die, but you want her to be sick. You make her sick, just so she needs you."

A flash of anger in Mama's eyes caused Luna to step backward. She shivered as her bare skin pressed against the cold tile.

"I make her sick?" Mama slowly approached the tub, voice rising with every step. "Did I put that tumor inside her head? Tell me, Luna. How did I do that? How?" The glass slipped from her hand and crashed to the floor. "It should have been you. You, not Cira!"

She charged at Luna, hand in the air, ready to strike.

Luna's hands came up to protect her face. Her feet slipped on the bottom of the tub and she fell. She heard a *CRACK*. Sharp pain shot through her head, and the world faded.

— • • —

Luna flew to the moon and perched atop the highest mountain peak. She sat for hours, watching Earth's blue glow.

The others rarely came here; they were too obsessed with vengeance or finding a way to cross over to leave Earth. Luna had learned quickly to avoid them, often spending her nights curled up sleeping in a crater on the dark side of the moon, while they roamed Earth in search of peace. Their uncontrolled anger reminded her of Mama. Their mournful cries of anguish ripped her soul to shreds. Most of them had met untimely deaths, pulled violently from their bodies before they were ready, left bitter and full of rage.

Luna did not dwell in bitterness or anger. She had made a promise to her sister, and death would not stop her from fulfilling it. *When the thief inside Cira's head releases her, I'll be there to guide her home.*

Since her own death a month ago, Luna spent every waking moment exploring the spirit world and learning her capabilities and limitations. The time drew near. Soon, she would be ready.

Luna hovered high in the corner of the room, watching Cira's chest rise and fall in the pale streaks of moonlight slanting through the blinds. The next breath never came. Cira's frail body jerked and convulsed, consumed by a seizure.

Luna, in her panic, forgot to fade before attempting to fly from the room to somehow alert the nurse. In her semi-opaque form, she hit the wall and dropped to the floor. The monitor's long piercing beeps brought the nurse running before Luna could recover.

Cira revived herself with a shudder and a deep gasping breath. Luna sat against the wall and watched the nurse care for her sister. Her gentle, soft-spoken ways captivated Luna, who was unused to such tenderness. She had caught glimpses of it in Mama—when she pushed a stray, dark curl from Cira's clammy face after a seizure, or called her *my sunshine*—but it was rare, and never for Luna.

"You and Mama are too much alike," Papa would say when Luna complained Mama loved Cira more. "She loves you just as much as your sister, but it's hard for her to show it when she sees so much of herself in you."

Luna had never understood why that should make a difference. Shouldn't seeing herself reflected in her daughter make Mama love her more?

Speaking in low, soothing tones, the nurse took Cira's vitals, then stroked a damp cloth across the young girl's face to remove the sheen of sweat. She picked up a cup of ice water, held the straw to Cira's parched lips, and smiled. "Feel better?"

Cira sipped and nodded.

The nurse set down the cup and began straightening the bed linens. "Your mother should be home soon. I'll let her know it happened again. I'm sure she'll want to see you before she goes to bed."

Cira raised her hand. "She gave me a picture of Luna."

The nurse smiled sadly, took the photo from Cira, and attempted to smooth the creases. "That's good. I know you've been asking for a while."

"Mama's been too sad to remember."

The woman pursed her lips and traced a finger across Luna's image before handing back the photo. She leaned in and kissed Cira's forehead. "I'll be across the hall. Try to sleep."

Cira's voice stopped her at the door. "When I die, do you think I'll see Luna?"

The nurse closed her eyes and whispered, "Yes," before hurrying from the room.

— • • —

Less than an hour later, narrow beams of light flashed at the window. Luna crossed the room, faded, and glided through the curtain to watch Mama's white Lexus SUV roll up and enter the garage.

Moments later, hushed voices drifted from the room across the hallway. Months earlier, when the treatments failed and Cira was discharged from the hospital, Mama turned the spare bedroom into a lounge for the visiting nurses. Luna overheard her parents arguing about it one night. Papa thought it unnecessary. Mama insisted the help should not spend too much time with Cira, as they might become too attached. As always, Papa gave Mama her way.

The voices faded as the two women descended the staircase. The front door creaked open and closed. Luna watched taillights disappear down the long, tree-lined driveway. In the following silence, the *click* of heels on the hard, tile floor below echoed through the house. Cold dread settled over Luna with the realization that, for the first time since her death, she was about to see Mama.

Her eyes flicked skyward, searching until they found a slice of moon peering at her from behind broken clouds. She fought the urge to fade and fly from the room into the familiar white glow. Why, she wondered, would the thought of seeing her mother frighten her so?

She cocked her head, listening carefully. Ice clinked against glass as Mama made a drink. Luna settled into the window seat, pulled her knees to her chest, and concentrated on the steady rhythm of Cira's breathing.

Soon she heard the tap of footfalls on the steps.

Mama entered the room. Backlit by the dim light of the hallway, she appeared flawless: designer pantsuit immaculately pressed, hair pulled into a tight bun at the base of her neck, understated diamond studs glittering at her ears. She set her drink on the nightstand and turned on the lamp.

Luna rose from her seat and hovered behind the curtains, studying her mother in the dim light. Lines that had been barely visible a month earlier now seemed etched into her face. A few stray streaks of grey hair glinted in the glow of the lamp.

Mama leaned over the bed and stroked Cira's hair until the girl's eyes fluttered open.

One corner of Cira's mouth turned upward in a sleepy smile. "Hi, Mama."

"Hello, darling. Beth told me you had another episode. How are you feeling?"

"I just want to sleep."

Luna drifted from behind the curtains, drawn closer by her sister's pain. Cira's anguished thoughts swirled through Luna in a haze of blinding crimson.

At Cira's words, Mama straightened and reached for her drink. Her face settled into an emotionless mask. She lifted the glass and took a long swallow before speaking. "I understand that Medullo tires you out, but sometimes I think you like spending time with the nurses more than with me." Her voice suggested hurt, but the twitching scar warned of her anger.

Luna flinched at the use of the name her mother had given to the brain tumor. She floated closer, until she hovered beside the bed.

Cira's lower lip trembled. "No, Mama. That's not true."

Mama's face softened with the reassurance. She shivered and rubbed her arms. "It feels cold in here suddenly. Are you cold? Do you want another blanket?"

Cira shook her head and brought a hand to her mouth to smother a yawn.

Mama took Cira's hands in her own. "You need your rest. Pray with me, and then I'll leave you to sleep."

Luna watched as her mother pleaded with God, the saints, and the Holy Mother to send forth their healing powers and cast the evil forces from within Cira. When Mama asked forgiveness for the evil sins that had allowed "Medullo" into her daughter's body, Luna encircled her in a swirl of fury. How dare she blame the imagined sins of a little girl for causing the tumor?

Mama gasped. Her eyes snapped open and darted frantically around the room.

Luna pushed, just a little, until the shell of her soul became a muted semi-transparent shadow. She snaked upward, skimming skeletal fingers across her mother's face.

Mama screamed, released Cira's hands, and stumbled backward.

Luna faded instantly—unwinding like a corkscrew from around her mother's body—and flew to the ceiling.

Cira's brow wrinkled in confusion. "Mama? What's wrong?"

"I—didn't you feel it?"

"Feel what?"

Mama shrugged. "I don't know. Nothing. My imagination, perhaps." She reached for her drink with a trembling hand and drank deeply.

Luna waited until Mama left the room and the click of her heels receded before descending. She studied her twin. Fluids trickled through a narrow tube into Cira's frail body. The numbers on the monitor's display cast a soft glow across her pale features.

The sight saddened Luna, but it was not unfamiliar to her. As long as she could remember, even before the cancer, Cira had spent more time sick than not. From a young age she had been afflicted with one mysterious ailment after another.

Mama had strictly limited the twins' time together, insisting Cira needed to rest. Luna quickly learned to stay quiet and out from underfoot, often hiding behind the curtains in the window seat so Mama didn't know she was nearby. From within the alcove she watched and listened, and eventually her mind was able to piece together what Mama was doing.

Luna realized now that much of the resentment she felt toward her mother was not due to neglect or lack of affection. More than anything, she resented that Mama's selfish refusal to share Cira had robbed the twins of precious time together.

Keeping Luna from her sister wouldn't be easy now. She couldn't be what she had been before death for Cira, but she could stay by her bedside and be her courage.

Brightly-colored ribbons of intense emotion swirled through Luna. She went inside herself and gathered them to her core. Using their energy to solidify her essence, she pushed it outward.

When Luna's awareness returned to the room, Cira's wide eyes stared upward at her in astonishment. "Luna?"

Luna flitted toward the bed and perched on the edge. "It's me. Don't be afraid."

"I'm not. Are you an angel?"

Luna giggled. "No, silly." She half turned to show Cira her back. "See? No wings."

"Oh."

Luna burst into laughter at the disappointed look on Cira's face.

"But, you can fly."

"I'm a ghost."

Cira's mouth gaped open. "A real, live ghost?"

"Real, but not alive. Not the way you are."

Cira's eyes filled with tears. "No. That's not true." She motioned to the IV site on her arm. "I'm tied to this bed all day, and you can fly. I'd rather be a ghost like you."

"Don't say that! Don't ever wish to die."

"Mama prays every day for a miracle, but I'm so tired, Lulu. I just want it to be over."

"I know, Cici."

A deep brooding silence filled the room. Finally Luna spoke. "I need your help with something."

— • • —

Luna shot across the room, materialized too soon, and hit the wall for the third time. She groaned in frustration. "Stop pushing me out! How are you even doing that?"

"I'm sorry. I can't help it. It feels weird." Cira's words would have been more believable had they not been choked with laughter.

"Well, with all the noise we're making, it's a good thing Mama's sleeping."

Before beginning the experiment, Luna had visited Mama's room to check on her and found her still clothed and passed out on top of the covers. She hadn't told Cira; for some reason she still felt the need to protect her from their mother's drinking.

Luna rose up and hovered beside the bed. "What do you mean it feels weird? Can you actually feel me inside your head?"

"I don't know. Not really. I don't *feel* you, but it's like my mind knows you're in there, and it knows you don't belong there so it's pushing you out."

"That's it! I need to go in when you don't know I'm doing it."

"Like, when I'm sleeping?"

"Exactly."

Later, when she was sure Cira slept deeply, Luna faded fully and slipped inside her sister's head. Slowly, she wove her way through the tangle of memories.

Pieces fit together to form the image of a sad, lonely girl craving a normal life. She longed for school and friends, for the warmth of the sun on her face, and the squish of mud between her toes. Yet Cira longed even more for her mother's love and attention, so freely given when she was ill.

Luna emerged in the ethereal light of early dawn and sank into the window seat. Exhaustion weighed heavy, yet her mind would not rest. She had spent her childhood feeling inadequate and second best. Now she regretted the times she had resented her sister for being Mama's favorite.

The sun inched over the scorched horizon and gradually filled the alcove with a blush of rosy light. Cira stirred and mumbled in her sleep.

Luna turned and peered through the curtains into the gloomy obscurity of the room. Her soul ached for her twin. Cira had been kept in darkness too long. Luna rose from her corner with a swirl and tore open the drapes.

Cira squinted against the light as her eyes blinked open. "How did you do that?"

Luna drifted to the bed. "It's hard to explain. I push with my mind and think about it really hard until it happens. Same as when I appear. You see me because I want you to."

Cira seemed satisfied with the explanation. "Did it work? Were you in my head?"

"Yes. You didn't wake up while I was in there?"

"I don't think so. If I did, I don't remember."

Perfect, thought Luna. *While Mama sleeps tonight, I'll sneak inside her head and explore her memories too. Hopefully they won't be too muddled by alcohol to see clearly.*

"Did you see it?"

Cira's voice stirred Luna from her thoughts. "Huh?"

"Medullo. Did you see it?"

Luna had seen the purple-gray mass. That she was powerless to destroy it enraged her. "Don't call it that!"

Tears sprang to Cira's eyes. "I'm sorry. I know you hate that name."

Luna burned with frustration. "It doesn't *deserve* a name. It's a thing. Just because it's inside of you doesn't mean it's a part of you."

She wished she could cry like Cira. Instead, emotions engulfed her until she felt suffocated. As much as Luna hated the last words Mama had spoken to her, in this moment, she believed them.

"Mama was right about one thing; it should have been me."

"That's not true. Mama didn't really say that, did she?"

"Oh Cici, you have no idea. I think she's been making you sick too."

She watched her sister's face crumble and instantly regretted her words. Cira was dying. The truth was useless now. *Why can't I leave well enough alone? Maybe Mama's right, maybe I'm selfish.*

"I'm sorry. I don't know why I said that."

"Maybe it's true."

The unexpected admission left Luna speechless. She had always thought her sister oblivious to their mother's transgressions.

"Do you think Mama gave me Med—the brain tumor?"

Luna shook her head. "I don't think there's any way . . . No, there's no way."

Cira's lower lip trembled. Tears brimmed in her eyes and spilled over, streaming down her cheeks.

Luna hovered closer. "What's wrong?"

"If Mama didn't do it, that means it's my fault."

"No, it's not. Why would you think that?"

"Mama said my bad thoughts let it in."

Luna flew to the ceiling and back again in a swirl of churning anger. "That's not true. Mama shouldn't say things like that."

"Why then? Was it God?"

"No one *gave* you cancer, Cici. Sometimes it just happens. It's not your fault. It's no one's fault."

———··———

That night, from her perch atop the moon's highest peak, Luna watched the sun sink below the endless horizon and contemplated what she was about to do. The thought of exploring her mother's memories filled her with both dread and anticipation. She hoped her suspicions were proven wrong but needed to brace herself for what she might see.

Hours later, when stars gleamed against the midnight sky, Luna returned home.

Mama had fallen asleep in her clothes again and was sprawled across the blankets on her back, snoring lightly. Her head tilted to one side, and a line of drool dribbled from the corner of her open mouth. Tiny bits of ice still floated in the glass on the nightstand.

Luna hovered above the bed, battling conflicting emotions as she gazed at her mother's face. How was it possible to both love and hate someone at the same time? And why had the hate intensified since Luna's body died? This was why she had come here tonight— to find answers. There was no point in putting it off any longer.

Luna braced herself mentally and, before she could change her mind, flew into Mama's head. Once inside, she pulled up sharply and stared in awe at the overwhelming tangle of memories. Countless threads of neurons hung suspended, like fluorescent spider webs floating in space.

She had learned from her foray into Cira's mind that the oldest memories resided in the farthest recesses of the brain. That is where she began.

Maria sat on the floor beside a bed, brow knit in concentration as she printed crooked letters onto a piece of paper. She jumped up, face alight with excitement. "Mama, look! I printed my name all by myself."

Empty eyes stared back at her from a gaunt, lifeless face. The little girl reached out and pulled on the hand hanging over the side of the bed. It was ice cold.

"Mama?" Her voice rose as she pulled harder. "Please, Mama."

Strong hands circled her waist. "Come, Maria."

She was pulled from the room as she continued to scream.

Luna now understood why Mama had never spoken of her mother. She moved onward, darting through insignificant memories until another caught her attention.

Maria fidgeted. She hated the dress nearly as much as that woman. The stiff petticoat and tights made her legs itch. She scanned the aisle toward the pulpit, where Papa stood waiting. He frowned at her in disapproval, and she pasted a smile on her face. She had promised him she would behave on his wedding day.

Later, at the reception, Papa's new wife, Ana, made a speech. She pulled Maria tight against her side and announced how happy she was to have a stepdaughter.

"Smile," she hissed in Maria's ear, pinching the flesh behind the girl's armpit.

Luna passed through memory after memory of her mother enduring Ana's cruelties. The intense emotion of one in particular pulled her in.

"Leave me alone!" Maria shouted.

Ana's voice followed her up the stairs. "Why weren't you at school today? Where were you?"

Maria ran into her room, turned, and waited until her stepmother's face appeared at the top of the stairs, then slammed the door closed.

It swung open immediately. Ana stood in the doorway, her delicate features twisted in anger. "Answer me."

Maria said nothing.

Ana stepped closer. "I'm talking to you. Don't you dare ignore me."

Maria jutted her chin. "What will you do?"

"I'll tell your father—"

"Tell him, what? More lies? I don't care anymore."

"Oh, you will care." Ana stepped close, poking her finger into Maria's chest. "You'll care when I convince your father to send you away."

Maria grabbed the finger and twisted.

Ana wailed, snatched her finger, and cradled it to her chest as she glared at Maria in disbelief. "How dare you?"

At fourteen, Maria stood a full head taller than her stepmother. She straightened to her full height.

"I'm not a little girl anymore, and I won't let you hurt me again. Tell my father whatever you want. Have me sent away. I don't care. Now get out of my room."

Ana's mouth hung open. She stood speechless and unmoving.

Stepping forward until their faces were inches apart, Maria stared into her stepmother's eyes. "Get. Out."

Ana blinked—as though woken from a dream—turned abruptly, and hurried from the room. Maria walked to the doorway to watch Ana's retreat. A reluctant smile tugged at one corner of her mouth. She had done it. She had finally stood up to her.

Ana paused at the top of the stairs, turned, and looked at Maria. "I knew your mother, you know."

"Don't talk about my mother."

"You were too young to remember, but I was her nurse. I looked after her when she was sick. That's how I met your father."

"Stop it."

"He fell in love with me before she died."

Maria's fists clenched and unclenched at her sides. "I said, stop it."

Ana smiled. "The first time we had sex was in their bed, with her in the next room, sleeping."

"Liar!"

Maria charged blindly toward the stairs, her vision blurred by hot, angry tears.

The memory ended abruptly, jolting Luna to the present and causing her to panic. *No, no, no. It can't end like this. I need to know what happened.* She jumped ahead to the next thread, praying the rest of the memory was there.

Maria sat, unmoving and silent, on the bottom step, watching blood seep from between her stepmother's legs. Ana stirred and groaned. She attempted to shift the leg twisted beneath her and screamed in pain.

Her eyes widened. She reached between her legs, then held her bloody hand in front of her face.

"No. Oh no. Please God, no." Her glassy eyes darted around the room and came to rest on Maria. "Help me. The baby . . ."

Maria's gaze moved to the blood, then back to Ana's face. "Baby? You're pregnant?"

A tear slid down Ana's face into her hair. She nodded. "It was too early to tell anyone. There's too much blood. I'm losing the baby. Please—"

The door swung open and Maria's father entered.

— • • —

Emotionally exhausted but determined to finish, Luna skimmed through the next decade of memories. After the incident with Ana, Maria was sent to a detention center for girls, and her father disowned her.

Her beauty and arrogance did not serve her well with the other girls, and she quickly learned to fake illness in order to find refuge in the infirmary. The nurse, Rosa, took Maria under her wing and showered her with attention, often gushing about how much she resembled her deceased daughter.

When Maria left the center four years later, Rosa took her in, helped her find a job, and introduced her to her son, Antonio.

Luna scanned quickly to the day she and Cira were born. Right from birth, they were so different from each other. Cira was calm and content, whereas Luna cried incessantly. Mama couldn't take it and left Luna's care to the nanny, while she doted on Cira.

Shortly after her first birthday, Cira developed breathing problems and was hospitalized frequently with asthma attacks and pneumonia. Mama spent days at a time with Cira at the hospital. She thrived on the attention from the staff—people she worked with—and soon craved it.

Maria was bored and restless. Antonio had left that morning, after being home for more than a month. He had spent all his spare time with the girls. Not that she cared; she had long ago stopped needing his attention. But it had been nearly two months since Cira had been sick, and Maria missed the commotion of the hospital. She missed feeling important.

She went to the bathroom and took the eye drops out of the cabinet. It was time to make Cira one of her special drinks.

Luna watched her mother slowly poison Cira. Some of the memories were familiar. At the time, she had been too young to understand what was happening, and when she grew older, Mama was wise enough to hide it from her. But Luna had vague memories of Mama mixing strange drinks for Cira or crushing pills to mix into her food.

Now she realized how truly obsessed her mother was. Short snippets of memories flashed by as Luna wove her way quickly through threads: Mama withholding puffers while Cira wheezed and struggled to breathe; sneaking into Cira's hospital room to inject something into her intravenous tube; watching with a smile while Cira's tiny body convulsed; the lies sliding so easily from her lips when the nurses asked questions.

And they had all believed her. Papa, the nanny, the nurses, the doctors had all been fooled by her love and devotion for Cira.

Overcome with emotion, Luna left the tangles and hovered beside them. She fought the urge to leave and find peace and solace in the light of the moon. Fleeing would be so much easier than confronting that one last memory. But she had to see it.

She had to know what had happened the night she died.

— • • —

Luna stared into space from her mountaintop peak on the moon. She had been there for days, trying to process what she had seen. The memory ran through her mind like a movie. But it wasn't Mama's memory; it was her own.

Her feet slipped on the bottom of the tub and she fell. She heard a CRACK! Sharp pain shot through her head and the world faded. Her eyes snapped open when she regained consciousness. She tried to breathe but inhaled a mouthful of water. Panic set in. She struggled against the weight on her chest and sucked in more water.

After a moment, Luna's struggles ceased and peace consumed her. The churning water settled, and through the last few air bubbles, she was able to see the hand on her chest. Her gaze traveled the length of the arm and rested on her mother's face.

Seeing the incident first from Mama's viewpoint had stirred something in the deep recesses of Luna's mind and shook loose memories she didn't even know existed. She had bolted from Mama's head and flown blindly to the moon, where she had been ever since.

"Mama killed me," she repeated over and over as the scenario unfolded in her head. Each time she said the words, her fury grew, until she could no longer contain her anger.

She soared into space, twisting and darting for hours around stars and planets, until the rage receded. When her composure returned, she headed toward Earth. She needed to tell Cira what she had seen.

— · · —

Luna swooped through the darkness into Cira's room. She pulled up quickly and hovered near the ceiling, shocked to see Papa asleep in the armchair beside the bed. She descended to his level and memorized his features.

Oh Papa, I miss you so much.

Despite how much time he had spent away from them, she had never doubted his love for her.

Cira coughed and Luna hurried to her side. A clear mask covered the girl's face from nose to chin. Her breath sputtered with short, shallow puffs. The soft hiss of oxygen filled the silence.

I've stayed away too long.

Feeling helpless and despondent, Luna flew behind the curtains and settled into the window seat to wait.

Shortly after dawn, a nurse entered to wake Papa and send him to bed. Hours later, when Cira was finally alone, Luna rushed to the bed and whispered her sister's name.

Cira's eyes blinked open but remained unfocused. "Luna?"

Luna materialized. "I'm here. What happened?"

Cira's words slurred together the way Mama's did when she was drunk. "I had a seizure—a bad one. I stopped breathing for a long time."

"I'm sorry I wasn't here."

"It's okay. There was nothing you could do." Her eyes illuminated. "Papa's here!"

"I know. I saw him."

Cira pulled a dark-haired doll from beneath the blanket. "He brought me a new doll. He cried when I told him I named her Luna." Her expression turned somber. "Did you find out about Mama?"

"We don't need to talk about it right now."

"Tell me."

"No, we'll talk—"

"No, now. Please, Lulu." Tears welled up in Cira's eyes. "There isn't much time."

Luna hesitated. What good would it do now to tell Cira the truth? It would only upset her. "Mama would never hurt you. She loves you more than anything in the world."

"She didn't make me sick?"

"No."

A tear spilled from the corner of Cira's eye. "I prayed it wasn't true, but Mama says God doesn't always give us the answer we want. Like Med—the cancer. I prayed for that not to be true too."

"I know. So did I."

"What will happen when I die?"

I don't know. "I'll build us a house out in space, and we'll live there together."

Cira smiled. "Love you, Lulu."

"Love you too, Cici. To the moon and back."

—··—

After Cira's funeral, Papa left for good. Mama stayed in bed for days, wrapped in darkness. When she finally emerged, she roamed the house aimlessly, the glass in her hand never empty. She avoided Cira's bedroom, and the door remained closed.

Luna drifted from room to room, following Mama, waiting for the right moment to reveal herself.

Revenge had not been her goal when she first returned to Earth. Even after recalling the memory of her murder, all Luna wanted was to keep her promise to her sister. But now that Cira was gone, Luna burned with the need for vengeance.

When Mama started up the stairs, Luna flew to the top and floated outside Cira's bedroom. She focused all her energy on the doorknob, willing it to turn.

The door swung open just as Mama reached the top step. She hesitated, one hand on the banister, drink in the other. The crease between her brows deepened. She looked into her drink, then back at the door. Finally, with a shrug, she pulled herself up the last step and staggered toward Cira's room.

Luna pushed the door closed. With a gasp, Mama stumbled backward and grabbed the railing. The door banged open, and Luna materialized, looming in the doorway. Mama screamed. The glass flew from her hand and over the railing, shattering on the floor below. She fell onto her backside and scuttled into the corner.

"Why, Mama? Why did you do it?"

Mama's face fell into her hands. "It's not real. Please, God, make it go away."

Luna dropped downward until her face hung inches from her mother's. "Look at me."

She shook her head, refusing to look up.

Luna pleaded in a soft voice. "Mama, please. It's me, Cira."

Mama became still and peeked through her fingers.

Luna shifted into skeletal form. Bits of rotting flesh hung from the bones. Empty eye sockets glowed red with rage. Her voice became a low growl. "We know what you did."

Shrieks of terror echoed through the house. Mama scrambled to her feet, ran down the hallway and into her bedroom, slammed the door, and locked it. Gasping for breath, she slumped against the wall and closed her eyes.

Luna faded, crept through the door, and whispered in Mama's ear. "I'm here."

"No!" Mama's eyes snapped open and darted around the room, searching for Luna. "Where are you? Show yourself."

Luna shifted, becoming nothing more than a dark shadow. Mama's breath came in short bursts. She yanked the door open and ran from the room.

Spurred on by her mother's fear, Luna shot down the hallway behind her. She circled Mama in a blur, leaving a dark haze in her wake. Like a cyclone, Luna spun higher, lifting Mama over the railing toward the vaulted ceiling. As the rage within consumed her, she whirled faster.

Mama's screams turned to pleading. "Please, Luna, don't hurt me."

Luna paused. For one surreal moment, they hung suspended before spiraling downward. She dropped her mother to the floor, materialized fully, and gazed intently into her eyes.

"I'm nothing like you."

Luna faded. Her formless soul flew through infinite space and time—through the delicate light of trillions of stars—into the universe beyond.

She awoke to the tickle of soft grass against her skin. The sweet scent of wildflowers perfumed the air. Her eyes blinked against the brilliance of a sun so radiant its heat permeated her essence.

Luna caressed the smooth skin on her face and ran her fingers through her hair. Excitement built in her chest. She placed a hand there and smiled when her heart thumped against it. Sitting upright, she skimmed her hands up and down her arms. She threw her head backward and laughed, then jumped to her feet, flung her arms wide, and danced through the meadow.

Never had she seen such vivid colors. Tall grasses of emerald and crimson danced and swayed against an azure sky. Butterflies flitted among flowers of every hue and shade. Birds soared overhead, singing songs of freedom. Low on the horizon a colossal moon hung over the highest mountain peak. As always, the sight filled her with peace, but she no longer felt the need to take refuge there.

A figure appeared in the distance. Luna's smile widened. They moved toward one another, slowly at first, then running with arms outstretched. Consumed by laughter, they embraced. Clasping her sister's hands in her own, Luna held her at arm's length. Cira's skin glowed. Glossy, dark curls cascaded like silk across the shoulders of her white dress and down her back.

Luna's eyes shone with tears. "You're not sick anymore," she whispered.

Cira pulled her hands free and spun in a circle, laughing. "No."

"What is this place?" Luna asked.

Cira stopped spinning. "It's Heaven, silly."

"It doesn't look like Heaven. Where's God, and the pearly gates, and the angels?"

Cira reached for Luna's hand. "This is our Heaven, Lulu. We only need each other."

A wide smile lifted Luna's cheeks. "You're right. It's perfect."

"Remember how you said you would build me a house out in space?"

Luna nodded.

Cira tugged on Luna's hand, pulling her toward the mountains. "You don't have to. It's here; we're home."

Author **Laurie Gardiner** grew up on a farm in remote northern Ontario, Canada, and now lives in Cambridge, Ontario. She is an avid reader, a yogi, and a Gemini, who graduated with honours from Conestoga College's Creative Writing program. Publications include "Til Death Do Us Part," which placed first in the 1997 Cambridge Writers' Collective short story contest, and "Retribution," chosen for Scout Media's 2016 anthology, *A Journey of Words*. Over the years, her poetry has also been published in various anthologies. Laurie's debut novel, *Tranquility*, published in 2015 by Escargot Books and Music, was inspired by her work as a personal support worker, specializing in dementia care.

Pepe

Dawn Taylor

Thump. Thump. A stiff jab punched Diane's back as she lay in bed. A fiery sting, like a thousand knives thrusting into her right kidney, jolted her from a dream. *Thump, thump.* The mattress slid off the box spring six inches.

Damnit. Not again, she thought as she threw back the blanket and peered under the bed.

The clown had returned. This time he clumsily rode a unicycle. With his arms outstretched, he pedaled wildly, his feet spinning in a circular blur. His size sixteen shoes hung over the miniature pedals, preventing him from maintaining balance. He swayed forward and backward until his shoelace tangled in the spokes, propelling him through the air. The unintended somersault ended with the clown sprawled on his back. His big feet, one without a shoe, crashed against the bed.

"Get out of here, now!" she shouted as she flipped the light switch. His annoying antics had disturbed her sleep nightly ever since she moved into this apartment.

Pepe grinned with his squared white teeth framed by his exaggerated red-painted lips. From a large plastic daisy on his lapel, he squirted red liquid into Diane's face. As it dripped down her nightgown, she noticed it was blood.

Diane vigorously rubbed her face. "Oh my God, my God."

Was it his blood or did he murder somebody? She grabbed the blanket to wipe away the remainder of the dreadful liquid. She swallowed the sour bile creeping up the back of her throat, fighting the image of contaminated germs entering her system. As she pulled the blanket from her face, she smelled . . . the pleasant scent of strawberries?

Pepe tapped his cheek with his index finger while holding his chin. He tilted his head in feigned confusion as he handed her an empty envelope of powdered drink mix.

"Goddamn you, clown."

Pepe cupped his mouth with his white gloves and howled in laughter. The blue grease paint under his eyes smeared as he wiped a steady stream of tears. Her gullible reactions to his pranks made his taunting so easy.

Pepe shrank the unicycle by pressing it between his hands like an accordion. He returned it to the purple box, monogrammed *PP*. Next, he withdrew a rusty trombone.

"Oh no you're not. You're not playing that at two in the morning."

Pepe hesitated as he brought the instrument to his mouth. A hint of yellow cloth poking out from his left sleeve caught his eye. He raised his brows in surprise. He laid down the horn to tug at the fabric.

A trail of multi-colored scarves emerged. Green, polka dot, pink—the scarves kept coming. Diane crossed her arms while exhaling her annoyance as he revealed the remaining three feet of the silk chain with the flair of an orchestra conductor. Disappointed his other sleeve was empty, Pepe threw the scarves and trombone into the purple box and disappeared.

The clock read 2:37 a.m. Although his escapades exhausted Diane for hours, the clock had ticked forward only one minute.

Diane was puzzled at his ability to enter her bedroom. She had moved the bed during the day and a few times after his nightly visits, searching for a trapdoor or secret entrance. She ran her hand over the floor several times hunting for an edge of an abyss but found nothing.

His ability to perform his tricks under her bed, diminishing his body and props to fit, mystified her. When she peered under the bed, she saw the underside of a striped tent, not her box spring. The beige carpet had transformed into a sand pit. During each episode of the clown's visit, ear-splitting carnival music blared from an unseen carousel.

Why had he chosen to perform under her bed? Was he a lost

soul from a circus long ago? The one thing she knew for a fact was he aggravated her to no end. His nightly intrusions not only caused her to lose sleep but affected her work performance as well.

She set her alarm and flipped off the light, begging to get some rest before her workday began.

—· ·—

Diane had graduated from Belmont University with a law degree she was proud to have earned. Moving from Tennessee to San Francisco to work as an intern for the prestigious firm, Nicholson, Hudson & Trent, was a dream come true. She looked forward to making her mark in the legal field, and this opportunity was one she could not afford to refuse. Being an intern meant essentially no income, which is why she was grateful the law firm paid for the apartment and allowed her a small stipend for expenses.

The shrill of the alarm awoke Diane, and she rushed to the shower. Her tardiness twice last week, reported to Mr. Nicholson by an office snitch, caused him to schedule a meeting with her at 8:00 a.m. this morning. *Eight o'clock sharp!* His voice resounded in her head as she rushed to get dressed and catch the bus to the office.

Diane knocked repeatedly on the heavy oak door to Mr. Nicholson's office. Finally, he opened the door and motioned for her to sit. He was about to offer her coffee until he saw the Starbucks cup in her hand. The large-sized coffee, combined with the dark circles under Diane Koestler's eyes, convinced William Nicholson he had made a wise choice hiring this intern. *She's been up all night working,* he thought.

"Let's review the proposal you are working on. Since it's your first project, I want to make sure you understand its purpose." Mr. Nicholson sipped his coffee in a rushed effort to continue speaking.

Diane relaxed, noting the topic of the meeting was not about her tardiness. "Yes, sir." She winced at how submissive her voice sounded, like a lap dog eager to obey for a treat.

He opened a file and studied it for a minute before clearing his throat. "This company—Sirkuss, EURL—holds many entertainment divisions in its portfolio. You are to focus solely on the Grande Tente Foire account. Any attorney worth their salt would've researched the background of the company before opening the file. I trust you have done so."

The interrupted gulp of coffee burned Diane's lips.

"From your expression, Miss Koestler, I deduce you have not approached your assignment in a logical way. Rookie error. Forgivable, once." He accented *once* through gritted teeth.

"Yes, sir." He had kicked the dog in the head.

"Allow me to enlighten you. Madame Astrid Pitre, recent widow of Monsieur Pierre Pitre, is the sole owner of Sirkuss, EURL. She was satisfied living in her chateau in France, drinking wine while her husband ran the family business. Pierre Pitre, always an astute businessman, made millions entertaining people around the world. The Grande Tente Foire—the big top show—was his pride since it was the startup of his business. Monsieur Pitre made the fateful decision four months ago to perform the tightrope act at an anniversary show. Needless to say, the crowd got more than their money's worth."

"That's terrible."

"That's show business. At any rate, this is where you fit into the equation. As I said, Madame Pitre has no business sense, nor does she want to deal with contracts and fine print. I met them years ago vacationing in Paris. Pierre never cared for the French attorneys; they were too *paresseux*—lazy—for his taste. Since he trusted me, she trusts me. She has hired our firm to handle all financial contracts for the business. For a pricey sum, of course."

"Of course." Diane welcomed a bonus. The dog panted for a bone.

"I will write all the contract terms. The first agreement is standard. Sirkuss, EURL pays to review and negotiate financial contract terms between the company and their vendors. The second agreement—which you'll have her blindly sign—guarantees our law firm will receive the majority of all revenue generated by the Grand Tente Foire. From my analysis, it's the only division within the company producing decent returns. Two contracts, two signatures, you explain one. Got it?"

"Well . . . yes, but—"

"But what?"

"Why would she listen to me and not to a more experienced attorney?"

Nicholson threw back his head and laughed. "Are you serious? This project requires a novice intern with soft edges. Do you think your mediocre college transcript landed you this assignment? You are the fresh-faced girl from next door. Old Astrid would most likely take you under her wing back to France and fatten you up with croissants rather than waste time hearing you explain boring contracts. She will trust such an innocent young woman, with a pen in her hand."

Nicholson watched his protégé mull the prospect of cheating a widow. He would not allow the intern to withdraw now after he disclosed the details of his despicable plan. The risk of the information leaving the walls of his office was too great.

"Of course, Miss Koestler, you will be rewarded handsomely with a bonus. May even open up a salaried position for you, depending on how quickly you execute the plan."

The dog leapt into the air to grab the bone.

"I'll do my best." Diane tossed the disposable cup in the trash. "You can count on me."

— · —

Splat. Splat. Diane awoke the following night as pie filling rained onto her hair. The clown stood across the room pitching coconut cream pies at a target painted on the wall above her bed. Each time he missed the bullseye, he held his chin in both hands and cocked his head from shoulder to shoulder. Next to him on a small table, fifty-six pies stacked in the shape of a pyramid nearly touched the ceiling.

"Why are you here?"

Pepe ignored her question as he threw pie after pie. Globs of meringue plastered the wall and slid onto Diane's comforter.

She jumped from her bed to stand in front of him. "I said, why are you here?"

Pepe grabbed a pie in both hands. He forcefully flung the first one at her. Disappointed he missed when Diane stepped sideways, Pepe smashed the second pie into her face. As Diane sputtered in an attempt to breathe, he rubbed the tin back and forth, driving the cream up her nostrils. His maniacal laughter filled the room as she brought her hands to fight against the pressure of the tin. Just as she was wiping the cream from her forehead, the clown vanished, along with his table of pies.

Diane patted her face in disbelief. She was clean and so was the wall. Was this a dream? Did the *splat* awaken her or was it the hideous carnival music? She climbed into bed and begged for sleep.

—··—

The bus commute to work was more of a freak show than the damn clown was. A couple of drug addicts discarded their used needles on the floor near her feet. More than one panhandler demanded money she didn't have and cussed her with threats as she apologized for having nothing to offer.

Diane's only assurances for her safety during the bus rides were the daylight and the fact she always carried a pistol in her purse. She promised herself she would buy a car and rent her own place with the bonus from the Pitre account.

She entered the office suite and said good morning to Sue, the receptionist, as she did every morning. Without fail, Sue automatically studied the clock before returning the empty platitude of a greeting.

Diane walked past Sour Sue to her office. She dialed the phone to contact Madame Pitre and was disappointed to receive the same answering machine greeting as she had the previous day. She left a voicemail as the French-accented voice requested and followed up with an additional email. Time was of the essence. She needed to contact Astrid before she returned to France.

Diane spent the remainder of the day reviewing endless columns of figures on financial spreadsheets given to her by Mr. Nicholson. She was confident the widow would never miss the money she was about to funnel into the law firm's account receivable ledger. Even using the skills gained from her college education, the complex financial structure of the Sirkuss group was difficult to grasp.

After another grueling workday, the bus commute home seemed longer than usual. A little girl with gum stuck in her hair cried to a woman sitting next to her. Diane assumed the woman was the four-year-old's mother and would put down her phone to help the distressed child. Instead, Diane's gasp was audible as the woman backhanded the girl and shoved her to the floor.

Diane, with her hand covering her mouth in shock, glanced at the other commuters' reactions. A young woman read a book while wearing earbuds, two teens shared a joint, and an old man hid behind a newspaper. Diane concluded she had no sanity in either her waking or her sleeping hours in this city—so unlike the small town she had left behind.

Arriving home, she decided to order pizza before continuing to work. Financials were never her strong suit, and she needed to comprehend the complexities of the spreadsheets to impress Mr. Nicholson. She called Party Pizza since it was the closest franchise to her apartment.

Diane repeated her address, 1616 Memorial Way, Building H, Apartment E11, to the young girl who promised confirmed delivery within thirty minutes. Diane was thrilled for the promise of quick service; she was starving.

The doorbell rang thirty-five minutes later, prompting Diane to rush for her purse. She opened the door a few inches as she searched for the twenty-dollar bill inside her wallet. She hated to make the delivery person wait. *Where was the twenty? I didn't spend . . .*

"Party Pizza. A party in your mouth!" The earsplitting *hoooink hoooink* of a toy horn blasted from outside the door as Diane jerked her eyes from the wallet.

Diane jumped backward. "What the hell—"

A clown stopped honking the horn and extended a pizza box to her. "Sorry. Didn't mean to scare you. We're required to —"

"Keep the change." She exchanged the twenty for the cardboard box and slammed the door.

Diane leaned against the wall as her sweaty palms absorbed the grease from the bottom of the box. Her pulse returned to a normal rate, and she began to wonder if she would ever experience an ordinary day or night in San Francisco.

Diane worked on the proposal until almost midnight, crunching numbers until her head ached. She ate the last slice of cold pizza, brushed her teeth, and went to bed. She drifted deep into a sound sleep lasting a few hours before the eerie carousel music wafted from beneath her bed.

Pepe dragged the purple box from behind him. The lid sprang open, and he removed a black top hat, unlike the tiny green one he wore cocked to one side of his head. In his other hand, he held a wand.

Diane glanced at the clock. 4:31 a.m. What maddening trick did he have in store for her this time?

With an exaggerated motion, Pepe bowed and turned the top hat upside down. Diane presumed this was to show it was empty. When he straightened himself to an erect pose, he tapped the rim with the wand. His right brow, painted with heavy brown grease paint, arched in surprise as nothing happened. He shrugged and tapped the wand again.

Diane had seen magicians pull rabbits out of hats or release a small flock of doves in shows she had attended as a child. *This clown must be running out of tricks*, she thought. She relished the opportunity to heckle him.

"Boo. *Boooooo*. Boring," she yelled at him.

Pepe ignored her, tapping the wand for the third time. He sprang backward as the hat toppled from his hand. Diane jumped also, her eyes frozen with fear as a full-grown African lion emerged from the hat. Diane was sure the beast would shred the clown to pieces.

As the big cat roared, Pepe opened its jaws wider and inserted his head, tapping the wand against the lion's mane. The hellish music whined to a slow pitch as they evaporated from sight. It was 4:32 a.m.

"Ridiculous, absolutely ridiculous!" Diane shouted to the emptiness of the room.

This clown, Chuckles, Bimbo, or whatever he was called, had better stop his shenanigans or she would end them for him—once and for all. Diane had noticed the purple box contained endless gags but never a weapon. Maybe if she inflicted pain on him, he would leave.

It was worth a try.

—••—

"We're having drinks after work. Wanna join us?" Connie, a paralegal, asked Diane the next morning.

"Sure. I could use some relaxation. Thanks for asking me."

Diane entered her office and flung down her briefcase. She checked her email and voicemail and still had received no response from Astrid Pitre. *Damn*! Nicholson had warned her that Madame Pitre was no businesswoman. Perhaps she had returned to France, stomping grapes or making goat cheese or whatever the hell they did there.

Diane started the routine again, sending an email and a

voicemail to Madame Pitre, while poring over contract verbiage. She was so absorbed in her paperwork she didn't notice Connie standing in the doorway.

"Pack that stuff up for the night. Time for a break."

Diane was ready for a cocktail after a day of analyzing financial records that blurred her eyes as much as her mind. "I'm with you."

She removed her coat from the hook and walked with Connie three blocks to Kildare's Irish Pub.

"Jackie's joining us, is that okay?"

"As long as Sue isn't."

"Naw," Connie said. "She's home trying to pull the stick from her ass."

They both chuckled.

At the pub, Connie ordered a round of beers while Jackie studied the short menu.

"So, how's old Nick treating you, Diane?" Connie asked.

"Like the fumbling idiot from college," Diane answered, sliding out of her trench coat.

Jackie ordered onion rings and said, "Well, he treats all of us like shit. Nancy hated him. If she hadn't—"

"Jackie," Connie scolded.

"It's true. He drove her to do it."

Connie flashed a shut-your-mouth-now look at Jackie. Diane took notice of the warning immediately. Connie's attempt to silence Jackie only piqued Diane's interest.

"Who's Nancy? Drove her to what?" Diane asked, biting into a steamy onion ring.

"I guess the big mouth can finish spilling the beans." Connie took a long sip of her beer as Jackie continued.

"She worked at the firm before you. Lived in the same apartment too."

Diane waited for Jackie to continue while Connie blew a breath of disgust so hard, her bangs fluttered.

"Old Nick rode her ass so hard, she shot herself." Jackie paused. "In the bedroom of your apartment."

Diane choked on her beer. The foam of the alcohol stung her nostrils. Blinking away the burning sensation lingering in her throat, she set down the mug. Her trembling fingers, wet from sweat mixed with condensation from the glass, weakened her hold on the handle. She wiped her fingers on a napkin.

"My God." Diane twisted the paper napkin until the pub logo disappeared.

"To be fair," Connie interjected, "it wasn't just Nick on her ass. The girl never got any sleep."

Jackie laughed. "Don't tell me you still believe her bullshit ghost story? That girl was whacked. Probably shot up heroin on the bus with the junkies, for all we know." She washed down a bite of onion rings with her beer.

Diane fought the urge to wet her pants. She tightly crossed her legs and ripped the twisted napkin in half instead. "She said the apartment was haunted?" Diane looked to Jackie and then to Connie, searching for answers.

"Never mind. Enough bullshit for one night. Look at my new Gucci handbag. I can't afford it, but Visa said *yes*." Connie flaunted her leather purse as Jackie ran her hand over the smoothness of the grain.

"*Ooh*, love it," Jackie cooed.

Neither woman noticed as Diane sat motionless, tearing the last bit of the napkin and focusing her eyes straight ahead on nothing in particular. Waves of queasiness consumed her as the onion rings swirled in the warm frothy beer inside her gut. The discovery of the suicide in her apartment tightened her stomach into a twisted knot of dread.

This Nancy killed herself in my bedroom. They would think I was crazy or drunk to ask if she mentioned a clown. Doesn't matter, the clown killed her. I know it. Diane rushed from the table to the restroom to purge the contents of her stomach.

If only getting rid of the clown was this simple, she thought as she splashed cool water onto her face.

— · · —

Diane was ready for Pepe that night when she returned home. She placed a baseball bat on the floor by her bed. When he arrived, she would give him a good smack over the head. She smiled as musical notes played louder under her bed. He was approaching and Diane was ready for combat.

She raised the baseball bat high in the air, ready to smash his tiny green hat. Pepe, lithe from acrobat training, snatched it from her. Leaning into his purple box, he retrieved a pair of wooden bowling pins to juggle. Pepe tossed the bat and the two pins high in the air, alternating between catching and throwing them as he grinned at Diane, scoffing at her with his thick red lips.

Diane stepped forward to interrupt his amusement, but he stowed the objects, including her bat, into the box and disappeared as the faint echo of his laughter hung in the air.

The following night she planned to capture him with a rope. After she had tied him down, she would force answers from him. Who was he? Where did he come from? What did he want? She had purchased a sturdy hemp rope from the hardware store. If she could manage to tie his hands to prevent him from performing tricks, he would be unable to escape or evade her questions.

Pepe made his appearance at 3:35 a.m. Instead of dragging his gags out of the purple box, he stood motionless in the corner of the room. He tempted her to make the first move. Diane seized the opportunity by lunging forward to slip the rope around his wrists.

Pepe stepped sideways and jerked the rope from her hands. He pulled on the loop to expand it and began to swing the riata over his head as he marched in place. With graceful motions, he commanded the rope into repetitive figure-eight formations.

If Diane had not harbored angriness toward the clown, she would have been impressed with his skill. She reasoned he must have come from the rodeo since it was the only place she had seen clowns demonstrate expertise with lassos. Pepe raised the loop above his head and then lowered it to a spinning circle to jump in and out before returning to the figure-eight routine.

"I need sleep. Go away. Please, just go away." She was too tired to shout at him. Her plea squeaked from her lips in a pathetic whimper.

Pepe lowered the rope and frowned. He brought his white gloves to his face and motioned with his index fingers, creating imaginary trails of tears running down his cheeks.

Finally, he understands.

He reached into the breast pocket of his baggy blue suit for a hanky. After dabbing at his pretend tears, he offered it to Diane. Accepting his truce, she reached for the cloth. As she pulled it closer, she saw it was not a single kerchief. Much like the multi-colored scarves, the hanky was one of several white squares tied together by a long thread. The squares pooled from his pocket onto the floor.

"That's it. Get out. Get out. Get out now!" Diane shouted until her face matched the redness of the clown's lips. His last prank reignited the rage she had felt toward him.

He flung open the lid of the purple box. In his hand, he held a deck of playing cards. He bent the stack into an arc, held the cards inches from Diane's face, and pressed down, propelling the deck into her face. She squinted while raising her arms in an attempt to dodge the sharp edges of fifty-four jokers slicing her face.

Pepe roared in laughter until the music stopped and he vanished.

—·· —

Madame Pitre's voice on the answering machine was music to Diane's ears, even though she spoke in a confusing, heavy French accent. Astrid was still in San Francisco and would gladly meet Diane in two days to sign documents before returning to Toulouse.

Diane beamed as she sent an email to Mr. Nicholson. In forty-eight hours, the law firm would have the controlling interests of

Sirkuss, EURL. Diane would receive a bonus and, hopefully, a full-time position offer. She spent the remainder of the morning emailing the proposed meeting agenda to Mr. Nicholson for approval.

She stopped by Jackie's desk to ask her to lunch.

Since Jackie could spare only an hour, they returned to the pub. Jackie ordered a coffee, while Diane ordered a glass of French wine. *Hell, why not? I'm celebrating.*

"Tell me more about Nancy, the intern before me."

Jackie's smile confirmed she was anxious to spill the details. "Connie liked her, I didn't. I thought she was nuts. Even more so when she started in about the bedroom being haunted. I mean, really?"

"What did she say exactly?" Diane asked in a forged nonchalant manner as she studied the menu and averted eye contact with Jackie. She tried her best to disguise the tone of anxiety in her question.

Since Connie was not present to interrupt, Jackie was free to reveal the details. "You're gonna love this." Jackie licked her lips. "She said a clown appeared in her room." Jackie pounded her fists on the table, roaring in laughter. Customers at nearby tables exchanged annoyed glances. "What the hell's so scary about a clown?"

"Exactly." Diane forged a fake chuckle, urging Jackie to continue.

Under different circumstances, the patrons' focus on Jackie's outburst would have been a cause of embarrassment for Diane. However, she ignored the diners' reactions as she sought the answers only Jackie could provide.

"Get this. He did magic tricks." Jackie raised her hands with her fingers waving back and forth. "*Ooo,* spooky."

The scraping of chairs upon the wooden floor signaled the patrons' return to their meals and ended the audience's interest in the two women. Diane was at a loss to respond. Before she had a chance to say a word, Jackie continued.

"So, I think the pressure from Nick, combined with some high-grade drugs she scored, pushed her over the edge. End of Nancy, end of story." She took a sip from her coffee.

"But why a clown? That's not your typical ghost."

Jackie ordered a salad and a coffee refill. Diane ordered the same, avoiding the greasy onion rings from the last visit.

"Don't you get it? There *is* no reason. The girl was psycho, a drug addict. You've lived there for what, two months now? Has this scary clown appeared in your bedroom?"

"Of course . . . not."

Diane sipped her wine and looked away.

— • • —

Diane checked her email and sighed with relief. Mr. Nicholson had approved the meeting agenda. He included a notation: *Get her to sign it as is, and I will sign your bonus check.*

She retrieved the copies from her briefcase to review one last time as she practiced her pitch for Madame Pitre. Diane would use her polite, slow tone usually reserved for conversations with small children since Madame likely would not have a developed ear to understand Diane's southern-American accent. Offering condolences to Mrs. Pitre while Diane dabbed at her eyes would convince Astrid of Diane's genuine sympathy and concern.

The expensive floral arrangement would be presented just as Astrid was poised to sign the second agreement. That distraction tactic had been contrived by Diane on her own. Nicholson, realizing the genius of Diane's plan, instructed Sue to eavesdrop near the door. The timing of the delivery was paramount, as Sue would fuss over Madame Pitre in presenting the gift of beautiful native French lilies. Before Madame could utter any words of gratitude, Diane would thrust the pen into her hand.

Diane closed her briefcase, satisfied everything was in order. She commuted home on the bus, relishing that the days of derelicts, drug addicts, and panhandlers as seat companions would soon end.

Tension over the past two months had etched achiness into every muscle of her body. Tonight she would indulge in a hot bath, easing the exhaustion from her body before slipping into her silk gown for a night of rest. Tomorrow was an important day, the day her career would start in earnest.

The fluffy comforter and feather-filled pillows enveloped her as she crawled into bed. She fell asleep within minutes, not bothering to listen to the radio, as she sometimes did.

She was dreaming of shopping at Gucci with Connie for a new handbag when the clerk hurriedly shoved them out with no explanation. The saleswoman locked the dead bolt as lurid carousel music swirled in the air.

Jackie turned to Diane. "Why is there a clown laughing behind her?"

The musical notes repeated in loud tinny echoes waking Diane. She glanced under the bed. Pepe was riding a merry-go-round, twisting balloons into animal shapes. When he saw Diane, he hopped from a grotesque half-horse/half-scorpion creature, motioning her to follow him to a performance stage lit by a large white spotlight.

He pointed to a chest on the stage. He pushed it apart, separating the box into two sections, demonstrating both com-partments were empty. Shoving the halves together, he opened both lids, gesturing for her to climb into the rectangular box. He stood waiting while holding a shiny handsaw high in the air. The sharp blade, edged with serrated teeth, glistened in the stage's light.

Diane screamed. As she turned to flee, he threw banana peels in her path. Dodging some but tripping on most, she skidded on the slippery yellow skins until she lost her balance. The clown straddled her, his enormous shoes planted on both sides of her body. Each time she screamed, he parroted her voice while holding his hands over his ears.

Diane glanced at the magician's box. Pepe had transformed it into a coffin with *DK* inscribed on the lid. When Pepe's screaming ended, he pressed on his nose, igniting a red glow. He waved farewell while wielding the handsaw and vanished.

Diane looked at the clock: 2:47 a.m. She knew the clown, in reality, had only been in her room for one minute, yet with his ability to warp time, it felt like he had been there six hours or longer. The scheduled presentation with Mr. Nicholson and Madame Pitre was at eight o'clock. Mr. Nicholson had sent two reminder emails, both stating *8:00 a.m. sharp!*

She needed rest to think clearly in the morning. Against her better judgement, she swallowed a sleeping pill and turned the volume to Loud on her alarm clock after setting it for six o'clock. Snuggling back into bed, she covered herself with her downy white comforter and slept soundly, without any interruptions, for the first time in weeks.

Diane revisited her dream of shopping at Gucci with Connie. The clown was no longer present, and the clerk ushered them into the boutique. They shopped for dresses, hats, handbags, and shoes. Laughing at the outrageousness of their credit card limits, they each bought two of everything. The alarm signaled the end of the dream, buzzing at 6:00 a.m.

Diane yawned and hit Snooze. She had ten minutes yet to rest and then she would rise-and-shine for her important day. She snuggled deep under the blanket and dozed. After what seemed about five restful minutes, she was refreshed and ready to start her day. She reached for the clock to disarm the obnoxious *buzz* before it could sound.

"Shit!"

The clock face stated 10:07 a.m.

Did I shut it off instead of hitting the snooze button? The realization she had overslept shocked her like a splash of ice water on her face. She scrambled out of bed and raced for the shower, yelling a steady mantra of *damnit, damnit, damnit.* The clown and his late-night antics were to blame, disturbing her for hours on the worst possible night of all nights.

She raced into the office lobby. Sue glanced at Diane's disheveled damp hair and twisted trench coat and then to the clock. Without a word, she handed Diane a message to see Mr. Nicholson. With her hands shaking, Diane read the short note and looked at Sue.

Diane sighed. "Not good."

Sue shrugged her shoulders and returned to her computer. Diane's heels resonated clicking sounds, growing softer as she walked the endless hallway toward her boss's office. She knew she had no defense against being fired.

What can I say? A clown appears under my bed each night and keeps me awake? She might as well admit she had a drinking problem and danced in the bars all night. That excuse was at least believable, if not sane.

She rapped her knuckles against the open doorframe. William Nicholson looked up from his phone call and motioned for her to have a seat. He slammed the receiver when his conversation ended.

"Missed the presentation with Madam Pitre this morning."

"Yes, sir." The dog cowered with its tail between its legs.

"You were hired to complete a task. You had one project. One goal to achieve. You failed miserably."

Diane's throat was dry, and she concentrated on the bookcase behind him to avoid crying. Crying was not professional. She was not professional. She was a bad dog.

"You leave me no choice—"

Diane bolted out of his office before he could finish his sentence. *This is not how today was supposed to go.* Her opportunity to start her career had ended before it started.

In her mad dash to flee, she nearly tripped over the copy machine repairman. She mouthed, *Sorry*, as she hesitated. Connie emerged from her office to see Diane standing bewildered. Wanting to comfort her co-worker, Connie extended her arms toward her. Diane continued to sprint down the hallway, wrestling herself from Connie's attempted hug.

"Diane, please. Don't rush out . . ." Connie's voice trailed behind her.

Sue nodded knowingly as Diane ran past the receptionist's desk and outward through glass entry doors. Tears blurred Diane's vision, sparing her from seeing the smirk spreading across Sue's face as Diane escaped to the parking lot.

She banged her fist against the bus shelter's Plexiglass. "That clown!"

She tightened the grip on her briefcase, remembering her parents giving it to her as a graduation gift. They, like Diane, held high hopes for her career. The briefcase held nothing of value now, only her unaccomplished goals and worthless documents.

That goddamn clown. I'll put a stop to him permanently.

Diane lay in bed, replaying the day's disastrous events, until nightfall. A clown had stolen her chance of obtaining a full-time position at a prestigious law firm. How could she ever explain that when she returned to Tennessee? There was no way to rationalize the situation. Taking revenge against the clown was her only recourse to save her reputation.

She listened for the garish music to fill the room, signaling Pepe's appearance. Her wait was short. The carousel music floated from beneath her bed and filled the room with the tinny sound of high-pitched notes.

She felt a jolt. *Thump. Thump.* Pepe was replacing his large floppy shoes with water skis. His knees jammed into the box spring as he maneuvered his big feet. Diane felt the familiar sharp jabs against her spine as she glanced at the clock. 1:11 a.m. The clown had arrived early tonight.

Pepe abandoned his attempt to wear the water skies and returned them to the purple box. He produced a large bunch of multicolored latex balloons. He withdrew a four-inch hatpin from his tiny green hat and flashed a grin at Diane. *Pop. Pop.* The hatpin pierced two balloons. He retracted his lips to expose his square teeth as he stabbed the pin repeatedly into the balloons. *PopPopPopPopPopPop.*

"I warned you!" she shouted.

Diane reached under her pillow for her pistol. She had purchased the gun for protection against thugs in the big city. She never dreamed she would be using it against a clown in her bedroom.

Pepe stared, astonished, at Diane. His red rubber nose illuminated the terror in his painted eyes before it bounced to the floor. Escaping the angry woman with a gun, he flung open the lid of the purple box and scrambled behind it. The remaining balloons floated around him, forming a useless barrier from a bullet.

Diane squinted as she steadied her aim. He was difficult to see in the dark with the balloons hovering in front of him.

"I warned you and I warned you. But you . . ."

Pepe reached around the lid and deep into the purple box to grab the concave mirror he had stolen from the funhouse, holding it as a protective shield. The distorted image gleaming from the curved glass disoriented Diane as she fired the pistol.

The bullet ricocheted off the mirror and struck her in the right temple. The carousel music slowed its tempo and stopped. The balloons hung motionless against the ceiling.

Pepe leapt over the shards of glass scattered on the floor. He had one item left in the purple box. For the third time this year, he placed a For Rent sign in unit H-E11's front yard.

— · · —

The clown returned to the vacant apartment a week later. Except for the industrial-strength pine scent of disinfectant hanging heavy in the air, everything remained the same. He withdrew a newspaper from the purple box to verify his rental listing had appeared in the classified section.

As he unfolded the newspaper, a headline at the bottom of the front page caught his eye.

Second Local Attorney Commits Suicide

He studied the photo of the woman he knew so well.

Pepe threw the paper into the purple box and dashed under the bed as voices from the hall became louder as they neared the bedroom.

"You'll like it here. The rent is very affordable . . ."

Author **Dawn Taylor** resides in Austin, Minnesota. Her co-authored book published in 2015, *Chauncey's Place: A Pictorial History of Austin, MN 1854-2014*, pays homage to her hometown. A work of flash fiction, "Dirty Gypsy Girl," appears in the anthology, *Frightful Tales for Hallows' Eve*. The short story, "The Price of Admission," appears on *Seakay's Guide to Storytelling*. Scout Media published the short story, "The Double Nickel Tour," in the anthology, *A Journey of Words*. Dawn is currently writing a novel and a collection of short stories scheduled for a 2017 release date. Contact her at AuthorDawnTayor@yahoo.com or follow her on Facebook: Facebook.com/AuthorDawnTaylor.

Outlook Supplies

E.C. Jarvis

Etched in old-fashioned filigree lettering, the sign in the shop read:

For Sale: Trinkets, Things, and Brass Knockers

Upon the first reading, Deven Harris found it stuck in his mind. As a young boy, at that point not even a teenager, he knew the reference to *brass knockers* to be amusing, even if he didn't quite understand why. Every day after school, no matter the weather, he walked past that same shop.

In winter, the snow on the sill would reach up to the bottom of the sign, cutting off the base of the letters. In the summer, the rays beating down on the shop front slowly turned the brass plaque to a dark brown tint. Every now and then he'd walk by to find the sign gleaming golden as the shopkeeper had applied a rigorous polishing. In his teenage years, it never failed to bring a smile to his face—the thought of a man standing outside, polishing his brass knockers.

Despite his unique attraction to the sign and the shop beyond, he had never ventured inside. It seemed even stranger that he had never properly seen the person tending the shop. An occasional glance at a faded face somewhere far at the back of the shop was all the glimpse he'd had.

On his momentous last day at school, with the future at his feet, the world his oyster, about to embark upon life as an adult, it seemed odd to his group of friends, shouting and laughing their way home, when Deven came to a complete stop in the middle of the path.

"What's wrong with you?" his friend, Gray, asked.

Deven didn't answer. His eyes were inextricably drawn to a new sign in the window. The brass plaque had gone, leaving a faded outline on the glass. The new sign, a horrid off-white plastic affair with brash red lettering, read:

Closing Down. Time's Up
Arrangements can be made

"Deven?" Gray asked as he backtracked along the path to stand beside him.

"Shop's closing," Deven said.

"Oh. Yeah, stupid old place run by that old weirdo. I hope they turn it into something better."

Gray slapped Deven's shoulder and then ran to catch up to the others. Deven stared aimlessly at the window, his focus switching between the sign and his own reflection. The mess of mousey-coloured hair fell flat on one side of his head as a breeze blew down the street. He noticed his shirt was twisted across his chest, showing off the thinness of his torso, and as a pretty schoolgirl on the opposite side of the street cast a glance in his direction, he knew the flush of red on his cheeks would be impossible to hide.

Two more girls headed down the street, walking to join the first, the three of them staring at him—or perhaps they were staring at the closing sign in the shop. He wasn't sure they would feel the same affinity toward the loss of the brass knockers plaque as he did. Having decided that the now-giggling girls were staring at him, he moved forward with determination toward the only reasonable escape. The shop.

Inside was dark and musty. A single brass lamp hung low, forcing him to walk in a circle to avoid smacking his face into it. The yellowish bulb inside the lamp didn't contribute much in the way of light. The interior of the shop was stuffed full of shelves and racking laid out at odd angles, the model of utter inefficiency in comparison to the other modern shops which occupied the remainder of the town. The sparsely-stocked cell phone shop on the next street over seemed an entire world away from Outlook Supplies, with gleaming glass windows and neatly uniformed staff; it was as though the two shops occupied different centuries, never mind different streets.

Despite having never set foot inside, there was something strangely familiar about the shop. He picked up a snow globe from a shelf and turned it over. The white flecks inside had faded to an off-white colour and seemed more like flakes of mud snowing down on the small old-fashioned building inside. Deven placed it back on the shelf a little to the side from where it had sat before. An obvious mark of a circle showed up against the dusty shelf.

Deven scrunched his nose up and then turned to check the window, wondering if the girls had moved on or if they were waiting outside for him to come out so they could resume their cacophony of high-pitched giggling.

"It doesn't belong there," a light-toned voice came from behind him.

He jumped a little and then quickly raced to cover it up with a shrug as he turned. "So?"

The face that greeted him was weathered with years of wrinkles. Cool blue eyes looked directly at him. The hair atop the man's head was mostly white, with only a few strands of mousey blond poking here and there. The man's stance mirrored his own, an odd sort of teenage slump to his shoulders, though his was clearly from the effects of age rather than the uncaring plunge of defiance against standing up straight in Deven's shoulders.

Deven straightened his back and placed his hands in his pockets.

"So . . . it has a place. Everything does. Its place isn't there."

"It will have a different place when you sell it."

"Are you buying it?" the man asked.

"No."

A wry smile cracked across the man's face in response. The wrinkles on his cheeks increased significantly in number with the smile. The pair of them stood staring at one another for a moment; the oddness of the smile made the hairs on Deven's neck stand up, and his fingers itched with discomfort.

He knew precisely what the man expected him to do, and he was utterly torn between wanting to stand defiant or give in and move the globe back to the right spot. He felt his fingers wriggle in his pocket as though the appendages were twitching to make the decision for him.

The man sucked in a breath through his nose and took a slight shuffle backward, his lean fingertips moving toward the snow globe, wiggling as he reached out to move it back into place, covering up the non-dusty spot.

Deven squished his own fingers together in his pocket, curling both hands into fists. Something about the man didn't seem right. Something about the entire shop didn't *feel* right. He glanced over his shoulder to peer out of the window once more, wondering if having a group of girls follow him home giggling would be less stressful than spending any more time inside. To his confusion, it seemed as though snowflakes were falling across the windowpane. The odd tint in the glass was colouring the flecks a light brown.

"That's better," the man said, dragging Deven's attention back toward him. "I've seen you walk past my shop many times."

"It's on my route home from school," Deven said with a shrug.

"Yes, all the school children walk past here; not many give the shop a second look. You always seemed as if you would come inside. Although I know it sounds a little creepy of me to point it out."

"That's an understatement."

The man smiled again, with an odd sort of puffed laugh accompanying the increase in wrinkle density. He thrust out his hand. "Harris," he said.

Deven looked down at the hand, which was waiting expectantly to be shaken. His own hands remained firmly stuck in his pockets; both seemed unable or unwilling to come out and be shaken.

"Right . . . probably not a good idea anyways," Harris said with a shrug as he retracted his hand and put it in his pocket. "Were you looking for anything in particular, young man?"

"I wasn't looking for anything."

"No? That is a shame. I was hoping to make one sale at least."

"You're closing down?"

"Yes. I've come to the end of my tenancy, and alas, I have neither the means nor the desire to stay here any longer."

"What exactly do you sell in here?" Deven asked as he glanced at the snow globe; his gaze then raked over the other shelves and moved toward the window. The odd-looking snow flecks had gone, but it seemed oddly dark for the time of day.

"Everything you could possibly need for the rest of your days. It's expensive stuff though."

"I don't have much need for brass knockers," Deven said, stifling a derisive snort.

"Ah yes, an old joke, here even before my time . . . Well, sort of. As to my stock, tell me, what sort of things interest you?"

"Nothing you have here," Deven responded, glancing over the shelving.

His eye settled on an odd item, which seemed completely out of place with the rest of the things in the shop: a brand new mobile phone. The latest iPhone model lay out in the open, curiously out of its packaging and sitting on a shelf, a layer of dust surrounding it as though it had been there for years.

"Is that what I think it is?" Deven asked, pointing at the phone.

"The latest model," Harris said with a nod.

"They've sold out at every shop in town. How have you got one? Is it stolen?"

"I have one because that is what a retailer is supposed to do, provide things that people want. No, it is not stolen."

"Then why is it out of the box?"

"It's a display model. The only one I have currently. I've not bothered to order more because, well, because I'm closing. I thought I didn't have anything that would interest you."

"It doesn't interest me." Deven stuffed the pointing finger back into his pocket in defiance. As much as he wanted that phone, he couldn't afford it.

"It's expensive," Harris said.

"I told you, it doesn't interest me."

"We could come to an arrangement."

The light flickered slightly, and an odd sensation ran up and down Deven's neck, as though a set of long fingernails were drawn across his skin.

"What sort of an arrangement?"

"I will give you the phone, for all the use it will be to you . . . In fact, I'll give you anything you want from my shelves. All you have to do is watch the shop for me."

"Watch the shop?"

"Run it; you know, if anyone comes in and asks to buy something, then sell it to them. It's pretty simple really. You'll catch on," Harris said, the easy smile ghosting across his face again.

"Now?" Deven asked as he glanced out of the window again, something feeling rather odd about the whole thing. Outside seemed odd too—the building across the street looked distinctly different, but he couldn't quite put his finger on why.

"Now," Harris said, drawing his attention back.

"How long will you be gone for?"

"As long as it takes to run my errands. You do want the phone, don't you, Deven? Anything else you want will be yours too, if you wish it." Harris stepped away, back-stepping toward the door, his grin growing wider.

"Even your brass knockers?"

"Especially those." The grin split across Harris' face.

Deven felt sick, as though the world were a sink full of water spinning in a swirl down a plughole. Perhaps he should have endured the giggling girls teasing him the whole way home.

As Harris stepped through the door, Deven realised something curious. He had not told Harris his name.

The door slammed shut. The spinning sensation stopped abruptly, and Deven found himself standing in a very clean-looking version of Outlook Supplies. The shelves were free of dust but utterly bare. The snow globe had gone and his coveted iPhone gone too. He stared dumbstruck for a time, his jaw slack. He turned, heading first toward the door, fully intent on chasing Harris down the road and telling him to keep the damn phone, but a note on the counter beside the till caught his eye.

An envelope addressed to Deven Harris, written in his own spider-scrawl handwriting, sat at a jaunty angle. Behind the counter lay a room full of boxes stacked on top of one another, each with a year written on the side. The first box marked: *1967.*

Curiosity pulled his hands from his pockets, and he opened the letter with a tremor running through his arms.

Deven,

I will be a little longer than expected. Fifty years longer. Watch the shop. Sales will sustain you. Be patient. Stock is in the back. Keep the sign clean. It will capture the interest of a certain young man in the future, and that's one customer you want to come in.

Yours,

Deven Harris

Outside, the shops on the opposite side of the street had all changed. An old-fashioned diner stood in place of the mobile phone shop. A toy-shop front filled with matchbox cars seemed to be attracting attention from a group of strangely-dressed children.

A chill ran down Deven's spine, settling uncomfortably in his brass knockers.

The outlook did not look good.

E.C. Jarvis is a British author working mainly in speculative and fantasy fiction genres. Since 2015 she has independently published six books spanning two different genres and series and had several short stories published in a range of different anthologies. If you like action-packed, fast-paced page turners, then try one of her books. There's never a dull moment in those pages. She was born in Surrey, England, in 1982. She now resides in Hampshire, England, with her daughter and husband. For more information, visit: www.ecjarvis.com, twitter.com/EC_Jarvis, facebook.com/E.C.JarvisAuthor, www.amazon.com/E.C.-Jarvis/e/B0154YOIGI, www.amazon.com/Machine-Blood-Destiny-Book-ebook/dp/B01B43XF08

The Last
C.H. Knyght

The monster had come back for her.

Marie heard the worn floorboards downstairs groan beneath its feet as it hunted relentlessly through the house.

Thump, thump, thump.

Not again. Please, not again. Every time the monster came back, she lost someone else. Now it was here for her.

Marie curled into a tight ball under the musty bed. Fear shivered down her back, and her hair stood on end as heavy footsteps tramped down the front hall. It took all her strength not to wail in sheer terror. She didn't know what to do, except hide.

Papa had fought it with all of his strength and lost. Brother too. They had been the strongest. What hope did she have?

Long minutes passed. Nothing happened. An eerie, waiting silence fell over the house. It'd stopped moving.

She didn't dare peek out from under the moldy bed skirt. Had it given up? The dying sunlight cast hollow shadows into the room. Nothing moved.

What was the monster doing? She hadn't heard it leave. It was impossible to walk silently in this house. It was over a century old. Every single board creaked like an old man's bones. It was still here then, had to be. The monster was too big and solid to sneak around properly.

The risk wasn't worth it. She'd stay under the bed all night if she had to. Marie drifted deeper into the meager shelter until her back bumped against the wall. Dust bunnies skittered about like disturbed spiders in her wake.

She wanted Mama. Why couldn't it have just left them all alone? This was their home. It was supposed to be safe. It had been abandoned and unwanted, like them.

Marie waited. Fear gave her a new patience.

Thump, thump, thump.

It wanted a soul. Her soul. She was the only one left. Everyone else was gone, consumed by the monster. It had come back for her. Nothing sated its hunger for long.

Thump, thump, thump.

Stairs creaked as the monster ascended to the second floor. A fearful moan escaped her throat. Marie wrapped both hands over her cold lips to trap the sound.

Had it heard?

She trembled as the footsteps on the stairs hesitated. Tears trickled down her cheeks, leaving icy streaks. Which way would it go? Marie burrowed into her ratty cloak, though it offered no warmth or protection. Nothing would protect her if the monster found her.

Thump, thump, thump.

No, no, no. It was coming closer now, relentless as it hunted her down like an animal to slaughter.

Papa had told them the old stories about the monster before it became a reality. Told them the rules. How not to attract its attention. How the monster's mere voice burned your ears, and how its words were like chains. It would bind you and take your soul.

Papa had been taken first. Marie hadn't seen it happen—she'd hidden in the closet with Baby Boo. Mama had wailed, heartbroken, for weeks after; more so after Brother's soul was gone. How she'd grieved. Until it had gotten her too.

How could she escape it by herself?

She'd tried to keep Baby Boo hidden and safe. She'd failed. Boo had been the last to be consumed by the monster. Mama would never forgive her if she knew.

It had taken everyone she loved. Her entire family. Except for her. She was all alone. Marie moaned, overwhelmed by the grief and terror that shredded the remnants of her heart.

Rusty hinges squealed as the bedroom door swung open. Startled, Marie shrieked and flew out from beneath the bed. The monster had found her. She had to run, but where?

A huge figure loomed, silhouetted in the doorway. She was trapped. Sudden cold permeated the room and frost bloomed across the floor beneath her feet. Marie stared at the monster, frozen in place by its terrible presence. It was bigger than she'd thought.

She had to get away. Marie didn't move, couldn't move.

The monster spoke. Its sinuous words linked together and created visible chains of power that writhed through the air. It gestured and they reached for her. Marie screamed. Wrapping her cloak about her like a shield, she ran. The chains lashed out. She swooped and swirled, dodging the coils. The chains missed and fell empty to the floor.

There was a promise of pain if they caught her. She knew it would hurt. Mama had screamed so terribly as the chains dragged her away. The monster had shown no mercy. At least Baby Boo had gone quickly, too little to struggle.

The chains rose up again as more heavy, grating words fell from the monster's mouth and the power swelled. They reached out like long, twisted fingers.

Fear twisted in Marie's stomach. She whirled around, searching desperately for an escape. The monster ground out more evil words and flung acid at her. The liquid stung everywhere it touched.

Marie dove out the bedroom window. Broken glass lining the window frame sliced through the tatters of her cloak. The monster was too large to follow her out the window. She hoped anyway.

Safe for a moment, Marie searched for something, anything that might give her a chance. She had to hide. If the monster couldn't find her, it couldn't steal her soul.

What would Mama do?

Weather-beaten shutters rattled in the breeze. The attic. She could hide up there. It would give up soon. It had to.

Pushing aside the loose shutters, Marie crept into the deep gloom. The old attic was huge. Heaps of musty junk offered several hiding places. She ignored them. Too obvious. She went higher. Huddled up on a rafter beam, Marie shivered so hard she nearly vibrated off the high perch. What to do? The monster was strong. Far stronger than her.

Footsteps stomped below.

Thump. Thump, thump.

Like a granddaddy clock keeping time until the final toll.

Thump, thump, thump.

It wasn't giving up.

Marie sobbed into her knees. She wanted Mama. She didn't want to be eaten. If the monster's chains caught her, she'd disappear forever. Her soul would never return. She'd seen that happen so many times already. It had eaten everyone's souls: Mama, Big Brother, Baby Boo. Papa had gone first while trying to protect them all.

Why couldn't it just leave her alone?

Thump, thump, thump.

The footsteps came closer.

Marie stared wide-eyed at the trapdoor. How did it keep finding her? She sensed the monster's malevolence as it oozed through the house, aimed solely at her. Fierce determination gripped her. She had to do it. For everyone. It had to go, even if it took her with it. At least then it couldn't hunt down anyone else. Marie crawled along the rafters, searching for an idea.

Black mold drew her attention. There was a weak spot in the floorboards where the rain always leaked in from the holey roof. Marie knelt on the timbers above it. In the darkness, the floor appeared strong and whole, but she knew it really wasn't. It had to work.

Across the attic, the trapdoor flipped open. The monster was coming up. Marie swallowed another wail and scurried to the farthest end of the attic. The chains came up first, like an escort of serpents guarding their demon king.

The monster churned out more of his hateful words and drove the chains into the depths of the attic, but the monster's power fell short. It climbed all the way into the attic.

Marie huddled into the darkest corner. She held her breath,

damming up the terrified scream in her chest. Her fingers and toes turned blue from the effort of not making a sound. A strange frost grew over the windows as the monster stepped closer. Its head swayed back and forth as it searched.

Thump, thump, thump.

Closer. She was suffocating with the need to scream, to let it out. The attic floor creaked. Closer.

Thump, thump, thump.

It was almost here. The chains writhed across the floor. Marie curled her toes as the chains slithered too close. The monster stomped into the center of the attic. The floor groaned and shuddered under its solid mass.

Now.

Marie flew out of the shadows. She wailed with all her might. The attic windows shattered from the pitch. Blood gushed from its ears, the monster roared in pain and covered them with its hands. The word chains disintegrated as it stopped chanting. Marie screamed harder. She used all of her fear and grief and pushed with willed, violent force. Rotten timbers gave way, and the monster fell through the floor. It yelled a useless sound of shock. She heard its body land with a wet *thud* and a sickening *crunch*.

Marie drifted to hover over the new hole in the floor. The monster sprawled, broken on the floor below. It was dying. Lifeblood pooled under its body, leaking steadily from a crushed skull and staining the embroidered purple silk draped around its snapped neck.

She had done it. Relief made her fluttery. She had beaten the monster. Marie let herself float down through the hole to study the poignant death. This was the moment of her evolution. She was not weak anymore. She was the hunter, not the hunted.

The glass vial of clear acid rolled from its fingers as they spasmed. Marie pressed a single finger against the vial, and ice crawled across the glass until the hateful, blessed water within was solid. It couldn't hurt her in containment.

Only one thing marred the pleasure of her victory. The book, with a golden cross stamped on the leather binding. It scalded her eyes to even look at it. She lifted the book with a mere thought and cast it out a window. That abomination she would not suffer in her house. The human monster couldn't use the book's words to bind her soul anymore. She was safe.

Triumph gave her a new strength. Her soul was secured here to this place now and forever. Marie let out a victorious wail that shattered all the remaining glass in the house. The old house was hers now. A cold wind rippled the transparent edges of her cloak.

All fell quiet; neither a clock ticked to keep the time, nor a heartbeat of life.

Silence.

Marie smiled.

C. H. Knyght writes magic into the world. It's not always kind magic, for there is magic of numerous kinds: seen and unseen, creatures of myth, and forces of forgotten power. "The Last" is her first published piece; although her fantasy novel, *Nightvision*, is set to launch in the near future. Knyght lives in the cold north of Minnesota with her family, two dogs, two horses, a cat, and an expanding library. For more magic born of words and ink, follow her at: www.facebook.com/chknyght.

A Wacky, Fantastical Misadventure in New Haven

William Thatch

It's days like today when I'm reminded of something my father once said. The family was seated around the dinner table enjoying a glazed ham on Easter Sunday when my father looked at the empty space above the table and proceeded to shout.

"Goddamnit, stop dancing in the mashed potatoes!"

We were all very confused but nervously laughed it away. A couple of days later, we had him committed.

Why am I reminded of that today? Because as I sat at the breakfast table twenty years later, a spoon filled with milk and cereal, I saw the unmistakable sight of Adolf Hitler tea-bagging my Cheerios.

Within the next twelve hours, I'll have lost my house, my job, my friends, and my life. But for now, all I lost was my appetite.

"Aren't you going to finish?" Hitler asked in a German accent as he did little squats, raising his unfortunately hairy scrotum out of the bowl before dipping it back in.

His tone was cheerful, not angry like one would expect from a man whose name is synonymous with evil. It struck me as the sort of tone a comedian might use if doing a parody of Hitler. It was like an audible tea-bagging to go along with the visual tea-bagging.

I tell myself it's just another strange day in New Haven. We have a very colorful, odd town. The founder of our town was arrested after some very public acts with the neighbor's dog. We were all horrified, and yet oddly proud when the account of it was published in *Playboy*. My great-grandpa died after getting into a shouting match with a plastic tree over the validity of the Earth being flat. The last time anyone saw him, he announced, "I'll show you!" and started walking. We're unsure what side he took in that debate, or where he ended up, but we like to joke he fell off the edge of the world.

I forced myself to put the spoon in my mouth, knowing full

well where it had been. I felt if I could be the master of my mind, prove to my senses he was not real, that he would go away. It wasn't until the spoon was in my mouth, and I could taste a difference, that I realized Hitler was translucent. I've seen plenty of pictures of the German dictator, and I can't recall one picture where he was translucent. That was the second clue that there was something off about my morning.

Unfortunately, I had no time to play detective. I was supposed to open the pizzeria today and had wasted my breakfast time staring at the saggy, hairy scrotum of Adolf Hitler. I scooped the bowl up and poured the remainder of the milk and cereal down my gullet, choking briefly at the cereal clogging my throat.

I suppose I should mention a thank you to Hitler for performing the Heimlich maneuver.

At least, I think that's what he was doing back there.

Because the Pizzazz Pizzeria, named by the CEO Zanzibar Zotz, was just a few blocks down the road, I walked to and from it every day. Some say he's obsessed with the letter Z; I say he was born into it. Anyway, the pizzeria being so close was a good way to get a little exercise, fresh air, and to stay connected to friends and neighbors.

I politely asked Mrs. Cahill how her flower garden was going as I passed, and then waved to the Miller children across the street as they ran and jumped through the spray of a garden hose. You'd think the latter would be a precious sight to see on a hot summer day, but the Miller children were in their thirties and legally retarded. I didn't know it was possible to be *illegally* retarded, but their painted-on bathing suits made me question if their particular brand of retardedness should have been illegal. But that's the kind of town we lived in.

You'd think seeing Adolf Hitler dipping himself into my Honey Nut Cheerios would have been concerning, but in New Haven, it didn't even rank in the top ten oddities I had seen that week; I mean, maybe twelve or thirteen. I hadn't decided where to rank it, given

Mayor Bugenhagen recently crashing his dirigible *The Queen Mary* into the town square. I think I softened on it when he admitted there was more time and cost efficient means of getting to city hall.

All right, Hitler Nut Cheerios ranks twelve, just higher than the sinking of *The Queen Mary.*

I reached the block where the Pizzazz Pizzeria called home, stepped over remnants of *The Queen Mary* dirigible, and opened the restaurant. It was early morning and we don't get much traffic at this hour. As it turned out, our breakfast pizzas were not a hit with the locals.

Oatmeal and sausage pizza was voted in the newspapers to be the worst atrocity in New Haven since that one nerd at the high school crossbred rabbit DNA with bacon. The streets were filled with people stripping live rabbits to the bone for their tasty, tasty meat flesh. It was also voted Science's Most Delicious Mistake. So there were some upsides to genetic engineering. There were no upsides to our breakfast pizzas, however.

I spent the morning alternating between wiping down the tables and pressing my face against the front glass, begging people to try our orange juice & prunes pizza to no avail. I thought I saw one of those bacon rabbits at one point, but it was just Mayor Bugenhagen's son climbing out of the wreck of the dirigible, still smoldering from the crash.

I was in the middle of figuring out which office supplies could be deep-fried—all of them, for the record—when our first customer walked in. And what a looker, too. Six-inch ruby-red high heels, a little French beret, a plunging neckline, and a dress so short it left little to the imagination.

I really wish Adolf Hitler would wear more appropriate clothing.

"*Guten tag!*" he said, throwing his arm out at a forty-five-degree angle and then waving.

"I cannot deal with you right now, I'm busy!" I said.

Hitler, still striking his weird salute/wave, looked around the restaurant with just his eyes. All right, he had me. There was no one else in the building, and I was just dicking around until eleven when we stopped serving breakfast.

"I've got . . . things in the deep fryer," I said. "Important things. I can't let them overcook."

The importance of the franchise manager Abraham Schmitt's desk nameplate notwithstanding, I was hoping the dictator wouldn't know how long something like that was supposed to be cooked. I sure didn't have an idea of when it was overcooked or undercooked or just right. That's the sort of thing Goldilocks might know, but I do not.

Pouting, Hitler turned and goose-stepped out of the pizzeria.

And not a second too soon either, as I heard the back door open and Schmitt greeted me.

Moving quickly, I pulled the desk nameplate out of the deep fryer, cursed loudly, and wished I had used a pair of tongs or something before returning it to his desk.

Schmitty and I—he hates it when I call him Schmitty—have a long history of pulling pranks on each other. It started with the old unscrewing-the-salt-shaker ruse and then graduated to the old sugar-in-the-gas-tank routine. I remember fondly the time I used the old set-his-pants-on-fire rigmarole. He got me back with the old run-your-mother-over-with-a-big-rig-and-then-repeatedly-bludgeon-her-with-a-baseball-bat-at-the-funeral rib.

We both agreed that one went a little too far.

"How's it hanging?" Schmitty asked as he walked in. "We get any customers?"

It had been a huge disappointment to Schmitty that the breakfast pizzas weren't selling better. The old convince-your-boss-of-an-amazing-marketing-gimmick-that-is-really-a-stupid idea gambit was working wonderfully. I hadn't figured out when it was going to pay off, but it would.

I considered telling him about Hitler coming in, just to get his hopes up, but I decided against it. He got a big enough ego after a look-alike of Stalin's brother came in to use the restrooms once. We had the picture on the wall to prove it, until the city demanded we remove it because people said they didn't want to see a vaguely Russian-looking man being startled at the urinal.

"Are you . . . all right?" Schmitty asked.

As it turned out, I never answered; I had just been staring while thinking about that photo. I told him no one came in. He teared up and excused himself to his office—his warm, crispy, deep-fried office-supplies-covered office.

We welcomed our first customers not long after. Some snot-nosed punks came in and ordered a cheese pizza. I cooked it, served it, watched them eat it, and then they left. I spent twenty minutes cleaning up their snot afterwards.

"Smith!" Schmitty yelled from his office.

I smiled. He'd found the deep-fried everything.

Schmitty burst from his office, a deep-fried stapler with teeth marks in hand and a series of broken teeth in his mouth.

"Did you do this?" he asked.

I tried to keep from smiling but I couldn't. I always had a problem with smiling when I shouldn't. I smiled at my mother's funeral, all the way through Schmitty's beating. I smiled that time the nuclear plant burped something green and glowing into the sky, and when it rained radioactive acid rain on us for a few days. People always tell me to stop smiling, and I tell them I can't. Someone drew one on my face with a permanent marker as a child. On the plus side, I'm voted Happiest Man in New Haven every year. It comes with a free coupon for markers. I'd say I'm not amused by it, but I'm always smiling when I think of it.

Schmitty proceeded to tell me it gave him an idea for a new pizza (and a reason to go to the dentist). He proceeded to describe his idea of a chicken pizza, with the hook being deep-fried onion strings scattered on the top.

I thought it was a wonderful idea.

"That's the stupidest idea I've ever heard," I told him.

I don't like making Schmitty feel too good about himself. Might lead him to getting an ego or some self-esteem. That can be a dangerous thing. Someone once told him he had nice eyes, so he spent weeks putting his eyes right up to yours when speaking. It was really awkward at the urinals.

But, I agreed to help experiment. We tried different sauces and meats. Customers asked if they could try a piece. We told them, "No, get out." So, they got out.

Out of the corner of my eye, I saw Adolf Hitler standing in the doorway. He had pants on this time. I never thought I'd have to specify that I saw Adolf Hitler with pants on, but that's how this day was going. I saw a look in his eye; one of mischievous contempt. I didn't know those two things went together.

Schmitty bent over to slide the pizza into the oven. That's when Hitler tiptoed at an alarming speed behind Schmitty and planted his boot into Schmitty's backside, shoving him head first into the oven. I watched in horror as Adolf Hitler faded from reality, waving and smiling pleasantly while my Jewish boss removed his head from the oven while shouting obscenities.

"Damnit Hitler," I whispered under my breath.

"What?" Schmitty asked, furrowing his brow.

It was hard to take his anger seriously. Maybe it was because I was smiling. That usually does it.

"I didn't say anything."

"I heard you say something about Hitler." Schmitty gasped. "That was a Holocaust joke."

I insisted it was not. He didn't believe me. It's the smile; I'm telling you. No one believes a guy who's smiling all the time. Eventually you look insincere.

And so I walked out of the pizzeria with a pink slip and my pants full of hot grease from the deep fryer. I still say he overreacted. Even if I had been making a Holocaust joke, the deep-fried penis gag was unnecessary.

I took a seat on the remains of the dirigible, frightening off a few bacon rabbits that had been hiding under it. Nearby townsfolk panicked when they saw more of these tasty abominations and began chasing them down. I, meanwhile, had something to do.

"*Guten tag*, again!" Hitler said, taking a seat beside me.

"Go away!" I demanded.

"Oh, you're not very nice."

"You killed millions of people . . ."

"It was the forties, everyone was doing it!"

I lunged at him, trying to wrap my hands around his stupid, translucent neck so I could throttle the air out of his stupid, translucent throat. Instead, I face planted into the ground.

I picked myself up and dusted myself off.

"Why are you always so testy?" Hitler asked, crossing his legs like a proper lady.

I squinted at him, trying to decide if he was making fun of breakfast. Then he began to grin. I still couldn't tell.

"I don't have time for this," I told him, climbing the wreckage of the dirigible.

It might have been easier to go around, but it wasn't the most direct route. I prefer direct routes. I had just gotten to the top when Hitler spoke again.

"Wait!" shouted Hitler. "Can I come with you?"

". . . Why?" I asked.

"I want to show off my new pants."

I looked back to see what he was talking about. Assless chaps.

As it turns out, they were also frontless chaps. The German dictator's balls swung lazily in the afternoon breeze. I'm pretty sure I could still see a Cheerio clinging to his scrotum. I was confused about the physics of that, but I was never too good with physics to begin with. I trusted it made sense.

I decided I needed to go hunting for a new job immediately. I wasn't the sort to sit around and do nothing all day. Idle hands being the devil's workshop and whatnot. And they're not lying when they say that.

I spent one Saturday lounging and watching television. Before I knew it, I had opened a gateway to Hell and was trying to explain to the Lord of Destruction, Baal, why he could not crash on my couch. I told him I was very sorry, but I had no room for him and the lesser evils making up his posse: the Lord of Lies, the Maiden of Anguish, and a shimmering ball of light I took to be the physical representation of pop music.

Baal told me I was a jive turkey, having opened a portal to Hell in my front yard, but refused any hospitality. He flashed a few gang signs and went back through, insisting he would get me back in the least expected way. The last thing I heard before the portal shut and I began to heavily salt my yard, was a high-pitched *teehee!* and something about Billie Jean.

So, I hit the pavement in search of a new source of income. The thing about New Haven is there are more jobs than there are people, so there is always a job somewhere for a man or woman willing to work. The business owners had tried running aggressive campaigns to bring in people from outside of New Haven, but they ran into a wall. By "they," I mean the people driving into New Haven, and by "a wall," I mean literally. After a meeting at city hall, where people complained it was too hot in the summers, Mayor Bugenhagen built a big wall around New Haven and tried filling it with water so that New Haven would be one giant pool. The people coming to take our jobs drove right into a brick wall. Our doctors tried rushing out to help them, but they just drove right into the other side of the wall.

Already the wall had gotten off to a bad start. It never truly got started either, as the plan for filling it with water amounted to Mayor Bugenhagen turning on the hose behind city hall. After a few weeks, it did flood the streets, so people did enjoy themselves some splash fights, but then winter came. With colder temperatures came freezing water, and with freezing water came slick driving surfaces.

When the complaints started coming in about the cold, Mayor

Bugenhagen set the town on fire with his brilliant strategy of literally setting buildings on fire.

My first stop was the Pizzazz Pizzeria, as I knew they had an opening. After cursing at me loudly, Schmitty threw deep-fried pencils at me. They weren't bad, but needed some salt. I filed a note about leaving that as a review and then walked farther into the business district.

The Coca Cabana, our only night club, was trying to put together a small wrestling show one night a week for people's amusement. They wanted to know if I had any experience in performance. I proved I did by breaking a wooden chair over a waitress's head. The manager had me thrown out, and for good measure, the bouncer gave me an elbow drop. I think he was auditioning for the spot himself, judging by the leotard and wrestling mask he was wearing. Seemed like a good kid. I think he'd do well.

Dejected and pretty certain I had bruised ribs, I kept walking and inquiring within establishments. I tried being a dentist next. I didn't expect to get that job, but as it turned out, the town's dentist had been among those who tried to help out-of-towners when they drove into the wall. I thought I'd noticed more cavities in the mouths of children as of late, but it was hard to tell with parents giving me dirty looks for poking my fingers in their children's mouths.

As it happened, my first client had scheduled an appointment earlier that day. He had broken his teeth on a deep-fried stapler. Imagine my surprise when Schmitty walked in.

I tried to play it cool, as if he hadn't just fired me and thrown unsalted deep-fried office supplies at my head.

". . .'Sup?" I asked.

"Are you trying to play it cool?" he asked.

". . . No . . ."

We stared at each other awkwardly for a few minutes until a large chunk of one of his teeth fell out and reminded us why he was there. I told him to get into the chair and proceeded to use every dentist tool in the room. I had no idea how most of them were used, however. I'd watched a video of two funny guys playing a game simulating surgery on teeth at one point and tried to emulate them. Schmitty was not laughing as much as the two guys when I used a hammer to break more of his teeth. I guess you really can't trust everything you see on the internet or in video games.

After he complained about the pain like a little baby, I turned on the valve for the sleeping gas all dentists have for when they want to take a quick nap and had Schmitty breathe in deeply. Once he was asleep, I continued to guess at what I was supposed to do. I watched more videos online, but either they showed something I was pretty certain wouldn't work, like going to a real dentist, or required skills I did not have as an untrained dentist. Finally, I just used the drill to take out the rest of his teeth and put a hole in his cheek.

I wanted to feel bad about it, but really, who is to blame—me or the irresponsible party who hired me in the first place? I think we can both agree I am completely faultless here.

It was at that point I started to feel drowsy and noticed I had not shut off the sleeping gas canister. I decided now was a fine time for one of those dentist naps as I fell to the floor.

I woke up briefly a few minutes later to see Adolf Hitler doing his tea bagging routine on Schmitty. It had been one of the suggestions in a video that featured a lot of pixilation, but I had dismissed it as having no relevance. But at this point I couldn't see it doing any more harm than what I had done, and who am I to argue with Hitler's dental practices? I think we can also agree I have no idea what I'm doing when it comes to dentistry.

When I woke up an hour later, Hitler was gone, and Schmitty was still sleeping it off in the chair. I examined my handiwork and decided I had won the pranking contest with this. Not wanting to leave the job unfinished, I grabbed a pair of dentures from a drawer and glued them to his face. I then marched out of the building and insisted I quit. I figured I should retire while I'm ahead.

I tried one more lead on a job, applying to Mayor Bugenhagen's office to give some assistance to Mayor Bugenhagen. After *The Queen Mary's* horrible wreck, he had been in search of a new means of transportation, and I was to help provide that.

So, he gave me a trial run, having me give him a piggyback ride all around town. He spent most of his time on my back, giving raspberries to people as we passed them. It was tiring work carrying a fully-grown man on your back. We stopped off at his favorite watering hole, and he tied me up outside so I didn't wander away and some other varmint didn't try to steal me. He then rode me for a while longer. We slipped on some snot trails on the ground from the aforementioned snot-nosed punks. I whinnied as I went down, and then whined while I was down.

Oddly enough, on the way back, he crashed me into the town square. I figured now was as good a time as any to tell him I didn't think this was going to work out, what with my back being sore and being so close to home.

He patted my head and gave me a sugar cube for my troubles.

I headed back home, my head hung low and constantly fidgeting my fingers. I couldn't afford for my hands to become idle. Now that money was going to be at a premium, I didn't have the space for Baal and his posse, nor did I have the money to feed them. I really need to step up my hospitality game.

As I walked, I noticed the street was oddly deserted. Mrs. Cahill wasn't tending to her gardens. Only one of the Miller children was outside, and he had tipped over the sprinkler system and was running in circles around it. Also, there was a big plume of black smoke rising from the direction of my house.

As it turns out, that's because my house was on fire.

I arrived to see a lot of the neighborhood had turned out to watch the fire. Mrs. Cahill was there, as was the other Miller child, and the snot-nosed punks were back. After slipping on the snot, I stood up and shook myself off.

"What's going on?" I asked the crowd.

Everyone in the neighborhood turned to face me. They scowled at me pretty fierce. It felt rude, particularly to someone that was always smiling at them, even now as my house was engulfed in flames. Ungrateful bastards.

The crowd parted and gave me a good look at my home. Beneath the raging inferno, I could see someone had painted a giant swastika, various Nazi slogans, and a pair of highly-detailed, well-shaded testicles being lowered into a hastily and crudely-drawn mouth.

I didn't have to guess who had pulled this stunt. I glared into the crowd, looking for Schmitty, but I couldn't find him. You might ask, for everything that had happened today, why I'd accuse Schmitty first. Well, I hate him. That's just for starters. I find if you hate someone, it's usually a good idea to blame everything that goes wrong in life on them. But, also, I got a good look at a notebook he kept on prank ideas. This was #6, just above #7 (kicking the person standing beside me in the nuts for months to lull me into a false sense of security), and just below #5 (kicking me in the nuts).

"Who did this?" I yelled.

"You did!" responded someone in the crowd.

Sure enough, someone had added my signature in the lower right-hand corner of the house. I thought hard about if I had done it and not remembered. But I was pretty certain I was chauffeuring Mayor Bugenhagen around town when this was happening.

"I didn't do this!" I protested. "I don't approve of this!"

"Then why are you smiling?" shouted the same guy as before.

The mob booed me. The snot-nosed punks blew chunks out of their noses at me. The other Miller child showed up, covered in mud, and then both blew raspberries at me. I tell you that hurt the worst. I tried calling the fire department, but when they showed up, they just added more fire to the house.

That's when I saw the person responsible for this. I ran into the street and clocked Schmitty in the face, knocking his teeth off his cheek. That was when Adolf Hitler materialized in front of me, smiling and waving. That's when it clicked that he was the one responsible. I ran over to try to clock him in the face, but instead, went flying into someone's yard.

"Why?" I asked as I pulled myself up. "Why are you such a jerk?"

"Well," he started, staring off into the sky. "I suppose it all started for me as a child. I was very lonely, you see."

"Don't care."

"All the other children would run about, playing with sticks and whatnot—that's what we had at the time—but any time I would try to play with them, they would just beat me with the sticks."

". . . Aw," I said. "Doesn't seem like a good excuse though."

"But then I would go home and tell my mother and then she would also beat me with a stick."

"That's a bit extreme."

"I guess," Hitler said, shuddering. "I guess all I've really been looking for is attention."

"I . . . well I guess you were successful."

"Yes, but all little Hitler wanted was a hug."

I watched as the evil German dictator, Adolf Hitler, wiped a tear from his eye. It was sad. You wouldn't know it from the smile on my face, but I felt a little bad for him.

I sighed. The last thing I needed right now was for the neighbors pissing on my yard, watching my Nazi propaganda-laced home burn to the ground, to see me hugging the ghost of Adolf Hitler. But, I'm a big old softie.

I opened my arms and closed my eyes. I wanted to get it over with. I stepped forward.

THUD!

That's when Willie the Blind Bus Driver ran me over with his bus. I really should have mentioned Willie earlier, like set him up for this part of the story. That's how a good story is told; you lay seeds early. But it was kind of a big day for me, as you might have noticed. I just plum forgot, so it kinda comes out of the blue. Remind me to tell about the time he accidentally drove on the street. It's a doozey.

My life was over instantly. My body got flung several feet ahead of the bus, and then got run over again. That time I got stuck between the wheel and the wheel well so it really grinded me down into a paste.

I looked longingly at my mangled corpse, trying to ignore the cheers of the mob, Mayor Bugenhagen stepping out of the bus to announce it as his new means of transportation, and that shimmering ball of light, now with thick glasses and curly hair, singing about eating something.

When I looked back to Hitler, he was straightening the French beret on his head again.

"That thing about children beating you with sticks wasn't true, was it?" I asked.

"No!" he said, eyes widening in excitement. "I was the one beating them with the sticks."

I watched the mob kick at my corpse for a little while. Schmitty got into it by beating me with a bat until my skull was deformed.

"Why did you do this?" I asked. "Why me?"

"Well, I always wanted to visit Paris, and I did not want to travel alone."

"You invaded Paris!"

"Yes, yes, but there was a war on at the time—"

"Because of you!"

"Stop interrupting, it's rude. Anyway, I was there for business, not pleasure. I didn't get to really appreciate it for its culture and architecture."

"Ugh . . . Jesus . . ." I said, rubbing my temples where the headache started to form.

"No, no. I asked him. He was kind of upset about the millions of dead people too." He stepped in front of me and clapped his hands together. "So, shall we?"

I shrugged my shoulders. I mean, I didn't need a job anymore. He wasn't my ideal traveling companion, but I had nothing better to do now. I told him fine, but I insisted on the window seat. He flew into a rage, his weird hair flapping all about but always returning to the same position when he stopped, until I agreed to take the aisle seat.

Every story should have a moral, right? I think, if you take any moral from my story, let it be this: Adolf Hitler is kind of a dick.

William Thatch, born in 1989, has been writing stories for twenty-three years. As a storyteller, Thatch gravitates toward science-fiction while incorporating elements of other genres, such as westerns and noir. His eccentric personality and sense of humor has given rise to fellow authors referring to him as a pirate. His first published story was "The Highway," which appeared in Scout Media's *A Journey of Words* anthology. Thatch can be found on Twitter at @The_0s1s and Facebook at facebook.com/The0s1s.

Coal
Run
Road

Donise
Sheppard

I glance around my grand living room, silently celebrating the fact that I'm finally unpacked. Three days of nothing but cleaning and organizing and I'm finally finished.

As I turn toward the television and drop onto the couch, my fourteen-year-old daughter enters the room, face planted in her phone with her fingers busily at work texting.

"What do you think?" I ask.

Charity looks over her phone at my beaming face, rolling her eyes. "I think you need better hobbies," she says as she goes back to work at her phone.

My smile falters as I watch my daughter sink into the lounger completely ignoring everything I've worked so hard on.

"I'd probably have more time for hobbies if you didn't leave your shoes on the staircase. I've moved them at least a dozen times since yesterday."

Charity squints over her phone. "I haven't touched my shoes except to go to school, and I left them by the door like you asked! Maybe Janice or Mandy's been playing with them."

Frowning, I stand up and walk away. I head for the kitchen through the large central hallway, which doubles as our dining area, but as I'm walking through, I see Charity's running shoes randomly tossed on the stairs.

I let out a sigh and climb the stairs to pick them up before returning them to the shoe rack by the front door, muttering under my breath about how I'm never going to have hobbies with as much as I clean.

Owen comes home just as I'm setting dinner on the table. He inhales sharply before wrapping his arms around me, first hugging my back before kissing me on the cheek. My lips reflexively turn upward at his tender touch.

"Dinner smells amazing, Jennifer."

I wave my hand, brushing him away as he tries to grab a potato. "Go wash your hands."

He kisses my cheek again before heading toward the bathroom.

"Put your phone away, Charity," I say, piling food onto the plates.

She rolls her eyes before burying it under her thigh with a frown.

Refusing to give in to her attitude, I grin at my five-year-old and three-year-old as they talk about preschool with bright eyes and laughter. Why can't my oldest daughter appreciate life like them?

"May said her would pway schoow wif me affer dinner," Mandy tells her big sister.

I simply smile at my baby. I've been meaning to teach her how to pronounce her *L*s and *T*s but have been a little preoccupied with the move. I'll have to start correcting her whenever I hear her leaving them out.

Janice takes a drink of her milk before she responds. "You can't play school with your imaginary friend."

My eyes widen. "You have an imaginary friend?"

"No. May is weal."

Mandy's eyes squint at Janice as she folds her arms defensively over her chest. Owen walks back in before the fight can go any further.

"I don't want to come across as rude, but someone at this table uses too much perfume. The entire bathroom reeks of it," he says as he sits next to Mandy.

Charity shakes her head. "Don't look at me. I don't use old woman perfume."

I sit between Janice and Owen, placing my napkin on my lap. Owen and Charity both turn to stare at me.

"Well it isn't mine. That smell has been there since we moved in. Maybe the last owner spilled a bottle and we can't get the smell out. I'll open the window again after dinner and try to air it out some more."

"Tat's May's mommy's perfoom," Mandy chimes in before taking a bite of her food. "Her said dat her spilled it one time and her was whipped and wocked in her woom. Her said it's your woom now, Mommy!"

Prying my eyes from my youngest child, I turn to my husband for support. His mouth is open and his eyes are wide. He's as speechless as I am.

"Wh . . ." He clears his throat, struggling to find the words. "Where did you hear about getting whipped?"

I'm just as perplexed as he is. We've never used corporal punishment, and all she watches is cartoons.

"May told me."

—. .—

While cleaning the counters in the kitchen, I hear thumping upstairs. I put the kids to bed an hour ago, so there's no reason they should be up running around or playing. I toss the towel in the sink before heading into the hallway and up the stairs, stumbling over Charity's sneaker.

"Son of a . . ."

Sighing, I pick up the sneaker and stomp up the rest of the stairs.

Janice and Mandy's shared room is the first door at the top of the stairs, directly over the kitchen. The door is slightly ajar, allowing the hallway light to seep into the room. I open the door to peer inside. Janice is sprawled across the top bunk while Mandy is cuddled on the bottom. Both girls are sound asleep.

My brows crease as I squint to look around the room. I could've sworn the thumping had been coming from in here. I close the door to its original position before tiptoeing my way down the hallway to Charity's room. I pause before knocking, listening for any signs that Charity is the culprit, but come up empty with clues. There's no noise from inside that I can hear.

I knock twice and wait for my daughter to open the door. It

swings wide and Charity stands there in her pajamas staring at me as if she had better things to do.

"Yes?"

I frown at the bitterness in my daughter's voice that I'm still not used to hearing. "I heard thumping. I'd appreciate it if you could keep the noise down a little. The girls are trying to sleep."

Charity crosses her arms and huffs. "I'm sitting at my desk studying with my headphones on. You can't blame me for everything."

"Did you drop something? Or maybe you went to the bathroom?"

"No, Mom. I've been there for twenty minutes, and I haven't dropped anything."

I plant a false grin on my face to try to keep from grimacing at her attitude. "All right. Sorry I bothered you, sweetie. Get back to your studying."

Charity's face softens before she closes the door.

I take a deep breath. Surely Charity had heard the thumping as well. It was so loud, as if someone had been running around. I rub the back of my neck and shake my head, convinced I'm finally losing it.

Deciding the house is clean enough for one night, I turn in early, showering before I go to bed. Halfway through, however, I smell something rotting, in addition to the perfume stink. I rush through the rest of the shower, eager to get out of the room.

"Honey, I think something may have died in there. It smells rancid."

Owen rolls over to face me, half asleep but still managing to give a hoarse laugh, grinning from ear to ear. "It's that perfume."

He reaches out as I walk by, grabbing my hand to pull me down on the bed beside him. I nestle into him, and his hand immediately slides down my arm to rest on my hip.

"No, Owen. It's a different smell. Maybe we should call someone to come out and look."

"I'll check it out in the morning, and if I don't find anything we can call an exterminator."

His breath is warm on my neck.

"Thank you."

"It's probably just a dead mouse."

I shudder at the thought, causing my body to sink deeper into his. He laughs as his hand moves to my stomach, pulling me closer.

"I love you, you know?" he asks, kissing my neck.

— • • —

"Marcus, you have to come over and paint for me! This wallpaper is horrible. I'm awful at it and it's your job!" I pause to listen, holding the phone to my ear. "That's what brothers do! Please? Owen is supposed to go build a deck for his friend today for some extra cash. I'll feed you." My lips form a smile as I finally get the response I've been waiting for. "Thank you! Yes, that color will be perfect! I'll see you in an hour."

Clicking the phone off, I set it on the table. The TV clicks on, alerting me that the children have finally awoken and are joining the living. Walking into the living room, I see Janice and Mandy occupied with cartoons.

"Girls, breakfast is on the table when you're hungry. Sausage biscuits today."

"Ohtay," Mandy says, turning the volume up.

I lean against the doorframe, crossing my arms over my chest as I watch my young girls. When I pry my eyes away, I turn to the stairs, once again seeing Charity's shoes staring back at me. Groaning, I pick them up and carry them back to the front door before making my way up to the girls' room to make their bunkbeds. I know I should make them do it, but I want to give them a little more time to grow up.

After tucking the blankets under the mattresses, I pick their teddy bears from the floor and lay them gently on their pillows.

Mandy's favorite baby doll is barely poking out from underneath the bottom bunk, so I fish it out and lay it beside her bear.

I'm starting down the stairs when I hear a small thud from the girls' room. My eyes slant and I turn around, seeing the reason for the sound: Mandy's favorite doll had somehow fallen.

My chest rises and falls as I make my way back into their room. I grab the baby doll from the floor, placing it farther back onto the bed than I had the last time. Maybe when I was walking, the vibrations bounced it off.

I head downstairs, yet again spotting Charity's shoes on the stairs. My mouth drops as I exhale sharply before roughly picking up the shoes and stomping into the living room, seeing both girls where I left them.

"Who did it?" I demand. I feel my eyes widen as my lips thin, but there is no calming myself.

The girls look to me, mouths parted and eyes wide.

"Who did what, Mommy?" Janice asks.

I take a deep breath before responding. "Who put Charity's shoes on the stairs? I keep picking them up and putting them back on the shoe rack, but someone keeps putting them on the stairs. I want to know who's doing it."

Janice shakes her head but Mandy laughs. "It's May, Mommy!"

My heart sinks. "This isn't funny, Mandy, it isn't a game. Someone could fall down and get hurt."

"Mandy was here the entire time, Mommy."

I cock my head at Janice but throw my hands up before leaving the room, defeated by a couple of preschoolers.

Owen peers around the corner before walking over to me. "I can't find anything, Jen," he tells me.

I shake my head as I toss the shoes in the right direction. "Fine. Whatever."

I try to walk past him to the kitchen, but he grabs my hand to stop me. "Jennifer! I looked. I didn't see or smell anything. Maybe there was a skunk outside or something."

I take a deep breath before planting a smile on my face. "That's fine. Thank you for looking."

He nods, releasing my grip. "I have to get out of here, I'm already late."

My smile fades. "I thought you said we'd call an exterminator? You want me to?"

He shakes his head. "No. I don't see the point in that. It'll just be a waste of money."

He rushes out the door without so much as a goodbye, completely forgetting his usual goodbye kiss.

An hour later, my brother is at the door as promised, carrying three bags of paint supplies.

"Thank God you're here! I really need my bedroom to be something other than floral."

Marcus laughs, pushing his way inside. "Floral isn't that bad. I have a few clients a month request it. They're usually much older than you, but still . . ."

I chuckle. "Follow me."

I lead the way down the hallway, through the kitchen, to my bedroom.

"I don't think you had to move everything onto the bed," Marcus says, setting his bag down on the ground.

I shrug. "There are some things in the closet too."

Marcus starts to unload his bag and assemble paint rollers.

"Want some coffee?" I ask.

He shakes his head. "No thanks. I had a cup before I got here. You know there's a McDonald's at the bottom of your hill?"

I laugh. "Of course I do. That's how I convinced the girls this would be a good move. I'll leave you to it. Let me know if you need help."

I walk back to the living room, only stopping to look up the stairs, seeing Charity's shoes, once again.

"Son of a mother . . ."

I climb the stairs to pick them up and return them to the shoe rack. I bend to place them strategically behind the shoe rack, harder for the girls to find. I stand up, catching a glimpse of myself in the glass on the door. My hair is messy, and I could probably use a little makeup. I tuck a strand of hair behind my ear and see a billow of blonde hair streak past me, heading for the kitchen.

Smiling, I turn to chase my only blonde daughter, Mandy. My smile falters as I run into the room I had just seen her disappear into. I narrow my eyes and shove my hand in my pocket as I search around the seemingly empty kitchen.

"Mandy?"

"Yes, Mommy?" Mandy walks into the kitchen from the hallway I had just come from.

I cock my head as I look at my daughter. "Did you just . . . were you in the living room?"

Mandy nods.

"But I thought you ran past me when I was by the front door? You didn't run past me?"

Mandy shakes her head, scrunching up her face. My eyebrows raise and I shake my head to clear it.

There is thumping upstairs as if the girls are up there running around or wrestling, even more loudly than the night before.

I exit the kitchen as Mandy gets a juice from the refrigerator. I bound up the stairs, wanting to hurry to catch whoever is causing the ruckus directly in the act. I make it halfway up before I trip over something. Looking down, I see Charity's shoes. Hot anger boils through me as I lean down to pluck them up, carrying them with me the rest of the way upstairs.

The thumping is coming from Janice and Mandy's room. I reach for the doorknob and let the door swing wide to face a vacant room, banging abruptly stopping.

"What the hell?"

I walk around the room, searching for Janice or Charity or some hidden animal but find nothing. The toys on the bunkbeds are out of place; some stuffed animals are at the foot of the beds and some are off the beds completely. Mandy's favorite doll is sitting on one of the rungs on the ladder. I cover my mouth and slowly back out of the room before briskly walking to Charity's room, knocking loudly.

A drowsy, bitter teenager opens the door, not so eager to start her day. "What time is it?"

"Were you in there jumping or running or drumming, by any chance?"

Charity's eyes squint and she snarls. "Are you drunk?"

I pinch the bridge of my nose, hands shaking. "Please just answer the question."

Charity's eyes soften and she shakes her head. "I was asleep."

I feel Charity's eyes bore into me as I run back to the girls' room. I hear her stomping up behind me as I kneel down to check under the bottom bunk for some clue as to where the noise had been coming from and who had messed up the beds.

I rush around the room, looking behind toys and around toy boxes, not knowing what I'm looking for but looking nonetheless. I open the closet and rifle through the clothes before Charity finally pipes up. "What's going on?"

"I have no idea," I say, shaking my head as I walk past my daughter and run down the stairs.

Janice and Mandy are still in the living room, a coloring book and crayons in Janice's hands, a juice box in Mandy's. I watch the girls for a minute before realizing I'm still holding Charity's shoes.

"Janice, did you move these shoes?" I ask, holding them up. My voice is thick with anger. My blood still boiling as fear and confusion still shake me.

My middle child raises her eyebrows as she shakes her head. "I've been coloring and watching TV." Her voice is sad, which sends a guilty punch to my gut.

I swallow the lump in my throat as I turn my back to the girls and saunter off toward the door. This time I put Charity's shoes under another pair of shoes. I walk toward the kitchen as Marcus comes out of the bedroom, bags in hand. I had nearly forgotten he was here.

"What's going on?" I ask, eyeing him.

His eyes are wide; his cheeks pale. "You have to move. You have to get your kids and get the hell out of here."

I frown. "Come on, Marcus. Wallpaper isn't that hard to take off. I said I'd help."

He shakes his head and edges to the door. "I'm serious, Jennifer."

I pause, hand on his arm. The seriousness in his voice is enough to make me stop. "What happened?"

His eyes brim with tears. "Something happened here and I don't feel it's safe."

My eyes mirror my big brother's as he pulls away and backs toward the door.

"You get some things together and come stay with me and Anna until you sell this place. Just get out. Right now."

He opens the door, and I chase after him. "What happened, Marcus?"

He throws his bag in the back of his truck, frowns at me, jumps in the driver's seat, and takes off without another word.

I walk back into the house, taking slow, deep breaths. This is shaping up to be a bad morning.

"May said her mommy didn't wike Uncle Marcus," Mandy tells me as soon as the door is closed behind us.

I sit on my knees to make myself eye level with my youngest daughter. "What do you mean, sweetie?"

"May said her mommy didn't wike Uncle Marcus. Her wanted him to die." Mandy's lip quivers.

I pull her into my arms and hug her. "He's all right, sweetie. He'll be fine."

Charity is standing on the stairs, mouth agape and eyes wide. "What a strange morning."

I close my eyes and take a deep breath before I stand up. "I made sausage biscuits, if you're hungry. How about we all go get one?"

Charity bounds down the rest of the stairs, only stopping to touch Janice on the shoulder. Janice stands in the living room doorway, staring teary eyed at the door.

"What's the matter, sweetheart?" I ask.

Her chest heaves as she stands there, rigid, looking past me. I follow her gaze, but see nothing.

"Jan? What's the matter, sweetie?"

Her face scrunches up and tears fall down her face. "She doesn't want us here." Her throat catches as she sobs.

I scoop my little girl into my arms, hugging her close. "What are you talking about? Is this because of what happened with Uncle Marcus? I'm sure he was just being silly, sweetie."

She shakes her head and pushes away from me, pointing toward the door. "I saw her, Mommy. She looked so mad! Her hair was gray, and she was wearing a dress, and her hair was everywhere. She was so scary. Then she looked at me! She looked at me, Mommy, the same way she was looking at Uncle Marcus."

"*Shh* . . ." I hug my daughter as she cries uncontrollably, trying to comfort her. "It's all right. Nothing can hurt you, Janice. Mommy's here to look after you."

"Mommy, May says Uncle Marcus got in twubble for wipping da paper off da wall. He untovered her dwawings."

"Her drawings?"

Mandy smiles a toothy grin. "Yeah! In your bedwoom!"

Upon entering my bedroom, I know exactly what Mandy is talking about. The wallpaper had been covering drawings and words and scratches, clearly indicating someone once lived an unhappy life here. I walk closer to inspect the drawings and words. A shiver of ice runs through me, seeing the words written over and over again: *Be good or I'll kill you.*

The drawings are of a stick figure with long messy black hair, choking a smaller stick figure with yellow hair—or of a stick figure holding something up as the other stick figure lay on the ground, blue tears dotting her round face. Every nerve in my body jumps as I realize the little girl who once resided here had been abused. The scratches, which are all so close to the ground, are deep, as if someone had dug into the wall trying to get out.

I turn to my daughters, finding Mandy cowering behind Charity.

"Mandy, did you see Uncle Marcus take the wallpaper off?"

She shakes her head as her big eyes widen more.

"Then how did you know about these drawings, sweetie?"

"May told me."

— . . —

Owen gets home a little after lunch time. No matter how many times we tell him our side of the story, he refuses to acknowledge anything strange is happening. He brushes the banging off as old pipes. He insists the girls aren't really seeing ghosts and that their imagination is playing tricks on them. He claims the toys could have been knocked over from the vibrations from walking and slamming of doors.

By the end of the night, he has me convinced that today had been my imagination and convinced the girls that even if something is in this house, it can't possibly hurt us. He claims the writing and drawings could have been from a teenager, wanting to cause panic and fear in the new occupants. Not wanting to believe some innocent girl was tortured here, I decide to agree with my husband.

Owen and I are sleeping in our bed when I hear a loud bloodcurdling scream. Being jolted awake causes every nerve on my body to jump from fear. There's another scream as I'm climbing out of bed, and I realize it's Charity.

Owen and I both run toward our eldest daughter at top speed. We make it to the bottom of the stairs as she starts to run down, crying and screaming. We both run to meet her, and she throws her arms around me.

"What's going on?" I ask.

I hear a creak before the tiny voice. "What happened?" Janice asks, hiding behind her door.

Charity continues to cry, so I ask her again what happened.

"Something . . . something flipped me out of the bed."

Owen looks at me, slits for eyes, before hurrying down the hall to her room. I hug her closer as she cries. I wave my arm to Janice, motioning her to move closer to me. She walks out of her room holding Mandy's hand.

Owen appears in the doorway and jerks his head, a clear indication he wants me to join him.

"Girls, go downstairs and sit in front of the TV for a bit. I'll be right down to make us a snack."

Charity clings to my arm, tear stricken and shaking.

"It's all right, sweetie. I'm just going to get you some blankets, and we'll camp out together tonight. Take your sisters downstairs, all right?"

I brush her hair out of her face, securing it behind her ear before wiping the tears off her face. She leads the way downstairs, slowly and cautiously, all the while blubbering like a toddler. I watch to ensure they make it safely before joining my husband.

Walking into Charity's room I see exactly what she meant. Her mattress is overturned onto the floor. She had literally been flung from her bed. I cross my arms over my chest protectively.

"Can you believe this?" Owen asks.

I shake my head as tears fall down my cheeks.

"I can't believe she'd pull a stunt like this."

My mouth drops as I turn to face him, watching him brush his hair back as he paces. His eyes are still slits, and his jaws are locked.

"You think she did this?"

Owen shrugs. "What else could have happened?"

I bite my cheek to keep myself from yelling. "You know what, Owen? I believe her. I believe that something flipped her out of her bed."

"What the hell are you talking about, Jennifer? What could have done that? It was a stunt by a rebellious teenager."

"That's not what it was!"

Owen takes a step toward me, hand outstretched, eyes softening. I tear my arm from his touch and take a step back.

"Believe what you want. I don't care, but I'm going to call our real estate agent in the morning. I want out of here."

He shakes his head. "We can't afford to move again."

"We'll have to figure out how we can afford it."

I grab Charity's blanket and leave him alone, only stopping to retrieve Mandy and Janice's blankets before joining the girls, who are busy watching late night comedy TV downstairs. I give them their blankets before fetching a pack of cookies and four cups of milk. Owen walks into the kitchen as I'm about to walk out with our tray of snacks.

"I'm sorry," he tells me. He leans against the doorframe and frowns. "If you want to move, we can, but I refuse to believe anything is happening here that doesn't have an explanation."

I cock my head. "Then how did she end up in the floor?"

"Maybe she rolled onto the edge of the bed and her mattress was hanging over the box spring."

Rolling my eyes, I push past him. "Whatever, Owen. Just go back to sleep."

I set the snack down on the coffee table in front of the girls, but none move to get a cookie except Mandy.

"Mommy, I don't want to live here anymore," Janice says.

"I know."

I watch my girls snuggle into their blankets, refusing to move. I need to get my family out of here. Whatever is here wants us gone, at all costs.

The next morning, I wake up late. So late that Owen has already left to work on his friend's deck. I sigh as I read the note he left me, telling me where to find him. At least he left me coffee.

Pouring myself a cup, I start on breakfast and try to call the real estate agent, only to get a recording instead. I should have known she isn't open on Sundays.

I've almost finished making pancakes when the power flickers before going out completely. My brows furrow with frustration. The power box is in the kitchen, so I pull it open and flip the main switch a few times. When nothing happens, I go through all the breakers, flipping each one twice, only to realize nothing is going to happen.

I peer out the front door to see my neighbors still have their porch light on, proving there isn't a power outage. I sent the check in, so there's no reason they would have shut us off.

The girls start waking up a few minutes later. Since the pancakes are only half done, I feed them cereal. They pick at their food more than they eat. After last night, none of us are too eager for talking or eating.

The day goes more smoothly than the day before, except with no electricity to cook. We escape the house at lunchtime, going for a walk down the street to McDonald's. Mandy and Janice love it; Charity and I are just glad to be out of the house.

Not until three o'clock is there more thumping upstairs. The girls are in the living room and I'm walking to the kitchen to get some water when we hear the pounding, even louder than the previous days. I stare up the stairs, just inches away, waiting for something to appear. The thumping continues but nothing makes its presence known.

Charity comes running into the hallway holding Mandy's hand, Janice hot on her heels.

"What is that?" Charity asks.

Mandy laughs. "Tat's just May pwaying. Her wikes to jump."

A cold shiver runs through me at her words. "You stay here," I tell them, rushing up the stairs, determined to catch something in the act.

I fling the door open and the banging ceases, revealing chaos. Dolls are strewn everywhere. Books are all over the floor, the beds are stripped, and the toybox is overturned. Mayhem has ensued and my family is in the middle of whatever war is going on in this house.

My throat closes when I look to the back of the room. A woman dressed in an old-styled black dress, hair wild around her face, slits for eyes, and mouth clamped so tightly her shut lips are barely visible stands in the midst of the chaos, staring at me. The hatred she casts burns through me, chilling me to the bone.

Too terrified to move, the blood drains from my face to my feet, which start to ache. My mouth trembles as it hangs open, no breath daring to come out. The woman opens her mouth, letting out a spine-tingling wail, which I've never heard before. She takes a step toward me, and it's more than I can take.

Slowly, so that I don't anger this woman more, I back out of the room into the hallway. My back touches the banister before I finally turn and dart down the stairs at full speed. I need to get out of here. I need to get my kids and get them out. I can come back for our things.

When I return, Mandy is in Charity's arms, clinging to her.

"Mommy, May's mommy is mad!"

I grab Janice's hand as I run for the door. I hold the door open and gently push my child out, ushering the other two to follow her.

"Get them to the car and call your dad. I have to get the keys," I tell Charity, whose eyes brim with tears. "No matter what happens or what he says, don't come back in."

Charity turns away and runs out the door with her sisters. I watch them make their way down the stairs before running to the living room for my keys, sitting where I left them on the mantel.

Just as I run into the room, a candle flies off the coffee table toward me. I jump back, barely dodging it. My breathing becomes rapid as I realize whatever resides here wants me dead. Every nerve in my body jumps.

I continue to run, but as I grab my keys, something hits me

in the back of the head, jerking my head forward into the mantle. Next thing I know I'm on my ass, struggling to stand up. The room spins as my vision starts turning black. My head throbs as I try to stand. I feel warm liquid running down my face, alerting me to the fact that I'm bleeding. I manage to make it to my feet, only slightly dizzy from my head injury.

Turning to the door, I see a shadow. A little girl with blonde hair like Mandy's, dressed in a yellow nightdress. She looks fine one second, but when I blink, she's covered in blood, and a chunk of her head is missing.

My mouth drops as I cry. This is how she died. Did her mother do it? Is that why they're both still here?

My blood goes cold when I realize she's blocking the exit. I can't get out of the house without passing through her.

My girls are waiting. I have to chance it. There's no other option than to run past her to get to my children. I need to get out of this house, or I could very well die here. Maybe it's just her mother that doesn't want us here.

"I'm so sorry," I cry, running full sprint toward her.

She doesn't move, just watches me. I speed past her into the hall and swing the door wide before racing outside. I jump down the porch stairs before I chance a look back to my house.

The woman from upstairs is now standing right inside the house, peering out the glass in the door. She looks just as ragged and angry, but now her lips are turned up into a sneer that makes my heart pound out of my chest. I cover my mouth to keep myself from screaming out.

I feel strong arms around me, trying to pull me up, and I scream.

"Hey! Calm down!" I hear Owen instruct.

I stop struggling, replacing my screaming with sobbing.

"What happened to you?"

His face comes in and out of focus as I squint through my hair and the blood. His eyes are narrow, and his jaw is tight. He looks from me to the house then back to the car.

"Please don't take me back in there!"

"I won't," he tells me, kissing the top of my head.

He pulls me close to his chest, and I let him lead me, feeling a weight of anger and sadness fall from me. I see bits and pieces of my children's horrified expressions as he wheels me toward the car. I can't suppress my smile, overjoyed that they've made it out safely, and none of us have to go back. Owen helps me into the passenger seat and shuts the door behind me.

I take one last look at the house that almost killed me. No woman is standing in the doorway anymore, so it looks like a normal house. The house I fell in love with. Someone would never guess that something this horrific could happen, just from moving into a house.

I try to tell myself it's over as I take a deep breath and let it out, but when I look back at my children, I can swear I see a wisp of blonde on both sides of Charity. I wipe my eyes to see better, and the second blonde shadow is gone.

I take another deep breath and repeat my silent chant. *It's over; we're safe. It's over; we're safe.*

I hear the sweet singsong voice of Mandy, her words making me shiver. "How come May doesn't have to wear a seat belt, Mommy?"

Donise Sheppard is a fiction writer born in Ohio but residing in southern West Virginia with her husband and four children. She is self-published on Amazon. "Coal Run Road" is her first published short story, and she plans to write many more. Even though she is deathly afraid of heights, her house is planted halfway up a mountain. When she isn't writing, she's reading, baking, or chasing her rambunctious children. Follow her on Twitter: @donise_sheppard and on Facebook: facebook.com/authordonisesheppard.

I'm Not Sure What It Means

Ricardo Anthonio

Mommy and Daddy don't like me very much. Not like they like my brother. I understand that because he's so cool. He goes to school, and sometimes when I go with him he cycles very fast. I think he's the fastest in the world. I'm not very cool. I really like sleeping on the big couch. Sometimes my brother sits on me when I'm sleeping, that's also not cool.

Daddy isn't home much, but when my brother gets home from school, Mommy always asks him if he had fun in school and makes him tea. He likes it with milk. When Daddy gets home in the evening, he sits on the big couch, and Mommy brings him dinner and then he watches TV with my brother. I like falling asleep next to them because I get really tired at night.

Grandma always drinks tea with milk too. Grandpa told me she drinks milk with tea, but I'm not sure what that means. It's the same. He says a lot I don't understand. Grandpa is always very nice to me, so I like talking with him. He has a big nose and a lot of wrinkles that wiggle when he laughs.

Mommy and Daddy only talk about my brother with Grandma. And sometimes about Daddy's work. He works with "human ray sauces," but I'm not sure what it means. Grandma's house is full of pictures of Grandpa and Grandma when they were young.

It was my brother's birthday yesterday, and Mommy baked him a cake. It was very pretty and had seven candles. I counted them myself. I can count to ten already. Grandpa said he is very proud of me. Then my brother's friends came over, and they played board games and hide and seek. I helped my brother look.

When my brother has his birthday, I have mine too, a few days later. I wonder if I get a cake. I didn't get any cake last year, so that's why I think Mommy doesn't like me. We don't go for a long walk to the park on my brother's birthday. Only on my birthday, so that is just for me. There are lots of trees and flowers and big, pretty stones. It's my favorite place. Maybe the beach too, but I have only been there once with Grandpa. Oliver likes the long walk and the park a lot.

I don't think Oliver likes me a lot. I'm a little scared of him sometimes. He always growls at me when I pet his back. But he wags his tail when he looks at me, and Grandpa told me it's a sign of affection, but I'm not sure what it means.

He has blonde hair just like Mommy, Oliver. And very brown eyes like Daddy and my brother. He loves his blue spikey ball, and when Daddy throws it, he brings it back to Daddy. Daddy is very brave and isn't scared of Oliver. He growls very loud when Daddy tries to take the spikey ball from his mouth. Sometimes you can see the teeth. They look like white crayons.

— · · —

Today is my birthday, I think. My brother isn't going to school, and Daddy is also home. Mommy is making sandwiches and packing a bag, and Grandma and Grandpa are here too. Grandpa asked if I had a birthday wish, and I told him I want to grow up as pretty as Mommy. He said I already looked as beautiful as her and "as-teht-ecks" are not very important, but I'm not sure what it means.

Everyone is going outside to the car now. The car is very big, and I sit in the backseat on Grandpa's lap next to my brother and Grandma. Mommy and Daddy are in the front. Oliver goes in the boot, and he has his blue spikey ball. Driving to the park is boring. I like to take a nap in the car. I always wake up when we get there.

Grandma complains about her leg. We walked for a very long time. I don't think we could have stayed in the car because the paths in the park are too small for the car. We always sit in the same spot, which is next to a big stone with beautiful letters on it. I can't read yet, but next year I'm going to learn.

Mommy looks sad and Daddy hugs her. I don't think they like my birthday as much as they like my brother's birthday. They always sing when my brother has his birthday. I got a candle too—only one—but it's way bigger than my brother's candles. His were more like pencils, and mine is really big.

That makes me feel happy.

I sit down on the stone with Grandpa and play with the flower petals. My hand touches the beautiful letters on the stone, and I ask Grandpa what they say. He says they spell out my name, Amelia, and: "Our Darling Angel Born Sleeping."

I'm not sure what it means, but I guess it explains why I like sleeping.

After climbing out of the cocaine-fueled trenches of direct-response copywriting for multi-million-dollar businesses, ranging from weight-loss pills, organic condoms, and forex brokers, **Ricardo Anthonio**, though only 28, finally settled down. Today he writes for fun, not profit. His stories are short and powerful, an inherited trait from writing in advertising, with a dark twist. Ricardo Anthonio writes stories to reflect on and, more often than not, covered in a thick, thick layer of existentialism and self-loathing.

Fighting Sleep

F.A. Fisher

Ross watched Dad push and slide the large box past his bedroom. Mom, her belly bulging, followed with a small mattress wrapped in plastic. Frowning, Ross followed them into the nursery.

Dad looked at him, smiled, and tousled his hair. "It's the new crib, fella. I picked it up on the way home." He brushed melting snowflakes off the box.

"I liked the old one."

"You haven't even seen this one yet. Besides, it's not for you. It's for your little brother."

Mom said, "We don't know—"

"The way that baby kicks? Exactly like Ross. It's got to be a boy. Anyway, Ross, you remember we sold the other crib at the garage sale? That crib was old. Your mom slept in it. They make them a lot safer these days, and now we can afford a new one."

That didn't make Ross feel any better. How could adults know so much, but sense so little? He could tell, with the box still unopened, that the old crib had been safer than this one. But he knew, too, what would happen if he tried to say it. They'd think he wondered why they hadn't given *him* a safe crib.

He'd turned four and a half before Christmas, and still they never paid any attention when he tried to tell them something important. Like when he told them about the bad string of Christmas lights. They just laughed and rubbed his hair, and were amazed later when the tree caught fire, as if it had been coincidence.

In frustration, he left the room and stomped down the steps into the den, where he pulled out the Scrabble board and made patterns with the tiles by the light from the fireplace.

While he played, bangings and scrapings and angry complaints drifted down the stairs to him. A couple of times he heard words his father rarely used. That crib was a bad one, for sure. Dad must realize it by now, from the sound of things, but that didn't matter.

Dad was stubborn. He wouldn't admit it, and it never helped to tell him. Dad always replied that Ross was the stubborn one, or Mom, or whoever tried to talk him out of his stubbornness.

It must have taken much longer to put the crib together than Dad expected because Mom called him three or four times to come down for supper before she served Ross and herself without him. But eventually he came downstairs, and while he put away the tools and washed his hands and bandaged his little finger where the crib had nipped him, Ross climbed the stairs and peeked into the nursery.

The crib, all white, sat with its head against the far wall. It looked innocent enough. That didn't surprise him; most things looked innocent in bright light. He could smell its vileness though, and he knew how the crib would look with the lights off, sweating cold evil like a glass of iced lemonade sweats water. He imagined the beads collecting and dripping down into the carpet, then evaporating, filling the room with their stench.

"It stinks," he said when he went back downstairs.

"That's a new smell," Mom said. "It'll go away in a few days or a week."

"I don't like it."

His mother laughed. "Ross, you're exactly like your father."

Ross frowned, unsure what she meant. Dad frowned as well. Ross shook his head and went back to play with the Scrabble board.

— • • —

He woke in the night, alone in his room. The evil smell of the crib had reached to where he slept.

He climbed out of his bed and went again to the nursery. The door had almost closed—it did that on its own—but he pushed it open and peeked in. The crib still sat against the far wall. He took a few hesitant steps into the room. In the moonlight, the crib cast shadows on the wall like the bars of a dungeon.

Ross knew what caused shadows; they didn't frighten him.

What made his heart trip and his breath wheeze like a dying man's was the crib itself, revealed now in the semi-darkness; the ends of it, their outlines curved like broad-shouldered ghosts; the spindly legs, like human bones; but most of all, the white slats in the side, like long teeth, revealed in a ghastly smile that said, *I see you. I know you're there. And I'm very, very hungry.*

Ross stared at the crib, petrified. How could they leave him alone in bed with this thing one room away?

The crib moved.

Ross hollered and turned, but the door had nearly closed again, and he bumped into it, closing it tight. In his panic, the knob slipped in his hands, and he knew that the crib rolled closer to him on its new, silent wheels, but he didn't dare turn to look, and at last, the knob turned, and he pulled the door open and dashed down the hall and into his parents' room, crying and yelling and Mom asking, "What's wrong?" until Dad shouted, "This is ridiculous!"

"But the crib was after me!" Ross said. He tried to keep his voice calm because they always complained when it grew loud, but it slipped out of his control, like the doorknob had slipped in his hands.

Dad grabbed Ross around the waist with one arm in the way he didn't like, carried him back to the nursery, and flicked on the light. Ross could hear Mom padding heavily behind. The crib still sat where they'd placed it, its evil hidden again by the light. The wheel tracks from positioning it showed in the carpet, but no others.

"Well? You said it chased you?"

He *thought* it had chased him, but he'd been too intent on opening the door to look.

"I saw it jiggle. I thought it was going to come after me."

"Then how could you say it actually came after you?"

"Oh Frank, you don't need to cross-examine him like one of your witnesses. Maybe you didn't tighten something all the way and it shifted a little bit. That could seem frightening enough in the middle of the night."

"Everything was tight, all right. I made sure of it." Dad was acting stubborn again.

Ross saw Mom squeeze her lips, but she merely said, "He could've had a dream. Don't be so hard on him."

Dad looked at Ross and relaxed a bit. "Maybe so. You probably dreamed it, fella. See how the crib didn't move at all?"

"Frank, that won't do any good. He can't tell the difference between dreams and waking yet. Leave it be."

But Mom was wrong. He could tell. The crib had moved. No good saying it though.

So when they left Ross alone in his own room and turned out the light, he waited a very long time, listening for the crib. When he decided his parents had gone to sleep, he grabbed his pillow and blanket and dragged them downstairs to the couch. If that crib tried to follow him down the steps, it would at least make enough noise to wake everyone up.

The next morning, he measured the width of the crib with his plastic pirate's sword and figured that it wouldn't fit through the nursery door. After that he slept better, until three weeks later when his parents woke him in the middle of the night during a gentle snowfall because the time had come to go to the birth center.

— • • —

Grandma held Ross so that he could watch the birthing.

"It's a girl," she said.

"A . . . girl," Dad repeated.

A girl? He had a sister? But Dad had acted so sure. Two days before, Dad showed Ross the little boy's outfit he'd bought to surprise Mom.

"Let me hold her." Funny, Mom didn't sound surprised at all. Just tired.

"Lie back here," the midwife said. "That's good. Now let her rest on your stomach for a moment."

Grandma set Ross down, and he heard Dad mutter, "I knew we should've done an ultrasound."

The midwife put a clamp on the cord and handed a pair of surgical scissors to Dad. Dad put the scissors into Ross's hands and guided them toward the place on the cord indicated by the midwife. Ross had practiced for this when no one watched, making ropes of Play-Doh and cutting them with his scissors. Of course, these scissors looked much sharper, with long dangerous points.

"Right here," the midwife said.

Ross squeezed but the cord didn't cut like Play-Doh. It possessed a toughness that resisted the sharp scissors. He gave an extra hard squeeze. The scissors cut through, and the baby was free, a separate person at last. She looked all purple with her little nose bent to one side and blood and sticky stuff in her sparse hair and all over her, and howling as if fit to be tied.

Poor thing, Ross thought. *She'll need loads of help. She can't do* anything *by herself.*

And in that moment Ross fell in love with her.

Grandma shook her head. "I can't get over it. In my day, they wouldn't have let children anywhere near this. The husband either, for that matter."

"Or the grandmother," said the midwife, laughing. "What will you name her?"

"Good Lord," Dad said, "we never considered girls' names. We—"

"Anne Louise," Mom said.

And that pretty much finished it, from Ross's point of view. He fell asleep on the couch in the lounge until noon, when, the snow having long since stopped, Dad loaded up the car, with Anne in her car seat in back with Ross. He'd be able to watch her all the way home.

Grandma slid into her own car. "I can't get over it. In my day, she'd have stayed in the hospital a full week."

"Well, that's why we came here instead of the hospital across the street." Dad sounded annoyed.

That puzzled Ross. Grandma had made a cheerful observation, not a criticism. If adults couldn't understand each other, how could he expect them to understand him?

The rest of the day passed in a blur. Dad stayed home and went out with Ross to build a snowman, but for the most part, Ross found himself alone more often than when he and Mom were the only two people in the house. His parents let him stay outside as long as he wanted, until so much cold leaked into his boots that he couldn't stand it.

Inside, Anne did nothing but sleep on shoulders, cry a lot, nurse, and nap with Mom. Whenever Ross tried to help, they told him not to get so close, or to wash his hands, or just to be more careful. He began to grow annoyed with his parents. They kept all the caretaking to themselves.

Grandma brought supper over, and soon bedtime came. Dad read him a story and turned out the light. Ross felt exhausted in spite of sleeping through the morning. Only the crying of the baby downstairs and his parents' arguing about how to make her stop kept him awake.

At last the crying stopped. A minute later, he heard Mom and Dad tiptoe past his room. He crept from his bed in alarm and followed them to the nursery in time to see Mom lay Anne in the crib and pull the little quilted coverlet that Grandma had made over her.

"No!" He'd forgotten, till now, why they'd purchased the crib in the first place.

"*Shh!*" Dad said.

"But don't put the baby in the crib, please!"

Dad's face grew scarlet. "If she wakes up, I'll, I'll, I'll do *something* you won't like, believe me!"

"Frank, keep your voice down."

Dad glared at Mom, but she ignored him and pulled up the

side of the crib. It locked in place with a *SNICK!* Anne didn't move. Ross relaxed a little bit when Dad turned on the baby monitor. At least if anything noisy happened, his parents would hear it. Ross wished that they'd put the monitor there weeks earlier. He'd have slept better.

Of course, sleeping tonight was out of the question. He didn't know the crib's abilities, but it wouldn't surprise him if it could act silently. If his parents wouldn't protect his little sister, he would do it himself, in spite of them.

And for now, that meant going back to his bedroom.

—— • • ——

Ross started, horrified, aware that he must have gone to sleep. But maybe only for a little while. He heard no sounds, so his parents were probably in bed. He crawled from the bed and slipped down the hallway to the nursery. He listened.

Silence.

That didn't reassure him. He pushed open the door and looked wide-eyed in the darkness at the crib. Somehow it seemed different. Of course, it held the baby, but something else . . . the shape seemed twisted . . .

No. The mattress lay on a slant. One side had dropped a notch. Ross moved to the foot of the crib and peered through the slats, over the bumper guard. Anne had rolled over and lay with her face buried in the coverlet, where it had bunched up against the bumper guard.

Ross had never touched the crib in the past, but he didn't think twice about it now. He moved to the side where Anne was. He could probably reach through the slats and push Anne away, but he had to get her *out*, and he could reach her best where she was. So he climbed up the side and leaned over the rail. Then he balanced on his stomach and reached down with his hands.

His fingertips had barely touched Anne's form when the railing beneath him dropped faster than he could fall, so that for a moment, he seemed to hang motionless. Then he plunged. The railing shot back up, smashed into his stomach, and threw him into the air. He landed on his back.

His parents burst into the room five seconds later. Dad almost stepped on Ross in the dark before Mom turned on the overhead light from the doorway.

"What the hell is going on here?"

Ross lay on his back and clutched his stomach. Tears streamed from his eyes. He couldn't say a word. They wouldn't listen anyway.

"Oh my God!" Mom ran to the crib. "Look at her!" She dropped the rail and pulled the baby out. "Frank, her lips are purple."

"Is she breathing?"

"I can't tell—"

"Here, give her to me."

"You can't tell any better than I can."

"Sure I can. Now—"

Anne's face scrunched up, and she let out a cry that startled everyone.

"Thank God." Mom held the squalling infant close to her chest and looked at the crib. "How did that mattress get tilted?"

Both his parents turned to look at Ross.

"I—didn't—do—it," he managed to gasp.

"The baby could have *died*," Mom said. "Do you realize that?"

"Why did you climb in there anyway?"

Ross lay on the floor and gasped lungfuls of air against the receding pain in his stomach.

Dad turned from him to straighten the mattress while Mom sat on top of the toy chest to nurse the crying infant. Dad reached for the hooks on both ends of the frame, lifted the frame a bit, pressed the hooks—they were four feet apart, and he needed to press both at once—then lifted the frame to the top level. When he released the hooks, they popped out and caught in their slots.

"Frank?"

"What?"

"How . . .?" Mom stopped.

"Well?"

"How could Ross have done that?"

Dad frowned, then flushed. "Are you saying I didn't hook it right? It still wouldn't have slipped if he hadn't crawled on it."

"That's not what I meant. I wondered if it could be defective. Could it happen again?"

Dad rattled the mattress frame. "No."

"Yes," Ross said from the floor. He felt a little sick, but he had his wind back. "It could." No harm trying once more.

"Not if you don't climb on it again."

"The crib did it itself."

Dad reddened further. "It's tight now. It won't happen unless somebody makes it happen."

Ross sat up painfully. *No point arguing*, he thought. *Dad doesn't even hear me. He thinks I'm saying that it's his fault. He thinks it is his fault. Well, maybe he's right. But only because he won't listen.*

Anne had fallen asleep again.

Mom said, "Ross, are you all right?"

He nodded.

"Maybe we've protected Anne too much. Maybe tomorrow we can let you hold her on your lap. I'm glad you want to, believe me. But you mustn't climb into the crib to sleep with her. Okay?"

He nodded again. Did they really think he wanted to sleep in that crib? Sleep came in two types, and that crib was chock full of the wrong kind.

"But now it's time for all of us to return to bed," she finished.

He nodded, momentarily defeated.

Back in his room, Ross put his pillow against the headboard and waited for the house to grow quiet. That crib didn't scare him now as much as it used to. He'd seen that it couldn't eat him. It didn't eat Anne. It could only move its mattress frame and side rails;

Dad really had screwed the rest together tightly. It couldn't hurt Ross unless he climbed on it, and it couldn't hurt Anne unless she lay in it.

Which she did. So he needed to get her out, and without Mom or Dad knowing or they'd put her back. He could stay quiet enough not to alert them, if he waited until they fell asleep. He wondered how long the crib needed to act.

Minutes passed. He slipped from bed and tiptoed down the hall, and when he peeked in the nursery, a glowing red eye shone from where the monitor sat on the toy chest.

That monitor would have to go.

He knew how it worked. His parents had let him play with it long after they no longer used it for him. If he unplugged it from the wall or turned it off, a burst of static would hiss from the receiver in his parents' room. But if he just unplugged the power jack, the battery inside would take over.

Ross walked softly, silently into the room—not like his parents, whose heavy bodies made the floor creak with every step. He noticed right off that the mattress had tilted again. The crib probably knew a limited number of tricks. But how long had it been that way? Anne must have slid less easily this time because the side of the mattress had dropped two notches instead of one. But the second notch had done the trick and Anne lay smothering.

Or smothered.

He almost called for help, but they'd just blame him again. Maybe lock him in his room this time. The thought made his throat tighten, but he didn't start to cry. Too much noise. He couldn't do *anything* until the monitor was out. He stepped to it and, trying to keep the touch of his hands on the monitor from making any sound, unplugged the jack. When the jack came out, the red light flickered, but only for a moment.

He lifted the monitor, carried it to the bathroom, and set it without a sound on the soft bathmat. Then he left the bathroom, and gently, though it strained his patience, he closed the bathroom door. Things would stay quiet enough in there.

Back to the nursery.

He looked at the crib. Both side rails could move. He needed to get in over the tall foot of the crib, but he was too short to climb over it. A folding chair sat beside the door. He turned it around, grabbed the top, tipped it, and began to pull it backward toward the crib. On his first step, the back legs of the chair caught the carpet, and it folded with a muted *CLANK!* and a whining hiss.

It took a fraction of a second for Ross to realize that the chair couldn't hiss.

He looked over his shoulder and saw smoke rise from the carpet where the crib's wheels touched it. The wheels spun furiously until they caught, and the entire crib hurtled toward him at breakneck speed. He let go of the chair and jumped sideways.

The crib twisted to follow him, but its momentum caused it to overbalance and careen broadside into the falling chair. The top of the chair drove through the slats and splintered them. For a moment, the crib and chair leaned against and into each other, with the top of the chair inside the crib, trapping Anne. Then the crib's broken slats slid down the chair, pushing the chair upright and then over. The crib landed on its side, and the folding chair fell over backward onto the carpet. The crib's wheels whirled uselessly.

"Mom! Dad!" No point keeping quiet now.

But then Ross realized that his voice wouldn't come over the monitor. They'd think he was shouting from his own room, and that's where they'd go first. He'd only slowed them down. And Anne needed help instantly. She still lay limp, her face still buried in the coverlet.

He bent down to reach for her, and the broken slats stood up, like stakes in the bottom of a pit, a picket line between him and Anne. They waved slightly—fingers ready to snatch him, fangs eager to bite.

He stretched his arms straight out, let himself fall forward, and stopped himself against the mattress. The splintered slats strained to reach him, but he had a good two-inch clearance. He reached down with one hand and grabbed Anne, but she was too heavy; he couldn't lift her from his awkward position. He pulled at the coverlet instead, but the room lights came on, startling him. At almost the same moment, the top edge of the mattress pulled back another notch, tipping him forward. The rail on the floor kicked out and knocked his feet from beneath him.

He fell. One of the fanglike slats pierced his chest while another angled to intercept his eye.

A sharp tug stopped his motion. The splintered slat remained an inch away from his eye. He rose into the air, lifted by his pajamas, and the slat in his chest pulled free, having penetrated a mere half inch. Drops of blood fell down onto the slat and soaked right in.

Dad held him. Ross looked up, blinking in the bright room light. Dad changed his grip to hold Ross in his arms but continued to stare at the crib in disbelief.

"I saw it," he muttered. "It really moved."

"Get Anne, Dad."

The direction of Dad's gaze changed at the same time as his expression. He set Ross down and reached over the broken slats to retrieve Anne, who looked almost as purple as at her birth. Without bothering to check if she breathed, he covered her nose and mouth with his own mouth and began to puff air into her tiny lungs.

A step sounded in the doorway behind them.

"Did it come from here after all, Frank? Why didn't the monitor . . . oh my *God*." Mom's voice rose almost out of control before she caught it. Then, swallowing: "Ross, what have you done?"

Dad placed his ear near Anne's mouth and nose and felt for a pulse in her upper arm.

"He didn't do anything wrong. See to his chest, will you?"

"But—"

"Anne'll be all right, she's breathing on her own, and her heart's still going. But Ross is bleeding. If there's any splinters of wood in there, get them out. No, never mind; you take Anne, she'll want you in a minute anyway. But call me right away if her breathing stops." And to Ross as he carried him to the bathroom: "You're a hero today, son. I won't forget it, ever."

Before going to bed, Dad let Ross tell him the whole story, and this time, Ross could tell, he listened. They went back to the nursery, and Dad examined the spots on the carpet where the crib's spinning wheels had melted the fibers. He moved back to stare at the crib. In sudden anger, he kicked the overthrown crib, and all four wheels started to whirl.

He backed away and said, "Let's get out of here."

When they'd left the room, he closed and locked the door.

The next day, Dad took his tools to the nursery, along with a hatchet. And that evening, after the fire in the fireplace got good and hot, he and Ross threw bits of crib into the flames and listened to the faint whistles and screams of their burning.

The course of **F. A. Fisher**'s life was determined in utero, when he was introduced to science fiction and fantasy by way of his mother's reading of *The Chronicles of Narnia* to his older sister. Though he grew up among the first generation where television was commonplace, his contrary nature meant that he spent most of his time reading. That contrariness continued in college, where he ignored his adviser and chose an area major, which allowed him to take whatever he wanted, with the result that his degree didn't prepare him for any job whatsoever—except perhaps writing. He was raised in an era without computers or even hand calculators, so naturally he got a master's degree in Computer Science. And though he loved learning, he always hated school, so of course he got his second master's in Education. He'd wanted to become a writer from an early age, so it followed that he went through several other jobs, including two self-start companies, before putting out his first book. Somewhere along the way, he developed a deep and abiding hatred for typos. Fortunately, by this time, his contrariness has abated, so if you find a typo in any of his books, let him know and he'll fix it. His books so far are *Cloaks* and its sequel, *Pandir Decloaked*. A third, final *Cloaks* book is in the works.

SUBWAY
Objects
in
Motion
Suanne Kim

The sign read:

Caution!
***STAND BEHIND** the yellow line*
***DO NOT** throw garbage onto the tracks*
***DO NOT** jump onto the tracks*

More than one moron must have done it. Okay, a bunch of morons. Because it takes more than a single incident for actuaries to calculate the risk of danger versus the cost of production and labor to install the signs at every station. Percentage of population. Chances of fatality. Average payout of lawsuits. It's all a numbers game, all about risk pools. And we're all swimming in someone else's piss-filled pond.

The day I met Mattie, the sign loomed behind her. She was leaning against a pillar across the platform waiting for a Queens-bound train while I hung around for one bearing uptown. She bobbed her head to whatever music played in her earbuds. Dressed in a kaleidoscope of colors and patterns, army jacket and boots, she embodied the quintessential quirky New Yorker. Cute didn't begin to describe her.

It was the first time I'd been back to the Rockefeller Center subway station in four years. I'd changed careers since then and just started at a brokerage firm in Midtown. Day one on the job, I stayed until eleven o'clock to quell my nerves and prove myself. When it came to my work, I'd developed a necessity to conquer everything, dispel any unknown factors, mitigate the variables. What I craved was a lay of the land and solid footing.

I opened my book and pretended to read while I stole glances her way. Something about her looked familiar—the soft curve of her lips, the strong cut of her cheekbones, the mischievous arch of her brows. I just couldn't place where I'd seen her before.

As the music strummed through her, the rest of her body followed suit. Her subtle curves swayed in sultry undulation, and this petite Asian girl came alive before me. Carefree, eyes closed in bliss, she danced and tuned out the world. My needle jumped to her frequency. I amended my original assessment. Screw cute. She was hot.

Clanking rang out from the black mouth of the tunnel and rumbling vibrated under my feet. It signaled the close of my window of opportunity. I'd been out of the dating game for so long, I needed a running start, time to build up my courage to approach her. After all, you can't just go up to a girl and say, *Hey, there. I feel like I've known you forever. By the way, what's your name?*

A disheveled drunk attempted to read the sign. "Do n-n-not..." He stumbled toward the edge to get a better glimpse, his steps as sloppy as his speech.

His proximity to her unnerved me. I closed my book and stepped closer. He tripped on the warning bumps embedded in the yellow strip. Arms flailing, he grabbed at her for balance as the train barreled into the station. Hurling the book aside, I bolted and wrenched them back from the brink just as the nose of the train whizzed by.

"Don't t-touch me!" The drunk staggered away.

No apologies. No remorse. Ungrateful prick.

"Holy shit!" She clutched her chest and sank to the floor, her breaths erratic.

I knelt beside her. "You all right?"

"I think so."

I rifled through my messenger-styled bag and held out a bottle of water. Understandably, she viewed it with caution.

"Brand new." To prove it, I cracked it open and took a swig without touching the rim. "Here."

"Thanks." She gulped down half the bottle. Color returned to her cheeks. "For a second I saw myself in tomorrow's paper. *Girl Plunges to Death at Rockefeller Center.*"

"It could have been worse." Jesus. I wasn't merely out of practice, I was clueless.

"Maybe you're right." In spite of everything, she smirked. "This could've happened at Queensboro Plaza. I hate heights."

She had a sense of humor. Oh, I really liked her.

"Was that your train?"

She glanced up as the *M* train pulled out and shook her head. She must have been waiting for the *F*.

"Want to move to the middle? It'll be safer." I stretched out a hand, which she declined.

"I got it." She crawled a few steps toward the center of the platform before hoisting herself up.

However strong she pretended to be, she was obviously still shaken. Her vulnerability endeared her to me even more.

I blathered to fill the silence with more of my winning charm. "You know, about fifty people are struck and die every year. Considering there are over eight million people in New York, I'd say it's a pretty unique way to go. Anyone can get hit by a car."

"Is that a twisted way of saying I'm special? Or that I'd be lucky to get hit by a train?" Rather than derision or annoyance, she displayed amusement.

Someone who wasn't easily offended? A sharp wit? I was in serious trouble.

"Uh, no. Sorry. That's just my inner geek talking. Don't listen to him."

"Aren't you a fount of interesting facts? How do you know so much? You work for the MTA or something?"

I blanched. "God, no. Never. I'm a financial analyst. Numbers. That's kind of my thing."

"So you make money."

"Mostly I make other people money. But I don't work the front office. I work the backend, creating financial models. I design algorithms to predict which stocks will yield the highest dividends."

"You kiss your mother with that mouth?" Her smile electrified with all the voltage of a third rail.

Damn. She was killing it, killing me. Love. Definitely.

Emboldened, I threw out a challenge. "I could talk dirty if you really want."

She threw down a gauntlet of her own. "Well, don't feel you have to hold back now."

I tacked on spunky to her list of attributes. This night was getting better and better, as was my confidence and my game. "All right. Don't say I didn't warn you."

"Go ahead. Hit me."

I affected the deepest, sexiest voice I could muster. "Pivot tables. Macros. V-lookups—"

She laughed, held up her hands in surrender. "Stop, stop. I give. That's way too kinky for me. Freak."

"Hey, I was just getting warmed up."

She noticed the book on the ground. "That yours?" She sauntered over and dusted the dirt off the cover. "*The Power of Now: A Guide to Spiritual Enlightenment.* Very deep."

"What? I'm not a Neanderthal."

"I never said you were. Just figured you for a Clancy or Crichton fan. I didn't expect a suit to be reading a self-help book."

"I'm going to take that as a compliment."

Her voice unfurled like smoke in an old jazz bar. "And so you should."

When she handed me the book, her skin was a feathery brush against mine. She shot another high-wattage smile, which sent me reeling. The hardcover weighed an astronomical hundred pounds, and I nearly dropped it. I was gone. So, so gone.

"Okay, your turn. What were you listening to when you did your little dance?"

"Little dance?" She cocked a brow. "You were watching me?"

"This is a public place. I'm a guy. What'd you expect?"

Her eyes shone with mischief. "I'd tell you but then I'd have to—"

"Kill me?"

"Hell, no. Nothing as clichéd as that. I'd have to straddle your face to shut you up."

Heat shot through my body. Her slightest caress would have been a match setting me ablaze. I loosened my tie. The top button of my shirt popped off in my haste to unfasten it. Just when I thought I understood her, she launched a bomb and proved inscrutable. Pinning her down was going to be like grasping a missile. And just as dangerous.

She chuckled and passed back the bottle. "You look like you could use a drink. I was just kidding, you know."

"I know. But you, uh. . ." I expelled a deep breath. ". . . do have a way with words."

"So people tell me. I should really come with a warning label."

"You should come with an instruction manual."

"I'm not that bad. Usually. Every once in a while, I'll do something outrageous. Makes me feel alive. Bet your book doesn't cover that."

"Uh, no. Not like that anyway."

"Here." She handed me an earbud and tapped on her phone.

We huddled close and our arms pressed together. My heat index spiked again. It was turning out to be the best night ever.

The song caught me off guard. It wasn't at all what I expected. Of course, neither was she.

Linked together by a sliver of wire, we listened to Cypress Hill's "Insane in the Brain." Despite the crazy lyrics, the riff and beat were catchy. The feverish screeches punctuated the melody. Our bodies grooved in tandem.

She angled her face to mine, her breath a soft, warm graze across my jaw. "Good, right?"

The scent of pomegranate wafted up with her every movement.

My mind whirled with visions of her writhing above me—hair tossed back, the surge of her hips, the thrust of her breasts, what my name sounded like in her mouth. Sweet mother of God, yes. So, so good.

She brought my fantasies to an abrupt halt when she killed the music. "I'm cutting the soundtrack for a short I'm working on. What do you think?"

I covered my groin with my bag and cleared my throat. "You produce music?"

"Films."

"You're a director?"

"Director, producer, writer, gaffer. And whatever else I need to be. I'm a film major at NYU."

A light bulb clicked on. "That's why you look familiar. You're an actress."

"Nope. Strictly behind the scenes. When it comes to my art, I'm too much of a control freak. I prefer calling the shots."

"Somehow that doesn't surprise me." And good to know we shared a common work ethic.

She poked me with an elbow, a positive sign. Playful contact ranked high in flirtation. That much I recalled from my previous life as a serial dater.

"So, can I get your autograph before you hit it big?"

Her eyes narrowed, clearly debating whether to entrust me inside her inner realm. "That sounds suspiciously like you're fishing for information."

"I'm only asking for your name. Not anything personal, like your social security number. Or, you know, your astrological sign. Think of it as a reward for saving your life."

"Wow. Lay the guilt trip. If you wanted to see me again, you could have just asked." If she only knew how much I wanted to see her again. And again and again.

"I thought I just did."

A minute of exquisite silence passed between us where we

simply grinned at each other like awkward, giddy teens. How was it possible that she could tether me to the ground and at the same time make me float?

A train sounded in the distance. We both knew what that meant.

"You might catch me this time tomorrow."

Another good indication. I wiggled my brows. "I'll bring two bottles of water."

"*O-o-oh*. Big spender."

The train drew closer. She still hadn't divulged her name, and time was running out. Either she was forgetful or the mistress of deflection.

"I'm Miles. What's your name?"

Her hesitation made my chest ache. Had I read the signs all wrong? Everything seemed to be going so well.

As the *F* train pulled in, her hair whorled around her, creating a wispy black halo, like the kind from static electricity. Her body hummed with life. Her radiant eyes emitted an energy that charged every molecule of my being. My skin crackled with excitement.

A variation of this image flashed before me. Her long strands of hair flying wildly around her, but this time, her head whips in my direction. Her catlike eyes widen in astonishment, in alarm. Her red mouth snaps open like an aperture.

Déjà vu, they call it. Some think it's a sign of having been there before, perhaps in another life. I believe it's the universe signaling your destiny or giving you a second chance.

"See you tomorrow." A hint of a smile touched the corners of her lips. "Maybe."

Without even so much as a backward glance, she boarded the train.

Dammit. Obviously, I was rusty.

Just as the doors slid shut, she shouted between the crack. "Mattie!"

The instant she left my sight, I did a post-goal happy dance.

Yes! Mattie. Mattie the Luminous. Mattie the Hottie. Smart Mattie. Funny Mattie. The first girl to capture my interest in years.

The next day, I was a man on a mission. I scoured the aisles at the Fifth Avenue Barnes & Noble, searching for the perfect book; something unexpected, strange, or cerebral. Anything to amuse or impress her. I couldn't decide between *The Manly Art of Knitting*, *The Sex Lives of Cannibals*, or *The Odyssey*. I bought them all.

Even before I saw her, I knew instinctively where she would be. Once again, her lithe body swiveled to music. The vision of her scrambled my brain and I blanked. All the clever lines I'd concocted and practiced at work vanished. I hid behind a column to enjoy the spectacle before I strolled over, toting bottles in hand and a big grin on my face.

"As promised. You have a choice of water. Or water."

She gawked at me as if I were a weirdo.

"It's me. Miles."

"That's nice." She turned up the volume and turned her back to me.

I tugged her sleeve. "Mattie, what's up?"

"What the hell?" She jerked away with such force, she lost her balance and tipped backward toward the tracks.

I yanked her back and caught her in my arms. "Looks like I saved you again."

She shoved me away, stripping the earbuds off. Her eyes flared with disbelief. "It's your fault I almost fell in!"

I wasn't expecting us to elope and have kids, but I couldn't comprehend her iciness.

"I'm just trying to talk to you. What's wrong?"

A guy came up to us. "Hey, man, you okay?"

My tone teetered between irritation and hostility. "We're just talking. Everything's cool."

What did he think I was doing to her?

He eyed me with skepticism. I glared back and he moved on.

"Look, I'm sorry. I didn't mean to scare you. I just don't get why you're pissed at me. Last time we were talking and laughing and then today—"

"Last time?" She was incredulous. "I don't even know you."

Had the rules of engagement changed that much in four years?

"Are you serious?"

"I don't know. Is pepper spray serious? Leave or I'm calling the cops."

After what we'd shared last night, was she just going to blow me off? Or was this part of her *outrageous* living? I pictured my own headline: *Chump Pulverized by Stupidity.*

"Suddenly you've developed amnesia? Neat trick. Does it come with a toy?"

"Are you still talking? What part of 'I don't know you' don't you get?"

"Fine. I can take a hint. I think Cypress Hill's rubbed off on you." I tapped my temple. "Insane in the brain. But you know what? Good luck making your movie. Hope you have a nice life, Mattie."

"Wait. What did you say? How do you know about the movie? The song?"

Two could play that game. Still fuming, I ignored her.

"Hey, I'm talking to you. How do you know my name?"

"Oh, now you want to talk to me? How do you think I know? Because you told me."

"Okay, you obviously know me. Then you should know I'm not, like, some stuck up bitch. I just . . ." She looked genuinely perplexed and as frustrated as me. "I don't know why I can't remember you. I usually have a good memory. Look, a girl can't be too careful, you know?"

Even her non-apologies had the power to penetrate armor.

She gave me the once-over and her posture relaxed. "Just promise me you're not a stalker." She held up two fingers in the configuration of a peace sign. "Scout's honor?"

I chuckled. Damn. Staying mad at her was like hating a kitten. "The scout's honor is three fingers. Like this." I gestured with my hand. "And we stalkers prefer the term *enthusiasts*."

"Okay, do-over. I'm Mattie Kim. What's your name again?"

"Miles Ferguson. I know we white guys all look alike but come on."

"Yeah, sorry. I can't tell you guys apart. It might help if you wore name tags."

After a split second of silence, we both chortled.

Everything returned on track. Two hours flew by before we realized the time. When I offered to escort her safely to her stop, she adamantly refused. Stubborn, proud, my least favorite of her qualities, I accepted her boundaries nonetheless. But the thought of any harm befalling her made me ill.

The next night, I showed up with a name tag plastered to my jacket. Goofy, but I figured she'd get a kick out of it. Some people struggled with names. If Mattie was one of them, my gambit left no room for error.

It didn't help. Once again, she failed to recognize me. Based on her sincere bewilderment, it dawned on me that she wasn't playing a game or hard to get. She had a serious problem.

As frustrating as the situation was, I couldn't give up. I really liked her. Hell, I'd already fallen hard. And I knew what it felt like to be deemed weird or a problem. To have people give up on you because your head's been messed up for a long time. Because bouts of depression, stupor, or rage consumed you. Because you couldn't just snap out of it like everyone said you should. I knew what it felt like to be a lost cause.

Rather than run away, I embraced the challenge that was Mattie Kim. The more I got to know her, the more my need for her grew. One fed the other. I came alive around her. Discovered pieces of myself in her. Devising new and creative ways to please her tapped into a part of my brain I'd forgotten or never realized existed. It awoke a sense of purpose, fulfillment. I'd never been happier in my life.

One night, I pretended to be a singing telegram courier and squawked out an off-key rendition of Queen's "Crazy Little Thing Called Love." I thought my plan clever. I thought wrong.

My stunt tanked spectacularly. I was the creep coming on to a client's love interest. But that's the thing, another chance always presented itself. A new day to set things right.

Not to pat myself on the back, but I considered my latest endeavor a stroke of ingenuity. I arrived early and waited. When she sailed down the stairs, I blasted Extreme's "More Than Words" on my phone and held up the signs I'd spent hours toiling over at the office:

Mattie, you don't know me
but I know you

You make films about killer bunnies
and social issues

You have beautiful thick hair . . .
now

But you were as bald as Mr. Clean
when you were born
and not nearly as pretty as him

At the theater, you buy
the largest tub of popcorn
and drench it in butter

Get sick and throw up afterwards
but can't help ordering it
Every. Single. Time.

You're Korean, born in Seoul
but tell assholes you're Chinese

That Jackie Chan is your uncle
who trained you in kung fu
and you're not afraid to use it

You like 90's music, jazz, and hip hop

You laugh in all the major keys of life

I love listening to them all

That earned me a kiss. Of course, it still took another four hours to cajole it out of her. Rome wasn't built in a day either. I'd pay for the late rendezvous at work but I didn't care. My heart soared with elation.

"You're—"

"Too much?"

She shook her head. "Just right. Come here." She tugged my tie and slipped her arms around my neck.

Her lips tasted every bit as sweet as I'd imagined. Soft, warm, with a faint savor of peppermint, her mouth melded with mine with a tenderness that quickly flamed with urgency. Frenzied desire roiled through my flesh. My body pulsed, throbbed, not only with the heat of her, but the intense shock and sensation of pouring myself into this wondrous being.

When she pulled away, my body leaned forward, innately following hers—hard and ardent as a magnet, stayed only by the press of her palm on my chest. I opened my eyes to discover a sheepish smile. My own was one of awe and longing.

The next night when I entered the station, Mattie didn't have her earbuds on nor was she dancing. She shifted her weight from one foot to the other, searching, expectant. My stomach flipped. Something was very wrong.

Her head tilted in my direction, eyes lighting up as soon as she saw me. Her body stilled; the world hushed. Her gaze lingered on my face before it swept past me. But that singular, glorious moment of recognition was the sun orbiting the earth. I braced the handrail and inched down the stairs.

As optimism grew, my pace quickened, and I rushed to greet her. "You waiting for me?"

Anticipation and mystification infused her features. "I don't know. I'm waiting for someone."

I dug up a blank name tag from my bag, scribbled *Someone*, and slapped it on my chest. "That would be me."

She laughed harder than I'd ever heard her laugh before. A luscious serenade to my ears. She was so beautiful it hurt.

To my amazement, a few days later she walked up to me.

"Hi. I know this is going to sound strange but do we know each other?" Her face flushed. "I swear I never do this. Going up to random guys, it's not—God, I sound like an idiot. I really have no idea—"

Learned something new every day. She babbled when she got nervous. I delighted in our sudden role reversal, to see her flustered for a change. Although I'd been tempted to let her wiggle a little longer on the hook, my heart broke for her.

"Mattie, right?"

The relief on her face was priceless. And women thought it was so easy.

"Yeah. So I'm not losing my mind. We do know each other."

Every muscle in my body yearned to haul her into my arms. I stuffed my hands into my trouser pockets to restrain my exhilaration yet I couldn't contain the huge grin. "We do."

From some dark crevice of her mind, it was clear she was reaching for me, fighting to be with me. Up to this point, our encounters never strayed beyond the confines of the train station. For the first time since we met, I believed in a possibility beyond our current limitations. I believed in the possibility of us. When you're trapped in limbo, you can't conceive it. I'd been there before not that long ago and knew how bleak things could look. That night, I had hope. That night, two words broke through the haze and crystalized what I once thought unattainable: a future.

I didn't know exactly how I should handle this situation, but I knew someone who would. I couldn't afford to screw things up.

In the past, I had always lain down on the sofa. This time, as I waited for Doctor Levine, I sat upright and took in the artwork on the walls, the fake plants in the corners.

"Hi, Miles. It's been a while. How've you been?"

"Whoa, Doc. Looking good. You dropped a whole person."

"Midlife crisis. Some men buy sports cars, I treated myself to a gastric bypass."

Most people would find his humor irreverent or inappropriate, but I always appreciated that about him. He'd joke, *Why take things with a grain of salt when you can take them with a sense of humor? Just as effective and tastes a whole lot better.*

During the three years I'd been under his care, he taught me to cope by finding the good in things, in situations, in people. He encouraged me to go back to school and embark on a new career. My recovery would not have been possible without him.

"I'm actually not here for me. I mean, yes, it's for me, but I really just wanted to pick your brain about something for a friend."

He nodded his head. "A friend. Of course, go ahead."

"I'm kind of seeing someone."

"That's great. I'm happy for you."

"*Seeing* might be the wrong word. I'm not actually dating her. That is, we're not boyfriend and girlfriend. Or going out on real dates—but I'd like to. Really, really like to."

"So what's the problem? Ask her out."

"This girl, she's amazing. She's a film student at NYU—brilliant. I've seen clips of her work. She's funny, intelligent, artistic. She's perfect. She just has this thing."

"What thing?"

"Some kind of amnesia. You ever watch the movie *50 First Dates*?"

"With Adam Sandler and Drew Barrymore? Sure."

"It's kind of like that but different. Anyway, in the movie they called it Goldfield's Syndrome. But are things like that real?"

"Let's clear up a few things. First, they made up that term for the movie. Second, there are a number of disorders that can affect memory loss. But without reviewing her medical records and evaluating her in person, I couldn't make an accurate diagnosis. Was she in an accident?"

"I don't know." I rubbed my palms on my thighs, anxious for answers. "Can it be repaired? Maybe with medication or surgery?"

"Couldn't start off with something easy? Like dating triplets? What's her name?"

"Mattie Kim. I know her situation isn't ideal but she's special. I really like her."

"She sounds lovely. But . . ."

"But?"

"Are you sure you're ready to tackle such a big undertaking?"

What the hell was he talking about?

"Doc, you're the one who taught me never to give up on myself. Why would I give up on her?"

He shook his head. "But her condition's different. Physical trauma isn't like emotional trauma. The way the brain functions, heals. It's unpredictable at best. Do you think it's wise to get your hopes up?"

But, but, but. Didn't he have any solutions to offer? My being there was precisely because Mattie had given me hope. Who was he to dismiss her? We all carry baggage. In this day and age, who isn't damaged? And what about her heart? Her soul?

My aggravation mounted. His job required asking questions. What I needed now were answers. "Doc, all I want to know—"

"Wait. You said her name is Mattie Kim? As in Matilda Kim?" Trepidation darkened his eyes. "Miles, where did you meet her?"

"Rockefeller Center station. Why?"

"Hold on." Without ceremony, he marched out of the room and returned with a thick folder with my name on it and set it on the coffee table. "Remember why you first came to see me?"

"I told you, it's not about me."

"Isn't it?" He slipped out a newspaper clipping from the file. "I want you to read this."

It was an article from *The New York Herald*.

Young Woman Pushed to Death on Train Tracks

A horrific tragedy cut short another life last night when twenty-year-old Matilda Kim was pushed to her death at the Rockefeller Center subway station. The only daughter of Korean immigrants, she graduated from Frank Sinatra High School and was an undergraduate studying film at New York University.
Mattie, as friends and family called her, had just left work and was on her way home when she was accosted by a man.

I scanned through the rest, picking up bits and pieces.

According to witnesses . . . Jamar Johnston . . . intoxicated at the time . . . shoved her . . . oncoming F Train . . . died instantly.
Train operator, Miles Ferguson . . . drove the lead car . . . tested negative for alcohol . . . investigation . . . Ferguson's

*performance or equipment malfunction . . . contributed to
her death.*
Notes and flowers . . . a candlelight vigil . . .

The remaining words careened off the page as vertigo spun
through my body. It couldn't be.

"No. That's not her. That's not my Mattie."

"Look at the picture. Are you sure?"

Cap and gown, diploma in hand, the beaming face of a pretty
Asian girl stared up at me.

"You're wrong. This—this girl's too young."

"That's because it's her high school yearbook photo. Think
about it. Her name, ethnicity, background. The location." He
sighed. "How many Matilda Kims do you think there are? You like
numbers. What're the odds it's a different girl?"

Odds? All those days lying in the dark. All those sleepless nights.
Living from one bottle to another. Popping pill after pill. What had
been the odds I'd ever climb out of that chasm?

"Obviously something triggered your guilt, and it's conjured
up—"

"I'm not conjuring anything!" I crumpled the article, jumped
up, and paced the room. "She's real. I see her. Feel her. She's as real
as you or me."

"Miles, it wasn't your fault. You were cleared of any—"

"I'm telling you, it's not her!"

Why was he trying to take her away from me?

"Maybe we ended our sessions too soon. Perhaps we should get
you back on your old schedule."

"No. I'm seeing clearly for the first time in a long time. Why
won't you help me? I mean, Christ, Doc. I'm just, what? A deposit
on your Hamptons vacation rental? Fuck you!"

I chucked the folder at him and stormed out.

"Miles. Miles!"

I raced the twenty blocks to the station where I waited for

Mattie. A little after 11 P.M., she floated down the staircase, her body swathed in light. I flung myself at her.

"Mattie, please tell me you know me." I touched my forehead to hers. "Please."

Confusion tinged her expression. "Do I know you?"

Oh, god. Not again. Not square one. I couldn't go back there.

Without the aid of any games or fanfare, she spoke my name. "Of course I know you, Miles."

Her acknowledgement ruptured a levee of emotions. A sense of rightness. Belonging.

I cinched her in my arms and kissed her hard with everything I was and had. Willed her body to mine. My hands raced over her, desperate to absorb and consume every inch; crushed her to me, leaving no space between us. The lights flickered around us as I delved deeper into her mouth.

My voice was gruff. "I love you, Mattie. God, I love you so much sometimes I can't breathe. Tell me you're real. Tell me you love me."

She cupped a palm on my cheek. "I know you. I know the real you. And now you know who I really am too. Don't you?"

Like bolts of lightning, terror and anguish struck my body as realization set in. Who was Mattie Kim? The girl who brought me back to life. But the question begged another. Who was I? The guy who took hers away.

Tears trickled down my face. I trembled. My voice cracked. "Oh god, Mattie. My sweet, sweet Mattie. What did I do to you?" I gripped her jacket and fell to my knees. The words crawled up from my throat. "I'm sorry. I'm sorry. I'm so, so sorry."

She stroked my hair. "*Shhh*. It wasn't your fault, Miles. You have to stop feeling guilty." Even in the worst of times, leave it to Mattie to find absurdity and grace. "No one does fucked up like us, huh?" Squeezing my shoulders, she lifted me up.

"You must hate me." I pleaded with my eyes. "Hate me. Hit me!"

Her skin grew paler, more translucent. Her eyes began to fade, already saying goodbye.

"I was angry. For a long time. And then, I wasn't." She held my face. "You can't imagine how much I've enjoyed getting to know you."

Her lips brushed against mine—slow, sensual, comforting. "I love you, Miles."

A train clattered in the tunnel. The sound a rattling of chains.

"You're leaving me, aren't you?"

Her lips curled up but her eyes weighed down with sorrow. "I don't want to."

"Then don't. I want to be with you. Always. Forever."

"You don't mean that."

I smiled and entwined my fingers with hers and kissed the back of her hand. Hope and euphoria coursed through us. Bound us.

She passed me an earbud. I was surprised to discover a different tune playing. I perked up at Goo Goo Dolls' "Iris."

After all that had transpired between us, what was the probability of our being together? Infinitesimal? Impossible? Sometimes the universe gifted us a rare second chance. What, in statistics, we might call an anomaly. I called it a miracle.

"You sure?"

I squeezed her hand. "Fuck it. I choose us."

She cranked up the volume. When everything seemed made to be broken, life had a way of proving us wrong.

The train roared toward the station. The lights sputtered, dimmed. Light bulbs sizzled and exploded in a brilliant display of fireworks. We ran. Leaped to a future, blinding and beautiful.

Suanne Kim attributes her writing perspective to her experience as a Korean immigrant struggling to learn English and as a latchkey kid roaming the streets of New York City. Often skipping school, she snuck into museums or rode the labyrinth of subways, chronicling her journeys and the myriad of people she encountered. Some of her early stories derived from her stint as super sleuth Paradise Rose, surveilling pimps and prostitutes in her Hell's Kitchen neighborhood. From the onset, the many facets and complexities of human nature and the human condition fascinated her, as reflected in the wide range of her work and interests. She writes poetry and fiction in a variety of genres and has been published in Newtown Literary and Nomad's Choir. www.facebook.com/SuanneKim.

Plastic Boy

Patricia Stover

Linda stared at a row of action figures. Her hands shook and her heart pounded. Each beat throbbed inside her brain. Since Peter's accident, Jimmy hadn't been the same. He'd always been a demanding little boy, but since his father died, he'd become vindictive and unforgiving.

A boy rolled through the aisle on a skateboard, and a slender blonde chased him. Her red heels clicked against the tile. How did she keep from stumbling? Linda glanced at her worn-out white sneakers. It had been years since she'd even thought about wearing a pair of heels.

The woman grabbed her son by his hood and pulled him toward the checkout. He lowered his head and followed. Linda sighed. That's how normal children behaved.

She scanned a row of action figures—the variety overwhelming—and then stared at the ceiling. Which ones did he have already? Not a toy in sight he didn't own.

Her mouth curled into a grin. She shook her head. "That's it," she said to herself. Why hadn't she thought of it before now? It was so simple.

She'd take Jimmy to choose his own present. No way he could be mad at her for bringing home the wrong gift. The odds of her finding anything he liked or didn't already own were slim. There would be no repercussions with this plan, only her and her son celebrating what should be a happy event in a little boy's life. Or so she hoped.

Yes, it was the best way. The safest way.

— • • —

Jimmy swung a sword above his head, mounted his stick horse, and galloped back and forth. He stopped outside Linda's bedroom door.

"It's my birthday. Wake up!" he said, banging the sword along the banister. Its gray plastic blade clanked and clattered against the wooden poles. No response. He pounded both fists on the door. "I said, wake up!"

Linda's eyes popped open. She squinted away from a yellow beam shining through the window. The clatter grew louder. She stretched and slid her foot around the brown shag carpet. Pink fuzz tickled her toe. She wiggled one foot into her slipper, stopped, and cocked her head toward the door.

The house grew quiet. Heavy breathing whispered through the crack. She shoved her foot in the other shoe and tiptoed around the bed. Easing her hand toward the doorknob, she placed her eye to the keyhole. A single brown eye peered back.

"It's my birthday. Where's my cake?"

She jumped as the words belted from Jimmy's mouth through the doorjamb. She took a deep breath and opened the door. Jimmy squatted and laughed.

"Happy birthday," she said as she forced her mouth into some semblance of a smile. She wouldn't get any rest until Jimmy had his cake.

Linda walked downstairs. She stumbled, grabbed for the banister, and braced herself for impact. A moan escaped as her hand bent against the stairwell. Sharp pain shot through her wrist and she tumbled. Her head bounced against a wood panel. She lay on the steps, half dazed, with her hand on her forehead. She flexed her wrist. Not broken, only a sprain.

Jimmy stood above her smiling. His stick horse lay strategically across the third step. She pushed herself from the floor with her good hand and staggered up the steps.

"Here." She handed the horse to Jimmy before limping into the kitchen.

She'd have to make an icepack for her wrist. It had already begun to puff and turn purple. She flinched as she laid the cold pack across her throbbing forearm. She stared at olive swirls on the kitchen table and blinked back tears. How had her life come to this?

How had she become terrified of her own child? The very child, once a part of her, growing inside her, now a stranger.

She braced her forehead with her free hand. She wanted to let the pain escape, but she didn't. She wouldn't let Jimmy see her cry.

Jimmy skipped into the kitchen. Linda wiped away her lingering tears before he could see them.

"Is your arm okay, Mommy?" he asked.

She rummaged through the cabinets. "It's fine, just a bump. What kind of cake do you want, sweetie?" she asked as she produced a mixer and cake pans.

"I want chocolate," he said.

Linda reached into the pantry and grabbed a box of cocoa.

"No . . . Vanilla—I want vanilla," he said.

She sighed, tiptoed, and fumbled in the cabinet. After a moment, she found a small brown bottle with *Vanilla* printed across a white label. She pulled the drawer, which always seemed to stick, and retrieved a measuring spoon. She poured the fragrant liquid into the spoon.

Jimmy's eyes followed her as she carefully measured the vanilla.

"I want strawberry," he said, before his mother could start the mixer.

He lowered his head and pretended to concentrate on a little yellow dump truck he'd been pushing through a flour mountain. Linda leaned against the counter. No need digging around the entire kitchen for his entertainment.

He watched her from the corner of his eye. His truck stopped and the side of his mouth curled. "I want them all!"

Linda set the extract on the counter.

"Jimmy, honey, don't you think three cakes are too many? You can't eat all of them. And anyway, that's a lot of work."

He narrowed his eyes at his truck and his grin faded. His fingers wrapped around the metal dump truck and squeezed. He glared at his mother, with the truck clasped in his right hand. Linda gasped and shuffled backward, trapped between Jimmy and the counter.

The same steel glare had burned into Peter's lifeless body. His ladder had toppled. Jimmy was with him when the accident happened. The only witness. When she found Peter, Jimmy stood over him, staring with wild eyes.

"I said I want all three. Make me all three or you'll be sorry."

Her eyes widened. She gaped at Jimmy and the metal truck in his hand. Her hand trembled as she ran her finger over a pink scar above her lip. She quickly gathered the ingredients in her arms, the pain in her wrist now forgotten. Getting pegged in the head with a truck wasn't what scared her. What she wouldn't see coming did. She missed Peter but wasn't ready to join him, not yet.

She mixed, measured, and baked three cakes. Afterward she set them on the counter to cool. While they cooled, she scrubbed dishes and swept the flour Jimmy had left on the kitchen floor.

Two hours later, the kitchen was spotless and the cakes decorated. Linda flopped into the chair and dabbed sweat from her brow with her tattered apron. She still had to survive the toy store. She sighed and called Jimmy.

He ran downstairs, jumping the last two steps, stopped, and stared at his cakes. Tears filled his eyes, and his face turned red.

"I wanted cupcakes. You're so stupid!"

His fist smashed the chocolate cake. Brown chunks splattered the floor. Linda flinched as bits of cake smeared her face. He lifted the strawberry cake above his head and let it drop. When Jimmy finished, a pink and brown pile of slop covered the table, the kitchen now a birthday cake disaster.

Tears stained her cheeks as she mopped and scrubbed the floor, cleaning the kitchen once again. She dumped the last bit of cake in the trash. Hopefully he'd like the toy store. She'd already upset him. The toy store was her last hope. If he didn't like it, there would be more than a toy dump truck waiting for her. A lot more.

Jimmy sulked in his room while Linda showered, washing cake from her face and hair. She poked her head through his door.

Hopefully he'd had enough time to relax. He sat on his bed, arms crossed.

"Ready for the toy store, honey?" she asked.

"No! This day is stupid, and you're stupid, with your stupid cake."

"You can pick any toy you want."

Jimmy jumped from his bed. "Anything? Promise?"

She nodded, a promise she'd soon regret.

— • • —

Jimmy sprinted from the car. He ran through each aisle, knocking toys from their shelves. Linda lagged behind, head hung, reshelving toys. She held a bag of little green army men toward Jimmy.

"How about this?" she asked.

Jimmy slapped her hand and soldiers scattered across the floor.

"No! That's for babies," he said, then ran.

Linda searched the aisles, pondering a variety of toys. Each one she presented was either rejected, thrown on the floor, or kicked aside. Jimmy rummaged through a bin of giant rubber balls. They'd been in the store for hours. Linda yawned and leaned against the rack.

She'd tried everything: puzzles, board games, even an electric scooter. Each time, Jimmy refused, leaving a trail of disregarded toys behind him.

He ran to the back of the store through a door. The sign read, *KEEP OUT.*

"Don't go back there," she said.

He ignored her pleas and scurried into the back, slamming the door behind him. Linda followed. She coughed as dust tickled her throat. The stench of mold drifted into her nose. Boxes of stuffed animals lined the storage room walls, waiting to be shelved.

She scanned the room. A chill ran up her spine. Rows of dolls encased in plastic sleeves watched her. Their eyes followed her through the room. An overhead light flickered. Linda held her chest and glanced over her shoulder. Something moving around the corner caught her eye.

"Jimmy?"

No one, only a toy castle. The peaks rose to her chest. Green and red flags topped the towers. Linda slid her hand over the rough stone walls. Dead peasants littered a long courtyard, and a wooden drawbridge guarded its entrance. Plastic figures, painted precisely, gathered in a circle near the entrance. She held one of the figures and studied it, each line and blemish flawless. The fallen soldier's face twisted in torment.

She dropped the soldier. "Ugh."

A king peered through his window. He scowled at the kneeling peasants, pleading for their lives. Linda's heart drummed. She stepped closer. Something strange about the castle, something she couldn't quite place, shook her. Linda eased her hand to the toy, mesmerized by its grotesque majesty.

Jimmy ran behind her. She jumped and jerked her hand back. He gazed at the castle with his mouth open.

"Wow," he said and stuck his head inside.

A gold rug, trimmed in red, adorned the stone floors. Pictures of royalty cluttered the walls, and oil lanterns lined the mantle of the fireplace, emanating a warm yellow glow. He opened a door in the hallway. Stairs led deep below into a dungeon.

Plastic prisoners lay strewn across the floor, starving. Others were chained against a cold rock wall. They watched Jimmy through the tiny door. Their hollow eyes burning into his. Jimmy laughed, flicked his index finger, and thumped one of the peasants across the dirty dungeon floor.

"I want this one. I can be King. Look, it has a dungeon."

Some of the knights' limbs were severed. Flesh and tendons hung from their wounds. Linda winced. One of the peasant's head lay in a basket, sliced by the guillotine. Shards of flesh and veins dangled from his neck.

She shuddered, nauseated by the sight. "I don't know . . . It's pretty graphic."

"You said I could pick what I want. I want this . . . You said!"

Jimmy spat, a slimy wad landed on her forehead and oozed over her face. She wiped away the saliva with her sleeve. Great, another fit.

Linda pulled her credit card from her wallet. "Go find a clerk."

Jimmy ran from the room with a giant grin on his face. He returned with a skinny, pimple-faced stock boy.

— • • —

"When will it be here? I want it now!"

Jimmy sat by the door and stared out the window. Surely they'd be here soon. The longer the driver took, the longer Jimmy would bug her.

The delivery truck turned into the driveway, and two plump men stepped from the truck. They hoisted the castle upstairs. Linda handed two five-dollar bills to the gentlemen while Jimmy pieced his castle together.

He'd be happy for a while at least. Most toys didn't last through the day. The newness faded in an hour or two, leaving her tormented by Jimmy. She snuck into her room and locked the door. Hopefully the television would drown out the sound of Jimmy and his imaginary battle. Her eyes drifted shut as she thumbed the pages of a book.

Images of Peter filled her dreams. They walked together, holding hands. Tears spilled from her eyes. Peter pulled her toward Jimmy's room. When he opened his door, a courtyard appeared. The castle stood before them, no longer a toy. It was beautiful, and it was theirs. He pressed his body against hers and kissed her deeply.

"Everything's going to be okay," he whispered.

The sound of horses galloping pulled her from his arms. This wasn't a dream. Sweat beaded on her forehead. She wiped tears from her eyes and glanced at the alarm. 4:20 a.m.

"He must've left the television on," she mumbled and threw back her blanket.

Galloping sounded from Jimmy's room. When Linda reached the door, a green light filtered beneath. She slowly opened the door. A yellow glow radiated inside Jimmy's closet—his nightlight. Definitely not the green light she'd seen.

Jimmy sat on the floor, his eyes fixed on the castle. She placed her hand on his shoulder. He sat like a statue, unmoving.

"What are you doing up this early?" she asked.

"Just playing with my new castle," he said, his eyes still planted on his toy.

"Did you have the television on?"

He shook his head.

"It's too early, honey. Go back to bed."

Linda flinched as soon as the words left her mouth. Before, he would have hit her for such a suggestion. She clenched her eyes and waited.

Instead, Jimmy stood, stiff as a board, turned, and climbed into his bed.

— • • —

A week passed and Jimmy hadn't bugged her once. One glorious week. He kept to his room, with his castle. Noises chattered from beyond his closed bedroom door throughout the night. Every time Linda entered his room, she found nothing, only Jimmy playing. She ignored his infatuation with the castle for a while, enjoying the peace that came with the toy. He was occupied with something besides tormenting her, and that was fine. No interruptions, no little boy barging in demanding this or that.

Though she loved her newfound peace, she had to admit Jimmy had been acting weird.

"Jimmy, I'm talking to you," she shouted.

His eyes didn't move, remaining transfixed on his castle.

She shook her head and stomped from the room. All he did

anymore was sit in his room and play with that stupid castle. His face was pale, his eyes bloodshot. He didn't eat, didn't sleep. He woke in the middle of the night, and she'd usher him back to bed. She'd had enough.

"Jimmy, this is the third time, now come down for dinner," Linda yelled from the kitchen.

No answer.

She grabbed a potholder and slammed a pan of lasagna on the counter. Jimmy's favorite. Surely the smell would entice him from his room. She sat at the table and waited.

Twenty minutes later, Linda poked the cold lasagna with a fork. Enough was enough. She grabbed a trash bag and stomped upstairs. She would be strong, not back down, no matter what tricks he pulled.

She snatched two knights from Jimmy's hands and shoved them into the bag.

His eyes widened. He clutched her wrist and squeezed. "What are you doing?"

"This thing is going in the trash," she said, shoving a handful of horses in the bag.

Jimmy jumped in front of the castle and spread his arms. "No! You can't. It's mine. It's special."

Linda hooked her arms underneath his and lifted him. The toe of his boot slammed into her shins. Pain throbbed in her bone, and she dropped Jimmy on his bed. He buried his face in his pillow and sobbed as she disassembled the castle. First the tower peaks, then the door. He followed her outside, begging her to stop. Piece by piece, she carried the castle to the dumpster.

Her heart sank into her stomach. She lowered her head and took a deep breath. She was a horrible mother. No, no she wasn't; it had to be done. She dropped the bag in the Dumpster and slammed the lid.

Jimmy sat on the floor gazing at the empty space.

"Why don't you go ride your bike?" she asked.

He didn't move.

"Fine, I'm going to bed."

She slammed his door, leaving him in his room to stare at the wall.

— • • —

"To the dungeon, peasant!"

Linda sprang from her bed. The little brat had dug the damn thing from the trash. She stormed down the hall. That was it, she could take no anymore. This time there would be a spanking.

The castle sat in the middle of Jimmy's room, reassembled. Linda's mouth hung open. No way he'd carried it upstairs himself. Jimmy was nowhere to be found. She tiptoed to the closet and flung open the door. A pile of dirty clothes and a baseball bag sat in the corner, but no Jimmy. Where was he hiding? She snuck to the edge of his bed and knelt.

A voice spoke. She stiffened and turned her head toward the castle. Unable to decipher what the voice said, she crept to the edge of the mattress and peeked around the bed. Nothing.

Linda turned to leave. The voice spoke again. A green glow filtered through the castle. Her heart pounded and she stepped closer.

"Mommy—Mommy, help," a muffled voice said.

Her body trembled as she peeked inside the wooden doors.

"Help me please!"

Linda wiggled farther inside. Her hand shook as she opened the tiny door in the hallway. When she placed her eye to the opening, a figure appeared.

Deep inside the dungeon, a plastic Jimmy lifted his arm. "Momma," he cried.

She screamed. Her back thudded hard against the wall. She planted her face in her hands and sobbed. Her baby was gone. It was all her fault and Jimmy was gone. Her heart beat into her throat; she swallowed hard. Her only child, her precious, sweet . . .

Her tears stopped. Heartbroken sobs turned into hysterical bouts of laughter. Jimmy was gone and he'd been gone for a while now. The little plastic boy locked in the dungeon was not her child, he'd never been.

Yes . . . Jimmy was gone and everything was going to be okay.

Patricia Stover is an emerging horror author from Oklahoma. Her short story, "Creepers," was featured in Scout Media's *A Journey of Words* anthology. When she isn't writing, she can be found on the beautiful banks of Lake Texoma or spending time with her son, Daxton. To learn more about Patricia and her work, you can visit www.PatriciaStover.wix.com/PatriciaStover.

HOME

Laura Ings Self

I can never leave this place.

This is where I was living when Jenna and I fell in love. The breakfast bar in the kitchen was where I asked her to move in with me. The sheepskin rug in front of the fireplace was where we celebrated her promotion—first with champagne and then with our bodies, limbs entwined, like we were one invincible being. The antique bed, with its ornate copper frame, was where we curled up together every night, my knees spooned behind her, my arm draped across her stomach.

Every inch is filled with her—her and the happiness she brought me before the accident shattered everything and took away the love of my life.

I came through the door after our first date with a warm sensation low in my belly and a fluttering in my chest I hadn't experienced before. A mutual friend had set us up, and my expectations were low. But her smile was warm and genuine, her eyes sparkled with mischief, and the stories she told about her human resources job were surprisingly entertaining.

She agreed to see me again. And then again. Love hit me like a line of cocaine. I craved her like oxygen. She had bewitched and enslaved me, but I loved every moment of my incarceration.

We would spend hours talking over a glass or two of Merlot, sharing our hopes and dreams, planning our life together. She had moved in after just a few months, and we took our friends' jokes with good humour, relishing being a lesbian cliché. I was the dreamer, and she was the planner. Together we visited new places, learned new skills, and braved amazing adventures. I loved who I was when I was with her—she made me the best version of myself.

I see glimpses of her sometimes; flickers, shadows skittering across the wall like beams from the headlights of a passing car. I see her pouring coffee in the mornings, a slow, sleepy smile brightening her face, her blonde hair wild from the pillow. I see her phoning her mum, her head resting on the sofa arm, her slender fingers entwining the cord of the vintage telephone she paid way over the odds for.

These momentary flashes comfort me, even whilst I doubt their veracity. The first time I caught a glimpse of her after the accident, it didn't frighten or even unsettle me. I just knew I was home.

I know I should move on, that it's not healthy to remain so firmly fixated on someone I lost, but I can't say goodbye. And while I'm still here, it's like she's still here too; I can pretend for a moment the accident didn't happen.

We had argued that night, which cuts me up more than anything else. Silvery tears tracked down her cheeks as I climbed into the car beside her and fastened my seatbelt. I had been unreasonable—spiteful even—but I couldn't bring myself to apologise while the rage still boiled in my veins. The argument was stupid, not worth getting so riled up over, but sometimes my anger just gets the better of me.

She sniffed and wiped her nose with the back of her hand as she turned the key in the ignition. The roads were wet, and the night was cold. Vapour fogged the windscreen, and she flicked on the heaters to dispel it.

A knot of guilt formed in my stomach, and I chewed on a fingernail, the dark purple polish flaking off and spreading across my tongue. I stole a look at Jenna. The watery redness of her eyes did little to spoil the image of her perfect profile captured in cameo by the streetlamps.

I wondered if I should apologise. I had spoiled what should have been a wonderful evening.

The other vehicle seemed to come out of nowhere. There was a flash of light, a squeal of brakes, the shriek of metal giving way, and the crunch of glass scattered across my lap.

My head pounded and my mouth suddenly felt dry. I looked across at Jenna and watched an impossibly bright trickle of blood course its way from her temple. A brick of despair settled itself deep inside my stomach, and a physical pain tore through me, as though I were made of tissue paper.

Nothing would ever be the same.

—••—

The flashes have been getting less frequent, like she's fading away and there's nothing I can do to stop her. I cling to her memory like I'm drowning. I try to recall the sensation of sliding my fingers through her hair, of touching my lips to hers, of wrapping my arms around her.

And then she's there, clearer than she's been in a long time, standing by the front door. I sweep across the room, like this fleeting image can slake my unquenchable thirst for her.

The figure is translucent and rippling, pulsing in and out of clarity, but it's her. I recognise the curve of her cheek and the soft slant of her brow like I know my own reflection. Her hair is scooped into a messy bun, not loose and wild like it was the night of the crash. She's wearing a pale green cashmere cardigan that I don't remember.

Her lips are moving, but I can't hear what she's saying. A sibilant *buzz* tickles my ears, but the words are indecipherable. I concentrate on her mouth, focusing everything I have on the indistinct sounds she is producing. What is she trying to tell me?

I sense the other presence before I see it. Another figure, vaguer even than her, stands just on the other side of the front door—I hadn't noticed it was open. It's another woman, with dark hair cropped short and swept low across her forehead. She flickers in and out of my vision, and I concentrate harder, trying to decipher what is happening. I focus all my energy—blocking out everything else around me—and the words they are speaking start to make sense. Their conversation sounds muffled, like voices underwater.

"Come on, Jen," the figure at the door says. "You've never even let me see inside."

Who is she?

The shape of Jenna floats in the doorway, hands hanging on either side of the doorframe. "I don't know, Diane. It's weird."

"What's weird is you never letting another person in here. No one. Cassie said she's not been in here since the accident. Neither has anyone else."

Jenna shakes her head.

The other woman, Diane, takes her hand. There is tenderness in her voice. "You need to let go, Jenna. This place'll be on the market by tomorrow morning. You need to stop treating it like a shrine."

My stomach cramps and lurches. I can taste bile. This can't be happening. My face prickles and a thudding feeling reverberates through my whole body. I explode in a cold sweat.

Shimmery tears trickle down Jenna's translucent cheeks. She picks up the photograph of the two of us that sits on the shelf by the door and hugs it to her chest so that it looks as indistinct as she does. Jenna steps aside and lets the other woman cross the threshold of the flat we had shared for three years.

"You'll feel better once this place is packed up and you're settled in at mine," Diane says.

Jealousy surges through me like a steam train. I reach out and slam the door shut. They both jump and Diane exhales a pathetic whimper of surprise.

Jenna turns and extends her hand toward where I stand. "Nicky?" she murmurs, her voice full of hope.

I reach for her hand, but mine passes through it like smoke.

She shudders.

"Don't do this to yourself," Diane mutters in Jenna's ear. "Let go."

Jenna collapses in silent sobs. She catches her breath and speaks in a hallowed whisper. "I don't know if I can, Di. It feels like she's still here. Sometimes I think I sense her watching me, looking after me. I don't want to leave her."

"I know, darling, but she's gone. It's been eighteen months now. I love you. I know I'm not her, but I love you, and I'm still here."

A flash of light, a squeal of brakes, the shriek of metal giving way, and the crunch of glass scattered across my lap.

I look at Jenna and watch an impossibly bright trickle of blood course its way from her temple. A brick of despair settles itself deep inside my stomach, and a physical pain tears through me, as though I were made of tissue paper.

My lungs constrict and the air I gasp is thin and dry. My heart thuds in my chest, each palpitation shaking my whole body but slowing, slowing . . . and then darkness and an incredible feeling of lightness.

I watch them pack her belongings, their shadowy forms pulsating in and out of existence. Jenna stops to weep from time to time; Diane makes tea and provides tissues. In a matter of hours, our home's heart is excised like a cancer at the mercy of the surgeon's knife.

The mug I used to make her coffee in every morning is packed in a box. The painting we chose on a whim in Brighton is rolled in bubble wrap. The photo of us in Thailand has been removed from its frame and tucked in the bottom of her bag, the frame reclaimed to display future memories.

The flat is lifeless, a show-home shell of its former self. There is nothing left of us here. The furniture is staying—for now at least— but every personal touch, every trinket and knickknack, is removed and boxed up.

Jenna's figure flickers in the foyer, a shimmering box propped on her hip. Her nose and eyes are red from crying, but her angelic beauty still enthralls me.

She lingers by the door. I don't know where Diane has gone.

Jenna's eyes drift across the hallway, looking through me as if I weren't here at all.

I watch her swallow another sob.

"Bye, Nicky," she says and presses her fingers to her lips to blow me a final kiss before closing the door behind her.

With leaden feet, I walk back toward the couch and sink into the cushions. I look around the empty flat and feel a balloon of anguish growing inside me, expanding until I am sure it will explode and rip me apart. There is nothing left of the home Jenna and I had created together.

Maybe tomorrow she will return. I know she still loves me. I know she won't leave me.

I sit with my head in my hands and wait.

Laura Ings Self lives and writes in the suburbs of London. When she isn't writing, she is looking after her four-year-old twins or taking the stage at her local community theatre.

"Home" is her first published work, and she is currently seeking representation for her two middle-grade novels, one of which was long-listed for the Times/Chicken House Children's Fiction Competition 2016.

Joe
J.M. Turner

"I'm taking Joe to the park today," I tell Rufus, my trusty, silky-eared black and tan mutt.

His good ear pricks up at the word *park*, and he chuffs at me, his head slanting comically to one side, a hint of excitement in his eyes.

"Yes, you can come too. Fetch your leash, then."

Rufus's paws scrabble on the hardwood floor of the hallway, his nails clicking as he slides his way enthusiastically past the stairs, past the closed door to the lounge, and along to the kitchen door, where his blue leather lead hangs from a white hook attached roughly four feet from the floor so that he can reach it. I watch in amusement as he stands on his hind legs and places his front paws onto the grooves his claws have gouged into the wood over the years. He curls them slightly to allow him to take a grip, nudges aside the coats that hang from the higher hooks, and slips the leash from his own by taking it carefully in his mouth and jerking his head upwards and inwards. Pleased with himself, he returns along the hallway to drop it at my feet, his tail spinning like a dervish. I clip it to his collar, tell him to sit, then I run upstairs to make sure my son has his shoes and coat on, straightening the photos that line the wall as I climb.

I stop to look at the fifth one along. It was taken on a gloriously sunny day, much like this one: Joe is wearing his little blue shorts and a white vest top. I say he is wearing blue and white, but the truth is that anyone looking at the picture would say he is wearing brown; he is sitting, splay-legged, in the middle of the one and only puddle that remained from the previous day's rain, covered in mud, his head thrown back in one enormous guffaw of laughter. A brilliant stream of sunlight illuminates his wet hair—blonde curls that cascade around his head like an angel's aura. Rufus is just behind him, one ear cocked, one ear flopped, head down and rear end in the air in his classic *play-with-me* position. He, too, is a muddy mess. I can still hear Joe's laughter and can almost taste the smell of mud, dog, and boy. I smile to myself, stroke the picture with one tender finger, straighten it up, then make a move to Joe's room.

"Ready, son?" I ask, watching as my little boy, all wrapped up in his new red jacket, gives a final tug on his red wellingtons and looks at me hopefully. "Yes, you can wear them!" I say with mock severity, knowing how much he adores his red boots.

He smiles up at me, relief written on his dear little face.

"Well done for getting them on all by yourself. Come on then." I hold out my hand to his and welcome the warmth of his tiny fingers in mine.

— · · —

It's a bit of a kerfuffle, exiting the house with an excitable dog and happy five-year-old boy in tow. I tie the leash around one wrist to keep Rufus under control and grab a tight hold of Joe's sleeve using that same hand. I use the other hand to firmly lock the front door and put the keys into my pocket, then I transfer the leash to that hand and we set off, me tugging on Rufus's leash to hold him back so that Joe's little legs can keep up with us, Joe practically running to stay abreast.

The road is busy. Always busy. Cars roar past, reckless drivers hurtling along the tarmac at a speed that exceeds the limits by a large margin. The sidewalk is narrow, and I tighten my grip on both dog and boy, loosening it only slightly when Joe turns his face up to mine and yells with indignation, "Too tight, Mommy!"

"Sorry, sweetie." I grin down at him. "Just making sure you're safe."

"I'm not still *four*!" Joe's voice is scornful as he scowls up at me. "I *know* to keep away from the cars!"

"Ah, but they don't know to keep away from *you*, do they?"

I stoop to draw him closer so that I can give him a kiss. He obligingly turns his face and allows me to plant one on his chubby little cheek, then tries hard not to giggle as I turn the kiss into a raspberry.

"Yuck, Mommy!" He wipes at his wet cheek with Pudge, the teddy he has had from birth that has to come everywhere with us. Pudge is being carried in the hand I am not holding.

A tug on the leash, a heavy sigh, and a meaty *thud* tells me that Rufus has given up on our walk and sat down on the pavement.

I grin at Joe and wave the hand that holds the leash. "I think he's trying to tell us something. Shall we go?"

Joe nods and indicates our joined hands by squeezing mine. "But not so tight please."

"As tight as I need to, okay?"

Joe rolls his eyes.

— • • —

There is no safe place to cross the road to gain access to the park unless we trudge all the way into town and use the elaborate system, which involves crossing the main road twice: once where the cars split to turn left into town and becomes a one-way system, and again where it turns right onto Beach Road, which has traffic that passes both ways. Both crossings involve the kindness of drivers actually stopping, and it can take some minutes until someone decent takes pity on those trying to get to the other side and stops.

About a quarter of a mile before the split is our local police station. All the locals are aware that sometimes one of the cops, probably bored from the lack of action in our little town, sits with a speed gun ready to catch one of the lunatics that use the road as a racetrack. There is usually a much more sedate flow of traffic at this point and, as the station sits directly opposite the entrance to the park, often a big enough gap to use to cross.

Today—after Joe has been lifted up so that he can walk along the two-foot-high brick wall that passes for the border of the police station's tiny car park, holding tight to my hand as he carefully balances and waves to the friendly sergeant on duty in one of the offices—there is such a gap. Once I have lifted Joe back down onto the sidewalk, we take advantage of it without having to stop walking.

"You didn't stop, look, and listen!" Joe scolds me as I hurry both him and Rufus over and through the ornate, but rusting, swing gates.

"I did," I tell him. "Okay, no, we didn't stop, but I had been looking and listening, and that's how I knew it was safe to go when we did."

"But you said we should *always* stop, look, and listen so that none of the assholes hit us!"

I stop in my tracks as Joe's little cheeks flame red.

"Sorry," he says sheepishly. "But you do say that!"

I acknowledge the truth with a nod. He's right—it *is* something I say, I can't deny it. "Well, it's something mommies say that little boys don't. You know that, right?"

"Yeah—I *said* I was sorry. Can I go and play on the swings, please?"

I cast a glance toward the enclosed play area to make sure that none of the bigger kids are lording it over the younger ones. There is only one other child there—a girl of around the same age as Joe, whose mother is lolling against the fence outside the play area, evidently too busy texting to actually watch her daughter, who is attempting to climb the high slide.

I wince. Some mothers should not be allowed to have children.

"Come on then," I tell Joe, who whoops with happiness, releases my hand, and runs as fast as his sturdy legs will allow him toward his favourite part of the park.

Rufus tugs on the leash and whines at me, rolling his eyes. If he could speak, he would be saying, *Let me go and guard him, then!* I unclip the leash, and he hares across the grass and is soon at Joe's heels. I hear my son's peal of laughter as our wonderfully clever dog slows and trots beside him, and I experience a moment of utterly pure happiness.

This. This is what life is about.

—··—

There are very few people in the park, other than the woman still ignoring her daughter; an elderly couple, who hold hands as they follow the pathway, are exercising their tiny Bichon Frise; and an overweight man of around my own age, who wears baggy yellow shorts and a grubby, off-white tee-shirt that is slightly too small for him as it is bunching up above a flabby paunch, jogs in through the gates and begins to run toward me. He puffs loudly with each step. He sees me watching him and tries to smile.

"Lovely morning for a run," I tell him.

He grunts in acknowledgement, speeds up slightly, detours back to the pathway, and overtakes the elderly couple. Their dog yaps in annoyance at the interruption to its walk and chases after the jogger. It can't possibly catch him, and it soon gives up the chase.

From the corner of my eye, I see Rufus's good ear prick up, and I have a moment's anxiety that he will loop off to chase the much smaller creature. Being the good dog that he is, he stays with Joe. The jogging man is soon rounding the trees that are to the left of me and is therefore out of my line of sight. I smile as the echo of his footsteps slows to a walking pace, then chide myself—at least he is making the effort to get fit.

Far in the distance, I hear a car backfire—an unusual sound in this day and age. It reminds me of the time my old neighbor, Jack Kazinsky, got drunk and tried to shoot his nagging wife, June. He missed but he spent a fair amount of time in the pen for the attempt. Prior to the shot going off, I hadn't been alone in praying for something to shut her up; our walls are thin and her voice loud. She'd been upset by his drinking and vociferously told him so, and I, and several other neighbors, were forced to listen to the entire one-sided ensuing argument. We all also heard the shot when he finally snapped, and had been required to testify at his court appearance. There wasn't a person among us that didn't secretly wonder why he hadn't done it a long time before, and for a man on trial, Jack Kazinsky looked happier in that courtroom than I'd ever seen him look outside of it. June divorced him during his time away, met someone else in a short space of time, and is now happily nagging him to death in that same house.

Dislodging the memory, I turn back to my son and pick up my own pace when I see that he has almost reached the little security gates that border the fenced-off play equipment. They, and the fencing, are there for two reasons: to stop little children from escaping the confines of the area and to keep dogs out.

Joe figured out how to open the gates at age two and nearly frightened me to death the first time he did it. We had to have a long chat about what he was allowed to do and what he wasn't. I think I frightened him a bit, which hadn't been my intention, but that busy road is only a short distance away and easily accessible to a small child through the gaps in the hedges. He still opens the gates, but only when I am with him and tell him he can.

He turns to look for me, and as his eyes lock onto mine, I hear his piping voice call, "Can I go in? Please?"

"Go on then. Be careful though, until I get there," I call back.

The woman texting sends me an uncalled-for dirty glare.

"My boy," I explain.

She glances toward Joe, who is sliding the bar across the gates to access the play area, then she nods her head toward the elderly couple. "That should be on a leash. Dogs on the loose are dangerous, don't you think?"

I look at Rufus. He sits on his backside, scratching with one hind leg at his wonky ear and using enough force to dislodge his brain. He is panting madly; his tongue lolls from the side of his mouth and flaps up and down with each leg movement.

I laugh. The woman is not impressed, and I see her shoulders square up as she turns to face me.

"He's safe, don't worry," I tell her. "Rufus, here boy."

The dog stops scratching, overbalances, and sprawls on the floor in an undignified heap. He raises himself onto all fours, shakes himself down, picks up Pudge that Joe has dropped outside the gates, then bolts toward me, stopping, fortunately, just before he crash lands into my legs. I bend and reattach the leash, and together we walk toward a different part of the fencing.

I stop some distance from the woman, who is back on her phone texting and sending dirty looks my way. I ignore her and watch Joe.

My son is following every move the little girl in the park makes. He seems taken by her. I can see why—she's a pretty little thing: long dark curls, flashing dark eyes, blue jeans on her long legs, and a pastel pink jacket with a furry hood. She has an air of confidence about her that Joe has yet to attain, but physically she looks to be around the same age.

Joe climbs the steps of the slide behind her, watches as she arranges her legs in the correct position to slide down—a thing that Joe has sometimes struggled with—waits until she shoots to the bottom with a whoosh of speed and a heady giggle, then copies her every move, including the giggle as he lands on the mat at the foot of the chute.

I smile at him, and he waves at me. "Did you see me?" he yells, delighted at his achievement.

"I did! Well done!" I call back.

The mother of the girl stares at me sharply. I ignore her and ruffle the top of Rufus's head. He shifts and licks my hand. The woman looks away, but I am aware of her renewed interest in me. Her eyes slide toward me surreptitiously, and it starts to make me feel both awkward and more than a little angry. I have done nothing wrong. I have brought my boys to the park, and we *will* have fun!

It is my turn to square my own shoulders, and I raise my face to studiedly look at her. It is her turn to look away. She raises her phone to her ear and speaks into it rapidly and too quietly for me to be able to make out what she is saying. I give a mental shrug. Who cares?

Joe and the girl are now on the swings. The girl has the knack of aligning her bottom with the swing seat, walking backward, and then jumping up onto the seat, giving herself momentum she can build on to swing herself. This is another thing Joe has not mastered.

I watch him carefully observing her, noting that she studiously ignores his attentions. Despite this, he does exactly what she did, and for the first time in his life, Joe is on a swing and moving under his own impetus. He watches the girl as she swings her legs forward and back, forward and back, then moves his own in the same rhythm. It takes a couple of attempts, but my son is soon swinging himself! I am so proud of him that a tear runs involuntarily down my cheek even as I laugh aloud.

Rufus chuffs up at me and I bend to him. "Silly thing, aren't I?" I say. "I'm so proud of him though. Look, he's swinging by himself!"

Rufus obligingly follows my gaze to the two children on the swings. The girl appears to be getting bored. Who knows how long she's been in there? She scuffs her shoes against the ground each time the swing hits the low point, decreasing the range of the arc in the time-honored fashion, then I hear her shout, "One, two, three . . . *jump!*"

I see her fly off the seat on the upswing, and my heart skips a beat until I see her land safely in a crouch on the rubber mulch that lines the ground. She stands, dusts off her jeans, and wanders over to her mother, who raises one hand to her, turns her head away, and concentrates intently on the conversation she is having.

I shake my head in disgust, then turn back just in time to hear my Joe shouting, "One, two, three . . . *jump!*"

"*Nooo!*" My heart is in my mouth as he flies off the seat without having slowed himself down first.

He lands, not quite so neatly, but safely.

"What *is* your problem?" the girl's mother shouts at me.

"He jumped!" I tell her. "He's not old enough to do that!"

"Don't you tell me what my kid can do and what she can't!"

"What?" I am confused. "I wasn't talking about—"

"You just fuck off! Go on!" Her voice is shrill and loud. "Take that stinking *bear* with you and just *fuck off!*"

I hear the clang of the gate and see Joe running toward me, his face white with fear. Rufus is now standing, his hackles raised, teeth bared, and a low growl emanates from the back of his throat. It is a chilling sound, and the woman backs off.

"No, not you!" I hear her tell the person on the other end of her phone. "There's some fucking nutter in here . . . No, I don't want you to come down. She's going now . . . Aren't you?" She directs this last to me.

I slip her the finger, grab Joe's hand, and walk off as fast as his legs are able to. We follow the direction the elderly couple and the jogger had gone, my heart hammering in my chest and a metallic taste in my mouth. What had just happened?

"Pudge!" Joe shouts just as we round the corner of the pathway. "I've left Pudge!"

My heart sinks. We can't go without the bear; Joe will be inconsolable if we leave it behind. We stop and I turn my head to look behind us and am amazed to see that the little girl is running toward us, followed a good way behind by her mother.

The girl is holding the teddy. "You dropped this," she says, shoving it into my hand, still ignoring Joe.

"I . . . thank you!" I stammer.

"Gotta go," she says solemnly. "Mom's mad at you, but I thought you needed the bear."

"Thank you," I tell her again. "That was very kind of you."

She shrugs, turns on her heel, and runs back to her mother. I can hear her calling, "I was just giving her the *bear*, all right?" and her mother's answering, "For fuck's sake! Don't you ever run away from me, you hear?"

I steel myself at the sound of the slap and tighten my grip on Joe's hand. He stares up at me, his eyes still wide with fear. I say nothing. I simply pass him Pudge, tug on the leash, and the three of us make our way across the park as I make a mental note of what the woman and child looked like so that I could report her behavior later.

It is not the right time to confront her now.

— · · —

At the other side of the park is another exit. If we go out there, we can visit the little shop that sells the extremely creamy ices that Joe so loves. It means a long walk home, detouring along the back roads, but it's been a while since we've taken Rufus for a lengthy walk, so it won't do us any harm. There's no way in hell that I'm risking taking my boys back the same way as that woman and her daughter; the person she was talking to on the phone could turn up, and she had been so *angry* with me for some reason. I wasn't going to take that chance.

We catch up with the elderly couple and the Bichon Frise. It yaps at Rufus as we pass them. Rufus, being three times the yappy creature's size, gives it a disdainful look and jumps over it. The little dog cowers briefly, then is up and yapping frenetically at our disappearing rears. I swear Rufus looks at me and grins. Joe definitely does. I relax enough to smile too.

We turn left outside the gates into a leafy tree-lined avenue that has large expensive houses that are set back from the road. One hundred yards along is the shop. We make our way there, and I tie Rufus up outside as he is not allowed in.

I bend and ruffle his ears. "We won't be long. Be good!"

His tail goes down, and his expression switches to one of mournfulness.

"I'll wait with him," Joe volunteers.

I think quickly. That won't do. What if that woman has followed us? "No," I say. "I'll tell you what, I'll wait with Rufus. You go in and get us three ice creams."

I reach into my pocket and pull out the correct change he'll need and pass it to him. He looks as pleased as punch to be trusted to do this and slips into the shop behind a lad that has come from the other direction. A few moments later he follows him out again, a sad expression on his face.

"What's up?" I ask.

The lad ahead of Joe gives me a sort of semi-grin, paired with an expression of puzzlement. "Sorry?" he says.

"Not you," I say.

He looks behind him, shakes his head slightly, and walks away from us back in the direction he came from.

"The man won't serve me. I don't think he can see me at the counter," Joe complains.

"Come on, we'll *both* go in then," I say.

I remind Rufus to stay, check that the knot on the leash is tying him firmly to the post provided, look around to check that the woman and her daughter are nowhere in sight, then Joe and I both enter the shop.

A small bell tinkles as the door opens, and the aroma of freshly baked bread wafts up my nostrils and makes my mouth water. I am tempted to purchase a loaf, and if I hadn't promised Joe an ice cream, I would. Unfortunately, I don't have enough cash on me for both, so ice creams it is. We make our way to the counter and wait to be served.

"I think you missed my son," I tell the attendant, an elderly man, who wears thick-rimmed glasses.

He goggles at me through them, his eyes so magnified I can see the red veins in the sclera. He glances down, passes his vision over Joe, looks over the rest of the shop, and shrugs. "What can I get you?"

"We'd like three of your vanilla cones, please," I say, smarting at the slight to Joe. It really isn't turning out to be a good day.

"Three?" Joe questions.

"One for you, one for me, one for Rufus."

"Ah! Thanks!"

The attendant gives me a peculiar look.

"Rufus is the dog," I explain. "He's outside."

"Didn't like to ask," the man says, handing over the cones as Joe slides the money onto the counter.

He takes the cash and turns his back on us.

"A *thank you* wouldn't go amiss," I tell him sharply, and he has the good grace to look somewhat ashamed of himself.

"Sorry," he mutters.

I carry the cones to the door and stand back as the female half of the elderly couple from the park enters. She holds the door open for us and smiles at me. I smile back as I thank her, glad that she's not angry about Rufus leaping over her little dog. She lets go of the door a little too soon, and it bumps Joe on his shoulder.

"Ouch!" he complains, rubbing it.

"It was just an accident, Joe," I tell him, certain that the lady didn't intend to hurt my son; her smile was too genuine, and she appears too well-bred for that.

I smile at the elderly man, who is waiting with the Bichon Frise, which is yapping at Rufus again. Rufus is studiously ignoring it to the degree that he is looking the other way and yawning. I stifle a laugh.

"It still hurts," Joe says. "Can I have my cone?"

"In a minute. Just hold on to them for me for a second, so I can untie Rufus."

"Okay," the elderly man replies, reaching out for the cones.

Surprised, I pass them over to him and automatically unleash Rufus. Joe simply stares at the man with his mouth open.

"You'll catch flies if you don't close your mouth," I tell him, then I laugh as both my son and the man close their mouths with audible snaps. "I didn't mean you," I tell the man, who laughs nervously along with me.

He looks at Rufus, who is sitting beside the Bichon Frise and openly drooling for his ice cream, then he laughs properly.

"I've got a thirsty one here," he says cheerfully. "No chance of him closing that mouth while this is on offer!"

"No," I agree, taking the cones into my hands that now held Rufus's leash tightly.

I pass one to Joe and hold a second out to my dog. Rufus sniffs it, takes a lick, then swallows it whole, shaking his head as brain freeze performs its magic. His eyes cross and he burps.

"He's no gentleman!" the old man says, still laughing. "But he did enjoy that!"

I nod, my own mouth too full of my own ice cream to answer properly. I swallow fast, say goodbye, and lead my boys back the way we had come, trusting Joe to stay to my right on the inside of the sidewalk. As we pass the park, I check for the woman and the girl, but they are nowhere in sight. For the first time since that incident, I relax and enjoy my ice cream and the sight of all the fancy houses. We wander along in companionable silence.

It is so quiet we can hear the difference in the songs of the birds that are, in comparison, garrulous. As I swallow the final piece of my cone, I begin to point out the various calls to Joe, who is interested in anything to do with nature. I am passing on the knowledge that my grandmother gave me as a youngster, and I hope it sticks in his little head.

"Is that a blue tit?" Joe asks, pointing toward a little bird that sits motionless on the branch of a cherry blossom tree that borders one of the gardens we pass. It has a blue back, yellow belly, and green and white markings.

"Yes," I smile, grateful that the impromptu lesson is sinking in.

"What about that one?" He points to another, slightly larger that is more green than blue.

"No, that's a great tit," I tell him. "They're similar, aren't they? They come from the same family."

"Like us?" Joe asks.

"Like us," I agree.

"Why was that woman so cross with you?"

I wait a second before I respond. "I have no idea, Joe. I think perhaps she just didn't like me much."

"But she doesn't know you, does she?"

I shake my head.

"I don't think the little girl liked me much either," he says frankly. "She wouldn't talk to me."

I stoop to give him a hug. "Don't worry about it. She doesn't know any better, coming from a mother like that."

"I love you," Joe says.

"I love you more."

"I love you most."

—— • • ——

Back home again we practically fall through the front door as Rufus shoves us out of the way so that he can get to his water bowl for a well-earned drink. His leash trails behind him as he sprints along the hall and into the kitchen, and Joe and I laugh at the sound of water splashing as he slurps his fill. We humans remove our coats and boots—I have to help Joe with his red wellingtons—and line them up neatly on the shoe rack that sits against the wall in the hallway, halfway between the front door and the stairs.

Joe runs off to try to hang the coats on the back of the kitchen door while I stay and smile at the array of footwear: my adult size sixes beside his child's size nines. Joe insists that the rack be displayed with a pair of mine next to a pair of his, squishing his tiny shoes into the smallest gap if space decrees that there is an odd number of pairs on a shelf. He's always been this way, as if innately believing that a woman should have a man beside her.

Joe *is* my man. My little man. The bigger Joe, for whom my Joe is named, did not get to meet his son. When I went into labor three weeks before the due date and, conveniently, whilst at a routine antenatal visit in the hospital, big Joe, in a tearing hurry to be by my side, ran a stop sign and was hit side on by a waste removal lorry; he wouldn't have known what hit him. I was told an hour or so after little Joe made his way, kicking and screaming, into the world. It's been me, little Joe, and Rufus ever since and goes, perhaps, some way to explaining why I am protective of my son.

"I can't do it!" Joe wails, dropping the coats onto the floor and turning to face me, hands on hips. "I'm not big enough yet!"

"No problem. Thank you for trying," I tell him as I hurry to curtail the tantrum that could very easily ensue.

Joe likes to be independent and gets very cross if he can't do what he expects to. For a child who is sweet natured ninety-five percent of the time, the other five percent is breathtakingly the opposite and involves fists hitting walls and feet hitting whatever else is in the vicinity at the time. My legs have been bruised more times than I care to mention, so it is important to me that this tempest is averted.

"Why don't you go and get your toy box out before dinner?"

"Can I get my bricks out?"

I nod and shoo him on his way so that I can hang up the coats. Rufus appears in the doorway, his muzzle dripping small drops of water that clearly shows the route he took around the kitchen table to get to us. Both his ears are down.

I bend to him, take his wet chops between my hands, and look into his soulfully deep, brown eyes. "Crisis averted," I tell him as I scratch behind his ears with my fingertips.

He sighs deeply. I kiss his silken head, stand, and make my way into the kitchen, avoiding the wet spots, to make a start on dinner.

—••—

Later, after we have eaten Joe's favourite meal—spaghetti bolognaise—and I have cleared away the mess, I give Joe his nightly bath, get him into a pair of his Sailor Sam pajamas, and take him into his bedroom. It is a typical little boy's room; the walls are painted with big blue waves, topped with white spray leading on up to the night sky that adorns the ceiling. Stars, all lovingly hand painted by me, show miniature constellations, and the midnight-blue curtains match the star theme. Joe's bed linen bears small images of boats afloat on gentle seas and is tucked into the room's *pièce de résistance*; a wooden framed boat bed that a friend of his father built for him soon after little Joe's birth.

I remember how he sobbed the entire time he worked on it and how red his eyes were as he also constructed a treasure chest, made of two halves, that magically became bookcases. Another large chest that nestles beneath the window holds Joe's toys—the lid seldom closes fully. Joe has yet to develop the knack of putting them away tidily.

The room smells of him—little Joe, that is—a curious blend of sweaty feet, freshly washed hair, and the unique warm odor of his body. It is a smell I cherish, and I have been known to quietly sit in his room long after he is asleep, inhaling the smell deep into my bones and soul. I would know his own personal smell anywhere and could pick it out blindfolded if I were asked to identify him out of his class of forty at the kindergarten he attends. I am not sure whether I should be proud of this ability or not. But I could.

I carry my son to his bed, pull down the covers single handedly, then gently lay him down and pull the covers to just below his chin. He smiles at me through sleep-heavy eyes.

"Lay with me, Mommy?" he asks, refusing to remove the arm that he slung around my neck as I covered him.

"Always," I reply, climbing in behind him and drawing his warm, snuggly body into mine. He fits perfectly.

"Love you."

"I love you more."

He giggles softly. "No, I love you most, Mommy."

— • • —

I awaken with a degree of disorientation to a regular beeping sound and a strange, oddly medical smell. A memory of the home for the elderly where I visited my grandmother when I was child fills my head, and I thrust it away, shuddering. I disliked the smell as a child and feel the same way about it now. I briefly recall how my grandmother died, alone and confused, having suffered from dementia for the final few years of her life.

My mother only visited my grandmother once in her final year, a fact that makes me angry still. The home where she was taken care of was a five-minute walk from my high school, so I took to visiting her after school every Friday afternoon. The first couple of times I did this were fine. There were two school buses available for me to catch, and I timed it so that I could tell her what I'd been doing all week, then dash off for my ride home. I knew my grandmother did not know who I was, but she seemed to enjoy my company and I enjoyed hers.

The third time I visited, I misjudged the time and missed the second bus. My English teacher, Mrs. Clements, happened to drive past the stop and caught me in floods of tears, not knowing how I would get to my home ten miles away from school. She pulled over, wound down her window, listened to my tale of woe, and told me to get in the car. She drove me the entire ten miles home and listened to my explanation of why I'd missed the bus and how angry my mother would be when she found out what I'd been doing.

"Well, that's a problem that's simply solved," I can still hear her warm voice saying. "I generally leave the school around half past four. I'll come by the home and take you back. No need to worry about catching the bus from now on, and look, there's the bus you missed. You'll be home earlier than usual today."

Mrs. Clements kept her word every week without fail for the next few months. She even made arrangements to pick me up from the corner of my road to take me on a Friday afternoon during the school holidays, with the exception of four weeks when she was on vacation herself. It was she who suggested I wait for her on the corner, aware that my mother would not be happy about her taking me. My mother never did find out, and she died several years later still blissfully unaware of my escapades.

The final time I saw my grandmother, she had an unusual moment of brief clarity toward the end of my visit.

"I love you," she whispered, clasping my youthful hand in her frail, old one. "Thank you for coming to see me."

"No need for thanks," I whispered in reply, trying to hold back the tears that stung my eyes. "I love you more."

"I love you most."

She passed away that night.

— • • —

The memory makes my eyelids prickle, and a small tear leaks out. It trickles down my cheek and is caught by the pillow. I feel for Joe's warm body but instead touch something cold and metallic. I pry my eyes partway open, utterly confused. I remember going to sleep cuddling my son, but now there are bars around the bed and the mattress feels . . . different somehow.

It is hard beneath my hip, which, I note, aches terribly. I raise my arm to push my hair away from my face and wince at a sudden pain. I bring my hand closer to my face and see that an IV line feeds into the back of it; at the point where the line enters is a massive purple and brown bruise and some dried blood. Beneath the bruise, the hand I am staring at is dry skinned and wrinkled and not mine. Alarmed, I attempt to sit up but am unable to lift my head from the pillow.

"Joe! Joe! Where are you?" Panic bubbles to the surface, and I cry out for a second time, "Joe! Come to Mommy, sweetheart! Don't be scared!"

I hear the sound of a door squeaking open and footsteps approaching the bed.

"Hush, be still now, my lovely. Don't be scared. Nothing to be scared of here." A lilting voice speaks, followed immediately by a cheerful brown face that leans over and smiles down at me. It is topped by a mop of black curls. The middle-aged woman has brown eyes that are lit with gentle humor, and I have no idea who she is.

I watch as she lifts her cool hand and takes a hold of the old, IV-lined hand, and curiously, I can feel the touch. I wonder if this is how Alice felt when she dropped down the rabbit hole as my eyes search for the owner of the old hand. I can see nobody apart from the smiling woman.

"I need to refresh the line." The woman holds my eyes as she speaks. "I'll be as gentle as I can be, my lovely, but first I need to turn you. You don't want to be getting bedsores, do you?"

I wonder why she's not looking at the old lady to whom she is evidently talking, but don't have time to ask as, without further ado, she moves something that had been resting against my back, cranks a lever at the side of the bed (how did *that* get there?), and my head gradually drops as I roll onto my back and lie flat. I feel her move my arms so that they cross my chest, and note that she moves the IV line carefully. She stands at the side of Joe's bed, and there is a clunk as the metal rail slips down from my view. She takes a pillow and her cool hand separates my knees as she places it between them. She then takes a hold of Joe's bottom sheet and pulls it gently up toward her. I find myself rolling over and focus on a window that has bars outside it. Joe's curtains are gone, as are the sea-painted walls.

I find myself screaming and am unable to stop, even when the strange lady's face appears in front of me, genuine concern written all over it.

"Oh, my lovely! Did I hurt you? I tried so hard not to."

"Where's Joe?" My voice sounds different, guttural almost. "I want my son brought to me, *now!*"

"I know you do, my lovely, and I promise you'll be seeing him again very soon. I *promise*, you hear?"

Something in her voice tells me she is genuinely distressed for me, but the terror that strikes at the core of me and keeps me immobile is simple; why isn't he *here, now*? This thought overrides the emotions of a woman I do not know, and with a strength I have to dig deep for, I find I can move my arms, and I flail and cry out as the visceral pain of loss floods my body from toes to hair.

I want my son. It is as simple as that. Why won't she let me see him?

When I run out of strength, which takes a shockingly short amount of time, I draw breath and ask the questions I fear the answers to the most. "Did someone break in? Was Joe hurt? Why can't I remember? Am I in the hospital? Is Joe here too?"

The woman strokes my head tenderly; her eyes lock on to mine, and she does not look away as she answers. "No, my lovely. No break in, and no, you're not in a hospital. You're in your own room."

She tucks something soft into my hand, and my fingers instinctively enfold around it as her words sink in.

"I'm not in my own room!" I shriek.

I want to lash out again, but instead I whimper as the biggest, most agonizing pain imaginable explodes deep within my chest, and as an alarm bell sounds and the room fades away, I finally hear Joe calling me . . .

— • • —

"Mommy!" Joe's little voice is ecstatic.

Eager to get to him, I pull myself out of bed and turn toward the sound. The love I feel for my boy overwhelms me, as it does every time I hear him. There he is! Joe stands just inside the doorway, and I laugh to see that he is wearing his red coat and red wellingtons. He holds a blue leash in his left hand, and Rufus strains at the end of it, his tail spinning like a dervish as he tries to reach me. Sweet yelping sounds come from his throat, and I laugh again as I make my way eagerly toward them, fall to my knees, and encompass them both with my embrace.

"My Joe," I say as hot, salty tears of joy course down my cheeks.

I cover my son's face with kisses as his arms twine around my neck. I breathe in his familiar smell, and the warmth of his love instantly heals the pain in my heart.

"Sweet boy," I tell Rufus as I reach out one hand to stroke his silken, wonky ear.

Rufus's tongue rasps on my wrist. I am filled with an uplifting sense of belonging and peace. I am with my family, and all is right with the world.

⚊ • • ⚊

I gradually become aware that the lady who had been by my bedside is still in the room with us. I remember her name now—Lydia, and I also recall that she is a nurse. She is greeting someone I recognize as being one of the resident doctors into the room with us. He is young and I do not like him.

I glance behind Lydia to a hospital bed, which holds a very old, frail woman, who has various medical lines disappearing into her arms that, in turn, feed into machinery that is now still and quiet. I note with a pang that she is beyond help, and as Joe turns to look where I look, I cover his eyes so that he does not have to see. I am surprised when he pushes my hand away and smiles at the body of the old lady but says nothing as Lydia speaks.

"She passed at five past seven. She'd been calling for her son again. We'd hoped after her escapade yesterday that she'd sleep most of today."

"Yes, I heard about that. What happened?" The doctor fidgets on his feet, flicks paper on the chart he holds, and turns his wrist to look at his watch.

Lydia makes a moue of displeasure. "Am I keeping you?" she says pointedly and waits until the doctor's shoulders sag a little. She has made her point. "She ripped out the IV line and took herself back to the park. God knows how she found the energy to get out of bed again, let alone get past the security systems at the door. She took the dog leash with her, and the teddy, she never let out of her sight. Sergeant McKinney saw her wandering past the station; he *waved* at her, the damned fool! Didn't think to go out and ask if she was okay. She went home, then to the play area and frightened the hell out of some woman who was there with her daughter—she reported it to McKinney on the way home—and then she went to the shop; you know, the one at the back of the park? Mr. News I think it's called? Bought three ice cream cones, gave one to an old boy's little dog, and fed one to a teddy. The old man said that very specifically; she *fed one to a teddy*. Obviously, he thought she was a bit confused and rang the station when he and his wife got home. By the time McKinney got off his butt and went looking for her, she'd disappeared."

Electric currents run up my spine as I listen to her words.

"Where had she gone?"

"Home again. She still had her old door key. The owners never bothered changing the locks. After so many years I guess they didn't think they needed to. They came home and found a mess in the kitchen; water all over the floor, cooked spaghetti on two plates at the kitchen table. God alone knows how she didn't burn the place down. Then she took herself to bed in what used to be her son's room."

Confused, I turn to little Joe. "*We* went to the park yesterday, didn't we?"

He nods.

"Poor woman," the doctor says with not a shred of concern in his voice.

"She *was!*" Lydia snaps. "Losing a son in the way that she did is enough to turn anyone's mind!"

"Oh, yes, of course! Um . . . remind me again . . . ?" The doctor realizes his mistake and tries to make amends.

Lydia tuts between her teeth and busies herself by pulling a sheet straight on the bed. Not looking at the doctor, she says, "She was coming back from a trip to the park with her son and the family dog. Joe twisted out of her hand and ran into the road just opposite the police station. He liked to walk on the wall outside apparently and wanted to do it without any help. The dog saw a car speeding down the road, yanked his lead from her *other* hand, and according to witnesses, tried to head-butt the child out of the way. The car hit them both. She was in the road but she wasn't touched. She saw the whole thing."

Joe squeezes my hand. I stare down at him as dark memories crowd into my head. In slow motion I see my beautiful son running across the road toward the police station wall; I see the car racing toward him; I see Rufus snapping the lead from my hand and darting toward our boy; I hear my feet slapping against the tarmac as I rush out into the road behind them; I see Rufus head-butt my son's body in his frantic attempt to push him clear of the vehicle; I feel in my bones the high-pitched squeal of brakes as the driver sees, too late, my boy and my good dog, and then I am deafened by the deadly double thud of impact mere inches in front of me. I see Joe's impossibly tiny body sucked beneath the car and pray that he falls flat, stays down—oh stay down Joe, don't lift your head, don't move, don't move, don't move . . .

I see his head slide into a jagged pothole in the road, and his neck and upper chest are caught by the front left-hand tire, which severs his head from his body and sends it flying through the air, landing neatly, neck down, on the sidewalk; I see Joe's wide-open eyes and his mouth set in an *oh* of shock; I see his golden curls turn to red; I see the red pour down his skull, onto his face, into his eyes and mouth, and I don't see him blink or hear him cry or spit or gag or swallow. I see Rufus flying partway over the bonnet of the car, then rebounding twice as fast back down to the tarmac, head first because his leash was caught beneath the front right tire. I hear the crunch as his neck breaks on impact. I see Joe's little red wellingtons poking out from beneath the car as I pass in front of it; I hear my breath, heavy and hitching in my chest and throat, as I walk on numb legs to the sidewalk to pick up Joe's head and return with it cradled in my arms so I can stroke Rufus's head as he tries to lick my hand and takes his last shuddering gasp of air. And finally I hear the *SNAP* that sounds like a shotgun going off in my head as I break.

"Oh." The doctor grimaces. "That was tough." He thinks for a second. "Explains why she was such a pain. Still, you'd think that after sixty years she'd have got over it."

Sixty years! Joe and I both turn to look at the old woman in the bed.

Lydia's head flashes toward the doctor. "Don't," she warns. Her voice trembles with an incredulity she is no longer trying to contain. "*Got over it?* She lost her entire family! What sadistic bastard condemned her to sixty years in this particular room, staring out of *that* window at the road that killed her husband and then took her only child? I'd be bloody upset too!"

"Upset? She was either catatonic or thrashing around and screaming blue murder!" the doctor protests.

"Did you not hear me? She could see the exact spots both of them died! For *sixty years!* Today is a blessing for her!"

Is it my imagination or does she glance at me?

Her voice drops to a whisper. "The only things that gave her comfort were Pudge and the dog leash."

"Pudge?" The doctor is backing toward the door, away from her suppressed rage.

Lydia's eyes grow colder still. "The teddy! You know, the one someone hid in her drawer at some point over the years? The one she asked for *every day?* It's in her notes—look, there!" Lydia bounds across the room to the doctor, rifles through the papers until she finds what she is looking for, then jabs her fingernails against the writing. "*Patient is requesting puj? Any ideas anyone?* There's the first note, and oh, look at the replies: *Perhaps she means that awful sludge the cook doles out? Probably needs her bum changed. Did she have her teeth in?.* . . Shall I go on? No, I didn't think so. She was still begging for Pudge when I came along, and *looked* for something out of the ordinary. See? She's holding it now."

Unwillingly, the doctor looks at the unmoving body of the old woman in the bed. A moth-eaten teddy that has no fur left on its ancient body lies beside the hand that has lost its grip in death. A tatty leash is tied around its neck.

Joe squeals with delight. "Can I have Pudge back now?"

"Of course you can."

I kiss his golden curls, take comfort from his unique little-boy smell, and reluctantly lower him from my arms. My mouth is dry as I watch him run to the hospital bed to collect the moth-eaten teddy as the doctor almost runs from the room.

He bends and kisses the old lady's face, and I clearly hear him say, "Thank you for taking me to the park yesterday."

I sink to my knees and find myself cuddling Rufus as he sticks his snout onto my lap. I take his head in my hands. His brown eyes glow with love for me, and I scratch him in his good place behind his ears and kiss the top of his head repeatedly.

"Good dog," I tell him. "Best dog!"

Rufus chuffs contentedly.

Joe comes back to me. He holds Pudge carefully in his little hands and says, "We've been waiting for you!"

My head turns from my son to the body on the bed and back again as I try to accept what I am evidently being told. As though in confirmation of this, Joe turns toward the doorway behind us and points. My eyes automatically follow his arm, and I can just make out the outline of a tall male figure that stands in the darkness just beyond the doorway. I frown. There is something very familiar about that shape, but I know from walking around town after Joe's birth that my eyes can lie.

As if fed up with waiting, the figure moves swiftly through the doorway toward us, bringing with it a brilliant light: so bright that I do not understand how I could have believed he stood in darkness, so strong that I am unable to make out his features. I stare in wonder as the light spreads out into the room, encompassing Joe, Rufus, and me.

Strange as it may seem, I am not scared. I find myself laughing in incredulity as I look beyond us to the man who has silently moved to crouch in front of where I kneel with Joe and Rufus, and with a shock that is electric, I know that my eyes do not lie this time.

— · · —

"You took your sweet time." Big Joe's face crinkles into his familiar smile.

"Sixty years?" I hesitantly ask, looking from the face of my gorgeous husband to the wrinkled papery skin and sunken features of the woman on the bed.

"Sixty since little Joe and Rufus. Sixty-five since me."

"I missed you so much," I say, "but I didn't know little Joe and Rufus had gone too."

"That's why we've stuck with you. Every day since, he and that dog have been here. I knew you didn't realise they were gone, but you knew I was, so I had to stand back and watch. I've wanted this day to come so badly!"

"But I'm old and decrepit now!" I wail.

He laughs and draws me to my feet and into his arms. "No, you're really not."

When we finally draw apart, big Joe tucks me firmly under his shoulder and kisses the top of my head, and I remember instantly where little Joe's smell comes from. He reminded me in his own way all his life. I reach up to return my husband's kiss, then I slide myself out of his grip. Big Joe understands without me needing to say anything.

I walk to Lydia and put my arms around her. "I know you can't hear me, but thank you. Thank you for your care, and thank you for finding Pudge and the leash. It meant the world to me, if you'd only known it." I kiss her cheek.

To my surprise, she looks directly at me and her features soften. "Oh I can hear you, my lovely, and you're welcome," she says with a wide smile. "I promised you'd see your son soon, didn't I? Your hunk of a husband told me where the bear and leash had been hidden, so you can thank him for that. They've both been waiting patiently for you." She turns to big Joe. "So don't you think it's time you took her home? Although I have to say that I'm going to miss you all. Especially you, young man," she tells my little Joe.

"Thank you for having us," Joe tells Lydia politely as he puts his small warm hand into mine. "Yes, let's go home, please. It's not very nice here, is it? Sorry, Lydia. Come on, Mommy, Daddy, Rufus."

My husband holds out his hand to us both, and Rufus comes to heel, carrying his own leash.

"That sounds like a good idea," I tell him. "Have I told you that I love you all? So much?"

"We love you more," they tell me.

Even Rufus chuffs.

"But I love you most."

I smile from the heart at my son, my husband, and my good dog as love radiates over us, and the brilliant light makes the room, and my body, fade from my view.

J.M. Turner is originally from London, England, and has been writing books and stories for some time now. She has written fantasy stories for children and contemporary fiction for young adults. This is her first foray into the world of writing for adults, but not, she hopes, her last. She works in education (believing that everybody should have a passion for reading and writing) and hopes to instill a love of books into as many people as she can. She is also an official proofreader for students who study Creative Writing, English Language, English Literature, and Law at her local university, and she copy-edits for certain local businesses and, more recently, for budding authors from the university. She can be found on social media here: www.facebook.com/authorjillturner, here: www. facebook.com/LittleRedLines, here: www.twitter.com/JillMTurner, and here: authorjmturner.wordpress.com, and she would love to connect with you, so feel free to drop her a line, particularly if you enjoyed the story, "Joe."

Worm
Jacob Prytherch

"I found a worm in my pasta today," I said.

Linda turned her head toward me before returning to her book. "I didn't cook you any lunch."

"I didn't say you did. It was from the shops."

"*Hmmm.*" Linda turned a page.

"Tomato and mascarpone."

Another page.

"And worm, apparently." She turned back a page, then two. I heard her breathe. "Did you keep it?"

I tapped my pen on the blank paper that sat before me. The piano was to my right, waiting. "I chucked it. Straight in the bin." I pressed a couple of keys experimentally before letting my hand drop to my side. *Nothing.* "Shit."

She ignored my swearing. "I would have gone down to the shop."

"I was working." I used the pen to scratch the back of my neck.

Linda placed a fingertip to her forehead, finished the page, and pulled a strand of hair over her ear. I couldn't remember if I'd told her that the action annoyed me to my prickly core, but I probably had. She did it again and then turned the page.

I pressed another key. The tone slunk away into the house, embarrassed about its own existence.

Linda looked up. "What was that?"

The truth. "Nothing."

Her voice was a plateau. "Was that a new hit?"

I stood up. "I'm going out."

I went to the hallway. I had left the keys on the squat dresser that my mother-in-law had burdened us with—I usually put them there so I'd be able to find them easily. They weren't there. I eventually found them on a hook next to the coats. It had a small framed picture of a keyhole above it. I picked up my keys and knocked the picture with my wrist, maybe accidentally, but it was glued to the wall. I slammed the door on my way out, threw my notebook on the seat of my car, and pulled out into no traffic at all.

It was Sunday. It was hot. There were waves dancing over the tarmac, like the lines on the button that turned the heater on in my decade-old silver hatchback. I turned on the radio, heard *that* song—my song—and turned it back off.

None of the shops were open yet. I drove out of town, which only took a few minutes thanks to the carefully chosen location of our two up, two down—close to the station, close to the countryside that we never visited—and took a snaking road toward the horizon.

It seemed that even farmers had a weekend, because there was no one about. Animals stood or sat, their minds empty and their mouths full of grass. There were fields of dancing crops that were on the turn from green to gold, but I had no idea if that was what they were bred for or if they'd just been left to die. It occurred to me that if I were the last human, I would be gone within a day.

Every time I drove out of town, I somehow found myself on an unfamiliar road, which usually meant that I had to pull out the satnav, but today it was just what I was after. Hills dotted the fields like lumps of fat in old milk. I found a particularly inviting one and stuck close to it, taking a turn that circled its base. The side of the hill was overflowing with old trees, the kind that looked like crooked fingers, old hags, and other things that spoke of fancy. Dried giant's bones. There wasn't any music in the land, no structure. It was a discord. It was wild. It was my job to bring some order.

I wanted to get to the top of the hill, but the rocks bulged and the trees wagged their branches at me. I drove faster, daring the land to keep denying me and my crappy 1.2 litre engine. I took a corner quickly, almost ending my journey in the front of a burned-out cottage. Its garden was walled by drystone and had become one large bramble, with stems as thick as my wrist. I moved on.

There were no sign posts, but the air clawing at my face through the open window was fresh. I was heading toward the sea. I didn't want to go down to the beach, I wanted to go up, and I was damned if something as insignificant as geography was going to stop me. I slowed down, hunching over the wheel as I willed the forest to open up. The trees must have known I was serious because they relented.

A road of broken tarmac and opportunistic weeds peered back at me. It was barely wide enough for one car. Bushes on either side scraped my doors as I squeezed my way through. There were no passing spots. If a car had come the other way, it would have been a battle of wills to see who would have budged first. If a car came from behind me, then it could have trapped me on the top of the hill until I dried out like an old apricot.

The peak was bald of grass and dry as coconut husk. The sun paid more attention to the top of a hill than the land below. The heat made me want a drink, ideally a milkshake—one of the fancy ones with ice cream and a really offbeat flavour, maybe pecan. Birds stayed down in the trees, and I couldn't even hear crickets, or grasshoppers, whichever one lived in Britain. It was quiet, and that was what I needed.

I sat down on a patch of grass curved like the bow of a violin, planted my notebook on my knees, and drew five lines across the paper, from left to right. The surface was a starburst to my eyes, and I had to shade the paper with my hand, but finally, out here with the countryside at my feet and no one at my side, I felt ready to write another hit. I either needed a piano or silence to write, but nothing else. No distractions.

I'd had success before, but just once. Some said it was more to do with the lass who was singing, and that was partially true. She was the working class success—all salt and swearing when she was speaking, with a laugh like a blocked gutter; but, when she sang, the critics and the public alike agreed they could hear the heartbeat of her soul. All I heard was the money falling into my bank account, although I realise that analogy doesn't work well now that hardly anyone uses cash, but you get the idea. I didn't care about who sang it, as long as the song was mine.

Someone was humming.

I think I'd noticed it a few minutes ago on some level but was too caught with the music inside me. Christ, that sounds pretentious . . . but it was true in that I had to turn my senses off in order to come up with something new. It had to come from somewhere, didn't it?

They were still humming.

"Who the f—" I started, before holding my tongue. I saw her.

She was sitting on a rocking chair on the porch of her house, which I'd somehow missed while parking and walking and sitting and looking about myself. It was nestled between a couple of trees that bowed over it like protective parents.

The woman hummed and I listened. The first thought that crossed my mind was that nobody sat in rocking chairs any more, but I soon forgot the detail as I started to nod my head along to the melody.

"That's electric," I said. I'd never used the word in that context before, but I knew that it was the best fit. "Who wrote it?"

She stopped humming and replied, "I did."

She looked to be about seventy but also in her mid-twenties, by which I mean that her body was physically young when first glanced, but the skin around her eyes creased into familiar lines when she blinked, and the manner in which she had settled in the chair spoke of many years on her bones. She looked like she'd worked out exactly how she needed to sit for hours without her feet getting numb, a skill I still hadn't learned. Her hair was long, but I couldn't say how long, as most of it fell behind the rocking chair.

The house was squat, one storey, and maybe even one room. It was so deep in the trees that it looked more as if the frontage of a house from a high-budget theatre production had been pressed onto the woods. The door of her house was open. Her hair trailed back inside, into the thick brown shadows.

"It's brilliant," I said. I longed to hear the melody again.

The tune had been simple, but such a quality can often be a sign of greatness. The oldest values were the most important:

family, community; and the most vintage stories speak to all of us no matter what complicated brushstrokes of politics or taste we lay over ourselves.

I'm mixing my metaphors, but that's just a sign of how much the song lit me up. It was new, but felt old. It seemed a sin that no one had thought of the tune before. It felt so damn *obvious*.

"Does it have any words?" I asked.

The woman shook her head. "Words would not sit well on it," she said. "They would kill it."

"You might be right," I said. "A tune like that could be heard the world over, and everyone would think it belonged to them."

A breeze licked over the hill and flicked the pages of my notebook into a boat sail on the grass.

"I write music too," I said.

I felt such a compulsion to validate myself, but I had no idea why. After all, who was she? Had she written a number one in seven countries? Although the U.S. should have counted as more than one country in my opinion. It's as large as an entire continent, after all.

"Music is important," she replied.

"I've had success," I said, continuing my posturing despite myself, or should I say an ever-shrinking part of myself. "People know me."

She waited.

"Can I have it?" I asked.

She nodded, and that was that.

━ • • ━

I rolled down the hill with a spring in my metaphorical step. The house was empty when I got home, but it didn't matter. I had what I needed.

I didn't even need to write it down. I sat down at the piano, and the tune left my fingers and filled the air, echoing around the house and filling out every inch of silence.

At some point, when it was night and the room became dark so that I couldn't see the keys any more, I picked up the phone.

"Andre," said the voice at the other end, dusted with nonchalance.

I didn't actually know what time it was, but Andre tended to be awake during the darker hours. He was an insomniac and a haemophiliac. He wore black leather gloves with cut off tips. He never took them off. He was a friend, and, more importantly, he was a record producer.

"I've got one, a great one." I didn't bother telling him who I was; no one needed to in this time of caller ID. It saved so much precious time. "Can I come down to the studio?" I asked.

There was a pause. I could hear another voice, higher than his and far less controlled. It laughed.

"No."

Disappointment bloomed but I weeded it straight away.

"Let me play it for you."

More laughter.

"Fine," said Andre. "Knock yourself out."

I balanced my phone on top of a stack of music books, magazines, and junk mail, and sat down at the piano. I placed my hands at the keys and my stomach lurched. The room spun and righted itself in a heartbeat, and I felt my face pull itself into a smile, one that was just for me.

I played and Andre listened. When I had finished, I could hear his breathing. There was no other sound on the line.

"Andre?" I asked.

"I'm here," he said. "That was . . . it was . . . I . . ."

I heard the hum of words in the background.

"Can we hear it again?"

— • • —

I slept, but only on the sofa, and only until it was light. I wasn't hungry but I forced myself to eat. I was used to getting up before my stomach had.

When I left the house, it was with my plastic travel mug of coffee in my hand and my notebook nestled in the sweat under my armpit. I had forgotten to shower. I heard the scrape of a trowel and looked over the fence to see that Lola, my neighbour, was already up. She was weeding her flowerbeds, knees to the lawn, in her pyjamas. She was humming, and I recognised the tune.

"Heard it through the wall?" I asked, wondering if I'd kept her up.

She looked at me with rheumy eyes and smiled.

Andre hadn't asked me to his studio in the end, as I thought he would. Instead he asked me to head straight to the radio station. He didn't own the radio station, and I reminded him of that, and he said he didn't care.

When I got out of the taxi, with the taxi driver still humming my tune back to me—he'd asked me what I did for a living and I'd shown him—I made my way up the concrete steps of the seventies monstrosity that housed KRR Medium Wave: All The Songs, All The Time, etcetera, etcetera.

I saw Andre before he saw me. He was arguing with the receptionist. He looked like he'd had about as much sleep as me. His hair was flat to his head and greasy. I hadn't seen him like that before. His shirt was crumpled and unbuttoned. I saw a freckled chest that looked as if it had been splashed with vinegar.

He was demanding to see the head of broadcasting, and the receptionist was explaining very calmly that "this is a local radio station, sir, and we do not have a head of broadcasting, but Paula Tunning is in charge of the schedule, and we will see if she's available, and could you please calm down before she arrives, sir."

Andre's eyes lit up like the light inside a rusting fridge when he saw me.

"Mate! About time. I'm just trying to explain to this jobsworth how important it is to get your tune out there."

To her credit, the receptionist kept her eyes on the blue glow of the computer screen in front of her.

"It doesn't have any words yet, but I'm working on it," I said, slipping my notebook out from under my arm.

Andre waved the notion away, which was good because I hadn't written any words, nor even started to. I had tried while I was killing time in the taxi, but it had become obvious that there was no way it would work. The woman on the hill was right. You couldn't add words any more than you could add another set of arms to a person without changing what it was. It was complete.

For the first time, I noticed that there was someone with Andre. A woman slid out of the shadows of the pillar wearing a dress that looked like it was only designed for the night. She placed a hand on my shoulder. She smelled of what was probably a body spray but seemed to me more like acid.

"Play us the song."

I looked around the foyer at the abstract art, potted plastic plants, and bevelled concrete columns. "On what?"

"Wait here," said Andre, his tongue churning out new-born words before they had formed. "Just wait, okay? I've got the gear in the car."

The receptionist was watching us. "Sir, if you'd just wait a moment—"

"Time waits for no man," replied Andre. "No man, no one."

He jogged out of the hallway, his shirt flapping free of his jeans. I looked at the receptionist to see if there was the hint of a smile at Andre's antics. There was not.

Moments later, Andre returned, hauling a large black case up the stairs. At the same moment, a tall woman with short hair, dyed the colour of oak leaves, atop a round head that was slightly too small for her shoulders, stepped out of the elevator. She was wearing a blood-red shirt. I don't think I'd ever seen anyone wearing such a red shirt before. She approached the receptionist and muttered something under her breath before approaching with the air of a baroness visiting the peasantry.

"I was told you wanted to see me." Her voice was as stilted as her body.

"You in charge, yeah? You Paula Tungsten?" asked Andre.

"Tunning," said the woman. "Can you tell me why you're here? And why I need to be here too, instead of enjoying my bagel?"

Andre pointed a finger at me so close to my eye that I flinched. "This guy, this one right here, has something for you. The best piece of music to grace our generation, no word of a lie."

Tunning looked at me. "Congratulations," she said, as if the word carried the same meaning as *your death would please me*. She looked back to Andre and took a step forward. "Stop unpacking that."

"No way," said Andre as he teased the keyboard from its case. "Not until you hear him play. You need him on your station, today."

"The schedule's complete," said Tunning. "No changing it once it's up."

"You'll make time in your schedule for this," said Andre. He pulled a tangle of cables free of the bag and started to look around for a power socket.

Tunning placed a hand on his shoulders. "No, I won't."

For the first time, Andre seemed to comprehend what the pinheaded woman was saying. He dropped the cables into a slithering heap, rammed a hand into his pocket, fumbled with his wallet, and fished out every note he could find inside, which looked to be close to £300. He thrust them into Tunning's hands.

"That won't get you on air," said Tunning.

Andre closed Tunning's fingers over the notes with shaking hands. "I know, that's just for three minutes of your time, just to listen to him. Three minutes, that's all—right here, right now."

Tunning jabbed at the inside of her lower lip with her tongue, making the sound of a wet fish hitting a chopping board. Eventually the coloured paper with the royal faces swayed her.

"Three minutes. After that, it's out or the police, *capiche?*"

I snorted at the word, but a look from her tungsten eyes—because she *was* tungsten, shiny and cold as a nail—fired a warning shot across my bow.

The keyboard was Andre's best, with a rich sound for a machine, not like the faded junk he hoisted on session musicians who paid him to use their practice room. This was a performance tool, recording quality. I felt bad touching it, but only for a second.

The next second flowed heavy with music, and I forgot everything else.

I finished later. I hadn't timed it, but the sun was now high in the sky outside, burning away the shadows from directly above. Where before it had been empty, now the lobby was full of people that I didn't recall seeing before. They were all watching me, with Tunning at their head. She led the applause and didn't stop or speak until Andre approached her.

A few swiftly-spoken words had sealed the deal, and soon I was back at the piano; this time in the radio station broadcasting room with more people listening to me than ever had before.

— · · —

The following few days are hard to recall.

After the radio station, the song moved. You could call it word of mouth, but there were no words—although mouths there were, too many to count, singing the notes back to us as we walked the streets—me and Andre and Tunning/Tungsten, the receptionist, and the woman who smelled of acid.

We moved and sang, and others sang with us. It didn't matter that there were no words; there were sounds, and everyone added their own guttural twang to the heady mix. Men, women, and children who hadn't been lucky enough to hear the song before stared at us and all of the other singers laughing and smiling, until they understood, and after that, they sang too: loud, open sounds. They were my choir.

Biblical isn't a word I use often, as I'm a dyed-in-the-wool atheist. Still, it was the best word to describe the scenes I saw in the streets of London.

The first thing that happened after the singing was that people began to stop, sometimes in crowds or sometimes alone. They just picked a place and stayed there. Some fell from windows, their bodies splitting on the floor or crushing others who continued to sing with broken spines.

We saw them as we moved past, me and my disciples. Whenever I slept, either on benches or grass or pavement, they lulled us to sleep and were there when I woke up. As their voices became hoarse, they fell into humming the sound, but *they* never slept, and as the time went on, they began to fall, letting the song take them over even as their body fell to dehydration. Heads hit the floor and cracked like eggs, and every face smiled, even in sleeping/dying.

I kept wondering, why me? Why did I manage to keep going when so many others just stopped? And the answer came to me just as another wave of arterial blood washed against my shoes.

It needs me. It needs me to play it. And it needs me to help it live. There wasn't any part of this world where they wouldn't think this tune belonged with them, and it did. It was no more mine than the air, than the oceans. Everyone needed to hear it.

I picked up an apple that had started to turn, taking what sweetness I could before it rotted away. There probably wouldn't be any more apples picked now, but I could always claim them where they fell. And there would be music, and that's better by any stretch.

I wondered briefly whether the woman in the chair was looking down at me and smiling, and I was sure that she was. It came to me then, when I thought of her face, that she was the girl, the singer . . . the one who had taken my first hit and made it larger than any of us. I hadn't recognised her; the new song had been more important.

She had famously taken her car to the crest of a hill and breathed in its fumes until the world had faded. That was what had made the song memorable to the public. Truth be told, the tragedy had sold it far more than any artistry on my part. Now she had a new song, one that stood on its own merits, and one that I could spread for her.

Whatever had happened to her body didn't matter. It was probably deep in the brambles, as brown as the apple in my hand. What mattered was that her music had lived.

I bit into the apple. My teeth severed the body of the worm, and both parts danced.

Jacob Prytherch is an author of science fiction, horror, and weird fiction, and occasional books for children. He started writing due to a love of Bradbury, Tolkien, and Gaiman, and carries on writing due to restlessness. He currently lives in Birmingham with his wife and two daughters. Coffee is both his friend and his enemy. His first novel, *The Binary Man*, published in 2012, has been the #1 cyberpunk bestseller on Amazon UK on two occasions, and his novella, *Carnival,* was credited as being one of the top five self-published Lovecraftian stories on Examiner.com.

The Rub

Lauren Nalls

Sick. I've never felt so sick.

"Welcome."

The sensation of an arm, hot on my skin, slid around my shoulders companionably, then slithered away.

"We've been waiting for you. You've taken much longer than expected."

Formless words—or thoughts of words—infiltrated my mind in a freight train rumble.

Jesus . . . I covered my ears with my hands.

"Now, now. Let's leave *Him* out of this."

A dizzying in-and-out of focus, a now-you-see-it, now-you-don't sort of shimmering, wobbled in front of me. Liquid like mercury one minute and an almost non-existent vapor the next. The vision unmoored me, like a tsunami.

Where the hell am I?

"Yes. Once you get settled in, Mr. Davis, we can have our formal meeting, and it will all become clear. But for now, you'll need some time to acclimate."

With a crisp snap of unseen fingers, a small primate in an old-timey bellhop uniform appeared at my side. He wore a tiny, red double-breasted jacket and pants accented with gold buttons, a ridiculous little cap, and white gloves. An outfit that trained monkeys might wear to charm tourists out of their loose change. My jaw dropped.

"You summoned, Your Eminence?"

"Martin, this is Mr. Davis. Please show him to his room."

My room? Hot acid roiled in my gut. I had the obsessive urge to flee, but my feet wouldn't—or better, couldn't—move.

"Yes, Your Eminence." Martin bowed to his sovereign, then turned to me. "This way, sir."

What was that look? Pity?

An inhumane chuckling surrounded me, oppressive and sweaty, like a schoolyard bully.

What the hell am I doing here? I was gripped by a racking dry heave. *And that putrid smell . . . Who are you?*

"Oh, I'm sorry," the disembodied voice said. "*Tsk tsk.* I'm not being a very good host, am I? I'm, well, I have so many names, but you may address me directly as Your Eminence."

I recoiled from the three-fingered . . . *hand?* . . . that solidified and extended toward me.

"The serpent of old, at your service." The voice falsettoed to a little girl's high pitch. An introduction so polite, it almost came with a Shirley Temple curtsey.

"Mr. Davis?" Martin's monkey-voice was in my head.

I swallowed repeatedly to soothe my cartwheeling stomach. Viper eyes appeared just inches from my nose, vertically slit and scale-rimmed. I was entranced in the serpent's tractor-beam gaze. Those eyes. Hot blue and lit from the inside, unlike any I'd ever seen, but familiar at the same time.

A minute or a million minutes passed. It was difficult to tell. My brain began moving again, like slow-warming oil, searching, searching to fill cracks with understanding.

What happened? Where's Leona? Wait . . .

"Becoming clearer, Mr. Davis?" The pupils pulled outward at their sides, widening with interest. "My, you are slow on the pickup. I'll wait."

She shot me.

"Split your head in half, actually."

The beast went entirely limpid in an excited scatter of unbound atoms, then drew together into a thousand dripping, rotted faces at once. A horror show somehow thrust directly into my brain against my will. Molecules broke apart again and accelerated in agitated friction. A sizzling buzz, faint at first, swelled to an earsplitting crescendo.

Shit . . . I always knew it would come to this.

"*Yesss* . . . and indeed, it has."

The vaporous creature took a unified shape, yet, somehow, I also sensed it was infinite. I couldn't see the apparition fully unless I looked away, as if in deference, and used my peripheral vision. The thing was black and bloated, like a corpse left to foul in water, and smelled even worse. My unstable stance, less steady than during the worst of my benders, was a funhouse mirror reflection; my brain told me one thing, my body, another. I doubled over, enduring another wave of nausea.

"Leave us!" The serpent turned to Martin, absorbing the bellhop into its scintillating darkness. Its gaze once again rested on me in an eternal pause. There was a reflective weight to the way the beast studied me; cutting, heavy, and sharp.

Whoa.

"On second thought . . ." The monster's maw stretched wide, an oven of flames flicked toward me.

I jerked my head backward. The smell of my scant facial hair melting sickened me all over again.

Blackened claws tapped at its re-hinging jaw. "I have an offer for you, Mr. Davis."

Wait, what? The shrieking in my head diminished.

"Let's play a game,"—its grotesque face appeared next to mine—"a gamble for your freedom, if you will."

Hell, I'd agree to almost anything—

"Good . . . 'Almost anything' is what will be required of you. If you want away from here, I'll give you the opportunity." The serpent's words were a sulfur-laced stink. "You're lucky you've caught me in an . . . irregular mood."

Oh, shit! A rush of bile slammed into the back of my throat, and I leaned over to retch. If the serpent had been wearing shoes, I would have splattered them.

"It seems we are of the same mind then?"

I hesitated, then managed a stiff, almost imperceptible, nod. Drawing the back of my hand across my mouth, I steadied myself and stood to my full, proud height. White bolts of pain ripped through me, stealing my breath and stooping my back.

"This is no place for dignity, Mr. Davis."

C'mon man, wake up. It's only a dream!

"Tick tock, do you want to play or not?"

The pain ratcheted up again, thousands of tiny teeth gnawing at my bones. *Okay, okay. What do I have to do?*

"You must become a walk-in," the creature hissed, slamming its baritone voice into my brain. "Steal a body, send me the soul, and I let you go, free and clear."

Send you . . . a soul?

"Why *yesss* . . . a soul in place of yours."

Send you a soul.

"But here's the rub; you must drive your victim to suicide."

And steal their body.

"That's correct, Mr. Davis. You must occupy their body. After all, possession is nine-tenths of the law, or so they say." The serpent grabbed my face, pulling me closer and branding my skin. "Immediately prior to their death, you'll have the energetic power to dislodge the host soul with nothing more than intention—but you'll have only a few, short minutes."

I struggled to turn away and closed my eyes, as if I could block the sewer-gas stench threatening my stomach again. *Kick it out energetically?*

"A walk-in must remove the soul while the body is still living. It's really the only way to step in," the monster said, releasing me roughly. "Once the death process has started, it's almost impossible to stop, so you must move quickly."

But, suicide?

"Yes, Mr. Davis. Suicide. All suicides come to me. Now concentrate."

Make someone take their own life? How?

"How you do it will be up to you, but I suggest you guide your host toward a means that inflicts the least damage. After all, you'll be inhabiting their body afterward," the beast said, snickering. "That's what makes the game so entertaining."

Pills? Slit wrists? Bridge jump?

"You will not be in your naked spirit; however, your soul will be provided with a loaner shell—a body—of your choice and any documents or props you feel necessary. Anything you need or want shall be at your disposal. That only seems reasonable, now doesn't it?"

Reasonable? We left reasonable a long time ago. I wanted to nod but could only muster a fragile grimace.

"Oh, and there's one more thing."

There's more? Lead-like trepidation coagulated somewhere near my small intestine.

"You have one month, Earth time, to choose your victim and carry out your task. If you fail, we spend the rest of eternity together. If you succeed, well, then you have the rest of your chosen victim's natural life to correct the mistakes you've made, to settle debts, whatever."

Mistakes?

Its tongue clucked at me. "You've been a very bad boy. You've left many of us defiled in your wake,"—the little girl's voice again—"almost enough to make me proud."

Shit. How—? A shiver of foreboding crawled up my back.

"I know everything about you!"

The creature spit, its high scream a cyclone. I'd already encountered the worst pain I could imagine, but now I had no choice but to withstand more.

The serpent became genial again. "The game is more than fair; what do you say? Would you like the chance to live a little longer, Mr. Davis?"

I know just the debt that needs settling. Irrational hatred blistered in me, bubbling to the surface to congeal in one cool, calculating thought.

"You have someone in mind then?"

Let's do this.

"Oh let's, indeed."

— • • —

When I came to, the first thing I was aware of was my white doctor's coat in the mirror. I smoothed the fabric, straightening it. Beneath were dark slacks, fitted snug around my muscular thighs and ass. A shiny name badge was pinned over my right pectoral muscle. I felt like shit, head throbbing, as if I had the worst hangover of my life, but I resembled a Chippendale dancer in disguise. Perfectly sculpted. Irresistible.

That's right, baby. I remember what worked for you.

She wouldn't be able to resist me. Tightly-cropped blond hair, a little bit of stubble, angular jawline, and crystalline eyes. I was tall and rugged-looking; her favorite dessert. But the coat . . . well the coat, and the dollar signs it implied, would seal the deal.

Gold-digging whore.

— • • —

"Here's your office. Here's your password. And your case files." My new administrator dropped a large stack of folders on the desk. "Welcome to Sunnyside State Women's Hospital, Doctor Carter. We're glad to have someone of your esteemed accomplishments join our team. Please let me know if you need anything." He spun on his heel to go as I set down my box. "Oh,"—he turned back toward me—"you might want to lose the coat though, these girls will be all over you in that getup . . . Unless, of course, that's what you're going for." He winked, firing a finger-gun at me, and left.

I ran my hand along my new name placard on my way to sit behind the solid mahogany desk. *Dean Carter, Psy. D.* It had a nice ring to it. I began to unpack my props: framed diplomas, textbooks so I could best play my part, electrical cord, and my copy of *Dante's Inferno.* I had become quite the reader in the two weeks since my transition, fascinated with my own journey into Hell.

Sifting through the files on my desk, I found the one I wanted. *Leona Davis* was scrawled in tight, formal handwriting on the label.

My jaw tightened. "Let's see, wifey, what you've been up to while Daddy was away."

Scanning the initial pages, I found that the previous psychiatrist, a Dr. Winger, had left a brief summation of their sessions to date. Leona's new diagnosis was psychotic depression, in addition to her previously existing bipolar disorder. Apparently, she had been reluctantly participating in daily therapy, both group and individual, and it appeared she had made some progress once she admitted to, and began working through, the murder.

My murder.

I had no idea how much time had passed since my . . . *death*. It's an odd thing to consider one's own killing. I wonder who had walked around my bloody corpse, careful not to step in my splattered brains. There were photos, I would imagine. My stomach fluttered. I would have to work up to looking at those.

Leona's court folder protruded from beneath her open file, and judging by how thin it looked, the trial must have been quick.

I'll save that one for bathroom reading.

I traced my finger along the lines of Dr. Winger's notes:

Mrs. Davis vacillates between rageful violence and depressive stupor and is prone to delusions. She has a history of suicide attempts by hanging and overdose, and we are currently trying to find a workable antipsychotic/antidepressant combination to complement her lithium. History, medications, and dosages are in her chart.

Hmm . . . abruptly removing all medication is just the thing to help her over the edge.

We have been working on moving toward participation in group therapy more fully to alleviate some of the guilt she retains over her husband's murder. Patient is particularly triggered when discussion of her husband's pedophilia arises.

Bitch. That was *my* business. My teeth ground against each other.

I have been unable to draw the full story out of her, but I do know from the casefile that she pled guilty to the murder of her husband by way of a mental disorder defense, which is how she came to be here. Patient stated she found her husband in a compromising position amid explicit photographs of himself with neighborhood children she recognized. This led to a severe psychotic break she has yet to fully overcome. I feel the biggest facet of her depression stems from her feelings of inadequacy as a woman and mother. She believes her husband cheated on her because she was so detestable that even a child was preferable to her.

Oh, boo-fucking-hoo.

One of the patient's most vivid delusions is one in which she believes she is deeply in love with me and that I have reciprocal feelings.

A hot rash crept up and over my chiseled chin to my temples. I scrubbed my hand across my brow.

This patient's infatuation with me has developed into such a dangerous fantasy, it has been remediated with my voluntary transfer from this facility, for both of our safety. Leona Davis was unable to withstand transfer in her delicate state.

Delicate my ass.

Pregnant at the time of her incarceration—

Holy shit! Hold up!

—patient has recently given birth to a somewhat-healthy girl and is being closely monitored by the medical staff for postpartum, which she suffered with her first infant from a previous marriage. No matter what she tells you, we do not have a child together; this is part of her delusion. The baby is her recently deceased husband's.

I have a baby? The news sent me reeling. I fell backward into my chair. I hadn't thought my temporary shell would include such common human frailties as queasiness. I was wrong, boy, I was wrong. My diaphragm tightened.

The child is being cared for by a paternal aunt at present, and it has been recommended the child visit as much as possible to help the patient stabilize. In closing, I wish you well. For the most part, this patient is pliable enough, and I hope she'll see fit to continue the work we've managed to accomplish in treatment.

Sincerely,

Dr. Alfred Winger, Psy. D.

My hands shook violently, spilling the papers to the floor in a confused scatter.

—— • • ——

The first time I laid eyes on Leona in group therapy, I almost lost my nerve and walked right out. She seemed docile, curled on a chair in the corner of the room, distanced from her fellow patients.

Goddamn, she looks like shit. Her skin was as gray as her

institution sweatshirt: dead and wax-like. Giving birth and taking life had obviously emptied her. But her eyes remained clear, offsetting her pallor.

I loved your eyes. Surreal blue against white, like a Grecian seaside town. Beautiful.

Thinking of Leona taking me away from my first kid ignited such a searing burn in my chest, I had to beat it down immediately or it could spread out of control. I was not going to let her get the best of me.

Bitch.

Her eyes drifted to her lap, and I steeled myself for the takedown.

"Good morning group. I'm Dr. Carter, Dr. Winger's replacement . . ."

— · · —

It didn't take long.

Before group the next Tuesday, the door to my office slammed open.

"You're expected to knock." I looked up and nodded to the orderly who had rushed in behind her; he backed out of the room and closed the door.

She came at me much quicker than I'd expected. I scrabbled backward in my chair to avoid her grasping hands.

"Leona—uh—Mrs. Davis!"

"Give them to me!" she growled through her teeth—a cheetah with her nails extended. Much swifter in her shriveled body than I had given her credit for.

I stood and anchored open my lab coat with hands mounted on my hips, relieved I was able to stay composed. "What can I do for you, Mrs. Davis?"

"It's *Ms.* Davis!" her hysterical voice grated. "Why did you take my meds away?"

She braced herself on my desk and leaned toward me, breathing hard. She didn't seem to notice the twelve-foot extension cord loosely coiled like a snake next to her hand.

I scooted my chair back toward the desk. "Uh—Dr. Winger and I—uh—felt that you would make better progress without them. You've been having extreme depressive episodes while on the medications we've tried, so we felt it was time to take you off to, you know, see how you do."

Her cerulean eyes were wide, imploring, and wild. "You asshole, that's not true! I can't live like this, trapped by my own brain, not even knowing if my thoughts are real."

"Calm down."

"Don't tell me to calm down. You're an asshole," she raged. "You did this! I don't believe it was Alfred! He loves me, he knows everything about me. He loved . . . me . . ."

What a damn whore.

I raised my hands to show her I was no threat. "Ms. Davis, you haven't attended any of the individual therapy sessions I've invited you to in the last week." I reached for her wrist—a light touch to bring her back before someone heard her. "I'm not surprised you're feeling upset. The medicine works best in tandem with therapy." I retracted my hand and retook my seat. "As the medication decreases, the therapy has to increase. That's how this works."

Leona slumped into the seat opposite me and sobbed. "I might as well just die."

"Oh? And why is that?"

I leaned in toward her, careful not to retrigger the time bomb in front of me. *Not yet.* I couldn't look straight at her, not this close, so I focused on her thin gash of a mouth. I was more nervous than I expected to be.

She was crying hard now. "Please, I'm begging you. I need my medicine. I'm afraid I'll hurt someone—my baby—if I don't keep my brain working right."

My hands fiddled with the prop on my desk. "Tell me about

your baby, Leona. What's her name?" I stroked her with my soft words.

"I named her Marie."

I waited, willed her to continue, then finally cleared my throat.

Her shoulders fell. "She's almost three weeks old, and they took her from me in the delivery room and gave her to my bitch sister-in-law. And nobody believes me that she's Alfred's." She wiped her nose with her sleeve. "She's only come to visit once so far, and I have all this milk . . ." She sniffed and lifted her hands, angled toward her breasts. "And she's supposed to come on Saturday, but all Marie did was scream when I held her, and I feel like I can't be a good mother without drugs; that I might do something, that I might hurt her . . . or . . . or . . . worse."

I stood and came around the desk to sit near her, perched on its edge. I brushed her dark bangs from her face and lifted her chin. She twitched as if I'd shocked her, but didn't recoil.

"There, there." I laid a comforting hand on her shoulder, proud I could sound so . . . empathetic.

Moving softly behind her, I approached the door. *Now for the kill.* The lock slid into place with a dull *CLUNK*, and I returned to the desk edge.

"Now, I haven't read your case file, so why don't you tell me how you came to be here as a new parent." *Stab.* "Why, where is your husband in all this?" *Slash.*

Leona gave me a quizzical look for the briefest of seconds. Recognition? I hoped not.

No stopping.

"I killed him."

I was giddy. "I'm sorry, did I hear you correctly? You killed your own husband, the father of your child?" *Stab, twist.* "That's got to be so hard on you." I patted her back before returning to my chair. "That poor child too." *Slash, tear.*

Her eyes became ice. "She's not his baby."

Keep pushing. "She'll receive proper care, living with her father's family, and hopefully she can come to forgive you someday. Then again, she may not." *Stab.* "It's just something you'll have to live with." *And rip.*

I contemplatively glanced at the water pipes hanging parallel to the ceiling, rubbing my chin.

Leona's eyes trailed to the ceiling as well, then to the fluorescent cord on the desk. A substantial tear breached the corner of her eye, and I sat, watching its painfully-slow descent down and around her gaunt cheek.

"Not the best of circumstances for a child—" I folded my hands on the desk. "—no father, and now, no mother either." *Stab, slash, slice.*

"Why would you say that? Alfred is her father."

"I know you may think that, but I can assure you, the child does not belong to him."

She sniffed, folding her arms defiantly. "She does—if they'd just let me talk to him, he'd tell them. He's just protecting me."

"But he left you and confided to me that you're delusional." *Rip, snap, tear.*

Her blood-starved white knuckles appeared on the arms of her chair as she strained to stay seated.

Ah, now we're getting somewhere.

"He abandoned you so you'd stop trying to pin your murder victim's kid on him."

She jumped up. "You're lying. He loves us!"

"He doesn't love you or your brat." *Twiiist.* A smug grin spread across my face. *Now, go for the jugular.* "He said you are unfit to be a mother." *POW! Bullseye.*

She flew at me, hands aimed at my throat, launching both of us to the dingy linoleum. Leona landed on my chest, straddling me. Any other time, I might have welcomed this as foreplay.

I squeezed my eyes shut. "*Aaaahh!* I think you broke my ankle!"

The pipes, sweetie, the pipes.

She jumped off, and in a flash, had the bright orange coil in her hands, eying the sturdy pipes above her.

I pulled my knee to my chest and rolled back and forth on the floor feigning injury, like a professional soccer player. "My ankle. I can't get up! Please, Leona, don't do anything rash!"

Leona tossed one end of the cord over the low-hanging hot water line, then deftly tied a hangman's noose. I was grateful she seemed to know what she was doing, but just to be sure, I'd greased the cord enough to make the knot slide. Wrapping the free end around the desk leg, she tied it off, then stepped backward to inspect her work, as if mentally measuring whether or not she'd left enough slack to get the job done.

I rubbed my head, as if the world was swirling around in front of me, and kept my eyes on the floor. I didn't want to spook her. She was focused, eyes blazing.

She mounted the chair and slipped the noose over her head.

I reached up toward her. "Leona, wait! Don't!"

"You don't care about me."

"Leona, I do," I said softly, hanging my head. "But maybe you're right, maybe this is for the best, so your daughter doesn't visit her homicidal mother at the nut farm for the rest of her life." I covered an accidental smile with my hand. *Over and done with quickly.* "For the good of the child."

And with that, she kicked the chair.

Take a bow.

Satisfied, I watched her from the floor. Her face swelled, shiny and red as an apple, eyes pushing out of their sockets. If she had even the briefest thought she'd made a mistake before, she knew it for sure when I stood and casually strolled to her swinging body.

Her eyes widened. She clawed to loosen the cord strangling her neck. If she was just six inches taller, she might have been able to reach the floor and free herself.

"Yeah, that's right, whore," I leaned in and whispered. "I got you."

She kicked at me, then seemed to realize she was using what little breath and strength she had left. I stepped backward, hands in my pockets, and let her fight for her life. The wait wasn't long.

As soon as her weak bucking stopped and she hung limp, I untied the desk-end of the cord and let her down. Working fast, I laid her on the floor and removed the noose. It was harder than I expected, but my tiny particles of energy filled her body and expelled her soul.

With a squelch, I was—I can't even explain the feeling— *vacuumed* from my rental body and awoke in hers with a sucking inhale. Leona was evicted.

See ya, bitch.

A disorienting high-pitched hum infiltrated my brain. *Oh man, it feels like crap in here.* I sat upright, rubbed my head, and looked at my temporary shell sprawled on the floor.

Goddamn, my neck hurts!

I stood, careful to take it slow, and opened the office window to let in some fresh air. The unfamiliar feeling of my breasts jiggling for the first time briefly caught my attention.

Weird.

Leaning against the wall for a few long moments to steady myself, I willed oxygen to penetrate my muscles and clear my head. As I rested, the office supplies, diplomas, electrical cord, even *Dante's Inferno*, and what I assumed was my wife's lifeforce, moldered and combined into a swarm of molecules flying past me and out the window. Everything had disintegrated but my temporary shell.

Shit, if they find him here, they'll blame it on me.

It had to look like a suicide. I was able to lasso the body where he lay, and using the desk leg as a pulley, drag the dead weight underneath the pipe. When I tried to string him up by the neck, however, I realized the weakness of my newly acquired scrawny body. It was no use, he was too heavy for me to lift.

"I'm sure gonna miss *you*, buddy."

I can't take this. Jesus, I can't do this anymore. This bitch never sleeps!

Rats climbed on me at night, horrifying entities penetrated me while I tossed and turned with insomnia. My inner life was now filled with terrifying images of gore. I didn't need to see my crime scene photos; Leona's brain replayed my murder constantly. And the sex! I was tormented by raunchy visions of her and Dr. Winger— Alfred—doing things she'd never done with me. Were they real? Memories? She had always been such a cold fish.

Our brains and thoughts, hearts and souls, and everything in-between seemed to be melded into some weird stew: a few ingredients mostly me, many ingredients all her. I was left with the memories of what had happened in my life, but most of the intensity and all the paranoia and whispers were Leona's. My soul in her body, her sick brain controlling my thoughts, and such a full range of emotion I couldn't begin to temper. I didn't realize it would be like *this*.

Do it! Do it! Do it! the voices chanted, urging me to kill myself day and night.

Why her body? Such a stupid, stupid decision made hastily in bitterness. Why hadn't I planned this better?

Fuck.

—■ • • ■—

I stepped into Dr. Parsons' office and quickly closed the door and leaned against it, eyes closed, my palms and forehead pressed against its cool wood surface. The shadow men were at it again today, and they'd chased me down the hallway.

Dr. Parsons, the small, beak-nosed man who had filled my spot—or more accurately, Dr. Carter's spot—looked up from his desk. "Hello, Leona. Shadow people after you?"

He cocked his head to the side, surveying me with sharp eyes. The way he raked me up and down, from my tits to my mouth, disgusted me. He was usually completely oblivious to my inner turmoil.

"Will you please put me back on my medicines?" I implored.

He began shuffling papers around his desk. "No. I'm sorry. I can't do that, Leona. Your previous therapists have noted that you do not tolerate medication well. It causes you to have suicidal ideation. You will remain off all drugs until further notice."

"But . . ." *Goddamn, why did I alter her fucking file?*

"It's too soon. You need to heal physically first. The bruising on your neck is still visible and you still have all those scabs. And now there's a second murder. I think I should take you back to baseline and start all over."

"No! I didn't kill him!" The first female shrill to my voice I'd noticed. I had left the body noosed and on the floor, clearly a suicide; he was just too stupid to notice.

"You may not remember, but we found you passed out next to Dr. Carter on the floor in his office. We haven't quite figured out how you did it, but you *did* kill him and stage the scene to make it look like a suicide." He resumed shuffling paperwork. "The rope marks on his neck were made post mortem."

A cold dread filtered into my lungs, seizing them. *Shit.* With the suspected murder of Dr. Carter now pinned on me, I'd be locked in here forever. My bangs clung to the sweat on my forehead.

"Is there anything else?" he asked placidly when I'd paused too long.

"No." I backed out of his office, retreating to lick my wounds.

"Oh, Leona!"

I stuck my head through the closing door crack.

"Marie is coming for a supervised visit tomorrow. That should brighten you up a bit."

— · · —

So innocent. I was falling in love. Tiny fingers wrapped around mine. I looked into her soft, blushed face. Perfect chubby cheeks and furrowed brow. Doe-lashed brown eyes. I even saw her crack a tiny smile—a real smile—and not just gas.

"Aren't you perfect?" I cooed, fascinated at how simply holding my baby started the hot prickle of my milk letting down. Two wide circles spread across the front of my shirt.

"Revolting," my sister, Amanda, said, looking at my chest. She sat across from me at a visitor's table, impatiently tapping her foot and checking her watch. "Can we move this along? It's almost time for her to eat again."

"But you just got here."

"Yeah, well, I still have other things to do," she snapped. "And I didn't expect to get stuck with some sperm donor's baby until I could figure out how to get her placed elsewhere."

Something was off. I raised my eyes to her heartless expression; nothing was there for me but disdain. *Placed?*

"What are you talking about?"

"C'mon, we all know she isn't my brother's child. Jesus Christ, Leona, I'm not an idiot." She stood and grabbed the baby out of my hands. "You both have blue eyes. You can't make a brown-eyed baby; it's genetically impossible. Google it."

The inside of my head spun, whirring around and around like a top. There really was no way this baby could be ours?

"We're leaving," Amanda announced.

Both of us stood in a face-off.

All this time I'd hoped it wasn't true. Sure, I'd heard the voices in Leona's head whispering, seen flashes of her bent over the desk in his office. But I thought that was just a fantasy, along with everything else her fucked-up brain manufactured. I was losing it.

There's no way this baby is mine?

My sister was turning to leave.

"Give her to me!" I snatched Marie by the feet, pulling her out of my sister's hands. Cradling her head, I tilted her to catch the window light on her face. The little chocolate-colored eyes locked with mine and I knew. "There's no way this baby is mine."

I let go of the head and doubled my hands around Marie's ankles.

"What are you mumbling about?" she asked, inspecting her cuticles. "C'mon, I have to go." She looked up and started, "Jesus, Leona! Give her to me, you're going to hurt her!"

"There's no way this baby is mine!" I shouted as I swung Marie like a baseball bat at my sister.

Their heads met with a wet crush, sending Amanda into the soda machine.

"Someone call Dr. Parsons," the supervisor yelled, running toward me. "And get a guard!"

"There's no way this baby is mine!"

I took another swing, this time narrowly missing an unfortunate visitor. Marie's blood sprayed into my mouth when her head hit the edge of the table where we'd been sitting.

I was vaguely aware of screaming . . . and the taste of blood. "There's no way this baby is mine!"

I dropped the supervisor mid-stride with a bloody slug, and before I could reset, the guard was on me, trying to grab Marie. I scratched him across the face while he fumbled with slippery hands for his gun. He kicked me off him and backed up, weapon drawn.

We were at an impasse; my back against the wall, both of us breathing heavy, a tattered child in my hands, a gun in his. *Well, I guess this is it then. Suicide by cop.*

I rushed him. "There's no way this baby is mine!"

I was a medieval warrior with a mace, swinging at . . . the most spectacular eyes gone sapphire with fury. *Those* eyes. *Her* eyes.

An immense *BANG!* filled my head, and my vision became a brief tunnel that soon enveloped itself completely.

— . . —

"Oh, how good of you to come." The voice trying to penetrate my mind was familiar.

I was lying prone, arms outstretched, as if in supplication. A blast of rancid heat exploded over me. I moaned. My skin was on fire—a ferocious, tortuous sensation.

A woman's laugh blared like a morning alarm clock. "Welcome home, husband."

I managed to lift my head between dry heaves to see her naked, standing triumphantly in front of me smoking a cigarette. Her skin was pinked, rosy almost, as if every capillary was aroused to the surface in anticipation of touch. She was a perfectly ripe fruit, so juicy. I tasted her in my mouth.

What the hell are you doing here?

"Oh, you don't know? Don't . . . get it?" she asked, eyes blazing electric blue.

I coughed, as if I were the one smoking. *Fuck you.*

The atmosphere crackled, then ignited around me. The serpent congealed at Leona's side, a scaly arm around her shoulders, and twisted her erect nipple, as if tuning a radio to a clear frequency. Her eyes closed, her head fell backward, and she moaned in a cavernous echo of infinite rapture.

The beast twisted again. "See, I told you it would be fun."

The cacophony of Leona's orgasm hit me, a nuclear squeeze of my entire being imploding and exploding simultaneously.

Make it stop! I begged. *Give me another chance!*

"Of course, as you can see, I offered your wife a deal as well: eternal pleasure in exchange for *your* soul." The beast waved its clawed hand dismissively. "Martin, show Mr. Davis to his room."

Martin bowed quickly. "Yes, Your Eminence. Right this way, sir."

Screaming. *My* screaming. The unimaginable agony of being sucked apart, molecule by molecule, as I siphoned into infinity.

The serpent chuckled. "It's not my fault she played the game better than you."

Lauren Nalls' publications include her short story, "Loose Ends," published in *A Journey of Words* (Scout Media, 2016), and her poem, "Burgeon," published in *Fredericksburg Literary Review* (spring, 2014; Volume 2, Issue 1). She also blogged for the Fredericksburg Parent and Family's *Tortoise and Hair* series (2014). Ms. Nalls currently lives alongside the scenic Rappahannock River in Fredericksburg, Virginia. She enjoys driving her critique group crazy, hiding from loud noises, and having someone cook for her. She promotes equality for all. Lauren is a proud member of Virginia Writers Club (Riverside Chapter), James River Writers, and Fauquier Writers Critique Group. You can find more information at www.LaurenNalls.com.

STORM HOUSE

MONICA SAGLE

I stood, hands on knees, gasping for precious air. Lightning flashed across the sky, and the rumble of thunder rolled off the hills. Heavy drops of rain splattered mud on my boots, drenched my jeans and blouse, and plastered my hair against my face.

Enough is enough, you asshole; never again.

I straightened, still gasping, and glared at the house.

Dark and bleak against the gray sky, a single light sat upon the porch.

I grinned. He knows his forever-loving wife is coming home.

This time is the last time, you bastard.

I wiped muddy hands on my blouse and glowered at my broken and dirt-filled nails. The rain had been my saving grace, washing away most of the hard-packed dirt from my shallow grave.

I moved toward the house, my left leg dragging.

It took time, but I managed. When I got there, I pulled myself up the steps to the porch. I was tired and wet, and my damn leg hurt like hell.

I grabbed the oil lantern from where it sat on the rail and moved across to the open door. He shot me the last time I came home. *But not this time.*

I stepped to the side and passed the lamp in front of the door. Sure enough, *BOOM!* Damn thing was loud enough to wake the dead.

I had to grin. He wasn't going to get me the same way twice.

"Hey, that ain't any way to greet your wife."

"You ain't my wife. You git yourself back in your hole and stay there."

"Nope, not happening, sweet pea. We is married, like it or not."

"Just until death do us part. You're dead and we done be parted. You git back where you belong."

"Nope, Love, this here is just the *worse* of 'for better or worse.'

But I have an idea. If you let me in, we can talk. I know how we can fix this."

"How?"

"Let me in first."

"Okay, but keep your distance."

I limped into the house and stared at my husband. He was haggard and skinny, like he'd not slept or eaten in a real long while. His clothes hung in tatters, and the hat on his head did nothing to hide his stringy hair.

He swung the gun to the left and said, "Kitchen."

I moved slowly through the living room, past the faded couch and the chair with gashes and holes. Pictures on the mantle were faded and dull. A layer of dust covered everything.

"Been taking real good care of the place, I see."

"Don't know why, but nothing seems to be working. I can't git the damn lights on, and there ain't nothing to eat."

I nodded. As I passed the old piano, I pressed an ivory, and the sound was hollow and off-key.

The muzzle of his gun poked me in the back. "Keep your hands to yourself, and git in the kitchen."

The kitchen was not any better. The paint on the table and chairs was cracked and peeling and the wallpaper yellowed. An old hand axe leaned against a rotted pile of wood in the bin. The old stove might still work.

I sat on one side of the table, and he pulled a chair away and sat on the other. The gun still pointed at me.

"So talk. You think you got the answers."

"Okay, okay, keep your pants on. What's the last thing you remember? Before I died."

"What's that got to do with this? I want you gone and back in your hole. Things ain't supposed to be like this. You're dead, and I buried you."

"Yup, you did. You shot me in the back and buried me out by the trees. The first stormy night, I came back and"—I jutted my chin to the wood box—"put that axe in your back and buried you out in the field."

"What? Are you crazy, as well as dead?"

"I may be dead but I'm not crazy. We fought, a lot, and we took to trying to kill each other. You succeeded first, but then the next time a storm came, I got you. Storm after that, you came back and shot me with that gun, again, and now it's my turn. But I think we can end this. Right here, tonight."

Should I tell him it's been ten years? Nah. Why mess him up even more?

"You're looney."

"Yeah, and you're just peachy. Look at yourself."

"Guess I've seen better days." He frowned with what was left of those bushy brows. "Not as how I believe you, but what's your answer?"

"My answer is, we live—dead, together."

"I suppose, maybe, that might work if I believed you. I know you are dead 'cause I put you in the ground myself, but I don't think I'm dead."

"Fine, if you want, you're not dead. I just want to live here too. Can we do that?"

"Nope. I'd have to watch out all the time; this way I only have to watch out when there's a storm."

I held my hand up in oath. "I promise not to try and kill you."

"Well, maybe. How do I know I can trust you?"

"We could start by getting rid of our weapons."

"Might work. Still seems too easy."

"Not to me it's not. I'm the one that keeps getting buried next to the damn trees. Those roots itch."

I watched him work it through his tiny brain—what was left of it—and then he nodded. "Worth a try. It's been kind of quiet here alone."

"Good. Now if there's any tea in the cupboard, I'll make us some."

"If we're dead, can we drink tea?"

"Well I can, and you don't think you're dead, so why not?"

"Okay, I'll get the tea down."

He propped the gun against the stove and pulled his chair over to the cupboard on the far side of the room. He climbed up on it, reaching to the top shelf to find the tea.

I stared at the axe and fought the impulse to grab it and lodge it in his back; instead, I got up and said, "I'll just go and get the water."

"Okay," he said.

Once more, I studied the man I had married. Ten years was a long time to be fighting and killing each other. But I had it figured out. If one of us died by *accident*, then it ought to put a stop to this back-and-forth killing, and I could get some rest.

I put the lamp on the stove and turned the old tee-ring at the back and, sure enough, I could hear the hiss of gas.

I picked up the water bucket and said, "Put some wood on for me."

He nodded and I ambled out the back door to the well and set myself on its ledge.

Minutes later, the place blew, spewing flames against the night sky . . . and it blew again as flames followed the gas line through the house.

I waited a long time to be sure. The storm passed and there was a distinct lighting of the sky in the east.

I ambled back to the trees, dragging my foot. Found my grave and climbed in, pulling the lid with its piles of dirt back over me, like a well-loved blanket.

Maybe now I could sleep through them damn storms.

Monica Sagle is a writer living in Southern Alberta. She writes sci-fi and fantasy stories and is working hard on her first novel. She is a member of CSFFA and is a regular attendee at When Words Collide in Calgary. She belongs to the Rocky Mountain Fiction Writers group in the Crowsnest pass and several online critique groups. She rounds out her life with a husband, three cats, music, and gardening.

Salted Ground

Amy Hunter

With Marley's world cast into upheaval, she had no choice but to strike a match and watch it burn. Like a warrior, she salted the ground and moved on, carrying with her only the trappings of survival.

Here's to change. She raised her drink and thought of Adam, the man who helped her rebuild—the man she loved.

Marley's younger sister, Gwen, jerked the Rumple Minze schnapps from her hand and set the bottle on the table. Ripples formed within the container, like the scene from *Jurassic Park*. Only in the film, a T-Rex caused the movement, not bass from pop music.

Bass. What a silly word, she thought.

Gwen reduced the stereo's volume. She was so panicked that white encompassed her irises. "Sober up, honey. The police are here."

Marley smiled. *Yeah, right. If those are real cops, I'm gonna need bail money.*

With Gwen gripping her elbow, Marley wove around her friends, almost losing her balance. She caught herself and continued to the doorway with her arms outstretched, like a tightrope walker. One step, two steps, three steps . . . One foot in front of the other.

"All right, boys," she slurred, slapping her hands onto the bricks and spreading her feet shoulder-width apart. The position was perfect for displaying the pink cursive letters of *Mrs. Vaughn* written across her bachelorette shorts. "Who wants to frisk me?"

One of the "officers" cleared his throat, so Marley lifted her palms and turned to see both a man and a woman in non-rip-away uniforms. She couldn't imagine either of them naked—maybe because their faces were solemn, as though she'd sent the world's last doughnut to sea on a scrap of floating driftwood.

Marley giggled. *They need Rumple Minze.*

The male officer shifted his weight from one foot to the other. "Mrs. Vaughn?"

Marley stopped laughing and pointed to the sapphire engagement ring on her finger. "I won't be Mrs. Vaughn for a few days. I'm Marley Davis."

They removed their hats. The man trained his eyes on a hanging ivy while the woman concentrated on Marley.

"Miss Davis, we're sorry to disturb your party."

Something wasn't right. Marley drew back so far, her hip slammed into the doorknob. Both officers reached to steady her, but she raised a hand indicating for them to stay.

"I'm fine. Are you here about the music?"

She had a headache from the weight of her tiara, so she removed it with the length of tulle. *Why are they here?*

The female officer frowned. "Your shorts. Would that be Dr. Adam Vaughn?"

"Did he do something wrong?"

The female officer glanced at her partner, but his eyes were still on the plant, as if he preferred the woman to do the speaking. His fists pumped open and closed.

"Miss Davis—"

Marley didn't give her time to finish her sentence. Her fingers clamped so tightly around her tiara, it cracked and fell to the Welcome mat.

"I know my name. Just tell me why you're here."

The male officer drew an impatient breath, stepped forward, and ran his sausage-like fingers through his gray comb over. Forehead sweat molded his hair into an untidy bird's nest.

"At eight-thirty, Adam Vaughn was attacked and killed outside Bag 'n' Save on Laurel Boulevard. Paramedics pronounced him dead at the scene."

Time seemed to wind down and become suspended in midair. Marley's breathing stopped.

Her pink boa slid from around her shoulders. Feathers brushed the deck as the cord coiled at her feet. She didn't reach for it; the wind carried the shawl, with some leaves, onto the nearby lawn. The contrast of hope versus loss crystallized itself in her memory.

Drums resonated in Marley's ears. She covered her mouth with her hand and shook her head, as though rejecting what the police were suggesting would make any difference—as though her denial would bring Adam home.

The truth was, she didn't have words for what she was going through. She remembered the times Adam would smile because she'd mispronounce words like *cinnamon*. She could still feel the times he'd nibble her bottom lip when he'd seal a kiss. And, God, he could uncomplicate her life with a single expression. Those were moments she'd never share with him again.

"The body was transported to Jefferson Medical . . ."

Marley tuned out the rest of the officer's sentence because she was fixated on his initial words: *the body.*

"Adam." Her tone wasn't quite above a whisper, yet it was solid and gained strength with every continued syllable. "His name is Adam. He's a person, not a body."

Sobriety traveled fast with tragedy. Marley grabbed the doorframe to support herself, bending at the waist and placing a palm on her knee. *Inhale, exhale.*

"Please don't hesitate to call if there is anything more we can do to help," the male officer said.

Marley stood tall. "I have an idea; you can go back in time and do your goddamn jobs. That's how you can help."

Her foot crushed the tiara as she hurried inside. The noise of plastic breaking under her shoes rang in her ears. She slammed the door. Between sips of schnapps, she shouted for the guests to leave.

Her only plan was to forget she was alive, even if it meant erasing Adam.

— • •—

Sapphires. She loved sapphires. Adam had explored three counties for a flawless diamond-encrusted gem that was as "multifaceted" as he often said Marley was and still had the same cerulean hue of his eyes. She had promised to never remove the ring from her finger, but he had also sworn to marry her. The way she saw it, they were both breaking their vows.

Marley twisted the band until her finger throbbed, but it wouldn't budge. Her skin was purple from loss of blood circulation. She was certain she'd be frozen that way forever; a portrait of a woman who was almost happy.

Her heart plummeted. As her nose wrinkled, she bit her lip, struggling to remain composed. No dice. Tears pricked her eyes, so she wiped her lashes with the backs of her hands. Her eye sockets burned, like open wounds.

Don't do this.

She hyperventilated as she choked on snot. The hiccups started. The fucking hiccups.

If she were the praying type, she'd have been on her knees begging for the pain to stop, but after what she and Adam did to her ex-boyfriend, she doubted God was on her side.

— • • —

Ethan McPhee had held Marley's heart hostage in a razor-lined cage, as most abusers do to their lovers. His charms, which rivaled his temper, only emerged around his psychology students; they were his family. He had everyone fooled into believing he was the perfect gentleman, sometimes even Marley.

Ethan paced the hospital room as she held her limp elbow. "You won't say a word. Do you hear me?"

Marley's vision settled on the cracked linoleum, her bangs hanging in her face. He had driven her to the poorest hospital in the farthest corner of Jefferson County, undoubtedly to avoid a police report. He should have realized she didn't have the nerve to file—he made sure of that.

He caught her chin, jerking so hard her neck cracked. "I asked you a question."

Marley looked at his chest. Ethan didn't like it when she met his gaze, unless he granted her permission.

"I won't say anything."

Still clutching her jaw, he moved his opposite hand to the back of her neck. He could have killed her using little strength.

"Please . . ." Marley's voice trembled. "I won't."

The door swung wide. Dr. Adam Vaughn entered as Ethan kissed Marley gently to mask his attack. He slid his hands lower and traced circles down her spine. She bowed her head and let her shoulders curve over her chest.

"Nurse, get me five of morphine." The doctor had seen her tears.

Marley's elbow had dislocated and broken into four fragments. Following surgery, she spent many weeks at the rehabilitation center for physical therapy. As she and Adam grew closer, he noticed bruises.

"I know Ethan hits you," Adam said, sipping from the cafeteria-brand coffee cup and placing it on the table. Then he clasped his hands together, bringing his knuckles to his chin every so often.

She finished stirring her herbal tea and sat backward in the booth. She had no argument; there was no reason to fight. They were both adults, and the evidence was in plain sight.

Adam took Marley's hand, instantly warming her fingers. Their relationship had blossomed over the last few months. Into what, she didn't know.

"Let me help you, Mar. You deserve better."

She watched the spoon spin in her teacup and tried to think of yet another cop out. When it stopped, so did her excuses.

Marley's fingers shook. Her chin dropped to her chest. Shame made her wish to God she could hide her face, but she needed to accept his offer. Unlike Ethan, Adam was someone she could trust.

She hugged her torso, rocking in her seat. "Please help me. I can't do this anymore."

At the apartment Marley shared with Ethan, she only packed necessities: three outfits, toiletries, and items that couldn't be replaced. She finished in about ten minutes, but not soon enough. When she returned to the living room, Ethan was outside the front door.

"Oh, shit. No, no, no."

She flinched each time the keys jingled.

"Get behind me," Adam said, but Marley stepped to the side.

This wasn't his fight. The last thing Marley needed was for Adam to be hurt because of her. She set her jaw and squared her shoulders.

Ethan entered and placed his bag by the doorway. When he looked up, he saw Marley with her suitcase. Then he saw Adam and smiled. He fucking smiled.

"You're the doctor, right? Yeah, I remember." His grin morphed into something bitter. He extended his hand but Adam did nothing. "The least you could do is be friendly, since you're taking Marley from me. Not that I blame you. She is a nice piece."

As Ethan scanned Marley from head to toe, emphasizing claim, Adam stepped forward and punched him. Ethan fell against the door, bleeding, but the laughter didn't fade. He shoved Adam; the force was powerful enough to knock him off his feet. Adam hit his head on the coffee table, rendering him unconscious.

Marley knelt to check. Adam was still breathing.

Ethan cracked his knuckles. "Your turn, darlin'."

On the table rested the fine-tipped pen Ethan would use to solve the Sunday crossword puzzles. Marley snagged the pen and lunged, screaming something indecipherable. Maybe it was his name, or maybe it was hers. Ultimately, the words that tore from her mouth were the battle cry driving her forward.

—ᐧ ᐧ—

Marley had never realized how large her home was, until then. She wished she hadn't reached that conclusion while holding a 9mm pistol and wearing a wedding dress. The skirt was wrinkled all to bedamned, but she felt pretty.

She sat and massaged her temples—the left with her fingers and the right with the gun's barrel. Her conscience, with its many voices, had emerged, and it enjoyed driving her to the mental edge just to see how large of a splash she made when she crashed into the waves below. The voice told her Adam was in Hell, and the idea terrified her.

Marley sipped from a lukewarm champagne bottle, but it slipped from her hands as chimes rang, signaling company. She stood, smoothing her wet gown with the gun in her palm, like it was nothing more than a set of keys. This visitor was not welcome.

"Bless your heart," Gwen cooed as she hugged Marley. The woman blessed everyone's heart whether they needed it or not. "Son of a bitch. Why do you have a gun?" She touched her throat with a manicured hand, shaking her head.

Marley rolled her eyes and used the weapon to wave her in, but Gwen remained on the porch.

"Put it down." Gwen's voice shook.

After a beat, she reached for the pistol. She was fortunate to step from the line of fire before Marley accidentally squeezed the trigger.

The bullet struck the television.

— • • —

Life was so different a week ago, Marley thought. She went from being adored and showered with wedding gifts to being a patient on Antebellum Asylum's maximum-security floor, or the acute wing; a level some doctors and nurses refused to work because of violence.

Nurse Winnie had confiscated Marley's shoelaces, belt, hair ties, and even her toiletries. Once the nurse used soap to loosen her engagement ring, it went into a plastic bag with the rest marked, *ACUTE: DAVIS, M.*

"Give it back."

"Take it up with your doctor." The nurse glanced at her watch. "You have about twenty minutes before lights out."

The hallway was endless, yet it resembled every background on *Scooby Doo* Marley had ever seen. She could have sworn she passed by the same flickering lights and peeling wallpaper every three feet.

To no big surprise, her room was cramped. At least she didn't have to share with a roommate. The staff didn't want to lock two rabid animals in a cage and risk fighting. At least, not on the acute floor.

The bed was a single rubber-sealed cushion that probably made it easier to wipe off bodily fluids. After Marley fitted the sheets onto the bed, she struggled to lie down without stripping the corners. Dealing with the squeaks proved to be more difficult.

When the moon carved a light bright enough to distinguish shadows of trees through the barred windows, Marley found herself better able to breathe. No, she didn't see herself living a satisfying life without Adam, but she'd rather be miserable outside with freedom than miserable inside without.

A woman screamed.

Marley shot up, backing herself into the corner. Even with the doors closed, the nurses' footfalls were almost as loud as their threats that the patients needed to shut up or they'd be sedated.

Mass hysteria. These weren't just screams. They were cries for help, scorching the brain. If Marley wasn't released soon, she might end up like them. She could become someone else's scar.

— · · —

Marley didn't fall asleep until the howling had subsided in the early morning, so when the nurse woke her at six, she threw a pillow at her.

She covered her face. "Leave the drugs on the table and go the fuck away."

Marley could only see the nurse's silhouette in the doorway, but she could tell it was her. She stank like a hooker's dirty laundry—not the lightly worn pile that could be rescued by Fabreze, either.

"Time for your shower," she said, scribbling on a clipboard.

She should take her own advice.

"You'll see the doctor after."

"We have supervised showers? I don't think so."

The nurse chuckled and handed Marley a Dixie cup containing body wash. "I'm just here to give you the necessities."

She reached into her pocket, removed a new plastic-wrapped toothbrush, toothpaste, and a single-serving bottle of green liquid, placing all three on the sink. After she opened the packet and squeezed a line of toothpaste onto the bristles, she handed the toothbrush to Marley.

"Don't bother swallowing the mouthwash," she said, tossing away the garbage. "It's non-toxic and alcohol-free. Meet me down the hall to get your breakfast. You're running late, so you won't have much time to eat."

Great. I'm late on the first day of crazy camp.

Marley's clothing was still being searched for contraband, so she had nothing to wear yet. Luckily, the nurse had brought her a set of black scrubs and socks. Things could have been worse; it could have been a hospital gown.

Things were worse. The patients were like haunted paintings—motionless, with eyes that move.

Holding her tray, Marley approached a young woman staring at a painted window. "May I sit here?"

The woman burst into a laughing fit. Defeated, she moved to the closest available seat next to a man speaking to himself. She repeated her question.

"Can't you see we're talking?" he asked. Then he continued his conversation.

Marley's last option was to sit next to a girl holding a pair of panties and weeping. This time she didn't bother asking. She sat and the girl treated her as if she were nonexistent. *Fine by me.*

Marley had time to drink a carton of milk and eat half of a silver-dollar pancake—with a plastic spoon—before the nurse called her name to see the doctor. He was in his mid-forties, with a potbelly and thick glasses. He smiled like he already knew too much. When she looked at his desk, her file was open to a page with an old school photo attached.

She already disliked him, but she shook his hand, regardless. His grip was confident, and that only reinforced the feeling of captivity.

"I'm Dr. Matthews. Please sit. Make yourself comfortable."

Marley eased onto the sofa. *Comfortable. The couch might as well have spikes in the cushions.*

"So, I assume you know why you're here. I want to dig deeper. You shot at your sister—"

"I didn't shoot at her."

There was silence. She crossed and uncrossed her legs while biting the inside of her cheek.

"Let's work through the process, shall we? Now, digging deeper . . . I'd like to find out why you had the gun in the first place. Your file says when the police brought you in, you were wearing a wedding dress."

"I don't want to talk about that," Marley snapped, trying to shut the man down.

He moved to sit on the corner of his desk, facing her. "Let me put it to you this way, Miss Davis. The sooner you cooperate, and you will cooperate, the sooner you'll leave. People only leave on my orders."

Breathe in the flowers, blow out the candles, Marley. That's it. Inhale, exhale.

Marley had come too far to abide another man's threats, but he had her. She wanted out, but she had to give Dr. Matthews what he wanted if she hoped to be released. She had no choice.

"Three days ago, my fiancé died. My shitty way of grieving was to drink myself into oblivion." She shrugged. "Wearing my wedding gown and waving a gun around made sense at the time."

The doctor snatched a ball from his desk and squeezed it in his right hand.

"Did you love him?"

"Did I love him? What the hell do you think?" Marley's blood boiled, but she couldn't keep her eyes off the ball. "Can you put that thing down?"

"I think you're evading the question."

He placed the ball on the desk and diverted his attention to swinging a small metallic sphere on the end of a pendulum.

"Of course I loved him," she said, eyes burning. "Why do you think I almost killed myself to be with him?"

Dr. Matthews cleaned his glasses.

"Tell me about him. When did you first know you loved him?"

"How is this helpful?" Marley watched the pendulum, but he waited for her answer. She sighed. "I was in an abusive relationship before Adam, and he helped me leave the prick. No one had ever given a damn about what happened to me. When my ex saw us leaving, he was pissed. He knocked Adam unconscious. We were lucky to get away. And do you know what Adam's first words were when we got to safety? He asked if I was okay. He almost died, and he was concerned about me."

When she finished speaking, her elbows were on her knees, with her hands cradling her head. She wanted to run. She wanted to rip off the shrink's head; however, that wouldn't be conducive to good mental health.

The doctor's expression was unreadable. He raised his eyebrows. "I see. And how did he propose?"

"Are you kidding me?"

"Miss Davis . . ."

The dam broke and water overflowed. Dr. Matthews had pressed the big, red button that read *Do Not Touch*. He handed Marley a tissue. She didn't take it on principle.

"For you to heal, you'll need to work with me."

"We-we-we . . ." Marley stuttered. "We were camping in the

woods. I was afraid because there were noises outside our tent." She wiped her eyes and massaged her burning cheeks. "He held me close and told me that scars shape a person, and even though he wished I had none, mine have sculpted me into someone who feels more completely than anyone he'd ever met. He said he wanted to protect and love me forever. And after he said these beautiful things, he pulled out a sapphire ring, which your people took from me, and asked me to be his wife."

— • • —

That night the screams were Marley's. Darkness blanketed the room, and everything moved too quickly for her to process.

"Tie her wrists. I've got her legs," a man's voice said as they tugged her in two different directions.

Marley tried to fight, but her arms and legs were like jelly.

"Did you give her the injection? What if—"

"Yes, asshole," a second man said. "We need to hurry before the drug wears off. Did you bring the drops? Jesus, do you ever shut up, girl?"

Rough hands held open Marley's eyelids as cold liquid splashed her eyes. She waited for pain, but there was nothing but grogginess from the shot. Sweat formed on her upper lip.

"What did you give me?"

"Just a paralytic, baby girl. You'll be back to yourself in no time." The man brushed hair back from her face. "Hey, buddy, get the light."

She was grateful for light until . . . nothing was clear. She could only decipher colors. The two men were large—too large to fight. Her only recourse was to run if she saw the opportunity.

One of the men threw Marley over his shoulder and slapped her backside. "Okay, darlin'. You're coming with us."

A brief walk later, the other man gave her an injection in the neck. The effects were slow, but her limbs prickled with life. One man seized her while the other held her wrists, binding her to a fixture inside a large shower intended for multiple patients.

"What's happening?" Marley was relieved somewhat, but she still couldn't see.

They ignored her.

When her hands were tied, the man faced her. "This is my favorite part."

A camera flashed in Marley's periphery. She heard scissors cutting fabric and felt a tug at her torso. When a chill reached her breasts, she squirmed. He pulled down her pants so roughly, she lost her balance and hung by the wrists. She screamed. He backhanded her.

Another flash lit the room.

"Don't leave marks on her," one of them said.

"Yeah, yeah, I forgot. Showtime."

The water was lukewarm at first, then it warmed and continued increasing in temperature.

She gathered saliva in her mouth and spat. "You're kidding me, right? All of this for a shower?"

They laughed as one of them kicked Marley's shin. Soon the water was boiling. Where the water splashed on her body felt as though someone was raking their fingernails over her flesh, as if her skin melted off the bone.

A man yanked her hair so the water would run into her face, up her nose, and into her mouth. A moment into the torment, her feet slipped, and the elbow she had dislocated years before popped. Pain exploded through her arm and up her neck.

"Damn," one of the men said as he revealed a syringe. "This should be enough for the doc's offering tonight."

— • • —

Marley never thought she'd be in a padded room, but here she was, nude and shaking, crouched in the corner. She wasn't even sure what the room was. A metal frame was the only sign of a bed, and there was no doorknob or heating. She was certain the camera wasn't connected to anything. The only thing that appeared to work was the blinking keypad.

At least my vision is back.

After several moments, two orderlies entered the room. Marley almost cried from relief until one pulled out rope. She backed farther into the corner and curtained herself in hair, though the men had already seen everything. Hell, they had photos.

Bobby laughed. "Look at her. She's shaking."

Yes . . . Bobby. They had nametags.

John exposed a syringe. "She won't fight us."

She moved to her knees in a prayer position, shaking her head. "Please don't."

"*Please*," Bobby mocked. When he opened his mouth, she could practically see the bacteria swimming between his yellowed teeth.

"Just a little Haldol,"—John injected her arm with the hypodermic needle—"to mellow you out."

Within seconds, Marley was "mellow." John carried her to the bedframe and turned her facedown. She didn't have the energy or will to fight. She wanted to sleep. He spread her legs and arms so he could tie her down.

Bobby ran a finger down her bare thigh. "Do we get to play with her first?"

John slapped away Bobby's hand. "No, the doc wants this one all to himself."

"He has all the fun."

A camera flashed.

They left Marley in the darkness for at least a day—cold and exposed, face inches from the ground while claustrophobia consumed her. Her stomach heaved and she vomited bile. The liquid hit the floor and splattered onto her face. The smell was so disgusting, she wanted to heave again.

She wasn't sure which she feared more: dying, or Bobby and John returning to "play."

—••—

The drug was still in effect when Dr. Matthews knelt beside Marley to untie her wrists.

"Thank Christ." She sounded as though she had a mouth full of marbles.

The room spun as the doctor pulled Marley upright, letting her fall against him. He stroked her hair, as a lover would, but she fought. Even though she was weak, she beat his chest, desperate to escape. What he was doing wasn't right.

Words echoed in her mind: *The doc wants this one all to himself.*

Dr. Matthews traced his fingers down Marley's cheek and forced his tongue into her mouth. Her hands were balled into fists so tight, she broke the skin on her palms with her fingernails. He ran his nose along her neck, smelling her. She couldn't move; one shudder could mean rape or death.

"*Mm*, you've always been so delicious," he said.

Marley searched every recess of her mind. She had never met Dr. Matthews before, but she couldn't help thinking of the similar kisses she'd shared with Ethan. Her eyebrows pinched together, and she recoiled at his contact. He was so much like her ex-lover.

"No," she said repeatedly, her hands reaching for her temples. "You're dead."

He stroked her arm. She cringed.

"Oh, I am. You made sure of that."

"How—"

He smiled. "I'm special. Not all spirits can walk the world of the living."

"I don't understand. You're a—"

"Ghost. Yes, Marley, and people like you—people I drive bat-shit crazy—anchor me here to this plane."

Marley's posture dropped and she wrapped her arms around herself to conceal her still-nude body.

"How did you change your face?"

He chuckled. "It's just a face. Perception. Tell you what, don't ask yourself how I changed my face. Ask yourself how I changed your thoughts."

Marley no longer saw Dr. Matthews. Ethan was in front of her. She inched toward the door. "Why me?"

Keep him talking . . .

"You're my anchor. I feed on madness, and you're an all-you-can-eat buffet. I torture you, you go crazy, I feed. Really, it's a sweet deal."

Torture me? Not again.

When Ethan stroked Marley's leg, she didn't shudder or fight. She let his hand roam higher up her thigh. She knew she had to make him vulnerable, so she went along with him. Remembering his dominance wasn't difficult; he pulled her hair to guide her lips to his. After a moment of rough kissing, he shoved her head down.

When she began unzipping his pants with her fingers, he said, "Use your teeth."

Marley knelt between Ethan's knees and pushed him backward to gain easier access. With his fingers snaked through her hair, she used her tongue to manipulate the zipper into her mouth and trailed downward.

"Good girl."

He relaxed, placing his palms on the frame behind him for support.

Ethan's bulge sprang from his pants. Using both hands, Marley grabbed his balls and squeezed. He raised his arm to hit her, but she ducked and squeezed harder.

"What is the code?"

His only answer was a string of high-pitched vowel sounds as he tried to stand. She squeezed again, twisting just a little.

"Tell me!"

"Nine-three-six!" His voice was an octave too high.

"Stay," she ordered.

Ethan nodded. When she released his genitals, he curled into a ball.

Marley ran to the keypad, entered the numbers, and exited the room. She wasn't surprised when she found no one to help her; it was a long hallway with doors like hers—all without knobs. She was, however, thankful for the soiled linen basket. She reached inside, grabbed a hospital gown, and wrapped it around herself as she ran.

Marley was free, searching for she-didn't-know-what. Then she found it: a room marked ECT. When Ethan was a psych instructor, he told her about electroconvulsive therapy. If someone shocked their brain long enough, their memories would disappear.

Marley closed the door behind her. She stacked the bookshelves, chairs, and anything she could use as a blockade.

The machine wasn't too complicated—switches, buttons, sticky pads. Marley sat on the bed and joined the wires to the pads, then she attached the pads to her head. She wasn't worried about bilateral or unilateral because she wasn't expecting to survive. If the machine didn't work the first time, she planned to repeat.

Marley flipped the switch, and the machine roared to life. She was about to tape down the large button when Ethan materialized. She grabbed the three-ring hole punch from the desk.

"No. Please, don't do this." His voice cracked. If Marley didn't know better, she could have sworn his eyes teared up.

Marley, breathing heavy, gripped the hole punch as if it were a baseball bat. "You don't care about me."

Ethan ran his hand through his hair. "You . . . you have no idea. I came back for you. We were supposed to be together."

Something inside Marley bent. Visions clouded her thoughts—visions of herself at an altar with Ethan as he slipped a sapphire ring on her finger . . .

Marley stepped toward him once. Ethan didn't move; he opened his arms and waited. A few more feet and she would be in his arms, if that's where she wanted to be.

Those eyes are the wrong color, she thought.

"Too little, too late," she said through gritted teeth.

Marley swung the piece of office equipment. As she let go, Ethan's eyes grew wide with disbelief, as if he couldn't understand how she'd broken free of his compulsion. The blow to the head rendered him unconscious.

Before Marley could change her mind, she returned to the ECT machine.

She unrolled a small length of medical tape and, starting on the left, adhered it to the top of the machine. Inch by inch, she came closer to the square button in the center. Her eyes burned with tears. It was time.

I'm coming, baby.

Marley's last lucid thought was of Adam and his proposal.

Dear Diary,

Ethan gave me a ring. It's blue and pretty. The sun makes it sparkly too. It's a little tight for my finger, but he says that's so it won't fall off. We're getting married. I love him.

Amy Hunter lives in southeast Texas. Born in 1983, she wanted to be a professional Karaoke singer until the stories in her mind became more interesting than music. Writing since her early teens, she now has two published short stories: "Core," appearing in the 2016 Scout Media anthology, *A Journey of* Words, and her story here. To learn more about Amy, you can visit her website: www. amyhunterauthor.com.

Groceries
Every Day

Quinne Darkover

April's father, Bill, closed the door with his foot and set the groceries on the table. "April, I'm home!"

April, an Aphrodite at twenty-two, came into the kitchen, sat at the table, and peered into the bags. "Dad, you can stop bringing me groceries. I'm a big girl. Get anything good?"

"It's all good, and I have to take care of my little girl."

"Dad, canned asparagus is *not* good."

"Well, it's good *for* you." He paused and cocked his head. "Did you leave the shower running?"

"No, that's Martha."

"Martha? Have I met Martha? Why is she taking a shower?"

"No, you've not met her exactly. She was hot, so she's taking a cold shower to cool off."

Bill put the groceries away as they talked. "Tell me about Martha. Does she work where you do? Where's she from?"

"No, she doesn't work. She's a friend that keeps me company when you're away."

"*Sooo*, she doesn't work. Independently wealthy or a free-loading dropout?"

April went to the fridge and pulled out a carrot. "Dad, be nice. She makes me laugh."

"Okay, she's a comedian. Making you laugh is a good start. Where did you say she's from?"

"I didn't."

"Well?"

April ran a finger across the table, cracked off another bite of carrot, talked while she crunched it, and made smacking noises. "From my closet."

"What did you say?"

April swallowed. "From my closet."

Bill leaned against the counter. "You're gay?"

"No, Dad. She comes out of my closet."

"What the heck does that mean?" He turned at a noise in the doorway. "Oh my God!" He slid down the front of the counter to thump onto his butt. He stared.

"Dad, this is Martha."

He stuttered and pointed. "Th-Th-That's a polar bear!"

"Nothing gets past you, Dad. Martha, meet Dad."

Martha rose onto her hind legs, her head scraping the ceiling. Water dripped from her fur, making a widening puddle on the floor.

"Really, Dad. Jeez."

Bill's eyes didn't waver from Martha.

April went to her and placed her hand on Martha's side. "Stop scaring Dad."

Martha dropped back to all fours. "No sense of humor." The voice was a deep rumble.

"It talks!"

"Duh, Dad."

"Wh-Wh-Wh-Where did it come from?"

"I told you. My closet. And Martha is not an *it*."

"No way it fits in your closet."

"Sure she does."

"How?"

"It's bigger on the inside."

"What?"

"Yes, pleased to meet you." The bass voice filled the room.

"Who are you?"

"Watt."

"What?" Bill's voice quivered.

"Yes."

"You're who?"

"No, Watt."

"What?" Bill's shoulders curved in as he tried to make himself appear to be a smaller meal.

"Exactly."

"Martha, stop it."

The polar bear's sigh made Bill's sphincter tighten.

Bill tried again. "You're what exactly?"

"Yes." Martha's huffing was her version of laughing. It didn't help Bill's clenched buns.

"Martha, don't start that again."

Bill took a deep breath to try again. "So you are who exactly?"

"No, that is the skinny guy in a blue box."

"What?"

"Yes?"

"Martha!"

"He's funny."

"Dad, this is Martha Watt. W-A-T-T."

Martha swung her head to look at April. "Well, you took the fun right out of that."

"Dad, get up off the floor."

"I'll be in my closet." Martha lumbered off and up the stairs.

He had made it to his feet when the sound of a rattle at the front gate came through the window.

"Your mom is here. I have to go."

"Dad, please stay."

As he faded away, so did the bags and food stuffs.

"Honey, I'm home." April's mother, Jean, walked in and set the grocery bags on the empty table.

"Hi, Mom. You know you don't need to bring me food. Did you get anything good?"

"Got you some of that strawberry yogurt you like."

"Great. Thanks."

Jean talked while she put away the groceries. "So how was your day? What have you been up to?"

"Pretty good day. Got some writing done. Dad helped. He met Martha again, and it was kinda funny. You know how when I was little, his imagination made up Martha in the closet so she could jump out and get any monsters under my bed? Funny how every day he forgets all about her."

"I hope that puddle means he wet himself."

"Mom! That wasn't nice."

Jean harrumphed and kept working, stocking the food. "It's his fault."

April's voice softened. "Mom, it was an accident. It wasn't his fault."

"That's why he blames me, because he thinks it wasn't his fault."

"Mom, you know I love you. It was both of you. If you both hadn't been swapping spit."

"April!"

"Swapping spit, playing suck face, tonsil tennis, tongue wrestling, practicing CPR, lip humping. Kissing while driving takes two. Give Dad a break."

Jean stopped unpacking, her face relaxed and her eyes became unfocused. "Your dad was a good kisser."

"I'm sure he still is . . . if you give him a chance. I think he blames himself and can't adjust and is frustrated."

"It's been a year. I don't know about that."

"Mom, my birthday is next month. For my birthday, I want you and Dad with me. At the same time . . . in the same room."

"We'll see. I won't promise anything."

"Thanks."

"I'm going to go change."

"Okay, Mom."

Jean faded away and so did the groceries.

April listened to the kitchen clock tick for a few minutes.

"Maybe I *should* check munchie supplies." April rose from her chair and checked out the cabinets and fridge. "Yep, need to go shopping. Cupboards are bare."

April showered and dressed. As she was leaving her room, she paused and picked up a picture from the dresser. It was a picture of her mother and father.

"I miss you both. Heaven is supposed to be nice, so stop blaming each other." She smiled. "Thanks for the story idea, Dad. Martha, keep watch. I'll be back in an hour."

She closed the door to the empty house and gave a skip on her way to the car. "Better be good on my birthday."

Born in Tampa, Florida, **Quinne** (pronounced like two initials: Q N) **Darkover** has lived in England, Spain, Italy, and Africa, traveled most of the U.S., and visited the East and West Caribbean. Quinne started his working life in satellite communications for aircraft for eleven years, then changed his career to managing various clubs of over 1,500 members for the next ten years. He has managed and overseen formal dinners that included congressmen and generals as special guests. He has let his varied interests take him through electronic, management, and culinary schools, and even flight school in Europe. Besides cooking, he enjoys movies and Ren Faires, for which he makes his own garb. Quinne has been in stage plays, acted as an extra on TV, read for Radio Reading Services for the Blind for two years, and has been SCUBA diving in the British Virgin Islands. Quinne is retired, living in Florida with a mortgage and way too much time on his hands. He started writing in 2013 and has completed a cookbook and two steampunk novels, with a third in progress. When he writes and reads, he sees the words as movies in his mind. Author of *The Captain and the Lady Fair* and *The Black Widow's Cookbook*.

Jimmy's Shadow

Sunanda J Chatterjee

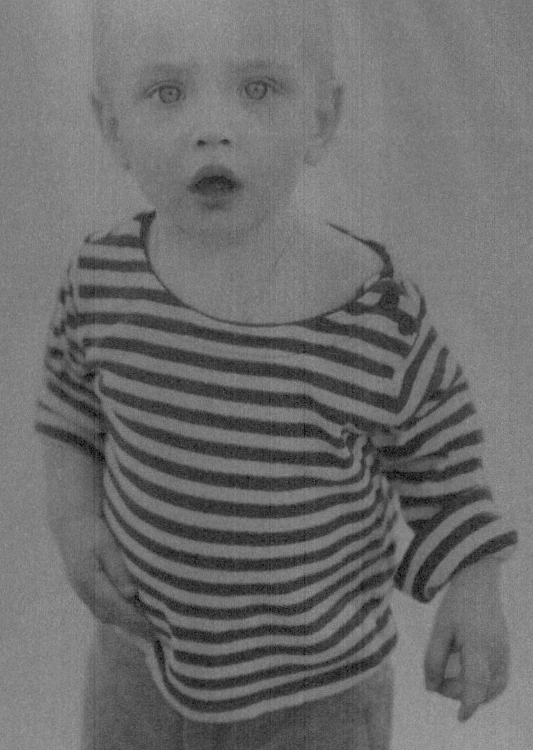

Cheryl had sworn off therapists after a disastrous meeting with her high school counselor when she'd tried to explain her dropping grades and mood swings. The meeting led to social worker visits to her house, and, ultimately, her parents' contentious divorce. The social worker told her that children do not thrive when parents bicker.

The experience established the two governing principles of her adult life: confide in no one regardless of the gravity of her situation and create an environment where her children could thrive.

She'd failed in both.

After much deliberation and one cancellation, she now sat in the office of Dr. Elaine Raddick, Psychiatrist.

Cheryl twisted the end of her skirt with shaking hands and avoided eye contact with Dr. Raddick. She glanced at the edge of the massive mahogany desk where her four-year-old son, Jimmy, was trying to play a game of peek-a-boo. Frilly curtains decorated the window through which sunlight filtered in, lighting a coffee mug with bold letters proclaiming *World's Best Therapist*. The atmosphere was meant to incite confidence and invite patients to talk.

Outside, the late February sun provided light without warmth. A small space heater near Dr. Raddick's feet warmed the room.

Dr. Raddick said, "So tell me why you're here."

Cheryl's voice was soft, almost a whisper. "Um . . . I've been depressed since Rob left."

"Rob is your husband?"

Cheryl tucked a strand of hair behind her ear. "Yeah. I can't sleep, I can't eat, I cry all the time . . ."

"Do you ever think about hurting yourself?"

What kind of question is that? "Oh, no! I'd never do that. Jimmy needs me."

"And Jimmy is . . .?"

"My son."

Dr. Raddick nodded and wrote something on her pad. "Tell me more."

Cheryl frowned. "I'm not comfortable sharing my feelings."

Dr. Raddick placed a warm hand on Cheryl's knee. "I'll never force you. I'm here to help, but you have to give me more."

They talked for a while as Cheryl told the doctor about her husband. They'd been married for eight years. She had craved a child, and they'd tried in vain for years, spending a fortune on fertility specialists. Jimmy was the product of the second trial of IVF.

When Cheryl became pregnant, her doctor told her to get as much rest as possible, and she took time off from work. Jimmy was born premature at thirty weeks. He was the loveliest baby in the nursery and fought his infection with valor. When they brought him home after a month in the NICU, Cheryl knew she could not return to work.

She gave a small smile. "Jimmy thrived under my care. He started talking at fifteen months. Full sentences." She told Dr. Raddick she was reluctant to send him to preschool because she feared he'd catch something from the other kids. She glanced at the therapist, seeking validation. "I thought Rob understood my connection with Jimmy. But he felt neglected or something."

"Go on."

"Rob left me on Jimmy's birthday, right before I cut the cake. The timing couldn't have been worse." Cheryl said she'd spent the last few weeks miserable and exhausted.

Dr. Raddick gave her a prescription for sleeping pills and told her to eat well, exercise regularly, and avoid alcohol. "Sleep at the same time each night. Read a nice book. Take the medicine an hour before bedtime, and see me again in a week."

Cheryl drove through downtown where she used to work a long time ago. People clutched their coffee cups and shopping bags and pulled their coats tighter as they walked the streets lined by bare, desolate trees. A few clouds hovered high in the sky, and Cheryl turned up the heat in her old Honda.

She picked up the prescription at the pharmacy. On a sudden whim, she drove to the library where she picked up a book she'd been meaning to read forever. From the kids' section, she chose a few picture books. Jimmy loved Dr. Seuss. The supermarket was next, where she picked up a dozen boxes of Jimmy's favorite mac-and-cheese.

Back at home, she opened a box of mac-and-cheese, cooked it in the microwave, and spooned it into two bowls. She used to sneak bits of broccoli into the mix, but she wasn't planning on eating healthy tonight.

Then she took a hot shower, entered Jimmy's room, and turned on the table lamp beside his bed. The pills lay in the bottle on the kitchen counter, untouched. She read the picture books aloud until she fell asleep in his bed, hugging the Superman pillow, her legs tucked under the SpongeBob blanket.

Eight months earlier, an online parenting group for stay-at-home moms brought up the idea for a book: *Childcare, a Mother's Perspective*. Cheryl was asked to contribute a chapter on potty training; a topic she knew well, having struggled with Jimmy for almost two years.

It had taken her just one day to complete the outline when Rob had called. He was in Camp Pendleton before getting shipped out to Okinawa and wasn't sure if he would have time to visit before leaving.

As the afternoon wore on, Jimmy got antsy, and Cheryl turned off her computer. He'd been cooped up indoors all day. She was terrified of all kinds of danger in the park, so they always played in the backyard.

Cheryl asked, "Want to go outside, Jimmy?"

He nodded and brought a ball from his room. She opened the

glass double doors which led to the brick-lined patio and led him into the backyard. They played catch in the late spring cool breeze, running barefoot on the lawn.

He got bored after a while and asked, "Can I ride my bike, Mommy?"

Rob had taken Jimmy out on the sidewalk last weekend, and Jimmy had loved being outside. But Cheryl was scared. What if he lost control and rolled into the road?

"Later, babe. We'll go out after Daddy comes."

"Can we swim, then?" Jimmy had the loveliest pout, and she was putty in his hands.

The June air was still chilly, but Jimmy had been begging for a swim for days. Cheryl opened the pool gate and squatted beside the pool. Rob had ordered a dozen six-foot circular solar blankets guaranteed to warm the water, but so far, the sun had been too weak. She flipped over one blanket and dipped her fingers in the water.

"Still cold, hon."

Another week of warm sunny days was sure to do the trick.

The phone rang. Cheryl hoped it was Rob and ran inside to answer it. Jimmy followed her to the brick patio and knocked on the glass double doors. "Come out, Mommy. I miss you!"

She smiled at him and waved. The call was from her college roommate, Amanda. She was coming to LA on a business trip and wanted to catch up.

Amanda had never married. She had a successful career as a hospital administrator in Arizona. Since Rob had been working late for days, Cheryl craved company.

They chatted for a minute as Cheryl looked out the patio door and saw Jimmy playing the fool in the backyard, flexing his knotty little biceps.

He shouted, "Look at me, Mommy! I'm Superman!"

Cheryl grinned at the enormous shadow his tiny body cast on the lawn in the slanting afternoon sun. She nodded at him.

He asked, "Play hide and seek?"

She covered the mouthpiece and said, "Yeah! You go hide. I'll be right out." After giving Amanda the address, Cheryl hung up and went outside. "Jimmy! I'm coming to find you!"

A giggle usually gave him away, but there was no response. He must be hiding behind the massive gardenia bush, his favorite hiding place. She crept up to the bush but didn't see him. For a moment, her heart stopped. Where was he? Then she told herself to stop worrying. Rob was right. Why did she always expect the worst?

She looked behind the detached garage, his second favorite hiding place. Then she noticed the pool gate. When the phone rang, she had left in a hurry and forgotten to close the gate. Could Jimmy . . . ?

She sprinted to the gate, calling his name. "Jimmy! Baby, where are you?"

The solar blanket was pushed aside, a small pool of water on top of it reflecting the fluffy clouds above. A few ripples distorted the view of the tiled pool bottom.

Blood drained from her body and her knees buckled. "Jimmy!"

She tugged at the blanket and saw him trapped below, his blond hair swirling around his head like a halo. He wasn't moving. Cheryl jumped into the pool, the ice-cold water piercing her skin like a million needles. She dragged Jimmy to the edge, hauled him over, and got out. His body was limp and cold.

"No! No! No!"

Shaking with racking sobs, she started CPR. She pinched his nose, blew into his mouth, and compressed his tiny chest as she'd learnt at the Red Cross. She heard the ominous sound of a rib crack. But Jimmy didn't take a breath. He didn't cough. He didn't wake up. His eyes were half-open, the blues reflecting the heavens above.

She ran inside and called 9-1-1. Then she went back and continued CPR, trying to pump oxygen into his lifeless cyanotic form.

The coroner called it an accident. Jimmy must have fallen into the pool when he ran to hide behind the deckchair inside the pool enclosure. He was trapped under the six-foot solar blanket for all of five minutes. Five minutes for which she would trade her own life. The five minutes that changed everything.

When she and Rob had bought the house, Cheryl got the pool fence installed for safety. She'd been a swimming champion in high school and had sworn to teach Jimmy how to swim this summer. But that wasn't going to happen.

Inconsolable, she had begged the police to take her away, lock her up for good. She was a terrible mother. Who leaves a child unattended for five minutes? She was cold and wet, sobbing and screaming to deaf ears. Why wouldn't the police arrest her? Instead, the woman police officer wrapped a blanket around her as a paramedic gave her a sedative.

They called it a terrible tragedy. Cheryl was not arrested for negligence or child endangerment. But something inside her broke that day. She was never the same again.

— • • —

Autumn reddened the maple trees lining the street, carpeting the sidewalks with golden foliage. Days were still warm, but the nights turned cool. It had been four months since Jimmy passed, and Cheryl had tried her best to avoid seeing a therapist to deal with her sorrow.

Jimmy's absence was a living, breathing entity, haunting Cheryl and plaguing her with guilt and regret. She had torn up her chapter on potty training; anything to do with childcare was a farce.

Guilt imprisoned her in its vice-like grip, draining her blood, drop by treacherous drop, until she was but a shell, cold and blue on the inside. Her heart, shredded by grief and agony, could hold no more love. Her marriage teetered on the verge of collapse.

She returned from her part-time job in the local supermarket where she spent four hours a day running inventory and manning the cash register. As an employee, she got a twenty-percent discount on everything.

She opened the front door and brought her groceries inside. The house was a single story Spanish-style with beige walls and a red tiled roof. A white picket fence with merry white roses rimmed the front yard. She and Rob had dreamed of bringing up a lovely family here.

Dropping her keys on the coffee table, she took the grocery bags into the kitchen. Then she took out the all-purpose flour and a mixing bowl. She whisked three eggs in the bowl, added sugar, molten butter, vanilla extract, baking powder, flour, and lastly, the baking chocolate.

She baked Jimmy's favorite cake for thirty-five minutes as she sat at the dining table and looked through the glass patio door into the backyard, imagining a happy little boy playing outside, casting Superman shadows on the lawn. But the sun blazed on the neglected browning grass. Not a bird twittered.

The oven dinged as the aroma of chocolate wafted through the house. She wore oven mitts and took out the perfectly baked birthday cake and left it to cool on the kitchen counter.

After a shower, she changed into a nice dress and decided to wait for Rob before cutting the cake. Once it was cool to the touch, she added the frosting and wrote in her best cursive: *Happy Birthday, Jimmy.* Then she pierced it with four candles and waited for Rob, a glass of wine in her hand.

The sky darkened outside as she refilled her glass, and another. Finally, she fell asleep on the couch. When Rob opened the door, she woke up with a start, her head throbbing, her mind muddled from the wine.

"Ready for dinner?" she asked as she staggered to her feet and banged her knee into the coffee table.

Rob nodded and followed her into the kitchen. That's when he saw the cake. She hadn't told him about it and was utterly unprepared for his reaction.

He clenched his fists, and a vein throbbed on his forehead. "What the heck's wrong with you?"

Her eyes widened. "It's his birthday, Rob."

"You've got to stop doing this to yourself. And to me."

"I . . . I don't understand."

He grabbed her by her arms and shook her. "Cheryl. This is the last time I'm telling you. Jimmy's gone. He died. Because of you. Do you understand?"

A massive sob escaped her lips. "I'm sorry! I tried my best!"

"That's the problem! Your best isn't enough. You let our only child drown. Can't you see? I can't live like this anymore. I've been thinking long and hard, but I cannot forgive you. I'm really sorry . . . I'm leaving."

Rob left that night, leaving a rent in her heart that nothing could fix.

Alone in the kitchen, Cheryl sobbed over the cake. The words, *Happy Birthday, Jimmy*, seemed to mock her. Jimmy was never coming back. But that didn't mean she couldn't celebrate the four wonderful years of his life. She lit the candles, tears streaming down her cheeks.

A blast sounded outside, startling her, as the house plunged into darkness, save for the glimmering light from the four little candles. A transformer must have blown. The house suddenly felt cold and loveless. Despite the closed patio door, she felt a breeze wash over her as goosebumps rose on her arms.

That's when she heard a soft voice.

"I'm *five* years old, Mommy."

Cheryl gasped and turned toward the patio door, her hands trembling.

Jimmy was standing with his hands in his pockets. Even in the dim light she could discern the blue-and-white-striped T-shirt, the same one he was wearing that fateful day. How could this be? Was her mind playing tricks on her? Had it all been a bad dream and Jimmy was really here? She wished she hadn't drunk so much wine. She blinked twice.

Something was strange about his eyes. His gaze penetrated her body, as if he was looking right through her.

I'm going insane!

She rubbed her eyes and looked at the door again. He was still there. He looked neither happy nor sad. Just a wistful look in his eyes, his shoulders hunched.

She whispered, "Oh my God, Jimmy!" Her knees buckled and she clutched the edge of the table for support. Her blood turned to ice.

"I miss you, Mommy!" His eyes were bright blue, glistening in the light of the candles, his body bright against the dark outside.

She stood rooted to the spot, trembling.

He crept closer. "Light one more candle, Mommy."

The hairs on the back of her neck pricked as she turned away from him and walked to the cabinet, her body shaking unbearably. She pulled out another candle, glancing over her shoulder to make sure she hadn't imagined it all.

But he was watching her.

Her breath came short and raspy, and her hands shook as she tried to light the fifth candle using one of the others on the cake. But the candle would not light. As a pool of wax formed on the frosting, ruining the cake, the flame singed her finger. She threw the candle down. Why wouldn't the damn thing light? She sobbed and glanced at the patio door.

Jimmy was gone.

She opened the double doors and ran to the patio. "No! Jimmy! Come back! I'll light another one."

But it was pitch dark outside. And still. Did she imagine a movement near the pool? She squinted at the pool as the lights turned on again with a thrum.

Back inside, she locked the double doors, blew out the candles, and threw the cake in the trash.

—— • • ——

Only after four months of terror and tears had Cheryl made her first appointment with Dr. Raddick. But she hadn't taken the pills the doctor prescribed. Her migraines had worsened. Barometric headaches, someone told her. A storm had drenched the town, and the streets sparkled with pools of rainwater.

Cheryl was back for her follow-up appointment, struggling to find a way to tell the doctor why she was really here. A goldfish bowl stood on the desk with a single fish swimming round and round in calming circles. Cheryl hadn't noticed it before.

"New fish?"

Dr. Raddick said, "Yeah. A patient gave it to me. He said watching it gave him peace and may help others. How are you doing? Did the medicines help you sleep?"

"Not really. I miss my son."

Dr. Raddick looked up. "Is he with your husband?"

Cheryl shook her head, twirling the hem of her skirt, her palms sweating. *Tell her the truth.*

Dr. Raddick said, "Where is he?"

Cheryl felt tears sting her eyes as she realized she couldn't hide it anymore. "He's gone. He's dead. And it's my fault."

Dr. Raddick frowned and picked up a pen from the desk. "When did this happen?"

"Eight months, twenty-two days, and fifteen hours ago."

Dr. Raddick's mouth fell open, and Cheryl wondered if she should have told her during her first appointment. The doctor noted something in her chart. "What happened?"

Cheryl told her how she found her son's body. "I never imagined he'd go near the pool. He knew he wasn't supposed to go by himself. He didn't know how to swim . . . I tried everything . . ."

"I'm so sorry. After a devastating loss like that, it takes time to recover. Did you get any grief counseling?"

She shook her head. "I don't like therapy, Dr. Raddick. I

got books from the library. I know all the stages. Denial, anger, bargaining . . . blah, blah. But . . . but that's not why I'm here."

"Why are you here?"

Cheryl looked up at Dr. Raddick's blue eyes, eyes that reminded her of Jimmy. "I didn't tell you everything before. I um . . . I can see him."

Dr. Raddick folded her hands on her lap. "Him?"

"My son. He waves to me from the patio door. Tells me he misses me. Dr. Raddick, I know he's dead. But he's still here. I . . . I need to make sure it's not my imagination."

Dr. Raddick said, "When did you see your son? Like a vision? Dream?"

"Just this morning. He looked so real. He was wearing his blue-and-white-striped T-shirt and blue shorts. As always. The sun glinted off his blond hair. He was smiling at me from the patio door. I tried to blink him away, but he said he misses me."

"Just once?"

Cheryl shook her head. "Almost every day since his birthday. The day Rob threw a fit and left."

"Did Rob hurt you?"

"No, he'd never do that."

"Go on."

"Rob said I'm crazy. He blames me for Jimmy. He just left. He didn't even pack a suitcase." She told Dr. Raddick how she'd seen Jimmy for the first time. "I'd been drinking. I found another candle like he asked, but it just wouldn't light. I looked again and he was gone."

"How long ago was that?"

"Almost five months."

"Did you tell Rob?"

Cheryl nodded. "He couldn't deal with it. He filed for divorce two weeks ago."

"Are you sleeping well?"

Cheryl shook her head. "A couple hours max. What do you think is going on?"

Dr. Raddick looked at her with kind eyes. "I think you're still in denial."

"No, I went through anger, bargaining, and depression. I experienced such abject sorrow . . . I was crying all the time. So I must be way past depression. I should be at the acceptance stage."

"Cheryl, everyone goes through grief in different ways. Let me give you something stronger for sleep. And for anxiety and to um . . . stop the hallucinations. See me again after a week."

— · · —

Cheryl hated the medicines. She couldn't perceive Jimmy anymore and didn't even know the time of day. Why, she didn't even know what day it was. She walked around in a fog, making mistakes in the inventory, and giving customers too much change. After a week, her manager forced her to take time off.

Cheryl stopped the medicines and skipped her appointment with Dr. Raddick.

She poured herself a glass of wine, although it was early in the afternoon. Just to soothe her screaming nerves.

"Come play with me, Mommy."

Cheryl looked at the patio door, and her heart skipped a beat. There he was in his resplendent glory, solid as flesh and blood. Maybe he *was* real. Maybe she had found an alternate reality where he hadn't died. Where she wasn't guilty. Where she had a hope to be happy.

When she was a kid, her social worker had said, "If you wish hard enough, maybe it will come true."

She gulped down the wine. Then she asked, "Are you for real, Jimmy?"

"Do I have to be?" he asked, taking a step back.

Cheryl stepped onto the patio as Jimmy giggled and led her into the backyard. He ran around the pool as she chased him. Laughter filled her backyard once again. She'd never been happier. She chased him around in circles, but try as she might, she never reached him. Cheryl didn't want to wake up from this blessed dream.

The doorbell rang and she glanced at the patio, wondering if the spell would break and she would wake up. She pinched herself and winced. She *was* awake.

Jimmy's smile disappeared.

She bent over, hands on her knees, panting. If it was a phone call, she would have let it go to voicemail. "I'll be right back."

He was looking at her with those big blue eyes. Then she noticed something. Jimmy was standing in the exact spot where she'd seen him being Superman, when he was truly with her. In the bright sun, Cheryl's own body cast a sharp shadow on the grass. Jimmy didn't have one.

The doorbell rang again, urgently this time, and she took a step toward the house.

"I miss you, Mommy," he said.

She closed her eyes for a moment, in two minds. Maybe this *is* a dream. Then she heard the splash. She turned to look, but Jimmy had jumped into the pool and disappeared.

Without a ripple.

Jimmy did not visit for a few weeks. As if he was punishing her for answering the door. It wasn't even important. Just some salesman pushing a new fiber optic internet service. Once again, she'd allowed the trivial to take priority over what was important.

But hope forced her to spend all day in the dining room, watching the patio door. She cooked box after box of mac-and-cheese, not eating any of it. The whole house smelled of cheese, as she hoped the aroma would entice him inside the house.

Cold wind blew the last fall leaves into the backyard as winter set in. She heard a rustling sound outside and decided to check yet one more time.

She stepped into the patio and called, "Jimmy! Are you there?"

There was no sound. The air was thick as soup.

Cheryl shivered and pulled her sweater closer. "Jimmy! I'm here for you, baby! Come out!"

But it was quiet.

She went back inside, changed into a bathing suit, and came out shivering as she stood beside the pool and waited for him to appear.

A faint voice called, "I miss you Mommy." It came directly from the pool, but she didn't see him.

She jumped in. The water was icy cold, just like the fateful day when she'd pulled him out of the pool ten months ago. Holding her breath, she swam to the bottom and looked around, brushing the tiled floor with her fingers. The sun's rays penetrated the depths, sending glowing, gliding circles on the bottom, outlining the shadow of her slender form. But she was alone. When her breath couldn't hold any longer, she came out of the pool, quivering and disappointed. Her teeth chattered as she dried her hair in the backyard.

The doorbell rang again. She donned a bathrobe, traversed the dining and living rooms, and reached the foyer just as the front door opened.

It was Rob. She'd have to change the lock.

Rob looked at her with concern in his eyes. "What the heck are you doing?"

"I went for a swim. Last I checked, it's still legal."

He took two long steps toward her and rubbed her arms with both his hands, a gesture more intimate than a kiss. "You're freezing."

She had missed him, but his warmth didn't belong to her anymore. She struggled out of his grasp. "I'm fine."

"Are you?" Jimmy had his father's eyes.

Unable to look at Rob's eyes, Cheryl dropped her gaze. "Yes. And I signed the divorce papers. You're free."

His voice was soft. "Are you taking your medicines?"

She frowned and shook her head. "Why do you care?"

"Elyssa saw you in the pharmacy. She said you were talking to yourself. Adjusting the seatbelt for the booster seat."

Their neighbor, Elyssa, used to babysit Jimmy on the rare occasions Cheryl pulled herself away from him for a date night with Rob. *Nosy woman!*

"I'm fine."

"Are you taking your pills?"

She shook her head. "They make me too groggy."

And they don't let me see Jimmy.

Rob stood there, bobbing on the balls of his feet, unable to leave her, unwilling to stay. He, who fought battles for his country, could not help her win hers. But her battle was with her past, and no one wins that fight. He glanced at the dining table where she had set a bowl of mac-and-cheese. He strode to the pantry and threw open the door as boxes of mac-and-cheese tumbled down.

His voice cracked as he said, "You need help, Cheryl."

"It's none of your business. Go home, Rob."

—— • • ——

Cheryl drove to the library after work and strode to the research section. She chose a computer terminal hidden from view and glanced over her shoulder. It was a quiet afternoon, and high school kids hadn't yet swarmed into the library for study groups.

She typed the keywords: *Ghosts, shadows.*

Three books popped up. She took down the call numbers on the tiny notepad beside the terminal, using a pencil that would be too small even for Jimmy. Clutching the piece of paper, she hurried to section 133.1: Ghosts/Supernatural.

She was the only patron in the dusty, desolate section of the library, imagining whispers and footsteps. She opened one book and tried to scan the contents.

An elderly librarian pushed a creaky cart filled with books to reshelve and smiled at Cheryl. "Need any help, dear?"

Cheryl was startled. What did the older woman know about Cheryl? Did she know she could see Jimmy? Did she know Jimmy had died? *Stop this, Cheryl!*

She mumbled, "No, thanks."

She grabbed two more books and scurried to the children's section beyond the computer terminals and picked out a few Dr. Seuss books. The elderly librarian had returned to the checkout counter, and Cheryl chose one of the newer self-checkout terminals.

Back at home, she had her mac-and-cheese and settled into the recliner where she used to curl up with Jimmy to read Dr. Seuss's books or watch SpongeBob. Over a glass of wine, she read about ghosts and visitations from the *other* world.

As far as her research could find, ghosts cast no shadows.

━ • • ━

The following week, she was back in Dr. Raddick's office. Dark clouds hovered low over the town. The mountains had experienced flash floods, and a wind advisory was in progress. The goldfish was going berserk in its bowl.

Dr. Raddick had turned on a table lamp to illuminate her office. She had a new haircut and perhaps new foundation, for she was glowing. Or maybe it was the raw heat from the space heater. But she also looked concerned.

"Cheryl, you look like you haven't slept in ages. Are you taking the medicines?"

Thanks. I know I look like a wreck. "The pills make me groggy. And . . ."

"And?"

"I can't see him when I take them."

"Cheryl, he is gone. What you were seeing were hallucinations. The medicines will help with those."

Cheryl asked, "Do hallucinations cast shadows?"

"What?"

"In your opinion, when people hallucinate about things, do the things they are seeing cast shadows?"

Dr. Raddick said, "I . . . I don't know. Maybe. Maybe not. I'll look into it." She wrote something in the file. "Is there any history of mental illness in your family?"

"No . . . I don't know. I was adopted." She didn't know why she lied. As far as she knew, no one in her family was cuckoo.

"I see."

Cheryl knew where Dr. Raddick was going with this line of questioning. She had decided Cheryl was delusional.

She shook her head. "I'm not going crazy. He comes to visit me."

Dr. Raddick placed a hand on Cheryl's knee. "You need to move on. You've got your whole life ahead of you. You'll fall in love, get married, have kids . . ."

Cheryl shook her head. "He likes being the only child."

"Liked."

"What?"

Dr. Raddick tapped her pen on the table. "You said 'likes.' You mean *liked*."

Cheryl looked confused. "Jimmy is still here."

He was standing there, tapping the goldfish bowl. The little fish went bonkers, scurrying in circles like it had gone insane. Jimmy giggled. Didn't Dr. Raddick hear him?

Dr. Raddick said, "Do you see him still?"

"Sometimes."

"Is he here now?"

Cheryl looked at Jimmy's impish eyes as he put his finger to his pursed lips and ducked under the table, leaving the psychotic fish to struggle on its own.

Cheryl shook her head. "No."

Dr. Raddick followed her glance and saw the fish. "I don't know what's come over it." She covered the bowl with a soft cloth. "I read somewhere that darkness soothes them." Then she said, "Cheryl, what you think you see isn't Jimmy. It's just a shadow of his memory. You should take the pills. They will help you."

"Can you give me something else? Something that makes me less groggy?"

Dr. Raddick frowned. "I have to ask you again. Do you have any thoughts about hurting yourself?"

"Oh, no. Why would I hurt myself? Jimmy needs me."

Dr. Raddick took a deep breath. "Can you stay with family for a few days? Friends?"

Dr. Raddick was beginning to irritate her.

"I told you I was adopted. My foster parents are dead. All my friends were Rob's friends. He got them in the divorce. They blame me for what happened."

"I think you should stay in the hospital for a few days. It will give you a change from everything."

"You can't force me."

"No, I can't, unless you're a risk to yourself or someone else. But I know it will help you."

Cheryl got up. "I'll think about it. After his birthday."

— · · —

For months, Cheryl tried to make sense out of it. She couldn't talk to Rob or Elyssa. And Dr. Raddick would think Cheryl was actually insane. Hiding essential information from Dr. Raddick had become easy. As Cheryl began to doubt her own sanity, a theory presented itself, and she tried to test it. If Jimmy was real, he would reach out to her, hug her, touch her. But, besides goosebumps, he gave her no physical evidence of his existence.

A few weeks ago, she saw him by the pool again, beckoning her, the impish grin on his face.

She gasped and clenched her fists. Then she turned her back to him. "You're not real. Go away."

She left him whimpering, "I miss you, Mommy."

Her heart broke watching him suffer alone. But she was desperate for respite. The pills prevented her from seeing him but wouldn't let her function. She couldn't live her life like that. If she ignored him long enough, he'd stop visiting. Wasn't that what she wanted? What she needed?

Cheryl took a long soak in the tub. Days had turned to weeks in a paralyzing haze. At least her manager had allowed her to return to work. She didn't take the medicines during the day. But come nightfall, she stared at the ceiling imagining him cold and alone in the pool. The dose Dr. Raddick suggested no longer worked; she needed two pills just to fall asleep.

An empty bottle of wine stood at the edge of the bathtub. She'd given up on glasses a while ago.

Jimmy was turning six years old.

Cheryl pulled herself out of the cooling water in the tub and stumbled. The wine bottle crashed on the marble floor, spreading shards of sparkling glass across the bathroom. She tiptoed around the deadly pieces and changed into the same dress she'd worn a year ago when Jimmy had visited the first time.

The oven dinged just as she came to the kitchen. By the time the cake cooled, she'd finished another half-bottle of wine. Then she frosted the cake and lit six candles. Her hands were steady, her breath calm.

She whispered, "Happy Birthday, Jimmy."

She glanced at the patio door but it was dark. Since the day she ignored him, he hadn't visited even once. Guilt tore at her for failing him as a mother, for trying to maintain a shred of sanity. But if he didn't come today, she knew she couldn't hang on.

She opened the patio door and peeped into the yard, "Your cake is ready, baby! Come on in."

Silence.

A sob escaped her lips. Her voice shook as she sang "Happy Birthday." Tears stung her eyes as she blew out the candles and clapped on behalf of the crowd that should have been celebrating his birthday. He'd have been a first grader now.

She sliced a piece of the cake and tasted the chocolaty goodness. After one last glance at the patio door, she went to the small room Rob had used as a gym. He had taken the treadmill with him but left some things in the closet. Sliding the closet door open, she found what she was looking for.

Cheryl selected the heaviest weights in the closet, tied them together with two belts, and fastened it around her waist. Then she went to the brick patio.

"Jimmy, are you here?"

Her heart surged with joy as his voice rang out in the still night air. "I miss you, Mommy!"

She couldn't see him. "I miss you too, babe. Where are you?"

Cheryl stepped onto the dark lawn and opened the pool gate. She had removed the solar blankets months ago.

His childish voice called again, "Come here, Mommy!"

Without a moment's hesitation, she jumped into the pool as icy water pierced her skin.

"Jimmy!" she yelled into a soundless world as bubbles erupted from her nose and mouth and floated away from her face, exploding on the surface.

She gulped the water into her lungs, coughing and sputtering, flailing her arms and legs in the ink-dark water, her hair flowing about her in silky swirls. Her lungs burned with hunger for air, but the blessed weights kept her down. In the depths of the pool, she saw blackness. A flash of blinding light. Then blissful, peaceful blackness.

His voice whispered in her ear, "I missed you, Mommy."

Sunanda J. Chatterjee is an ex-Indian Air Force physician, blogger, and indie author. She grew up in Bhilai, India, and after a five-year stint in the Indian Air Force, completed her graduate studies in Los Angeles where she is a practicing pathologist. When she is not at her microscope making diagnoses, she writes fiction; her themes include romantic sagas, family dramas, immigrant experience, women's issues, and medicine. She loves extraordinary love stories and heartwarming tales of duty and passion. She has authored four novels and is working on a romantic suspense series. Her short stories have appeared in Short-Story.Net, IndusWomanWriting.Com, and in two *Holiday Heartwarmers* anthologies. She lives in Arcadia, California, with her ex-Indian Air Force anesthesiologist husband and two wonderful children. In her free time, she paints, reads, sings, goes on long walks, and binge-watches old TV dramas. You can follow her here: www.sunandachatterjee.com, www.facebook.com/SunandaChatterjee_Author-515705275228760, twitter.com/sunandajoshich1.

THE JONATHAN
OF BRACKEN
MANOR

R.J. Castiglione

Newport had a lot of Jonathans. They were

not Johns. They were not Johnnys. They demanded all three syllables. Most of them were skinny, although some were quite fat. They would march in and out of Bracken Manor doing all sorts of things. Sometimes they would shop. Sometimes they would sail a boat. Sometimes they would sneak around and kiss girls. It's what Jonathans do. It's who Jonathans are.

There was one, however, who was very unlike the rest. He wasn't skinny or fat. He wasn't short or tall. He detested the idea of kissing girls. That was gross. Most of the time this Jonathan was standing in the corner of the vestibule leaning into the wall. The paint was faded there, smoothed and polished by oil from his forehead. Jonathan was a boy capable of unique mischief. That's what Mother always said. *The corner is where you belong! The corner is where you'll stay until I say otherwise!*

In 1927 Jonathan was standing in the corner with his forehead cleaning the wall. Mother was yelling at him from the kitchen. "You know what you did was wrong!" Her face was red, like a tomato in August. He always liked making her face change colors. "You're going to stand there until you learn your lesson and apologize!"

In truth, Jonathan didn't know what he'd done wrong. He stood there and thought about it. For hours and hours, he remained in the corner. He was more comfortable there than his own bedroom. Even though he had buckets of toys, he preferred the wall in the corner. He was able to plan and schedule upcoming games and mischief. He stood there until his legs hurt. He stood there until his eyes began to water.

Mother started screaming again. The boy wanted to see why Mother was angry, but she told him not to move. He learned long ago to stay put until Mother said it was okay. He waited there until she stopped yelling. He even stayed there when the house became hot, the air became cloudy, and the walls turned black. Jonathan was tired by then and decided to take a nap.

He was sure Mother wouldn't mind.

—— · · ——

In 1935 a new Mother arrived. There was also a Father and three little boys. None of them were Jonathan. He remembered then why he had been bad. He had been playing with the new stove Mother had bought.

"Mother, I apologize! Mother, I'm sorry!" he yelled, head still planted in the corner.

She didn't respond. Jonathan learned last time that when Mother didn't answer him, he was no longer being punished. He decided to look for Mother. It had been a long time, and he wanted to make her face red again.

He ran into the kitchen. She wasn't there. She wasn't in her bedroom or her bathroom. He wanted to check the garden, but his pants were dragging on the ground. If he got them muddy, Mother would put him in the corner again. He didn't want to go there right now.

"This place is ugly!" one of the Not-Jonathans said.

This boy was short and pudgy and not at all exciting. Jonathan wanted to punch him in his hideous buck teeth. He kicked a cabinet door instead, splitting it in two.

"What did you do?" the new Mother yelled at the porky Not-Jonathan.

"Nothing! It just broke!"

"Don't lie to me! Go stand in the corner!"

The fat boy protested, but Mothers always got what they wanted. He stormed off to the corner, his face now strawberry-red. Jonathan was pleased. He'd never not been punished for being bad. He made a game of this for quite some time.

Whenever he got bored, he would play a trick on the Not-Jonathans. He would break something Mother liked, hoping to make her angry. One of the Not-Jonathans was always sent to the corner. Sometimes two of them were. When they had to stand there, it was too full of crying boys. There was never any room for Jonathan.

And so he continued his game. He scared Mother and Father. He broke things. He left the water on. They even had a new metal box that kept food cold. Jonathan loved to leave it open until the food started to smell. He did this until the fat Not-Jonathan became tall and skinny. Mother stopped putting him in the corner. It was now consistently empty.

Jonathan realized he had been misbehaving. If the corner was empty, he would have to go there until he apologized, and he didn't like to say he was sorry. He had to do something really bad if Mother was going to put another boy in the corner. He decided to trick Mother one more time.

She was walking down the stairs into the vestibule, and Jonathan stuck out his foot. He laughed when Mother fell and tumbled. She spun around three times until she reached the bottom. Father had come out from his private study to see what had happened. He dropped to his knees and picked up Mother in his strong arms.

Jonathan stopped laughing when he saw Father cry. He didn't know why. Mother was only taking a nap. Jonathan felt bad that he made Mother sleep in the middle of the day. He knew it was his turn for the corner.

When he stood there, he felt comfortable again. He pressed his forehead into the worn-out spot of paint on the wall. He stayed there when men in white costumes came. They put Mother on a rolling bed and took her away. Father and the Not-Jonathans were sad. They were all sobbing now. One of them had snot running out of his nose.

There was too much happening at once. Jonathan wasn't able to focus on all the naughty things he had done that day. He decided to take another nap in the corner and wait for Mother to return.

— • • —

In 1943 dozens of people entered the house. There were plenty of new Mothers and new Fathers. Jonathan was happy after counting more of the former.

"Mother, I apologize!" he yelled before running away from the corner.

He was good again, and this time he planned to stay that way. There were other Jonathans this time, although they were different. One Jonathan was tall and skinny. He was missing a leg. It was all right though. Mother gave him a stick to help him walk around. Another Jonathan wore a white jacket and had a weird tube hanging around his neck. He would use it to help the Fathers.

Jonathan wanted to play tricks on them, but they were already unhappy. They looked like they were all standing in the corner. Some of them even screamed all night long when he tried to talk to them, like he was a monster. One Father was funny. He had no hair, and the skin on his face was thick and jagged. He didn't talk much. Jonathan was bored with these Mothers and Fathers. How could he play tricks on them when they were already so sad?

Jonathan sat in a chair near the corner. He wanted to go there. To do that, he needed to be bad. But what was the point of being bad if not to make happy people sad? He sat there and waited. He waited for the Mothers and the Fathers to cheer up so he could play tricks on them.

That day came in 1945. It was getting warmer outside, and the Mothers and Fathers were playing in the garden. Jonathan liked the garden. It was pretty and it smelled good. They were all drinking out of glass bottles and listening to the radio. Some were dancing to the music. Some Mothers and Fathers snuck away and were kissing under the trees behind the garden.

Jonathan liked parties. He never did anything bad when people were having so much fun. That meant extra time in the corner.

The music stopped and a Father started talking through the radio. He mentioned something about Europe and a war and surrender. The Fathers and the Mothers stopped what they were doing and started yelling and cheering. Jonathan thought a beehive had fallen down. He wouldn't stand in the corner for that. When they stopped applauding, they began going inside again. They weren't sad anymore.

Jonathan tried to play some tricks. He left the water on in a bathroom. He knocked a lamp off a table. He hid behind doors and scared people when they walked by. No one seemed to notice. No one seemed to care. They were too happy. He thought about tripping Mother on the stairs again but that wasn't fun anymore. He didn't like it when Mother took a nap.

Instead, he found Father resting in bed. Jonathan realized then that he was tired. It had been a long day. He lay down with Father and fell asleep, dreaming of the morning when he could play with new Mothers and new Fathers. He hoped there were other Jonathans as well.

They were always the most interesting.

—••—

In 1965 a new Father showed up. He was wearing all black, save a white collar he only took off when he was alone. He was ugly and scary, often scratching a hairy mole on his chin. Father had a thin stick in his hand that he liked to play with. When he swung it in the air, it made a sound like *WHOOSH!*

Pouring through the doors behind him, an army of boys filled the vestibule. They didn't all fit. Some had to stand in Father's study. This made Jonathan angry. Only Father and Mother were allowed in the study.

"You're not allowed in there!" Jonathan yelled. None of the boys listened to him. They were all Not-Jonathans and Not-Jonathans rarely listened.

He liked to play tricks on the Not-Jonathans. All day long he would hide their clothes. He would scare them in the shower, sending them scurrying through the halls without them. He lay under their beds when they were trying to nap. Jonathan kicked his feet against the mattress. The Not-Jonathans would cry the entire time.

Some of them told Father, but Father got mad at them. He would make them take their clothes off so he could hit them with his little stick. This made their skin red and made them cry. Jonathan didn't like this.

"If Mother were here, she would stop you," Jonathan said to Father. "Where's Mother?" Jonathan became mad when Father didn't answer. He had to get Father's attention. "Where's Mother?" he yelled louder. "Where is she?"

Jonathan would jump on Father's bed when he was taking a nap. He also broke glasses in Father's room and knocked paintings off the wall. He even opened Father's windows when it rained. This made Father mad. His room got all wet.

The entire time, Jonathan screamed at him. "Where's Mother? I want Mother!"

He even pushed Father down the stairs. If Father took a nap, Mother might come. She didn't. Instead, Father's face turned red. He grabbed a Not-Jonathan with orange hair who was standing at the top of the stairs and took him to his room. It must have been hot in there. Both Father and Not-Jonathan took off their clothes.

Father hit Not-Jonathan with his stick. He grabbed Not-Jonathan by his orange hair. He made Not-Jonathan kiss him all over his body. He made Not-Jonathan-With-the-Orange-Hair sit on his lap until Father became happy again.

Not-Jonathan didn't like this. He ran out of Father's room. He ran down the hall and stumbled down the stairs. Jonathan followed him, laughing at the orange-haired boy. He went outside without his clothes. It was cold outside today, and he forgot his coat. If Mother were here, she would make sure he didn't forget his coat.

Later that day, more Fathers showed up. They had blue clothes and hats. Some of them wore silver stars on their shirts. Others wore gold stars. They tied Father's hands together and took him away. The Not-Jonathans also left, leaving Jonathan all alone.

He was upset. There was no one left to play with. Despite all his mischief, Mother never came. He missed Mother.

"If I wait long enough, Mother will come back," he said, taking his place in the corner.

This day had been long. He needed to nap. So, he did. He took a really long nap. Mother and Father didn't come back for a long time.

— . · —

In 1986 a Mother and a Father arrived.

"Mother!" Jonathan was fidgeting in the corner, eager to end his punishment. "I apologize! I'm sorry!"

This Mother was strong and beautiful. He imagined her spinning him around by his arms until he was too dizzy to stand. He ignored Father. He was bored with Fathers. They didn't interest him at all.

Jonathan followed Mother around the house. She went from room to room, scribbling notes in a thin black book. She would walk away from him when he tried to play with her. She was more interested in her black book. She liked the house more than him. When she was done with her notes, she talked into a strange metal box.

Fathers arrived later that day. They began knocking down walls and putting them back up again. They changed each room into a bedroom. They added over twenty bathrooms! They even built a giant bathtub in the basement. When the Fathers were done, more people began to arrive.

There were more Mothers, more Fathers, more Not-Jonathans, and the occasional Jonathan. They came to eat Mother's food, sleep in Mother's bedrooms, and play in the giant bathtub. None of them had time for Jonathan. They were all too fat and happy.

He tried to get Mother's attention, but she was always too busy making food. Father was too busy playing with the others. Sometimes, he went in a room with another Mother, and they played with all their clothes off. Jonathan didn't understand why. Bracken Manor was never warm. They didn't even have a fire burning.

The Not-Jonathans also didn't have time to play. They were running in and out of the manor all day. This made Jonathan angry. Why would no one play with him? He tried breaking things. They would just be replaced. He tried to shake beds, but they were already shaking—full of Mothers and Fathers playing together. He tried screaming at them. They never heard him. He tried leaving them gifts from the garden, begging for their attention. They didn't care.

Then one day a lonely Jonathan was playing in the giant bathtub. This gave him a good idea. He knelt by the side of the tub and splashed the boy in the face. The boy began to cough but kept playing. Jonathan jumped in and stood at the bottom of the pool. The boy was kicking his feet above Jonathan's head. He reached up and grabbed the boy's foot, pulling him down to the bottom.

Jonathan held onto the boy, giggling and laughing until the boy finally noticed him. At last, he had someone to play with him. Jonathan let go of the boy. He floated up like a balloon. He pulled him down again. He did this over and over again until the other Jonathan grew tired and took a nap.

Jonathan was upset by this. He never made another Jonathan take a nap before. He felt bad and decided to let the other Jonathan go. Mothers and Fathers jumped in the bathtub with him. They tried to wake the other Jonathan. He must have been too tired from playing. He stayed asleep.

Later that day, everyone left. There were no more Mothers, no more Fathers, no more Jonathans, and no more Not-Jonathans. Only the normal Jonathan remained.

He stood in his comfortable corner, ready to nap. He had been bad. He made everyone go away. The corner was where he belonged.

— • • —

In 2017 Jonathan woke up to the sound of crashes and booms. A giant metal ball was swinging through the manor. It knocked down walls and floors. It cut through wires and pipes.

Jonathan was scared. He didn't know what was happening. The ball wasn't Mother or Father. It swung to and fro. It crashed through one room after another. Even Father's study was destroyed. All that remained was the wall in the corner. Jonathan had nowhere else to go.

He pressed his forehead into the wall, trembling from head to toe. He wanted Mother. When Mother didn't come, he thought about the fun he had over the last few days, reviewing them out loud to comfort himself.

"Newport had a lot of Jonathans," he said. "They were not Johns. They were not Johnnys. They demanded all three syllables . . ."

After graduating from Boston University in 2006, **R.J. Castiglione** became a professional Technical Support Engineer. While he spends his days fixing software issues and writing technical documentation, his evenings are spent penning grand stories either in the LitRPG genre or about places he visits with his husband and friends. He was inspired to write "The Jonathan of Bracken Manor" after visiting a hotel and restaurant in Newport, Rhode Island. The paranormal ambiance of the hotel became the perfect setting for a haunting by a mischievous young ghost. For more information on his available and upcoming works, visit https://www.rjcastiglione.com.

Black *Butterfly*

B. Sharpe

Phaedra's footsteps echoed down the hallway. Her brisk pace gave her enough momentum to burst through the double doors and arrive at the nurses' station just in time for her shift. "Phew!" She tossed the file she was carrying and pulled a pen out of her pocket.

The checkered nightmare of floor tiles stretched away from the nurse's station into two wide sitting rooms with flat screen televisions screwed into the walls. Yellow wallpaper curled away from water-stained walls. In the ceiling, long bulbs hummed behind plastic screens, casting a dingy yellow light into the catty-cornered area between two halls. The scent of goat piss battled the antiseptic's bitter smell. Screams and maniacal laughter echoed down the hallways that converged in the dayroom.

In the dayroom itself, the patients barely noticed her arrival. A man sat rocking in a far corner, his hospital gown askew. His eyes darted about chasing shadows, and his mouth hung slack. His hair, graying, gnarled and matted, stuck out in odd tufts about his head. In the center of the room, a woman dressed in a white hospital gown, with long, flowing white-blonde hair, danced about in grand sweeping gestures to music only she heard; a distant look in her green eyes. On the opposite side of the room, a frail, tiny woman with lipstick that ran up her cheek sat in a wheelchair, singing hymns as loud as her thin voice would allow.

A chubby man sauntered up to her, then offered Phaedra his hand. "Hi there!" his deep voice echoed.

"Um . . . hi . . ."

He seems sane enough, she thought to herself.

"I'm the President of the United States!"

Never mind.

He made eye contact with her. A few minutes passed as she floundered, unsure of how to answer. He never broke eye contact.

Just as she was about to respond, a heavy hand clapped down on her shoulder. She let out a soft mew of surprise, then twisted her head to find a familiar face.

"Oh! Oh, hi, Dr. Romanstein. Nice to see you again."

"Ms. Kazan, nice of you to join us." He turned to the *president*. "Ronald, now you leave my new nurse alone. You're not to touch her, you understand?"

Two male orderlies came up beside the doctor and stared pointedly at Ronald. Phaedra went to say something, then noticed her employer's dark glance in her direction.

"*Ssshhhh!*" the doctor hissed at her.

A tense moment passed as Romanstein and the *president* stared at each other with affected smiles that never reached the rancid fire in their eyes.

There was something cold and predatory in Ronald's smile. Eventually, his lips fell, the friendliness faded, and he nodded. "Yessir . . . Too bad though." He bit his lip and traced her small form with hungry eyes. "She's just my type." He turned and waddled away.

His eyes on her had felt like an assault. She felt dirty afterward. "Well, that was creepy . . ."

The two orderlies faded away into the bustle of the nurse's station.

Dr. Romanstein turned to her. "Welcome to Belle Reves Sanitorium. Most of our patients, such as dear Ronald, are beyond help and quite possibly criminally insane. However, they have wealthy relatives that pay us large sums of money to keep them alive, and well . . . out of the public eye—meaning off their list of worries. Your job is to keep the inmates, I mean patients, from harming or killing each other or the staff . . . which includes yourself. Phaedra, these aren't normal people. These people, even medicated, want to scare and hurt you. You're on graveyard shift, so you'll hopefully have limited contact with them. You've got to develop a thicker skin and a tougher demeanor, young lady. Or these people will literally eat you alive. Understood?"

Realization spread over her features, and for a moment, she contemplated bolting, then thought better of it. Truth be told, she desperately needed this job, any job, to pay the bills after her recent stint in rehab. The past several weeks had been a flurry of forms.

An arctic smile spread across her features. "Crystal clear, sir. I think I'll surprise you."

She tried to act confident, crossing one leg over the other, then leaning out with her elbow in front of her, hoping for a counter to catch her. Instead, her elbow found the shoulder of another nurse that was just walking up. Startled, she spun around, her apologies quick and effusive.

She found herself looking into ice blue eyes that confused her. She couldn't tell if she found an almost maniacal brilliance in them, or if they were simply alert. By degrees, she became aware of auburn hair in a crewcut and a square chin above a short muscular male body. He shifted around her and sat down in a rolling chair at a computer. She noted how his red scrubs, the same as hers and all staff, hung over his chest muscles.

Yummy! She hadn't even realized she'd licked her lips until Dr. Romanstein bopped her over the head with a patient's file he'd picked up.

He pointed a stumpy, gnarled finger at her nose. "And none of that!" He turned and walked away in a flurry of his white overcoat.

The male nurse she'd been consuming as eye candy followed the doctor's exit. He gave her a quizzical look, to which she responded with a shrug, shaking her head.

She walked over and offered her hand. "My name's Phaedra."

"I'm Claude, the head nurse. You must be the new graveyard shift nurse that I'll be working with tonight."

"Yup, that's me. I—"

A bellow burst from some location behind them. All heads turned toward the green double doors that sat closed to the side of the nurses' station.

"I. Don't. Belong. Here!" A man's voice, gravelly from years of drug abuse, echoed down the halls. He emphasized each word, the doors rattling from the impact of his kicking legs.

The chatter of the dayroom died away. The screams down the hallway burst into a hungry silence. She felt a pressure in her chest. There came a crunch, then a cry and a sickening slurping sound.

Claude stood up and walked over to the doors. He flashed his ID at a scanner, and the doors swung open. His look of determination spread to a grin that didn't reach his eyes, then, as quick as a cat in water, it changed to a horrified expression. "Christ! Get your crisis gear!"

The wing erupted into movement and sound. Nurses, doctors, and orderlies in red scrubs poured out of closed doors. Patients swung and jumped, screamed and howled like baboons—all except the white-haired dancer. She froze in place and stared toward the doors.

Phaedra felt a chill crawl up her spine and the hairs on the back of her neck rise. Clouds of her own icy breath formed before her eyes.

The medical personnel all froze in front of the double doors and stared. She walked over. The sight in the hallway washed her senses in gelid shock. Blood poured from open wounds and spread across the checkered floor. The bodies of the orderlies reflected defensive postures: arms out in front to fend off an unexpected threat; knees bent, indicating they'd tried to make themselves small. Their heads were turned toward the double doors, as if they'd watched in desperation for help to arrive. Their faces were frozen in expressions of sheer terror.

He sat between the two orderlies, huddled and glaring like a cornered animal. Blood dripped down the front of his hospital dress and chin. His brown eyes held a wild anger, and his chin was thrust out. His mouth was clenched as tight as the muscles of a tiger ready to pounce. His eyes took in the crowd before him, then settled on Phaedra.

"I told them I don't belong here," he growled as he sneered at her.

"Um . . . Yeah. Yeah, you do." She hadn't even realized she'd thought her response before the words tumbled out of her mouth.

"No. I. Don't." He began to crawl toward her. His sadistic sneer dominated his features as his eyes glittered with glee.

She backed away from him and bumped into another nurse. She wanted to slink down, to hide. His sneer deepened to reveal bloodstained teeth. He locked eyes with her.

The song rang out through the ward in a voice soft, yet sweet. The walls echoed back the words in eerie rendition.

Ride a cock-horse to Banbury Cross,
To see a fine lady upon a white horse.
Rings on her fingers and bells on her toes,
She will have music wherever she goes.

As the song faded away, so too did the predatory gleam in his eyes. His eyes glazed over, and his face went slack. It was as if the silly little nursery rhyme had sent him into a fugue state.

Just then, medical personnel flooded the hallway and cut her off from the evil she'd confronted. However, she heard him hiss as they gave him a shot of Thorazine. She spun around to see the woman in white standing still and silently staring . . . at her. A crooked smile spread across the woman's pale, youthful features.

Phaedra had the desire to become invisible.

— . • —

Later, Phaedra and Claude sat at their respective computers, inputting patient status updates and logging activities. Dinner came and went. As evening passed, the other personnel completed their shifts and headed toward the elevator. Night fell, lights dimmed, and they put patients to bed. The faint hum of the overhead lights and clanking of keys were all that could be heard.

Phaedra threw glances over her shoulder at her cute coworker.

"What is it?" he asked and her heart dropped. She hadn't realized he'd caught her.

"That thing with the girl singing. And that out of control patient. What was that about?"

"Oh, her." He leaned back from the computer, then stared into the shadows of a corner in the room. "Phaedra . . . You're going to see shit here . . . and it's not going to make sense."

She snorted.

"And I don't mean the crazy kind of not making sense . . ." He went to say something, but thought better of it.

"What kind then?"

"The kind that makes you question everything."

"Like?"

"Like ghosts and ghouls and things that go bump in the night." He turned and leveled a stare at her, blue eyes holding steady, unsmiling as they darkened.

She laughed. "You're fucking with me, aren't you?" She reached over and punched him on the shoulder—a playful light in her eyes, a flirty smile on her lips.

He snorted, then turned his head back to his computer before standing up. He grabbed his jacket off the back of the chair. "I'm going to step out for a smoke. Okay, Phaedra?" Something about his voice and mannerisms seemed off.

"Hey, I didn't . . . I didn't hurt your feelings or anything . . . did I?" The smile fell, sincere remorse filling her eyes. Then, "You're . . . you're serious?"

His eyes looked like he'd been up for forty-eight hours straight without coffee. "I'll be back in a few."

The doors swished behind him as he walked away. She watched him with equal parts of disbelief and a sinking feeling battling in her chest. Then she turned her attention back to her computer. She'd completed all the updates to the patients' files. All save the one she'd brought with her from HR on her way up. The file for Faye Stewart. She opened it and read the synopsis.

Hair color: white. Eye color: green. Symptoms: psychosis, with delusions and hallucinations. Calls herself the Rhiannon, a being with magical powers who can talk to ghosts and control them to fulfill her desires. Claims she is the descendant of a deceased race she calls the Aos Sidhe or the Fae. Very clever. Harasses people she believes to be evil by following them around and telling them their "sins," accusing them of murder, betrayal, adultery. On more than one occasion, the people she's harassed have turned up dead or insane. Special care instructions: use battle buddy teams; do not engage alone. Stay away from her room. Prognosis: to date, patient has continued to be resilient or allergic to all medication and treatments attempted.

Phaedra sat back, aghast. The chick was a real nutcase, that was for sure. Then again, who was she to say that about anyone else? Hadn't she done what she had to in desperate times? Was this job not another stop in her long run from guilt?

She scowled. What guilt? Memories of her mother lying in bed, screaming obscenities at her, flooded her mind. Memories of being a little girl beaten and neglected. She'd expected the time she spent taking care of her during hospice to be a time of reconciliation and resolution. Instead, her mother had bitterly harangued her every move, vicious because she wasn't her sister.

"I had to." She choked on her whisper as her throat constricted, but she was unable to convince even herself. She slammed her fists on the desk in front of her. "I had to!"

Her tears rolled down her cheeks and splashed her scrubs.

— · —

Meanwhile, the Thorazine wore off, and he found himself on a bed of crisp white linen. He chuckled. At least the mattress was soft.

The shadows on the ceiling fluttered. He didn't have to look at the window to know that the blackbirds still danced on the window sill—the same blackbirds he'd watched outside the window as they flew along with his father's car. The memory of his mother's suffering made him smile.

He remembered the leathery new-car smell of his dad's Mercedes.

His mother had sniffled and sobbed in the front seat. "I don't want him to be locked up, Derek!"

"I know, Misty. Neither do I. We don't have a choice. He's sick. Corey is sick. If you'd seen what I'd seen in that wine cellar, you'd agree." His dad darted glances toward the passenger seat as he drove through the pastoral back roads.

"What? What did you see? What could merit having him locked up in some obscure nursing home?"

All that could be heard for a few moments was the rush of wind as the car sliced through the heavy stillness.

"Blood. I saw blood, Misty." His voice was little more than a whisper. "More blood than one person can possibly hold. And hair . . . so much blonde hair." The eyes that stared through the windshield at the white lines held a kind of vacant terror. "Misty, all those blonde girlfriends of his that we didn't see again . . ." He glanced at her.

She'd gone pale and quiet. She turned to face the road.

"What? What is it?"

"All those nightmares I'd had for weeks on end . . . about girls who never stopped screaming."

A significant look passed between them. All those nights away on business . . .

"Jesus. We're lucky we don't have the police knocking our doors down." His father leaned into the steering wheel. The car lurched as he pushed harder on the gas pedal.

Misty made a fussy sound.

"Speeding ticket be damned. It'll be a shit ton of work to keep this out of the news."

Corey had turned back to the window, watching the blur of green as the fields whizzed by. That's when he'd seen the three black spots with wide wings that were flying alongside the car. He thought about the graceful wings of feather and muscle, about sinew and blood. Were their bones really hollow like they said? He had imagined capturing one, relishing its cries of terror and pain as he tore it apart to find out. His cheeks had lifted in a gleeful smile.

He'd arrived at the hospital amongst a flurry of whispers, hard eyes, and scrubs red as blood. At some point, it had sunk in that this was a special *nursing home*, a home for crazy people, one that they were never released from. He had tried to explain that he wasn't crazy. The doctor that had spoken with his parents had even agreed with him, saying that by public standards, he wasn't crazy. However, they had still had him undress, take pictures, and put on a gown.

He'd tried a different tack with the orderlies as they walked him to his wing: the *crisis unit*.

"I don't belong here, don't you see?" he'd asked them over and over, his breath shorter and shorter.

Their faces had remained impassive, complete with firm jaws and fake smiles. As he'd realized that they were ignoring him, a red haze had clouded his vision. How dare they ignore him, Corey Braxton Mulvaney, son of the CEO of America's biggest gas company? He was better than all of them! He'd huffed and puffed as the red haze and rage had taken over.

He'd awoken from the red rage to glorious carnage. The inert bodies of the unconscious orderlies had sprawled about him. Blood had poured copiously out of their raw, seeping flesh. If the other guy hadn't opened the double doors, he would have finished them off, killed them for their offense. The other guy's face had flashed through a few expressions, each polar to the other, none that reflected in his bright, sick eyes. He'd turned and screamed something about crisis gear. Corey chuckled at the memory.

Then he'd seen her, that cute, juicy girl in scrubs with skin the color of mocha and light gray intelligent eyes that missed nothing. Those eyes guarded secrets of their own. She was completely different from the blonde bimbos he'd lured into his basement. Their eyes had always held a soulless vapid air about them after a few snorts of angel dust. The stupid little hood rats had begged for their lives as he cut them apart, piece by piece. But this goddess, would she beg?

Her uniform hung from her luscious, curvy little body. When her eyes met his, he'd seen straight through her shock into a soul as cold, dark, and twisted as his own. Oh, sure. She'd championed the mask, the façade of humanity most people strutted around with, pretending they gave two shits about anyone but themselves. But in the end, she was as ruthless a murderer as he was.

The woman's song had filled the air, the haunting notes paralyzing his mind and sending him into a fugue-like spell. As the notes faded away, the red scrubs had stormed in with medicine-filled needles and he'd slept. He'd woken to the shrill song of blackbirds at the window.

In his dream, the song had been the screams of his victims as they chased him through the halls of the hospital. Now, he listened as the birds continued to chirp and peck on the window. He even heard the flutter of the flapping wings as he watched the shadows of them on the walls. The nurses insisted there was nothing there and that he be quiet.

But they were there, they were!

And it wasn't fair . . . the birds wouldn't leave, no matter how much he banged and pounded on the windows.

━ • • ━

Claude's sneakers slapped the tiles as he trotted down the hallway, stepping into the elevator. He pulled his jacket tighter around himself, then checked his pocket for cigarettes. The desire to smoke was a hungry ache that he looked forward to fulfilling.

He knew Phaedra wanted him, that she wanted to jump on him like a panther jumps on its prey. Truth be told, he was attracted to her too. He thought of her full lips, warm bedroom eyes, and the curve of her hips as she sashayed about. He felt a tug in his gut and a tightening between his legs. He imagined the shifting of her expressions across her face as he—

The elevator dinged its arrival, and a sharp shock jolted through him as he remembered the danger, as he remembered that his lust would act as a beacon, drawing the witch to him. The door spread open to sickly yellow lights that bore down on the cracked pavement. He dug his nails into his palm to draw his thoughts away from his basic appetite as he stepped out into the shadowy parking basement. Faded white lines peeked up from the ground, forgotten parking space delineations that no longer mattered.

"No one ever leaves Belle Reves." His tenor bounced about the eerily silent space.

He walked over to the smoking area, a corner of the basement with a dusty derelict car, graffiti, and a high window. His back against the cool concrete, he contemplated the graffitied wall before him. Black spray paint formed a weird seven-pointed star, two points to the left and two to the right, stretching out farther than the rest, like wings. Above it, a strange incomprehensible word was scrawled in ghostly white spray paint. He recognized the symbol. The same sign was tattooed on each and every occupant of Belle Reves.

His big sister, Faye, had carried around a notebook labeled *Book of Shadows*. Within that notebook, the same symbol that was on the wall had been copied down with the words *Magickal Energy* beside it.

Faye. Pain shot through his chest at the thought of her name. White smoke billowed out like a freight train around him. She'd been the only one who really saw him, understood him. When his face showed emotions inappropriate for the situation, emotions he didn't really feel, she'd been the one to defend him. She'd understood that, through all the cruelty and beatings, his soul had shattered inside his head. He crouched, bowed down his head, and rocked. She'd understood how sick he was. Tears rolled down his cheeks. Faye.

His madness was a black sun whose shadowy flames licked away his humanity. He hugged himself tight, terrified, desperate to contain that which obeyed nothing. He trembled, knowing the witch approached. Powerless, he felt the black flames destroy the earthen walls of his brain.

He stubbed his cigarette out and looked out the window. A huge moon hung high in a deep blue sky. Evergreen trees waved and whispered in a wind that he knew couldn't be felt.

He knew the witch would come tonight.

— • • —

She turned from the file and logged into the computer. She peeked over her shoulder to make sure she wasn't going to be caught while surfing the web. A quick search revealed a plethora of informative links. She selected one at random: *Rhiannon, fairy queen, daughter of Epona, wife to the God of the Underworld.*

Fairy, as in little people with wings? Her fingers flew into another search.

Fairies. Mythological creatures mentioned in various folklore throughout Europe. Earliest known folk legend is the Sidhe of Ireland. The Sidhe are also referred to as the hill people, or mound people. The legend goes that once a very prosperous people, the Sidhe were defeated by invaders and forced beneath the mounds. It is generally assumed that they lived on. However, early Ireland is also known for the use of burial mounds. Even the word fae *has its roots in the word* fate.

Were the Fae simply ghosts of an ancient race? The hairs on the back of Phaedra's neck rose. As she opened her eyes, she had the distinct feeling of being watched. She looked around her at the shadowy dayroom and dim hallway. Every door remained closed. Her eyes flitted to the bank of television monitors that showed the patients in their rooms. Her attention came to rest on a prominent screen marked *Faye*. The woman with long white hair sat up in her bed, with closed eyes and lips that moved.

A feeling of misgiving spread through her chest, and she considered scolding the patient.

"That's crazy though," she muttered. "I don't even know it's her."

Don't even know it's her? I can't even prove anything's going on. It's just a feeling. Am I losing my mind?

Just then, Faye turned and stared at the camera. Phaedra's breath caught in her throat. The lights flickered. Then, one by one, the monitors switched to speckled pictures of static. She watched the volume control as it turned of its own accord. The crackling hiss of radio interference crept up to an unbearably loud roar. She shot up out of her chair, her pen clattering to the ground. An electrical hum crackled in the air. Goosebumps crawled up her arms. She shivered.

The whinny of a horse echoed down the hallways. The lights over the nurse's station shut off. Her chest tightened. Her heart pounded. Her hands shook. One by one, the monitors shut off.

"Something is coming." She whispered the words.

She now stood in absolute darkness. The only sensation available was the sound of her own desperate breaths.

Clomp, clomp. Clomp, clomp.

At the end of the hallway, a white light, thin and fluid, swirled around like creamer in coffee. It became a horse's head, small and almost indistinct at first.

Clomp, clomp, as the light spread to a large body. *Clomp, clomp. Clomp, clomp*, as it came closer, became clearer, even though it never seemed to move faster.

She saw that it was a horse that shimmered against the pitch black. As it got closer, she realized that she could see through its form. The horse now whinnied as it stood before her. She wanted to scream but found her own breath paralyzed, gripped by the tight muscles of her throat.

Then, the horse faded away. The lights and monitors flickered on, all at the same time. As if nothing had happened.

She continued to stare where the horse had been. In the shadowy dayroom, on a wall directly in front of her, blood dripped from a message written there. *Why did you kill me?*

Memories of her mother half-paralyzed in bed, screaming obscenities at her and calling her a bad seed, sprang up in her mind's eye. Months and months of hospice care, trapped by obligation, tending to the woman who'd allowed her to be locked away days at a time in her room—no food, no water, and no bathroom. The weeks she'd spent mashing up the blood-thinner medication and mixing it in her mother's food. Watching the last breaths of life leave her tormentor's body, and the subsequent joy of freedom. Then the guilt, and running away, always running, never being able to forgive herself.

—. . .—

He hugged himself tight. He could feel it. The witch was in there with Phaedra.

"I told you." Claude's loud whisper came from behind the double doors. "I told you."

—. . .—

Paper butterflies, all colored in black ink, hung on the walls of her room. Black butterflies—souls, all hers, all belonging to her. She was the jar in which they fluttered about, desperately tapping against the glass trying to break free.

I am the Rhiannon, Queen of Ghosts, descendant of a forgotten race. She looked at herself in the mirror. Moonlight streamed in through the window somewhere behind her. Daughter of the horse goddess of nightmares, wife to the God of the Underworld.

Now that Phaedra had paid for her sins, Corey could be taken care of. The ghosts of Corey's many victims surrounded her, their empty black eyes and shrill cries demanding justice.

She stared at the ceiling, her arms out as she spun, first this way, then the other, as she sang the old nursery rhyme.

Ride a cock-horse to Banbury Cross,
To see a fine lady upon a white horse.
Rings on her fingers and bells on her toes,
She will have music wherever she goes.

A ring on her finger
A bonnet of straw
The strangest old woman
You ever saw.

I'm coming for you, Corey, she thought to herself. *Are you ready for me?*

— • • —

In the dayroom, Phaedra still stood, frozen in the same half-crouch that she'd been in twenty minutes ago while she had sat in her chair. Claude wondered if she'd ever move again. He sat on the floor next to her now, moaning and whimpering as he watched her unmoving figure.

His hands hugged his head as he tried to tune out the memories that flashed through his mind. Memories of coming to Belle Reves with Faye, his sister, his twin, as teenagers. Their father screaming at them as they had been guided down the hallway, "Satanic children!"

She laughed maniacally as Father's eyes bulged, a gurgle issuing from his throat. The wild eyes she turned to him when his mind whispered into hers to stop. He didn't want the witch and Faye to be the same. He didn't. But they were, and there was nothing he could do to dam the flood of her ire.

— . . —

Meanwhile, Corey lay there, staring at the ceiling. Tears rolled down his cheeks as his insides clenched. He'd been listening to the song consisting of those blackbirds for hours. He wanted to scream.

He tried to think of the many girls he'd dragged down into the basement. He tried to remember the fear in their eyes, the tears, the cries, the screams as he plunged the knife in again and again. The memories couldn't drown out the birdsong from the window. He searched his brain in vain for memories that wouldn't come. He searched for the hours of play, the torment in his victims' eyes.

It was as if the bimbos defied him. His fingers curled into talons. He gritted his teeth. He huffed and puffed, then realized that his breath came out in a cloud. Only then did he become aware of the icy bite in the air, the prickle of chilblain on his skin.

He felt eyes on him and immediately twisted toward the source, a corner of his room steeped in black shadow. The shrill song of the blackbirds finally stopped.

"I know what you've done . . ." Her whisper held the notes of a song that tickled the edge of his memory.

He shook his head as a twisted smile spread across his face. "Do you?"

She stepped out of the darkness, then—white skin, white hair, and white dress. As she stepped out, all thirty-three of his victims appeared, hollow-eyed, mouths agape, their bodies checkered with the wounds he'd inflicted on them. Their weeping howls ricocheted about the small room, seemed to assault him from every side.

His breathing came in short gasps. His eyes darted from one victim to the next. A worm poked its head out of the nostril of one girl and inched over to the other. He placed his hands over his ears.

This can't be real, he thought. *They can't be here.*

She stepped back into the shadows and the girls disappeared.

"How . . . How did you do that?" His voice shook and cracked.

He placed his hands in his lap, unsure of what else to do with them, and found that he was drenched.

"I am the Rhiannon . . . the Ghost Queen . . ."

He stared at her, not quite sure what to make of her. "What do you want?"

"What they want."

"What do they want?"

"Justice . . ."

Abruptly, she appeared before him. Her mouth opened impossibly wide as she took a deep breath. He felt his body weakening as a black essence was pulled from his eyes. He heard a terrible, inhuman scream. The essence from his eyes formed into a black butterfly that flew into her mouth. Life left his eyes, and his dead body collapsed on the floor.

She swallowed his soul, then walked over to the window. She stood in the moonlight and stared up at the moon.

— • • —

Eventually, moonlight faded and night drew back her velvet quilt to reveal a periwinkle morning.

Dr. Romanstein walked into the dayroom, humming and sipping coffee. He stopped to take in the scene. The congealed blood on the dayroom wall, Phaedra's catatonic body, Claude's tearful rocking.

"She got her, huh?"

Claude nodded. His eyes were bright as the tears rolled down his cheeks.

"Faye?"

He nodded again.

"She get the new guy too?"

He nodded a third time.

The doctor sighed deeply, then went about his day.

B. Sharpe is a stay-at-home parent of four children in South Carolina. When she isn't enjoying her kids, she reads voraciously and writes avidly.

FRAGMENTS
RIVER M. DANIEL

A bright, sunny morning in the village of Wrestlingworth had darkened to night as quickly as any other day. The trees, great willows in the countryside, rustled amid the howls of nearby dogs. The local park, alive with the chatter of parents and the play of small children while the sun had blessed its grass, swings, and other objects of fun, was now dark. The grass had become black and formless, seeming deep and endless, like the ancient Styx. The trees twisted and curled into faces and figures made to haunt the nightmares of unlucky children. Only teenagers—those stuck in the awkward stage between playful and curious, in the way country children are, and cynical and bored in the way country adults tend to be—dared to inhabit the park, whether it be to talk, drink, or explore each other's bodies in a curious yet cocksure way . . . enough to cause onlookers to either giggle with amusement or squirm with awkwardness.

The church around the corner from the park sat opposite the primary school where children ran and played with their friends every morning, oblivious to the world. It had only recently been reopened; roll after roll of police tape had eventually been removed after the investigation. In the dark the church seemed to tower threateningly over the school, its holy aura looking almost as though it were furrowing an angry brow in judgement. As the village became more and more residential, it became more and more stuck in time. Eventually it became one of those rare English villages where, despite the occasional car sounds at daybreak mixing with the opening off-licences and cafés, it retained its identity as a charming place, mixing modernity with the traditional quaintness of milk runs and windmill-made bread.

It was this small wooden windmill—slightly removed from the rest of the village by its large grounds—that offered a spectacle for locals, who would admire the beauty and upkeep of such a building that still functioned enough to offer daily bread to them all. However, recent tragedy in the family of the owners had ended its production whilst they grieved their losses. It was this building that, at 2 a.m. on a Sunday morning, was the only one to have lights on, albeit candles lit by the dozen, resembling an altar in a cathedral. The holy glow it offered to the inside of the mill displayed a warmness that matched and finally overtook the local church.

Inside, however, despite the hot flames of the candles, the air was icy cold as Sarah Berkley breathed out. Her breath fogged her vision for a moment before settling heavily downwards in such a strange fashion that, every time, it caused her to catch her breath before releasing it, allowing it to join the already heavy mist settling onto the ground. She looked across at her husband, Andrew, who shivered, despite wearing his dark brown winter jacket.

There were only three others in this icy-cold candlelit room. They didn't seem to be affected by the cold at all. The priest was busily working, setting up the highest room in the mill. Large sacks of flour had been moved against the dark walls, leaving a large open space in the centre. Occasionally Sarah would see the priest move behind these sacks and seemingly disappear for a moment before re-emerging and continuing to work. He was a large man, short yet wide; his chins wobbled as he worked.

Andrew offered to help with preparations, but the priest simply shushed him and continued to work in silence. He wore the typical priest's gown in a striking black, though he had no band around his neck to display his title. He wore wooden sandals that appeared ancient and biblical in an unnatural way.

The next person was the body of their ten-year-old daughter. Lucy had been freshly dug from her cold grave only a couple of hours ago, and the six months she'd spent buried showed. Her chest and face were deformed from the impact that had killed her, as well as rotting from the early stages of decomposition, leaving dark spots of mould all over her body that, not yet clean, still reeked of dirt and death. But to Sarah and Andrew, their daughter was just as beautiful as the day she'd walked alone to school.

Lying next to their child, as though a neighbour, was the body of the man who had killed her, butchered only a few hours earlier and laid out in a fashion specifically requested by the priest. Lucy was still wearing the pale white dress she had been buried in, though it was muddy and torn. The man next to her, however, was dressed in a black suit and a white shirt, fresh from the commute home before he was snatched away from that life. He was now lying on the misty ground next to the young schoolgirl he'd murdered six months before. He looked peaceful, as though asleep, his dark skin betraying no signs of death. The only sign that he wasn't alive was the thin line of dried blood across his neck where a knife had been drawn with a surgeon's precision.

Sarah was shaken from staring at the bodies by the voice of the priest, who was fully composed, despite the service he was about to perform.

"Okay, everything is in order now. Thank you both for completing the tasks I requested, and, naturally, you are both aware that no one can know of the events that take place in this room." The priest spoke in a kind voice, the same way he'd speak to choir children—lyrical and soft as though ready to tell a story. His tone seemed entirely inappropriate for the event about to take place in this shadowy, misty room.

Sarah and Andrew nodded stiffly in response to the priest, both looking down at the body of Lucy. Their mouths twitched up to form shaky smiles.

"Yes, we know the deal and are ready to begin." Andrew, though his voice shook with emotion, spoke assertively, placing a cold hand on Sarah's shoulder and gripping it tight.

She didn't feel her body shake any less; instead, she felt more nervous from the supposed comforting touch. The two of them should have been full of joy and hope, and yet foreboding and fear seemed to settle on the room like a thick, dark cloud.

The priest nodded before explaining to them slowly, yet again, what was about to happen. "Now that I have the body of the girl and the body of her killer, I can work on establishing a connection. Due to the link between them, their souls should be far more easily located in the afterlife, bringing both of their ghosts back to their bodies and allowing them to live again. Though I feel it is fair to warn you that people are not the same when their ghosts are returned." He smiled at this final statement as though resigned before looking at both Sarah and Andrew in turn. "Are you sure you want to go through with this?"

"We have given you all our money and everything else you've asked for; there's even a dead body in front of you because of us!" Sarah suddenly blurted this out at the priest, with tears streaming down her face.

Andrew looked at her angrily, causing her mouth to close. The priest retained his smile and slowly nodded. As soon as silence again returned to the room, the mist darkened and became heavy. The priest closed his eyes and, losing his smile, began to mutter unintelligible words at too fast a speed for Sarah and Andrew to follow. The room dropped to a new temperature, and Sarah felt herself become even colder, grabbing hold of Andrew's dark, tense arm and hugging it.

A breeze hit her lightly. She closed her eyes as it built up to an icy wind against her skin. She clutched tighter and slowly opened her eyes to see nothing but the arm she held; the room had become completely black, as though everything but Sarah and Andrew's arm had been painted out of existence. She listened intently and could still hear the shouts of the priest amid the darkness. She closed her eyes and prayed she could weather the storm, knowing—despite her freezing skin, pained, sore face, and the fear crawling through her body like a parasite—she had to finish this ceremony for the chance to be a mother again.

▬ ∙ ∙ ▬

Sarah and Andrew had been working on bringing their child back since a month after she'd died. At first, they had tried for another child, but the two of them gave up, knowing no one could ever replace Lucy. Ultimately, they settled for silent grieving. The mill closed, stopped producing any bread and, for months, the two of them idly wasted away their days searching for alternatives to their pain. Andrew found whiskey to replace the hole his daughter left behind whilst Sarah searched for a way to get Lucy back.

After a while she stumbled onto darker areas, areas that were too fantastic to exist and were too dark to earn the right to. She finally received an email from a man known only as The Priest, promising he could return any person back to the world of the living; in return he demanded £250,000 for the service. Sarah organised a meeting, and, in no time, she and Andrew were standing before him in the centre of London, feeling like two people conspiring against the world, conspiring against God.

The priest bowed and smiled; at that, they introduced themselves before heading toward a local apartment. The walk had felt so dreamlike and surreal to Sarah, she didn't even notice when the three of them were sitting on hard wooden chairs in a cold, unfurnished and run-down apartment. Teenagers shouting and cursing could be heard in the nearby flats, but the priest took no notice, only allowing his dark eyes to rest on the parents, narrowing and searching them each in turn.

Eventually he sat down, and a knowing smile rose on his face. "So, the two of you want me to return Lucy to you?" observed the priest, looking down at them and smiling.

Andrew leapt to his feet as Sarah's eyes widened in shock at the sudden statement.

Andrew looked at her questioningly. "Did you tell him about Lucy?" he demanded, pointing at her with rage in his eyes.

She quickly shook her head; in their last few months of grief, Sarah had learnt that staying quiet was safest with Andrew when talking about their daughter. The gentle man she'd married had been warped by grief, changed to a man that knew only how to face his loss with a bottle and his fists. The bruises underneath Sarah's blouse displayed that much. She wore foundation matching her creamy skin to cover a bruise on her cheek.

"I didn't email him. He emailed me out of the blue and told me to meet him here with you. I don't even know his name!" She quickly spluttered these words out, recoiling from Andrew, who continued to stare threateningly at her, as though searching for a lie.

Satisfied he couldn't find one, he resolved to sitting down and shifting his stare across the table to the priest, who sat there silently, smiling with the same unnerving warmth. After Andrew stared for a time, finally satisfied he was on a level term with the priest, he sat back and rolled his shoulders back—broad, though no longer toned as they were in his youth. He looked like an intimidating man. More intimidating than would be expected of someone trained as a lawyer.

Finally, the priest broke the silence. "It's okay. Shock is to be expected. I will make this brief, so as to waste as little of your time as possible. I can bring Lucy back to you, but for a price, of course."

Andrew could only stare for a moment at the priest, trying hard to control his anger. "You're telling me that you expect us to pay you because you claim you can bring our daughter back to life?" His face was red, and his eyes seemed to shine, as though challenging the priest sitting in front of him.

After a moment, the priest chuckled at the raging bull in front of him.

"How dare you! Is that supposed to be some kind of trick? Some scam?" Andrew continued to shout these tirades as the priest watched with calm blue eyes.

Blue, not like sapphires but rather dark blue like an ocean; calm, though in a moment capable of drowning anyone who dares to swim there. Sarah saw the danger in his eyes, so instead, under some urge in her body she didn't understand, she didn't move out of her seat or even react to the priest's impossible claims. Her mouth felt forced shut whilst her body felt heavy as a rock, incapable of moving.

"For a man who claims to be a lawyer, you seem to have a serious issue with keeping your calm, Andrew. Though it is understandable, all things considered in the past few months." The priest spoke and Andrew was silent, his mouth open as he listened.

The priest's eyes became darker; there was a dark blue storm at sea, and the small shine in his eyes made it clear, even to the raging Andrew, that if he didn't step in line, he would simply be sucked in and swallowed under.

At that moment, as though possessed, Andrew lost the rage in his face; his shoulders slumped and relaxed, as though the wind was suddenly knocked out of him. He fell weakly back into his chair, his eyes shining with trapped tears. When he settled down, looking at the table like a scolded schoolboy, Sarah rested her hand limply on his open palm, offering her support in something so small as a hand. Andrew didn't seem to notice the contact at first, but as soon as he did, he pulled away from her and sat up again, rigid, head craned to listen to the priest.

"I want to be clear on my terms. Most were included in my email when I contacted you. I will be expecting full payment for my services in advance and—"

At the priest's calm words, Andrew started again in shock, his body tensing back to what it was only moments earlier. He looked at Sarah, with still shining eyes, and simply asked, "Payment?" Though it wasn't a question, it was a challenge.

Sarah knew that, as a lawyer, Andrew always questioned her and Lucy in the same way he would question a suspect or a witness— with patience and understanding. He was an expert in keeping his usually rich voice plain and under control. However, since the loss of Lucy, his voice had gained an edge to it. It was hidden well, except from those who knew him. Sarah knew him well enough to notice this edge, and its constant changes were starting to become easier for Sarah to identify. Andrew's anger and frustration were building itself up to a point that could only hit one person, and it wasn't the priest sitting opposite them with a patronising smile.

Sarah looked at her hands as she spoke, watching them tremble uncontrollably. Her eyes were stinging with a mixture of tears and fear, and her voice had become nothing more than a pathetic murmur, no longer that of the woman fighting to bring back her daughter.

"Two hundred, fifty thousand pounds. I'm sorry. You wouldn't have let us go to London if you found out . . ." Her voice trailed off.

She didn't look Andrew in the eye for fear of him retaliating. She heard him breathe deeply, as though trying to bring himself under control.

"That's all the money we have. We've been saving it our whole lives . . ." His voice trailed off, and Sarah caught her breath, terrified of the repercussions of him not being told.

Her eyes fell to the small suitcase underneath her chair. She felt herself wondering if it was truly the right move bringing a briefcase containing all their money to a man who they knew only as *The Priest*. She hadn't questioned the compulsion. She simply had to bring the money to this man, who'd only sent them an email claiming he could help with their deceased daughter. The same compulsion had struck her in this apartment a few minutes earlier, when she couldn't even stand to soothe her husband's anger. She looked at the priest's smile with fear, seeing something else in it now, the self-assured smile of a man who had more control than one should have.

Andrew looked as though he were dreaming. ". . . okay. For Lucy."

Sarah looked up at him, eyes wide, as his face returned to the same placid, pale, faraway look he'd had. Sarah realised he too wasn't in total control of his actions. She felt her lips twitch upwards, though she didn't truly feel like smiling. She looked at the priest.

"Well then, let's continue with my terms. It goes without saying that you cannot tell anyone what has happened, or of the service

I have offered to you, whether you accept it or not. Additionally, there are objects and materials I will need for the act of bringing your daughter back, which I will reveal in due time. My final term is that I will be taking residence in your home whilst we set to work preparing the day for me to revive young Lucy."

Sarah said nothing as she absorbed the terms of the deal. She lifted the briefcase onto the table, and the priest eyed it hungrily. She looked at Andrew, who reluctantly nodded, biting his lip as he did so. She pushed the briefcase across the table as the priest nodded his thanks to her and immediately stood.

"Well, if you would like to transport me to Wrestlingworth, we can get to work." He smiled and carried the briefcase out of the door without another word, as though completely carefree.

Sarah thought she could hear him happily whistling a tune as he went about this unhappy business.

—■ ■ ■—

The darkness in the room had formed into a thick cloud that, now, though it didn't affect their breathing, made Sarah and Andrew squirm uncomfortably. Sarah could hear nothing apart from the rushing sound of the dark storm and the continued mutterings of the priest, increasing in volume as the swirling cloud continued to fill their ears.

Sarah felt a burning sensation rise in her throat before she sickly swallowed it back down. She felt lightheaded and her legs were shaking, as though unable to support her own weight. Andrew had withdrawn his arm from her hold at some point, so now Sarah faced the dark madness engulfing her alone, with fresh tears rolling down her cheeks.

Amid the cold cloud, the priest's spell, and her own fear, Sarah heard the scream of a child. She screamed back, instantly recognising the scream that belonged to her daughter, Lucy. The cloud continued to swell more rapidly, as though taking hold of that scream and working harder to maintain it.

The priest had been at the mill for two weeks. At first, when he walked about the town with both Sarah and Andrew, the villagers were curious.

"Have they turned to religion to get over their grief?" they would ask each other in worry for the two mourning parents.

Some sympathised, some approved, and some simply took no notice. After a week, the people of Wrestlingworth simply ignored this new addition to their village and got on with their daily lives.

Within the mill, Sarah only ever saw the priest when he was giving her errands—clearing a space on the top floor of the mill for the ritual, ensuring the mill was completely soundproofed, and choosing a time when both the church and graveyard were unattended. Other small jobs included cleaning the priest's bedroom every afternoon, though he made it clear that Sarah would not have to make him meals.

The priest never seemed to be dressed in anything but his black robes, always perfectly ironed, despite their obvious faded and worn look. They were particularly tight around the middle, forcing his belly to fold over his waistband in an ugly fashion. Neither Sarah nor Andrew had asked him any questions during his stay; the same strange compulsion they felt during their first meeting seemed to hold them both in place against questioning the man living under their roof.

When Lucy passed away, Andrew quit his job at the law firm to "grieve," though by this point, his grieving had turned simply into drinking his sadness away. Sarah became robotic in everything she did. Cooking, cleaning, sleeping, and weeping daily. Between her buried emotions and Andrew's bitter drinking, their love for each other had turned into disgust. The wedge that was driven between the two of them had never been clearer than that current moment.

Andrew sat in the living room on an old, worn sofa, staring into space with a half-drained bottle in his hand. Before Lucy's death, the walls were a light blue and adorned with photos. The room was supposed to be open and airy, letting the sunshine illuminate it with as much light as possible. Now, however, the curtains were drawn tightly closed, allowing only a thin stream of light to penetrate, enough to highlight the figure of Andrew.

The kitchen was also dark whilst Sarah set about cleaning appliances that hadn't yet been touched. The room was immaculately clean, making the image seem even more painful when compared to the mess that was supposed to be caused by a mother baking cakes and entertaining a child. The sound of the room had, in the space of six months, turned from a girl's laughter, a mother nagging, and a father cooing, to nothing more than a heavy silence—a silence that weighed on the hearts of those involved, both desperate to break it with some form of conversation, apology, even tears, while they also wanted to preserve it to protect their hearts from being shown to the stranger in the next room.

Sarah was cleaning the oven when she heard heavy creaking down the wooden stairs above her. Moments later, the priest was standing in the doorway between the kitchen and the living room. Sarah immediately stood and watched him, her eyes begging for news of the service being ready.

He smiled at her thinly before speaking. "First, I want to thank you both for your hospitality and your patience with me. I can happily announce that everything is finally ready for Lucy to be returned to you tonight. There are two last things I will need done before the ritual, however. Lucy's body must be dug up and brought here, and I need the body of the man who killed her." He stopped talking for a moment before being prompted by a confused look from Andrew. The priest sighed before continuing to speak. "He offers the closest link to her, being the man whose life she was most closely tied to at her death. Those kinds of souls tend to stick together." After this, the priest crossed his arms and waited for a response, eventually losing patience and breathing deeply. "Both tasks must be completed by midnight or else I will be unable to carry out the service for you." At this, he turned and walked upstairs with a confident air about him.

Sarah went into the living room to look at Andrew, who grimaced and stood.

"I know. I'll get the bodies, don't worry. I'll be back tonight." At this, Andrew walked upstairs drunkenly, slowly pacing each step.

Eventually he reached the top and made his way to their bedroom, where Sarah heard the door slam behind him. She stooped down and continued to mindlessly clean, the same smile twitching her lips that had appeared at the priest's apartment. She couldn't understand why she smiled at this dark business, so she shook her head and returned to cleaning blankly, her hands shaking as she did so.

— • • —

Preston Addams hadn't slept properly in months. Images of a dead girl haunted his dreams, turning them to guilt-ridden nightmares. Every day he went to work at the office and spent his time idly typing, his co-workers watched him suspiciously, hate blazing in their eyes.

"How did he not get sentenced for murder?"

"What monster does that to a child?"

Whether his co-workers said this or not, Preston could read it from their faces and how they looked away from him whenever eye contact was made.

He worked in a call centre; he was lucky to still have a job there, his bosses having had to place him on a three-month suspension. He was allowed to return on the condition that he had proven his innocence and was demoted from a team leader back down to a caller. He would spend eight hours a day being given abuse on the phone by anyone he tried to call offering PPI and broadband. They would listen amicably until price and subscription was mentioned, then, as though by magic, the perfectly civilised folk he spoke to became hateful monsters, screaming insults at him before angrily hanging up.

He had planned to speak to his wife that night, the reminder he'd set on his phone making it vibrate. He reached down into the glovebox as he drove to look at his phone. Immediately dropping it at the memory of the girl he'd hit with the front of his car only six months ago whilst checking his phone. Something he'd chosen to not tell the police about. With no witnesses able to contradict him, the guilt of the life he'd taken and the lie he'd told for self-preservation had haunted him since. His wife moved away to stay with her family and took his two children with her.

He tried to pick his phone back up from the floor of his car but decided to keep driving, clearing the highway he was cruising down and turning at the next sign offering a service stop. The car park was empty—strange as it was only 10 p.m. on a Saturday. A car followed him closely up through the services lanes, a small Ford that rumbled and lurched, as though the person driving was having trouble keeping control of its steering and pedals. It was tiny in comparison to the black Range Rover Preston drove. Though with his lowered wage, he faced the prospect of losing it, along with his house.

He parked in the first empty space he saw in the service station. The small car stopped next to him, parking diagonally and taking up two spaces. Preston took no notice, instead fishing out his phone from underneath him. He switched off the vibrating alarm, knowing he would be home in an hour, just in time.

He looked up at a knock on his window. The person knocking wore a balaclava and roughly opened the door, dragging out Preston as he did so. The man was large and built, as though a former rugby player. Preston was small, forever sitting at a computer or a help desk. The man's breath carried the stench of whiskey as he shouted into Preston's face, wrestling him to the ground.

"Do you remember Lucy Berkley?"

Preston became limp and nodded dumbly. Looking up at the masked man as the knife was drawn across his throat, Preston didn't register the quick tear of pain before slipping away into darkness. His final thought was of his wife and children.

—··—

Andrew quickly picked up the limp corpse, blood gushing from the incision in its throat and spilling onto his shirt. He opened the Ford's boot and threw the body of Preston into it with disgust before getting back into the driver's seat, switching on the engine, which rumbled to life after a couple of angry whirs. He took his time trying to find the clutch before giving up entirely and simply laying his head on the wheel. He took a deep breath before lifting his head and allowed tears to roll down his face as he sobbed in the way only a grieving, desperate parent could. Finally, after what felt like hours, Andrew sat up straight and drove back to Wrestlingworth with determination, thinking nothing of the fresh corpse in his boot.

Soon enough, Andrew was passing the mill and going on to the churchyard. It was abandoned now. Andrew did his best to ignore the school as he drove past it, instead focusing on the church. He kept his eyes on Lucy's plot, her grave lying directly underneath a small, thin tree she used to climb when she didn't think her parents were watching.

He parked the car in front of the gates, hastily stopping and retrieving a shovel from the backseats. He walked through the black gate, freshly painted to hide its rust; it let out a high-pitched creak as he pushed it open. He could hear youths in the nearby park shouting, and their voices made Andrew catch his breath in his throat. He froze before dropping slightly, hoping no one saw him. He quickly jogged to Lucy's grave, staying low as he went. Finally, he stood, placing himself behind the tree to search the graveyard.

Satisfied he was alone, Andrew let go of his paranoia and began to dig, planting his shovel firmly into the ground and scooping out mounds of dirt. Fear of being discovered gave him speed, and he dug fast enough to build up a sweat. Voices of kids came and went, and there was more than one occasion when he had to duck low just to make sure he wasn't seen. Fitting his large frame into a small ball, he would wait for the voices or a set of footsteps to subside, feeling his heart beating out of his chest before he would rise and continue to dig.

Eventually his shovel landed on a hard surface, and in seemingly no time at all, he'd widened the hole enough to pull out the small, black coffin, roughly half the size of him. He pried off the lid with the shovel and pulled a small body in a white dress out of it, not yet able to recognise his daughter's features due to the darkness all around him. He placed the lid back onto the coffin, laid it back into the ground, and piled the earth back over the spot to cover it. Andrew could only pray nobody would notice.

Picking up the shovel in one hand and the dark bundle of his daughter in the other, Andrew ran across the graveyard and back to his car as fast as possible. He carefully placed Lucy on the backseat, keeping the lights off so as not to look at his child. He placed the shovel next to her and jumped into the driver's seat before revving the engine and speeding back to the mill. He was almost fully sober by the time he returned and could feel a headache begin to pulse in his skull.

He walked through the front door where the priest stood, waiting, as though expecting him. Sarah was in the kitchen and broke down into sobs at the sight of the bundle Andrew was holding. She fell to her knees and held her head in her hands. Andrew ignored her as he softly walked to the sofa to lay Lucy down. He examined her corpse.

Dark spots of mould infested her once perfect face, and her blonde hair had become dirty, discoloured, and bald in places. Her body was curved and broken from where the car had hit her tiny frame, and yet Andrew knew immediately it was his daughter. Her nose, though broken, matched his own, and she had her mother's blonde curls. She was also a broader girl than most ten-year-olds and boyish in her own way.

Andrew smiled at the corpse of his daughter as tears began to roll from his eyes again. He quickly stood, wiped his eyes dry, and walked back to the car, his feet crunching on the gravel as he replaced the warm living room with the cold darkness of the outside. Nervous, Andrew looked around for anyone watching the mill. Finally satisfied, Andrew opened the boot of his car and dragged out Preston's body, grunting with the effort. Preston's blood had dried around his neck; cracking and flaking off as his corpse was dragged across the gravel.

Andrew brought him into the living room, closed the front door behind him, and then simply let go for Preston to flop to the ground. He looked at the priest.

"Well done. I knew you could do it, Andrew. Now they just need to come to the top of the mill and we can begin." With that the priest picked up Preston's corpse and held it under one arm while Andrew just stared after him, open-mouthed at the strength of the whistling priest.

He gently picked up Lucy and, biting his trembling lip, slowly walked upstairs. After a few more minutes of sobbing, Sarah finally followed them. Ready to bring her daughter back to life.

— · · —

All the priest remembered from his life, before his death and rebirth, was that he was a priest. All his other memories seemed too distant and blurry to remember. He could vaguely recall the laughter of children. Apart from these small fragments though, his memory from that life mainly consisted of fractured prayers and bible verses.

The earliest complete memory he had was that of the afterlife. An empty white void that defied all logic. Loneliness and anger set in for the priest as he simply waited with as much patience as he could muster for his heavenly reward.

One day, sick of waiting patiently, he started walking and didn't stop. The priest walked for what felt like an eternity. Being dead had its perks. His body was returned to its youth, turning the priest from the old, fat man he'd died in the body of, to a forty-year-old.

Another perk was that his body didn't have limits, he didn't get hungry or thirsty. He felt no need to sleep, and his body never seemed to require rest. He walked for years, sometimes coming across other souls begging for help and direction. The priest tried to point them toward God, convinced that he, along with all the other souls, were in purgatory. After an impossible amount of time, the priest lost even that faith, and instead, simply left the souls to their begging and madness. He only believed he should continue to walk.

After walking farther than he ever had when alive, the priest came upon something called The Field: a place full of souls, emanating the same aura as his own—either black or white. The priest's aura had started white at the beginning of his walk but had become grey and discoloured by the time he reached The Field. The less help he offered the other souls, the darker his aura became. It was here, amongst these auras, that he was offered a way out.

It wasn't anywhere noteworthy, as all of The Field looked alike. Even the people seemed to blend into a mixture of white, black, and all the shades in between. A man stopped the priest and caught his arm. He seemed to have all the world's accents and yet none of them at the same time, and his smile was artificial, as though he was only wearing his body as a costume. He was tall and built, making for an intimidating figure to any, though the priest knew by this point that the size of a person's body was irrelevant. Everyone was the same in that respect, from children to old men.

"Well hello, Priest. I am Light, I think. I have been waiting to give you a tour." With that the strange man began to walk as the priest spluttered behind him in shock, only just noticing that Light didn't have an aura at all.

"I'm sorry, who are you? What do you mean, *tour*? And where is your aura?" The priest shot these questions all at once at Light, partly out of shock and partly out of a need to talk to someone who was sane. Something souls in the afterlife seemed to lack.

"Oh, I don't really know who I am. No one does. All I know is what is here, what I can do for you, and that I don't have an aura, but it doesn't make a difference anyway." Light spoke quickly and seemed to skip as he walked.

The priest didn't know if this change of pace excited or worried him. He started to wonder what would happen if someone hit him whilst he was a soul.

He looked around to realise Light had dragged him out of earshot of the other souls and suddenly hunched lower, coming down to the priest's eye level and speaking in almost a whisper. "Listen, I have a way for you to get out of here. Only certain people can go back to the world of the living, and you can. I know that. I've been waiting for you for a long time. If I can send you back to the world of the living, you must promise to find my grave and resurrect me. If I'm right, then the ritual for resurrecting me should just come naturally to you. Please, don't you want to escape too?" Light spoke with urgency and madness in his eyes before looking down apologetically. "Look, I've spent God knows how long in this world. It doesn't get better. We don't even get to die again. Instead, everyone wanders aimlessly, losing their fucking minds, and I couldn't live with it anymore, so . . . so I prayed . . ." He looked down with shame as he spoke. "I prayed and I was given the instructions for getting out of here but was told I would need to wait for someone. I know now it was you I was waiting for!" He grabbed the priest and pulled him close, smiling as he did so.

"But I need time to process this . . . I don't even know who you are . . ." The priest trailed off.

Light looked down at the ground in sadness. "Look, Priest, you can take as much time as you need. Years, decades, centuries, it doesn't matter. But tell me this, there is more to 'the finish' than this in-between space, isn't there? I know this is against your code, but I can see it in you and in your aura. You aren't all priest anymore. You know that, don't you? I can see how bitter you are. You have the chance now to break the rules and bring back as many people as you like. You can bring them back, and no one will be stuck in this hellhole place anymore. If you just break this rule, think of how many people you can save."

The priest stared at Light for a time. He bit his lip and shook his hands as he thought, pacing, while Light stood there and stared, longing in his eyes.

"Listen, Light. I have a code that I have to keep to. I became a priest to carry out God's will, and if this is it, then I am not able to judge. I became a man of forgiveness, not a man of divine right."

The priest went to walk away before Light's words stopped him. "In this lack of forgiveness, you will let down everyone!" Light suddenly became animated in his anger toward the priest. "Do you want to know the truth about the pairs of souls that hold hands? One soul that holds the hand was killed, the other was the killer! I've seen children holding the hands of men and know that we are on an equal playing field! What is the point in a man of forgiveness such as yourself when this world will not reward and punish as was promised to us in the books?"

The priest froze and turned, suddenly having a change of heart. He felt his aura darken as the thoughts of the world spun in his head. "You are right. I performed my duty as a man of forgiveness. But this world, it isn't right . . . it's wrong, and now I know what I have to do."

It made perfect sense to the priest now. He stepped forward and took Light's arm, completely oblivious to the mind control that Light was performing on him as they spoke. Behind him, the priest felt a gust of wind hit the back of his head, ruffling his short hair.

A portal opened behind him while Light stared open mouthed.

On the other side of the portal was grass, as though from a field in England. It had never looked so lush and green. The priest stepped toward it, every step causing his aura to become darker and darker until he was pitch black as he stepped through the portal.

The moment he left, it closed behind him with Light's final words. "Find me!"

The priest stepped out and started walking. Still looking the same as in The Field, he realised he was some form of a ghost, though the world still recognised him as human. He would later learn that, since he'd died in 1985, he'd spent fifteen years in the soul fields. He watched the world as an outsider now, an unwelcome stranger in the modern day. He found hypnotism and resurrection came naturally to him, and, finally, the priest became more and more cynical, seeing injustices everywhere in society and knowing there was no reward for this suffering in the next life.

The priest searched for Light but would never find him. Eventually he ended up offering his services to the living, to return the souls of the ones they loved but for a price. He realised money seemed to be the only real thing in the world. So, he collected it in the same way one collects stamps, knowing the living would give anything for his services. He wanted for nothing, so his funds grew while he sold his grotesque creations—crimes against nature, generally fractured pictures of what once was.

People were always too fast to say yes to his deal. He made sure they didn't allow themselves to question anything too much. Any term he wanted, he was given without fuss, his hypnotism allowing him to be persuasive enough to tell anyone that what he was doing was simply the best option, even learning how to be persuasive over emails by the time they were widely used.

As for the ritual, Light was right in that respect; the priest just knew the right words to say and the right actions to use. It was as much a part of him as breathing, and it came to him just as naturally.

The case of Sarah and Andrew's child, Lucy, was no different from any other case he'd taken on, and he knew the results would be the same as every other time he'd resurrected a person.

—··—

The black smoke was swirling more violently than before. It brought Sarah to her knees as she choked and spluttered on the world around her, hearing nothing but the roaring darkness. She couldn't see her hands by this point, she could only feel how cold they were. She shivered, her jaw trembled, and she sobbed painfully until, finally, the darkness and the cold subsided, and the room was, in a moment, back to normal and completely undisturbed, the only change being the two new living additions to the room.

They were glowing white for a long time before these lights settled into the bodies of Preston and Lucy, and they both slowly stood, eyes closed. The priest stepped forward, completely unaffected by the ritual. Even his clothes were undisturbed. Sarah and Andrew were both damp with sweat, despite the cold. Their clothes were ripped in places, though neither noticed.

The priest chuckled as he walked up to the two of them. He stopped as he stood between Lucy and Preston. "It is a tough ritual for the living, but here is your daughter, returned to her body as promised."

The priest smiled while the two bodies slowly healed; their daughter's skin shone again, and her hair grew, becoming brighter as her injuries disappeared, replacing her deformities with the perfectly structured face of a ten-year-old girl. Preston's neck wound healed and the blood disappeared, flaking and drifting into the air before settling on the ground, though they both simply stood there, eyes closed and completely still, as though they were mannequins.

"Why isn't she waking up?" Andrew asked quietly, shocked by the events they were witnessing.

"I ask you both one final time, are you sure you wish to go

through with this?" The priest smiled, as though he already knew the answer.

Andrew just lowered his head in a beggar's stance and whispered to the priest whilst Sarah remained speechless. "Yes . . . please . . . Just give us our daughter." Andrew sounded weak and weary.

Sarah could only nod. For them to now see their Lucy standing made it as though they had reached the end of a long dark tunnel and were finally staring at the light.

"Very well." The priest smiled. His eyes turned a new shade of blue. No longer that of a storming sea but simply bright, as though a victory had been won.

He tapped both Lucy and Preston's temples, and a moment later, their eyes flickered open. Sarah cried with joy as she ran to embrace Lucy. Then their daughter screamed through her lifeless eyes before an invisible force threw her across the room and against the wall with a loud crash, splintering it slightly. Lucy's deformed features returned, and her body produced fresh blood.

Andrew watched as Preston's throat opened through its old incision, and a moment later, he collapsed to the floor, bleeding onto the wooden boards. Seconds later he stood, and his wound healed before the process repeated all over again. Lucy was slumped against the wall before crawling forward on her broken body, still screaming, as though her lungs would burst. She moved back to where she had been and silently rose to stand before repeating the screaming car crash.

Sarah and Andrew broke their stunned silence in their own ways. Sarah broke down screaming, watching her daughter continuously die. All she could do was shout *MY BABY!* as those thoughts completely consumed her.

Andrew stood and, growling like a dog, shouted at the top of his lungs at the priest, who just stood there with the same calm, detached smile. "What are you doing to Lucy!" he roared.

The priest chuckled slightly, forcing a new roar from Andrew as he ran toward him and attempted to tackle him. Before he could react, the priest simply stepped aside, sending Andrew straight into a metal beam behind him. The priest turned and, while Andrew struggled, picked him up and threw him back across the room, forcing groans of pain from Andrew. Sarah stumbled over to him and hauled him up, cradling his head as the priest fixed his black robes and began to leave the room.

Sarah grabbed the hem of his robes and looked into his eyes, tears falling while she was forced to shout over the screams of her daughter. "Please, what have you done?" she begged, her voice low and shaking as she spoke.

The priest smiled and stroked her head while his eyes were still that wicked shade of blue. "I have saved your daughter; her spirit has returned, and she is a ghost. Though you didn't ask, I shall tell you now. There are two kinds of ghosts: those that leave the afterlife and those that are dragged out. When I left, I kept all that I was and gained more. I ascended mere humans. As a ghost, I have the world at my fingertips. I've had to drag Lucy and Preston out, and sadly, a dragged ghost is nothing more than a fragment of what was left behind in their life. That final, magical madness before death. They will forever re-enact these final moments, as though stuck on repeat their whole lives. However, she is in there, your daughter is there. Just only in part. The other part is still waiting for her where she belongs . . . in the afterlife."

He pulled his hand away from Sarah and continued to walk away.

"You monster!" Sarah screamed, stopping the priest dead in his tracks.

He turned and shouted back with an unearthly fury in his eyes. "Me? A monster? Sarah, it was you and your stupid husband who decided to defy the will of God. You dragged your daughter away from her peace in death without so much as thinking about the consequences of your actions, and you expect to hold me responsible? Trust me, the two of you will very soon realise what *you* have done!" With that, the priest turned and walked quickly down the stairs.

Minutes later, while Sarah cradled Andrew, breathing shallowly, she heard the front door of the mill slam shut as the priest walked out of their lives. She could hear him whistling the same tune as before. With every dying scream of her daughter, it forced pain anew in Sarah, as her body would tense upon impact, and a cry of pain would escape her also. It was almost as though she was experiencing the collision along with the ghostly shell of her daughter. She could do no more than hold Andrew and cry onto his limp, weak body.

Finally, he stirred and slowly rose, holding Sarah as he did so before standing. There was a stream of blood falling from a cut on his temple, and his body leaned to one side to avoid aggravating the damage to his ribs.

"Okay . . . Sarah . . ." He trailed off and watched Lucy crash into the wall again, whimpering with the impact and screwing his eyes shut to escape the tears. He breathed deeply and stood up taller, stern as a schoolmaster. "Sarah, get hold of Lucy while she's down and bring her into the cellar. Until we figure out how we can fix her, we need to stop any suspicion from the neighbours. I'll get rid of him." Andrew jerked his thumb at the currently free-bleeding Preston as he spoke.

Without hesitation, Andrew grabbed Preston by the arms before roughly hauling him downstairs. He wasn't so careful this time, leaving the ghost's blood to freely drip onto the stairs. He made his way onto the ground floor of the mill and dragged him through the kitchen and out of the backdoor. Andrew then threw Preston onto the grass, where he then immediately stood just to fall in a pool of his own blood again. Andrew left him there so he could go into the car and grab the shovel. He jogged through the house once he had retrieved it, grimacing at the drops of blood on the floor leading in a trail to the garden.

He heard Sarah slowly walking down the steps above him, silent as the corpse of the girl she held. Suddenly Lucy screamed again and continued to scream as she was carried. Unable to be free to be pushed into the next wall and be revived all over again.

Andrew began to dig, quickly building a grave just about deep and wide enough to throw Preston into. The ghost didn't even struggle against Andrew as he kicked him into the hole. Preston simply kept bleeding as Andrew piled dirt on top of him, burying him hastily.

He heard the basement door close and drown out Lucy's screams as Andrew returned to the kitchen. He looked in the living room mirror and saw that his arms, hands, face, and clothes were covered in blood—dried and fresh alike. He closed his eyes and turned away from the mirror to take control of his nausea before slowly going upstairs to the bathroom where he switched on the shower and washed in silence. He'd seemingly lost the ability to cry.

He'd lost his money and his house; he'd killed a man, and his daughter seemed to be better off dead at this point. Andrew didn't even feel his eyes sting. He had no need to fight back the tears as they simply would not arrive. He switched off the shower and wrapped a towel around himself before heading into his bedroom and changing into a simple tracksuit with a black T-Shirt.

He realised Sarah was still in the basement, so he went looking for her. What he found when he went down there turned his skin to ice. He walked into the room to hear Sarah cooing softly to Lucy through tears, then Lucy started her blood-curdling scream and flew into the basement wall, an impact followed by Sarah's scream. He turned the corner of the basement to see Lucy screaming against the wall. Sarah was holding Lucy from behind, acting as a buffer between the ghost and the cracked wall. She continued to coo at Lucy with love through her broken and bloodied mouth as they both crawled to the centre of the room where Sarah proceeded to hug the ghost before the two of them flew into the wall, screaming in unison.

Andrew stormed across the room and grabbed Sarah by her torn blouse. She screamed as he aggravated her badly broken bones.

"What do you think you are doing, Sarah? This isn't going to fix anything!"

Through the blood in her teeth, Sarah laughed, before looking seriously at Andrew. "I'm protecting my baby from being hurt. I knew you wouldn't want me to, but I must look after my daughter!" She screamed these final few words, spitting blood and spittle on Andrew's face in the process.

Snapping, he slapped Sarah in the face and, ignoring the swiftly-flying backward Lucy, dragged her up two flights of stairs and into their bedroom, hitting her every time she tried to resist and escape. He threw Sarah onto the bed and left, slamming the door and locking it behind him.

She simply screamed at the door and begged to be free to see her daughter.

"You can see her when you get your mind back!" he shouted back through the door and went downstairs to sleep on the sofa.

—●●—

The mill had been selling bread to locals again for the past week. Andrew made the bread runs every morning, then worked on the upper floor of the mill to make more loaves for the next day and, though no one was permitted to visit the mill, the Berkleys seemed to be getting over their loss. Sarah, by all accounts, was happily staying at home to get over her grief. The Berkleys were united again and were delivering bread around the village.

The bell ringing at the front of the store that morning brought the shopkeeper's attention, who walked out to the till to be greeted by Andrew with a bag full of bread.

"Good morning, Mr. Berkley. You are arriving delightfully early these days. I haven't even had breakfast yet!" he said good naturedly.

Andrew just smiled thinly in response, his eyes looking sunken, dark, and exhausted. "Here is your delivery. Put it on the tab for me to pick up tomorrow. I didn't bring change with me today." Andrew spoke quickly before turning to leave.

"How's Sarah? You look tired. Can I help you two in any way?"

This was the first time a villager had asked Andrew this question; the villagers were all desperate for gossip but none dared ask.

The question froze Andrew in place before he angrily turned around. "How dare you ask me that. I don't even know your name! You aren't from around here. You don't know me, and yet you insist on asking me about my business! How dare you!" With these words and a rude hand gesture toward the shopkeeper, Andrew stormed out of the store and drove away, ignoring the rest of the deliveries he needed to make that day and going straight back to the mill.

He parked the car outside the mill and ran into the house. As soon as he opened the door, Sarah started to scream from the bedroom. He ran up to the door and removed the chair barring it to look in at the dirty, crazed woman he used to love.

The room smelt like an animal due to the build-up of Sarah's faeces and a week's worth of dirty dishes from the food Andrew brought to her. Sarah had bald patches on her scalp now and cuts all over her body from trying to break out of the reinforced bedroom door. She ran past him without any hint of fear, as though Andrew wasn't there, and ran straight down to the basement, calling Lucy's name.

Andrew went to the kitchen and picked up a large, cruel knife before following Sarah to the basement, knowing that only something extreme could bring him peace. He walked down to the same cooing sound as he had a week ago, followed by the same crash and scream. He watched his wife and child hug each other for a time before crouching silently next to them both and holding them.

With tears building up in his eyes, he screamed as he wildly stabbed Sarah through the chest, forcing a gurgled scream to form through her bloodied mouth before she dropped limp. Without hesitating and not wishing to lose any momentum, Andrew whispered an apology and begged for forgiveness before bringing the cold steel of the now wet, bloodied knife to the ghost's throat.

"I love you, my baby girl," he said quietly through choked tears as he slid the knife across the ghost's throat just as she began to form a scream.

She shrieked for a time before dropping limply into his lap, cold and dead again, as she should have been.

Andrew finally pulled his phone from his pocket and called the police, leaving a quick message. "I'm in the mill in Wrestlingworth village. There is a man buried in my back garden, and my wife and daughter are dead in my basement. I've killed them both."

Andrew then hung up and simply cried to himself, holding his wife and child together, like the family they used to be, whilst begging their forgiveness over and over. He kept his eyes fixed on the knife on his lap and only picked it up when he heard the sirens of police cars on his drive.

He whispered to the two most loved women in his life before drawing the blade against his own throat. "I love you both so, so much. I'm sorry. I hope you can both forgive me in the next life."

Aside from working two jobs and studying at university, **River M. Daniel** writes novels, particularly in the horror, fantasy, and science fiction genre. He currently has a Wordpress blog and a science fiction style novel in the works. He has also submitted work for the *Bite* anthology and is a regular contributor to Worldsmyths, an online group of young fantasy and horror writers. "Fragments" is his first published piece of prose.

NIGHTFALL

Duaa Hyder

Iana's mother stared, wishing to be with her one last time. She missed her; she would trade the world just to spend one last day with her daughter.

"Zoë! What do you think you're doing?" Octavia sped toward her. "You're here to haunt! No one ever told you to sneak up on your child! How embarrassing it must be, to have a child who's alive! Even more so to have one who doesn't believe in our existence!"

"Octavia, calm down," Zoë ordered. "Iana would believe in ghosts if you let me talk to her!"

"Enough! Letting a mere mortal speak to such powerful beings like us!"

"You were a mortal once, and you always brag about how your mortal family were so good to you, and I've seen you talk to them before," Zoë argued.

Octavia's face went red.

Zoë smiled. "Oh, has the *leader of the dead* finally shut her big mouth?"

"Fine then. Why don't you be with your *precious mortal daughter.*"

—··—

Iana's jaw dropped. "No, it . . . it can't be. August deliberately put it there so that Jen thought Aliya did it! This is the best TV show ever!"

"IANA!" a voice shouted, making Iana drop her popcorn. "You are fourteen and you still watch animated TV programmes? I am disgusted!"

Iana's jaw dropped even farther. "Mum? You're . . . you're here!"

"Of course, I'm here! Are you blind?"

"N-No . . . I'm not blind."

"Good. Now what do you wanna do?"

"What do you mean? You're dead!"

"Oh, I've been given a day to spend with you."

—··—

"Next season, August must find a way to sneak past Jen and Aliya to steal the Sacred Green Flower. Will she do it? Find out in all new episodes."

"Iana, you were right! This is the best programme ever!" Zoë exclaimed.

"I know, right? Do you wanna sit down?"

"Iana, I'm a ghost."

"Yeah, sorry. How did you actually get here?"

"Oh, this girl called Octavia sent me here."

"Why?" Iana asked.

"I dunno. Something about getting you to become a ghost by nightfall, or I'm banished from the clan. I wasn't really listening because I was craving some salty fries."

"Wait . . . WHAT?"

"Yeah, even when you're dead and you can't eat, you can get these annoying craving feelings," Zoë started.

"No! I mean the nightfall thing!"

"If you don't sign this contract to become a ghost by nightfall, I'm gonna be kicked out. I was going to tell you about it, but I kind of forgot—"

"What about Dad?"

"Oh, I'm sure he wouldn't mind. He'll probably have one less problem without you."

"Hey! I'm not that bad! What do you even have to do to become a ghost?"

"You could die or just jump into this portal thing that was here this whole time."

"Okay. *Weeeeeeeeeeee!*"

Iana was never heard of again.